COLLINS' 2/6 NOVELS

FULL LIST OF TITLES

In shape and bulk they are identical with the 7/6 book

Mr WELLS has also written the following novels:

Love and Mr Lewisham.
Kipps.
Mr Polly.
The Wheels of Chance.
The New Machiavelli.
Ann Veronica.
Tono-Bungay.
The Secret Places of the Heart.

Marriage.
Bealby.
The Passionate Friends
The Wife of Sir Isaac Harman.
Mr Britling Sees It Through.
The Soul of a Bishop.
John and Peter.
The Undying Fire.

The following fantastic and imaginative romances:

The War of the Worlds.
The Time Machine.
The Wonderful Visit.
The Island of Dr Moreau.
The Sea Lady.
When the Sleeper Wakes.

The Food of the Gods.
The War in the Air.
The First Men in the Moon
In the Days of the Comet.
The World Set Free.
The Invisible Man.

Numerous short stories collected under the following titles:

The Country of the Blind.
Tales of Space and Time.
Tales of Life and Adventure.

The Stolen Bacillus.
The Plattner Story.
Tales of the Unexpected.

Twelve Stories and a dream.

A series of books on social, religious, and political questions:

Anticipations (1900).
Mankind in the Making.
First and Last Things.
New Worlds for Old.
A Modern Utopia.

The Future in America.
God the Invisible King.
The Outline of History.
Washington and the Hope of Peace.

The Salvaging of Civilisation.

And two little books about children's play, called:

Floor Games and Little Wars.

THE RESEARCH MAGNIFICENT

BY

H. G. WELLS

LONDON: 48 PALL MALL

W. COLLINS SONS & CO. LTD.

GLASGOW MELBOURNE AUCKLAND

Manufactured in Great Britain

CONTENTS

THE PRELUDE

THE STORY

THE PRELUDE

§ 1

THE story of William Porphyry Benham is the story of a man who was led into adventure by an idea. It was an idea that took possession of his imagination quite early in life, it grew with him and changed with him, it interwove at last completely with his being. His story is its story. It was traceably germinating in the schoolboy; it was manifestly present in his mind at the very last moment of his adventurous life. He belonged to that fortunate minority who are independent of daily necessities, so that he was free to go about the world under its direction. It led him far. It led him into situations that bordered upon the fantastic, it made him ridiculous, it came near to making him sublime. And this idea of his was of such a nature that in several aspects he could document it. Its logic forced him to introspection and to the making of a record.

An idea that can play so large a part in a life must necessarily have something of the complication and protean quality of life itself. It is not to be stated justly in any formula, it is not to be rendered by an epigram. As well one might show a man's skeleton for his portrait. Yet, essentially, Benham's idea was simple. He had an incurable, an almost innate persuasion that he had to live life nobly and thoroughly. His commoner expression for that thorough living is 'the aristocratic life.' But by 'aristocratic' he meant something very different from the quality of a Russian prince, let us say, or an English peer. He meant an intensity, a clearness. . . . Nobility for him was to get something out of his individual existence, a flame, a jewel, a splendour—it is a thing easier to understand than to say.

One might hesitate to call this idea 'innate,' and yet it comes soon into a life when it comes at all. In Benham's case we might trace it back to the Day Nursery at Seagate, we might detect it stirring already at the petticoat stage, in various private struttings and valiant dreamings with a helmet of pasteboard and a white-metal sword. We have most of us been at least as far as that with Benham. And we have died like Horatius, slaying our thousands for our country, or we have perished at the stake or faced the levelled muskets of the firing party—'No, do not bandage my eyes'—because we would not betray the secret path that meant destruction to our city. But with Benham the vein was stronger, and it increased instead of fading out as he grew to manhood. It was less obscured by those earthy acquiescences, those discretions, that saving sense of proportion, which have made most of us so satisfactorily what we are. 'Porphyry,' his mother had discovered before he was seventeen, 'is an excellent boy, a brilliant boy, but, I begin to see, just a little unbalanced.'

The interest of him, the absurdity of him, the story of him, is that.

Most of us are—balanced; in spite of occasional reveries we do come to terms with the limitations of life, with those desires and dreams and discretions that, to say the least of it, qualify our nobility; we take refuge in our sense of humour and congratulate ourselves on a certain amiable freedom from priggishness or presumption; but for Benham that easy declension to a humorous acceptance of life as it is did not occur. He found his limitations soon enough; he was perpetually rediscovering them, but out of these interments of the spirit he rose again—remarkably. When we others have decided that, to be plain about it, we are not going to lead the noble life at all, that the thing is too ambitious and expensive even to attempt, we have done so because there were other conceptions of existence that were good enough for us; we decided that instead of that glorious impossible being of ourselves, we would figure in our own eyes as jolly fellows, or sly dogs, or sane, sound, capable men, or brilliant successes, and so forth—practicable things. For Benham, exceptionally, there were not these practicable things. He blundered, he fell short of himself, he had—as you will be told—some astonishing rebuffs, but they never turned him aside for long. He went by nature for this preposterous idea of nobility as a linnet hatched in a cage will try to fly.

And when he discovered—and in this he was assisted not a little by his friend at his elbow—when he discovered that Nobility was not the simple thing he had at first supposed it to be, he set himself in a mood only slightly disconcerted to the discovery of Nobility. When it dawned upon him, as it did, that one cannot be noble, so to speak, *in vacuo*, he set himself to discover a Noble Society. He began with simple beliefs and fine attitudes and ended in a conscious research. If he could not get through by a stride, then it followed that he must get through by a climb. He spent the greater part of his life studying and experimenting in the noble possibilities of man. He never lost his absurd faith in that conceivable splendour. At first it was always just round the corner or just through the wood; to the last it seemed still but a little way beyond the distant mountains.

For this reason this story has been called *The Research Magnificent*. It was a real research, it was documented. In the rooms in Westhaven Street that at last were as much as one could call his home, he had accumulated material for—one hesitates to call it a book—let us say it was an analysis of, a guide to the noble life. There after his tragic death came his old friend White, the journalist and novelist, under a promise, and found these papers, he found them to the extent of a crammed bureau, half a score of patent files quite distended, and a writing-table drawer-full; and he was greatly exercised to find them. They were, White declares, they are still after much experienced handling, an indigestible aggregation. On this point White is very assured. When Benham thought he was gathering together a book he was dreaming, White says. There is no book in it. . . .

Perhaps too, one might hazard, Benham was dreaming when he thought the noble life a human possibility. Perhaps man, like the ape and the hyæna and the tapeworm and many other of God's necessary but less attractive creatures, is not for such exalted ends. That doubt never seems to have got a lodgment in Benham's skull; though at times one might suppose it the basis of White's thought. You will find in all Benham's story, if only it can be properly told, now subdued, now loud and amazed and distressed, but always traceable, this startled, protesting question, *'But why the devil aren't we?'* As though necessarily we ought to be. He never faltered in his persuasion that behind the dingy face of this world, the earthy stubbornness, the baseness and dullness of himself and all of us, lurked the living jewels of heaven, the light of glory, things unspeakable. At first it seemed to him that one had only just to hammer and will; and at the end,

after a life of willing and hammering, he was still convinced
there was something, something in the nature of an Open
Sesame, perhaps a little more intricate than one had
supposed at first, a little more difficult to secure, but still
in that nature, which would suddenly roll open for mankind
the magic cave of the universe, that precious cave at the
heart of all things in which one must believe.

And then life—life would be the wonder it so perplexingly
just isn't. . . .

§ 2

Benham did not go about the world telling people of
this consuming research. He was not the prophet or
preacher of his idea. It was too living and intricate and
uncertain a part of him to speak freely about. It was his
secret self; to expose it casually would have shamed him.
He drew all sorts of reserves about him, he wore his manifest imperfections turned up about him like an overcoat
in bitter wind. He was content to be inexplicable. His
thoughts led him to the conviction that this magnificent
research could not be, any more than any other research
can be, a solitary enterprise, but he delayed expression;
in a mighty writing and stowing away of these papers he
found a relief from the unpleasant urgency to confess and
explain himself prematurely. So that White, though he
knew Benham with the intimacy of an old schoolfellow
who had renewed his friendship and had shared his last
days and been a witness of his death, read the sheets of
manuscript often with surprise and with a sense of added
acidation.

And, being also a trained maker of books, White as he
read was more and more distressed that an accumulation
so interesting should be so entirely unshaped for publication.
'But this will never make a book,' said White with a note
of personal grievance. His hasty promise in their last
moments together had bound him, it seemed, to a task he
now found impossible. He would have to work upon it
tremendously; and even then he did not see how it could
be done.

This collection of papers was not a story, not an essay,
not a confession, not a diary. It was—nothing definable.
It went into no conceivable covers. It was just, White
decided, a proliferation. A vast proliferation. It wanted
even a title. There were signs that Benham had intended

to call it *The Aristocratic Life*, and that he had tried at
some other time the title of *An Essay on Aristocracy*.
Moreover, it would seem that towards the end he had been
disposed to drop the word 'aristocratic' altogether, and
adopt some such phrase as *The Larger Life*. Once it was
Life Set Free. He had fallen away more and more from
nearly everything that one associates with aristocracy—
at the end only its ideals of fearlessness and generosity
remained.

Of all these titles *The Aristocratic Life* seemed at first
most like a clue to White. Benham's erratic movements,
his sudden impulses, his angers, his unaccountable patiences
his journeys to strange places, and his lapses into what
had seemed to be pure adventurousness, could all be put
into system with that. Before White had turned over
three pages of the great fascicle of manuscript that was
called Book Two, he had found the word 'Bushido' written
with a particularly flourishing capital letter and twice
repeated. 'That was inevitable,' said White with the
comforting regret one feels at a friend's banalities. 'And
it dates . . . Yes—this was early. . . .'

'Modern aristocracy, the new aristocracy,' he read
presently, 'has still to be discovered and understood. This
is the necessary next step for mankind. As far as possible
I will discover and understand it, and as far as I know it
I will be it. This is the essential disposition of my mind.
God knows I have appetites and sloths and habits and
blindnesses, but so far it is in my power to release myself
I will escape to this. . . .'

§ 3

White sat far into the night and for several nights turning
over papers and rummaging in untidy drawers. Memories
came back to him of his dead friend and pieced themselves
together with other memories and joined on to scraps in
this writing. Bold yet convincing guesses began to leap
across the gaps. A story shaped itself. . . .

The story began with the schoolfellow he had known at
Minchinghampton School.

Benham had come up from his father's preparatory
school at Seagate. He had been a boy reserved rather
than florid in his acts and manners, a boy with a pale face,
incorrigible hair, and brown eyes that went dark and deep
with excitement. Several times White had seen him

excited, and when he was excited Benham was capable of tensely daring things. On one occasion he had insisted upon walking across a field in which was an aggressive bull. It had been put there to prevent the boys taking a short cut to the swimming place. It had bellowed tremendously and finally charged him. He had dodged it and got away; at the time it had seemed an immense feat to White and the others who were safely up the field. He had walked to the fence, risking a second charge by his deliberation. Then he had sat on the fence and declared his intention of always crossing the field so long as the bull remained there. He had said this with white intensity, he had stopped abruptly in mid-sentence, and then suddenly he had dropped to the ground, clutched the fence, struggled with heaving shoulders, and been sick.

The combination of apparently stout heart and manifestly weak stomach had exercised the Minchinghampton intelligence profoundly.

On one or two other occasions Benham had shown courage of the same rather screwed-up sort. He showed it not only in physical but in mental things. A boy named Prothero set a fashion of religious discussion in the school, and Benham, after some self-examination, professed an atheistical republicanism rather in the manner of Shelley. This brought him into open conflict with Roddles, the History Master. Roddles had discovered these theological controversies in some mysterious way, and he took upon himself to talk at Benham and Prothero. He treated them to the common misapplication of that fool who 'hath said in his heart there is no God.' He did not perceive there was any difference between the fool who says a thing in his heart and one who says it in the dormitory. He revived that delectable anecdote of the Eton boy who professed disbelief and was at once 'soundly flogged' by his head master. 'Years afterwards that boy came back to thank—'

'Gurr,' said Prothero softly. '*Stew*—ard!'

'Your turn next, Benham,' whispered an orthodox controversialist.

'Good Lord! I'd like to see him,' said Benham with a forced loudness that could scarcely be ignored.

The subsequent controversy led to an interview with the head. From it Benham emerged more whitely strung up than ever. 'He said he would certainly swish me if I deserved it, and I said I would certainly kill him if he did.'

'And then?'

stopped, trying to defend his head with the horse rearing over him. It beat him down with two swift blows of its fore hoofs, one, two, lifted him up in its long yellow teeth and worried him as a terrier does a rat—the poor old wretch was still able to make a bleating sound at that—dropped him, trampled and kicked him as he tried to crawl away, and went on trampling and battering him until he he was no more than a bloody inhuman bundle of clothes and mire. For more than half an hour this continued, and then its animal rage was exhausted and it desisted, and went and grazed at a little distance from this misshapen, hoof-marked, torn, and muddy remnant of a man. No one it seems but a horror-stricken child knew what was happening. . . .

This picture of human indignity tortured Benham's imagination much more than it tortured the teller of the tale. It filled him with shame and horror. For three or four years every detail of that circumstantial narrative seemed unforgettable. A little lapse from perfect health and the obsession returned. He could not endure the neighing of horses; when he saw horses galloping in a field with him his heart stood still. And all his life thereafter he hated horses.

§ 6

A different sort of fear that also greatly afflicted Benham was due to a certain clumsiness and insecurity he felt in giddy and unstable places. There he was more definitely balanced between the hopelessly rash and the pitifully discreet.

He had written an account of a private struggle between himself and a certain path of planks and rock edges called the Bisse of Leysin. This happened in his adolescence. He had had a bad attack of influenza and his doctor had sent him to a little hotel—the only hotel it was in those days—at Montana in Valais. There, later, when he had picked up his strength, his father was to join him and take him mountaineering, that second-rate mountaineering which is so dear to dons and schoolmasters. When the time came he was ready for that, but he had had his experiences. He had gone through a phase of real cowardice He was afraid, he confessed, before even he reached Montana he was afraid of the steepness of the mountains. He had to drive ten or twelve miles up and up the mountain-side, a road of innumerable hairpin bends and precipitous banks, the horse was gaunt and ugly with a disposition to shy, and he confesses he clutched the side of the vehicle and speculated how he should jump if presently the whole turnout went tumbling over. . . .

'And afterwards I dreamt dreams of precipices. I made strides over precipices, I fell and fell with a floating swiftness towards remote valleys, I was assailed by eagles upon a perilous ledge that crumbled away and left me clinging by my nails to nothing.'

The Bisse of Leysin is one of those artificial water-courses which bring water from some distant source to pastures that have an insufficient or uncertain supply. It is a little better now than most because of a certain exceptional boldness in its construction; for a distance of a few score yards it runs supported by iron staples across the front of a sheer precipice, and for perhaps half a mile it hangs like an eyebrow over nearly or quite vertical walls of pine-set rock. Beside it, on the outer side of it, runs a path, which becomes an offhand gangway of planking at the overhanging places. At one corner, which gives the favourite picture-postcard from Montana, the rocks project so sharply above the water that the passenger on the gangway must crouch down upon the bending plank as he walks. There is no hand-hold at all.

A path from Montana takes one over a pine-clad spur and down a precipitous zig-zag upon the middle of the Bisse, and thither Benham came, fascinated by the very fact that here was something of which the mere report frightened him. He had to walk across the cold clear rush of the Bisse upon a pine log, and then he found himself upon one of the gentler interludes of the Bisse track. It was a scrambling path nearly two feet wide, and below it were slopes, but not so steep as to terrify. At a vast distance below he saw through tree-stems and blue haze a twisted strand of bright whiteness, the river that joins the Rhone at Sion. It looped about and passed out of sight remotely beneath his feet. He turned to the right, and came to a corner that overhung a precipice. He craned his head round this corner and saw the evil place of the picture-postcards.

He remained for a long time trying to screw himself up to walk along the jagged six-inch edge of rock between cliff and torrent into which the path has shrunken, to the sagging plank under the overhanging rock beyond.

He could not bring himself to do that.

'It happened that close to the corner a large lump of rock and earth was breaking away, a cleft was opening, so that presently, it seemed possible at any moment, the mass would fall headlong into the blue deeps below. This impending avalanche was not in my path along the Bisse, it was no sort of danger to me, but in some way its insecurity gave a final touch to my cowardice. I could not get myself round that corner.'

He turned away. He went and examined the planks in the other direction, and these he found less forbidding. He crossed one precipitous place, with a fall of two score feet or less beneath him, and found worse ahead. There also he managed. A third place was still more disagreeable. The plank was worn and thin, and sagged under him. He went along it supporting himself against the rock above the Bisse with an extended hand. Halfway the rock fell back, so that there was nothing whatever to hold. He stopped, hesitating whether he should go back—but on this plank there was no going back because no turning round seemed practicable. While he was still hesitating there came a helpful intervention. Behind him he saw a peasant appearing and disappearing behind trees and projecting rock masses, and coming across the previous plank at a vigorous trot. . . .

Under the stimulus of a spectator Benham got to the end of this third place without much trouble. Then very politely he stood aside for the expert to go ahead so that he could follow at his own pace.

There were, however, more difficulties yet to come, and a disagreeable humiliation. That confounded peasant developed a parental solicitude. After each crossing he waited, and presently began to offer advice and encouragement. At last came a place where everything was overhanging, where the Bisse was leaking, and the plank wet and slippery. The water ran out of the leak near the brim of the wooden channel and fell in a long shivering thread of silver. *There was no sound of its fall.* It just fell—into a void. Benham wished he had not noted that. He groaned, but faced the plank; he knew this would be the slowest affair of all.

The peasant surveyed him from the farther side.

'Don't be afraid!' cried the peasant in his clumsy Valaisian French, and returned, returning along the plank that seemed quite sufficiently loaded without him, extending a charitable hand.

'Damn!' whispered Benham, but he took the hand.

Afterwards, rather ignobly, he tried to explain in his public-school French. '*Pas de peur*,' he said. '*Pas de peur. Mais la tête, n'a pas l'habitude.*'

The peasant, failing to understand, assured him again that there was no danger.

('Damn!')

Benham was led over all the other planks, he was led as if he was an old lady crossing a glacier. He was led into absolute safety, and shamefacedly he rewarded his guide. Then he went a little way and sat down, swore softly, and watched the honest man go striding and plunging down towards Lens until he was out of sight.

'Now,' said Benham to himself, 'if I do not go back along the planks my secret honour is gone for ever.'

He told himself that he had not a good head, that he was not well, that the sun was setting and the light no longer good, that he had a very good chance indeed of getting killed. Then it came to him suddenly as a clear and simple truth, as something luminously plain, that it is better to get killed than go away defeated by such fears and unsteadiness as his. The change came into his mind as if a white light were suddenly turned on—where there had been nothing but shadows and darkness. He rose to his feet and went swiftly and intently the whole way back, going with a kind of temperate recklessness, and, because he was no longer careful, easily. He went on beyond his starting place toward the corner, and did that supreme bit, to and fro, that bit where the lump was falling away, and he had to crouch, as gaily as the rest, Then he re-crossed the Bisse upon the pine log, clambered up through the pines to the crest, and returned through the meadows to his own hotel.

After that he should have slept the sleep of contentment. but instead he had quite dreadful nightmares, of hanging in frozen fear above incredible declivities, of ill-aimed leaps across chasms to slippery footholds, of planks that swayed and broke suddenly in the middle and headed him down and down. . . .

The next day in the sunshine he walked the Bisse again with those dreams like trailing mists in his mind, and by comparison the path of the Bisse was nothing, it was like walking along a kerbstone, it was an exercise for young ladies. . . .

§ 7

In his younger days Benham had regarded Fear as a shameful secret and as a thing to be got rid of altogether. It seemed to him that to feel fear was to fall short of aristocracy, and in spite of the deep dreads and disgusts that haunted his mind, he set about the business of its subjugation as if it were a spiritual amputation. But as he emerged from the egotism of adolescence he came to realise that this was too comprehensive an operation; every one feels fear, and your true aristocrat is not one who has eliminated, but one who controls or ignores it. Brave men are men who do things when they are afraid to do them just as Nelson, even when he was seasick, and he was frequently seasick, was still master of the sea. Benham developed two leading ideas about fear; one that it is worse at the first onset, and far worse than any real experience, and the other that fear is essentially a social instinct. He set himself upon these lines to study—what can we call it?—the taming of fear, the nature, care, and management of fear. . . .

'Fear is very like pain in this, that it is a deterrent thing. It is superficial. Just as a man's skin is infinitely more sensitive than anything inside. . . . Once you have forced yourself or have been forced through the outward fear into vivid action or experience, you feel very little. The worst moment is before things happen. Rowe, the African sportsman, told me that he had seen cowardice often enough in the presence of lions, but he had never seen any one actually charged by a lion who did not behave well. I have heard the same thing of many sorts of dangers.

'I began to suspect this first in the case of falling or jumping down. Giddiness may be an almost intolerable torture, and falling nothing of the sort. I once saw the face of an old man who had flung himself out of a high window in Rome, and who had been killed instantly on the pavement; it was not simply a serene face, it was glad, exalted. I suspect that when we have broken the shell of fear, falling may be delightful. Jumping down is, after all, only a steeper tobogganing, and tobogganing a milder jumping down. Always I used to funk at the top of the Cresta run. I suffered sometimes almost intolerably; I found it almost impossible to get away. The first ten yards was like being slashed open with a sharp sword. But afterwards there was nothing but joyful thrills. All instinct, too, fought against me when I tried high diving. I managed it, and began to like it. I had to give it up because of my ears, but not until I had established the habit of stepping through that moment of disinclination.

'I was Challoner's passenger when he was killed at Sheerness. That was a queer unexpected experience, you may have supposed it an agony of terror, but indeed there was no fear in it at all. At any rate, I do not remember a moment of fear; it has gone clean out of my memory if ever it was there. We were swimming high and fast, three thousand feet or so, in a clear, sweet air over the town of Sheerness. The river, with a string of battleships, was far away to the west of us, and the endless gray-blue flats of the Thames to the north. The sun was low behind a bank of cloud. I was watching a motor-car, which seemed to be crawling slowly enough, though, no doubt, it was making a respectable pace, between two hedges down below. It is extraordinary how slowly everything seems to be going when one sees it from such a height.

'Then the left wing of the monoplane came up like a door that slams, some wires whistled past my head, and one whipped off my helmet, and then, with the seat slipping away from me, down we went. I snatched unavailingly for the helmet, and then gripped the sides. It was like dropping in a boat suddenly into the trough of a wave—and going on dropping. We were both strapped, and I got my feet against the side and clung to the locked second wheel.

'The sensation was as though something like an intermittent electric current was pouring through me. It's a ridiculous image to use, I can't justify it, but it was as if I was having cold blue light squirted through every pore of my being. There was an astonishment, a feeling of confirmation. "Of course these things do happen sometimes," I told myself. I don't remember that Challoner looked round or said anything at all. I am not sure that I looked at him. . . .

'There seemed to be a long interval of intensely excited curiosity, and I remember thinking, "Lord, but we shall come a smash in a minute!" Far ahead I saw the gray sheds of Eastchurch and people strolling about apparently unaware of our disaster. There was a sudden silence as Challoner stopped the engine. . . .

'But the point I want to insist upon is that I did not feel afraid. I was simply enormously, terribly *interested*. . . .

'There came a tremendous jolt and a lunge, and we were both tipped forward, so that we were hanging forehead down by our straps, and it looked as if the sheds were in the sky, then I saw nothing but sky, then came another vast swerve, and we were falling sideways, sideways. . . .

'I was altogether out of breath and *physically* astonished and I remember noting quite intelligently as we hit the ground how the green grass had an effect of *pouring out* in every direction from below us. . . .

'Then I remember a jerk and a feeling that I was flying up again. I was astonished by a tremendous popping— fabric, wires, everything seemed going pop, pop, pop, like a machine-gun, and then came a flash of intense pain as my arm crumpled up. It was quite impersonal pain. As impersonal as seeing intense colour. *Splinters !* I remember the word came into my head instantly. I remember that very definitely.

'I thought, I suppose, my arm was in splinters. Or perhaps of the scraps and ends of rods and wires flying about us. It is curious that while I remember the word I cannot recall the idea. . . .

'When I became conscious again the chief thing present in my mind was that all those fellows round were young soldiers who wouldn't at all understand bad behaviour. My arm was—orchestral, but still far from being real suffering *in* me. Also I wanted to know what Challoner had got. They wouldn't understand my questions, and then I twisted round and saw from the negligent way his feet came out from under the engine that he must be dead. And dark red stains with bright red froth——

'Of course !

'There again the chief feeling was a sense of oddity. I wasn't sorry for him any more than I was for myself.

'It seemed to me that it was all right with us both, remarkable, vivid, but all right. . . .'

§ 8

'But though there is little or no fear in an areoplane, even when it is smashing up, there is fear about areoplanes. There is something that says very urgently, "Don't" to the man who looks up into the sky. It is very interesting to note how at a place like Eastchurch or Brooklands the necessary discretion trails the old visceral feeling with it, and how men will hang about, ready to go up, resolved to go up, but delaying. Men of indisputable courage will get into a state between dread and laziness, and waste whole hours of flying weather on any excuse or no excuse. Once they are up that inhibition vanishes. The man who was delaying and delaying half an hour ago will now be cutting the most venturesome capers in the air. Few men are in a hurry to get down again. I mean that quite apart from the hesitation of landing, they like being up there.'

Then, abruptly, Benham comes back to his theory.

'Fear, you see, is the inevitable janitor, but it is not the ruler of experience. That is what I am driving at in all this. The bark of danger is worse than its bite. Inside the portals there may be events and destruction, but terror stays defeated at the door. It may be that when that old man was killed by a horse the child who watched suffered more than he did. . . .

'I am sure that was so. . . .'

§ 9

As White read Benham's notes and saw how his argument drove on, he was reminded again and again of those school-boy days and Benham's hardihood, and his own instinctive unreasonable reluctance to follow those gallant intellectual leads. If fear is an ancient instinctive boundary that the modern life, the aristocratic life, is bound to ignore and transcend, may this not also be the case with pain? We do a little adventure into the 'life beyond fear'; may we not also think of adventuring into the life beyond pain? Is pain any saner a warning than fear? May not pain just as much as fear keep us from possible and splendid things? But why ask a question that is already answered in principle in every dentist's chair? Benham's idea, however, went much further than that; he was clearly suggesting that in pain itself, pain endured beyond a certain pitch, there might come pleasure again, an intensity of sensation that might have the colour of delight. He betrayed a real anxiety to demonstrate this possibility, he had the earnest-ness of a man who is sensible of dissentient elements within. He hated the thought of pain even more than he hated fear. His arguments did not in the least convince White, who stopped to poke the fire and assure himself of his own comfort in the midst of his reading.

Young people and unseasoned people, Benham argued, are apt to imagine that if fear is increased and carried to an extreme pitch it becomes unbearable, one will faint or die; given a weak heart, a weak artery or any such structural defect and that may well happen, but it is just as possible that as the stimulation increases one passes through a brief ecstasy of terror to a new sane world, exalted but as sane as normal existence. There is the calmness of despair. Benham had made some notes to enforce this view, of the observed calm behaviour of men already hopelessly lost, men on sinking ships, men going to execution, men already maimed and awaiting the final stroke, but for the most part these were merely references to books and periodicals. In exactly the same way, he argued, we exaggerate the range of pain as if it were limitless. We think if we are unthinking that it passes into agony and so beyond endurance to destruction. It probably does nothing of the kind. Benham compared pain to the death range of the electric current. At a certain voltage it thrills, at a greater it torments and convulses, at a still greater it kills. But at enormous voltages, as Tesla was the first to demonstrate, it does no injury. And following on this came memoranda on the recorded behaviour of martyrs, on the self-torture of Hindoo ascetics, of the defiance of Red Indian prisoners.

'These things,' Benham had written, 'are much more horrible when one considers them from the point of view of an easy-chair'; White gave an assenting nod—'*are they really horrible at all ?* Is it possible that these charred and slashed and splintered persons, those Indians hanging from hooks, those walkers in the fiery furnace, have had glimpses through great windows that were worth the price they paid for them? Haven't we allowed those checks and barriers that are so important a restraint upon childish enterprise, to creep up into and distress and distort adult life? . . .

'The modern world thinks too much as though painless-ness and freedom from danger were ultimate ends. It is fear-haunted, it is troubled by the thoughts of pain and death, which it has never met except as well-guarded children meet these things, in exaggerated and untestable forms, in the menagerie or in nightmares. And so it thinks the discovery of anæsthetics the crowning triumph of civilisation, and cosiness and innocent amusement, those ideals of the nursery, the whole purpose of mankind. . . .'

'Mm,' said White, and pressed his lips together and knotted his brows and shook his head.

§ 10

But the bulk of Benham's discussion of fear was not concerned with this perverse and overstrained suggestion of pleasure reached through torture, this exaggeration of the man resolved not to shrink at anything; it was an examination of the present range and use of fear that led gradually to something like a theory of control and discipline. The second of his two dominating ideas was that fear is an instinct arising only in isolation, that in a crowd there may be a collective panic, but that there is no real individual fear. Fear, Benham held, drives the man back to the crowd, the dog to its master, the wolf to the pack, and when it is felt that the danger is pooled, then fear leaves us. He was quite prepared to meet the objection that animals of a solitary habit do nevertheless exhibit fear. Some of this apparent fear, he argued, was merely discretion, and what is not discretion is the survival of an infantile characteristic. The fear felt by a tiger cub is certainly a social emotion, that drives it back to the other cubs, to its mother and the dark hiding of the lair. The fear of a fully grown tiger sends it into the reeds and the shadows, to a refuge, that must be 'still reminiscent of the maternal lair.' But fear has very little hold upon the adult solitary animal, it changes with extreme readiness to resentment and rage.

'Like most inexperienced people,' ran his notes, 'I was astonished at the reported feats of men in war; I believed they were exaggerated, and that there was a kind of unpremeditated conspiracy of silence about their real behaviour. But when on my way to visit India for the third time I turned off to see what I could of the fighting before Adrianople, I discovered at once that a thousand casually selected conscripts will, every one of them, do things together that not one of them could by any means be induced to do alone. I saw men not merely obey orders that gave them the nearly certain prospect of death, but I saw them exceeding orders; I saw men leap out of cover for the mere sake of defiance, and fall shot through and smashed by a score of bullets. I saw a number of Bulgarians in the hands of the surgeon, several quite frightfully wounded, refuse chloroform merely to impress the English onlooker; some of their injuries I could scarcely endure to see, and I watched a line of infantrymen go on up a hill and keep on quite manifestly cheerful with men dropping out and wriggling, and men dropping out and lying still until every other man was down. . . . Not one man would have gone up that hill alone, without onlookers. . . .'

Rowe, the lion nunter, told Benham that only on one occasion in his life had he given way to ungovernable fear, and that was when he was alone. Many times he had been in fearful situations in the face of charging lions and elephants and once he had been bowled over and carried some distance by a lion, but on none of these occasions had fear demoralised him. There was no question of his general pluck. But on one occasion he was lost in rocky waterless country in Somaliland. He strayed out in the early morning while his camels were being loaded, followed some antelope too far, and lost his bearings. He looked up expecting to see the sun on his right hand and found it on his left. He became bewildered. He wandered some time, and then fired three signal shots and got no reply. Then losing his head he began shouting. He had only four or five more cartridges and no water-bottle. His men were accustomed to his going on alone, and might not begin to remark upon his absence until sundown. . . . It chanced, however, that one of the shikari noted the water-bottle he had left behind and organised a hunt for him.

Long before they found him he had passed to an extremity of terror. The world had become hideous and threatening, the sun was a pitiless glare, each rocky ridge he clambered became more dreadful than the last, each new valley into which he looked more hateful and desolate, the cramped thorn bushes threatened him gauntly, the rocks had a sinister lustre, and in every blue shadow about him the night and death lurked and waited. There was no hurry for them, presently they would spread out again and join and submerge him, presently in the confederated darkness he could be stalked and seized and slain. Yes, this he admitted was real fear. He had cracked his voice, yelling as a child yells. And then he had become afraid of his own voice. . . .

'Now this excess of fear in isolation, this comfort in a crowd, in support and in a refuge, even when support or refuge is quite illusory, is just exactly what one would expect of fear if one believed it to be an instinct which has become a misfit. In the case of the soldier fear is so much a misfit that instead of saving him for the most part it destroys him. Raw soldiers under fire bunch together and armies fight in masses, men are mowed down in swathes, because only so is the courage of the common men sustained, only so can they be brave; albeit spread out, and handling their weapons as men of unqualified daring would handle them, they would be infinitely safer and more effective. . . .

'And all of us, it may be, are restrained by this misfit fear from a thousand bold successful gestures of mind and body; we are held back from the attainment of mighty securities in pitiful temporary shelters that are perhaps in the end no better than traps. . . .'

From such considerations Benham went on to speculate how far the crowd can be replaced in a man's imagination, how far some substitute for that social backing can be made to serve the same purpose in neutralising fear. He wrote with the calm of a man who weighs the probabilities of a riddle, and with the zeal of a man lost to every material consideration. His writing, it seemed to White, had something of the enthusiastic whiteness of his face, the enthusiastic brightness of his eyes. We can no more banish fear from our being at present than we can carve out the fleshy pillars of the heart or the pineal gland in the brain. It is deep in our inheritance. As deep as hunger. And just as we have to satisfy hunger in order that it should leave us free, so we have to satisfy the unconquerable importunity of fear. We have to reassure our faltering instincts. There must be something to take the place of lair and familiars, something not ourselves but general, that we must carry with us into the lonely places. For it is true that man has now not only to learn to fight in open order instead of in a phalanx, but he has to think and plan and act in open order, to live in open order. . . .

Then with one of his abrupt transitions Benham had written, 'This brings me to God.'

'The devil it does!' said White, roused to a keener attention.

'By no feat of intention can we achieve courage in loneliness so long as we feel indeed alone. An isolated man, an egoist, an Epicurean man, will always fail himself in the solitary place. There must be something more with us to sustain us against this vast universe than the spark of life that began yesterday and must be extinguished to-morrow. There can be no courage beyond social courage, the sustaining confidence of the herd, until there is in us the sense of God. But God is a word that covers a multitude of meanings. When I was a boy I was a passionate atheist, I defied God, and so far as God is the mere sanction of social traditions and pressures, a mere dressing up of the crowd's will in canonicals, I do still deny him and repudiate him. That God I heard of first from my nursemaid, and in very truth he is the proper God of all the nursemaids of mankind. But there is another God than that God of obedience, God the immortal adventurer in me, God who calls men from home and country, God scourged and crowned with thorns, who rose in a nail-pierced body out of death and came not to bring peace but a sword.'

With something bordering upon intellectual consternation, White, who was a decent self-respecting sceptic, read these last clamberings of Benham's spirit. They were written in pencil; they were unfinished when he died.

(Surely the man was not a Christian !)

'You may be heedless of death and suffering because you think you cannot suffer and die, or you may be heedless of death and pain because you have identified your life with the honour of mankind and the insatiable adventurousness of man's imagination, so that the possible death is negligible and the possible achievement altogether outweighs it.' . . .

White shook his head over these pencilled fragments.

He was a member of the Rationalist Press Association, and he had always taken it for granted that Benham was an orthodox unbeliever. But this was hopelessly unsound, heresy, perilous stuff; almost, it seemed to him, a posthumous betrayal. . . .

§ 11

One night when he was in India the spirit of adventure came upon Benham. He had gone with Kepple, of the forestry department, into the jungle country in the hills above the Tapti. He had been very anxious to see something of that aspect of Indian life, and he had snatched at the chance Kepple had given him. But they had scarcely started before the expedition was brought to an end by an accident; Kepple was thrown by a pony and his ankle broken. He and Benham bandaged it as well as they could, and a litter was sent for, and meanwhile they had to wait in the camp that was to have been the centre of their jungle raids. The second day of this waiting was worse for Kepple than the first, and he suffered much from the pressure of this amateurish bandaging. In the evening Benham got cool water from the well and rearranged things better;

the two men dined and smoked under their thatched roof beneath the big banyan, and then Kepple, tired out by his day of pain, was carried to his tent. Presently he fell asleep and Benham was left to himself.

Now that the heat was over he found himself quite indisposed to sleep. He felt full of life and anxious for happenings.

He went back and sat down upon the iron bedstead beneath the banyan that Keppel had lain upon through the day, and he watched the soft immensity of the Indian night swallow up the last lingering colours of the world. It left the outlines, it obliterated nothing, but it stripped off the superficial reality of things. The moon was full and high overhead, and the light had not so much gone as changed from definition and the blazing glitter and reflections of solidity to a translucent and unsubstantial clearness. The jungle that bordered the little encampment north, south, and west seemed to have crept a little nearer, enriched itself with blackness, taken to itself voices.

(Surely it had been silent during the day.)

A warm, faintly-scented breeze just stirred the dead grass and the leaves. In the day the air had been still.

Immediately after the sunset there had been a great crying of peacocks in the distance, but that was over now; the crickets, however, were still noisy, and a persistent sound had become predominant, an industrious unmistakable sound, a sound that took his mind back to England, in midsummer. It was like a watchman's rattle —a nightjar!

So there were nightjars here in India, too ! One might have expected something less familiar. And then came another cry from far away over the heat-stripped tree-tops, a less familiar cry. It was repeated. Was that perhaps some craving leopard, a tiger cat, a panther?——

'*Hunt, Hunt;*' that might be a deer.

Then suddenly an angry chattering came from the dark trees quite close at hand. A monkey? . . .

These great, scarce visible, sweeping movements through the air were bats. . . .

Of course, the day jungle is the jungle asleep. This was its waking hour. Now the deer were arising from their forms, the bears creeping out of their dens amidst the rocks and blundering down the gullies, the tigers and panthers and jungle cats stalking noiselessly from their lairs in the grass. Countless creatures that had hidden from the heat and pitiless exposure of the day stood now awake and alertly intent upon their purposes, grazed or sought water, flitting delicately through the moonlight and shadows. The jungle was awakening. Again Benham heard that sound like the belling of a stag. . . .

This was the real life of the jungle, this night life, into which man did not go. Here he was on the verge of a world that for all the stuffed trophies of the sportsman and the specimens of the naturalist is still almost as unknown as if it were upon another planet. What intruders men are, what foreigners in the life of this ancient system!

He looked over his shoulder, and there were the two little tents, one that sheltered Kepple and one that awaited him, and beyond, in an irregular line, glowed the ruddy smoky fires of the men. One or two turbaned figures still flitted about, and there was a voice—low, monotonous—it must have been telling a tale. Further, sighing and stirring ever and again, were tethered beasts, and then a great pale space of moonlight and the clumsy outlines of the village well. The clustering village itself slept in darkness beyond the mango trees, and still remoter the black encircling jungle closed in. One might have fancied this was the encampment of newly-come invaders, were it not for the larger villages that are overgrown with thickets and altogether swallowed up again in the wilderness; and for the deserted temples that are found rent asunder by the roots of trees and the ancient embankments that hold water only for the drinking of the sambur deer.

Benham turned his face to the dim jungle again. . . .

He had come far out of his way to visit this strange world of the ancient life, that now recedes and dwindles before our new civilisation, that seems fated to shrivel up and pass altogether before the dry advance of physical science and material organisation. He was full of unsatisfied curiosities about its fierce hungers and passions, its fears and cruelties, its instincts and its wellnigh incommunicable and yet most precious understandings. He had long ceased to believe that the wild beast is wholly evil, and safety and plenty the ultimate good for men. . . .

Perhaps he would never get nearer to this mysterious jungle life than he was now.

It was intolerably tantalising that it should be so close at hand and so inaccessible. . . .

As Benham sat brooding over his disappointment the moon, swimming on through the still circle of the hours, passed slowly over him. The lights and shadows about him changed by imperceptible gradations, and a long pale alley, where the native cart track drove into the forest, opened slowly out of the darkness slowly, broadened, slowly lengthened. It opened out to him with a quality of invitation. . . .

There was the jungle before him. Was it after all so inaccessible?

'Come!' the road said to him.

Benham rose and walked out a few paces into the moonlight and stood motionless.

Was he afraid?

Even now some hungry watchful monster might lurk in yonder shadows, watching with infinite still patience. Kepple had told him how they would sit still for hours—staring unblinkingly as cats stare at a fire—and then crouch to advance. Beneath the shrill overtone of the nightjars, what noiseless gray shapes, what deep breathings and cracklings and creepings might there not be? . . .

Was he afraid?

That question determined him to go.

He hesitated whether he should take a gun. A stick? A gun, he knew, was a dangerous thing to an inexperienced man. No! He would go now, even as he was with empty hands. At least he would go as far as the end of that band of moonlight. If for no other reason than because he was afraid.

Now!

For a moment it seemed to him as though his feet were too heavy to lift, and then, hands in pockets, khaki-clad, an almost invisible figure, he strolled towards the cart-track.

Come to that, he halted for a moment to regard the distant fires of the men. No one would miss him. They would think he was in his tent. He faced the stirring quiet ahead. The cart-track was a rutted path of soft, warm sand, on which he went almost noiselessly. A bird squabbled for an instant in a thicket. A great white owl floated like a flake of moonlight across the track and vanished without a sound among the trees.

Along the moonlit path went Benham, and when he passed near trees his footsteps became noisy with the rustle and crash of dead leaves. The jungle was full of moonlight; twigs, branches, creepers, grass-clumps came out acutely vivid. The trees and bushes stood in pools of darkness, and beyond were pale stretches of misty moonshine and big rocks shining with an unearthly lustre. Things seemed to be clear and yet uncertain. It was as if they dissolved or retired a little and then returned to solidity.

A sudden chattering broke out overhead, and black across the great stars soared a flying squirrel and caught a twig, and ran for shelter. A second hesitated in a tree-top and pursued. They chased each other and vanished abruptly. He forgot his sense of insecurity in the interest of these active little silhouettes. And he noted how much bigger and more wonderful the stars can look when one sees them through interlacing branches.

Ahead was darkness, but not so dark when he came to it that the track was invisible. He was at the limit of his intention, but now he saw that that had been a childish project. He would go on, he would walk right into the jungle. His first disinclination was conquered, and the soft intoxication of the subtropical moonshine was in his blood. . . . But he wished he could walk as a spirit walks, without this noise of leaves. . . .

Yes, this was very wonderful and beautiful, and there must always be jungles for men to walk in. Always there must be jungles. . . .

Some small beast snarled and bolted from under his feet. He stopped sharply. He had come into a darkness under great boughs, and now he stood still as the little creature scuttled away. Beyond the track emerged into a dazzling whiteness. . . .

In the stillness he could hear the deer belling again in the distance, and then came a fuss of monkeys in a group of trees near at hand. He remained still until this had died away into mutterings.

Then on the verge of movement he was startled by a ripe mango that slipped from its stalk and fell out of the tree and struck his hand. It took a little time to understand that, and then he laughed, and his muscles relaxed, and he went on again.

A thorn caught at him and he disentangled himself.

He crossed the open space, and the moon was like a great shield of light spread out above him. All the world seemed swimming in its radiance. The stars were like lamps in a mist of silvery blue.

The track led him on across white open spaces of shrivelled grass and sand, amidst trees where shadows made black

patternings upon the silver, and then it plunged into
obscurities. For a time it lifted, and then on one hand the
bush fell away, and he saw across a vast moonlit valley
wide undulations of open cultivation, belts of jungle,
copses, and a great lake as black as ebony. For a time
the path ran thus open, and then the jungle closed in again
and there were more thickets, more levels of grass, and in
one place far overhead among the branches he heard and
stood for a time perplexed at a vast deep humming of
bees. . . .

Presently a black monster with a hunched back went
across his path heedless of him and making a great noise
in the leaves. He stood quite still until it had gone. He
could not tell whether it was a boar or hyæna; most
probably, he thought, a boar because of the heaviness of
its rush.

The path dropped downhill for a time, crossed a ravine,
ascended. He passed a great leafless tree on which there
were white flowers. On the ground also, in the darkness
under the tree, there were these flowers; they were dropping
noiselessly, and since they were visible in the shadows, it
seemed to him that they must be phosphorescent. And
they emitted a sweetish scent that lay heavily athwart the
path. Presently he passed another such tree. Then he
became aware of a tumult ahead of him, a smashing of
leaves, a snorting and slobbering, grunting and sucking,
a whole series of bestial sounds. He halted for a little
while, and then drew nearer, picking his steps to avoid too
great a noise. Here were more of those white-blossomed
trees, and beneath, in the darkness, something very black
and big was going to and fro, eating greedily. Then he
found that there were two and then more of these black
things, three or four of them.

Curiosity made Benham draw nearer, very softly.

Presently one showed in a patch of moonlight, startlingly
big, a huge, black hairy monster with a long white nose on
a grotesque face, and he was stuffing armfuls of white
blossom into his mouth with his curved fore claws. He
took not the slightest notice of the still man, who stood
perhaps twenty yards away from him. He was too blind
and careless. He snorted and smacked his slobbering lips,
and plunged into the shadows again. Benham heard him
root among the leaves and grunt appreciatively. The air
was heavy with the reek of the crushed flowers.

For some time Benham remained listening to and peering

at these preoccupied gluttons. At last he shrugged his shoulders, and left them and went on his way. For a long time he could hear them; then just as he was on the verge of forgetting them altogether, some dispute arose among them, and there began a vast uproar, squeals, protests, comments, one voice ridiculously replete and authoritative, ridiculously suggestive of a drunken judge with his mouth full, and a shrill voice of grievance high above the others. . . .

The uproar of the bears died away at last, almost abruptly and left the jungle to the incessant nightjars. . . .

For what end was this life of the jungle?

All Benham's senses were alert to the sounds and appearances about him, and at the same time his mind was busy with the perplexities of that riddle. Was the jungle just an aimless pool of life that man must drain and clear away? Or is it to have a use in the greater life of our race that now begins? Will man value the jungle as he values the precipice, for the sake of his manhood? Will he preserve it?

Man must keep hard, man must also keep fierce. Will the jungle keep him fierce?

For life, thought Benham, there must be insecurity. . . .

He had missed the track. . . .

He was now in a second ravine. He was going downward, walking on silvery sand amidst great boulders, and now there was a new sound in the air—— It was the croaking of frogs. Ahead was a solitary gleam. He was approaching a jungle pool. . . .

Suddenly the stillness was alive, in a panic uproar. '*Honk!*' cried a great voice, and '*Honk!*' There was a clatter of hoofs, a wild rush—a rush as it seemed towards him. Was he being charged? He backed against a rock. A great pale shape leaped by him, an antlered shape. It was a herd of big deer bolting suddenly out of the stillness. He heard the swish and smash of their retreat grow distant, disperse. He remained standing with his back to the rock.

Slowly the strophe and antistrophe of frogs and goatsuckers resumed possession of his consciousness. But now some primitive instinct perhaps, or some subconscious intimation of danger, made him meticulously noiseless.

He went on down a winding sound-deadening path of sand towards the drinking-place. He came to a wide white place that was almost level, and beyond it under clustering pale-stemmed trees shone the mirror surface of some ancient tank, and, sharp and black, a dog-like beast sat on its tail in the midst of this space, started convulsively and went slinking into the undergrowth. Benham paused for a moment and then walked out softly into the light, and, behold ! as if it were to meet him came a monster, a vast dark shape drawing itself lengthily out of the blackness, and stopped with a start as if it had been instantly changed to stone.

It had stopped with one paw advanced. Its striped mask was light and dark gray in the moonlight, gray but faintly tinged with ruddiness; its mouth was a little open, its fangs and a pendant of viscous saliva shone vivid. Its great round-pupilled eyes regarded him steadfastly. At last the nightmare of Benham's childhood had come true, and he was face to face with a tiger, uncaged, uncontrolled.

For some moments neither moved, neither the beast nor the man. They stood face to face, each perhaps with an equal astonishment, motionless and soundless, in that mad Indian moonlight that makes all things like a dream.

Benham stood quite motionless, and body and mind had halted together. That confrontation had an interminableness that had nothing to do with the actual passage of time. Then some trickle of his previous thoughts stirred in the frozen quiet of his mind.

He spoke hoarsely. 'I am Man,' he said, and lifted a hand as he spoke. 'The Thought of the world.'

His heart leapt within him as the tiger moved. But the great beast went sideways, gardant, only that its head was low; three noiseless instantaneous strides it made, and stood again watching him.

'Man,' he said, in a voice that had no sound, and took a step forward.

'Wough !' With two bounds the monster had become a great gray streak that crackled and rustled in the shadows of the trees. And then it had vanished, become invisible and inaudible with a kind of instantaneousness.

For some seconds or some minutes Benham stood rigid, fearlessly expectant, and then far away up the ravine he heard the deer repeat their cry of alarm, and understood with a new wisdom that the tiger had passed among them and was gone. . . .

He walked on towards the deserted tank, and now he was talking aloud.

'I understand the jungle. I understand. . . . If a few men die here, what matter ? There are worse deaths than being killed. . . .

'What is this fool's trap of security?

'Every time in my life that I have fled from security I have fled from death. . . .

'Let men stew in their cities if they will. It is in the lonely places, in jungles and mountains, in snows and fires, in the still observatories and the silent laboratories, in those secret and dangerous places where life probes into life, it is there that the masters of the world, the lords of the beast, the rebel sons of Fate come to their own. . . .

'You sleeping away there in the cities! Do you know what it means for you that I am here to-night?

'Do you know what it means to you?

'I am just one—just the precursor.

'Presently if you will not budge, those hot cities must be burnt about you. You must come out of them. . . .'

He wandered now uttering his thoughts as they came to him, and he saw no more living creatures because they fled and hid before the sound of his voice. He wandered until the moon, larger now and yellow tinged, was low between the black bars of the tree stems. And then it sank very suddenly behind a hilly spur and the light failed swiftly.

He stumbled and went with difficulty. He could go no farther among these rocks and ravines, and he sat down at the foot of a tree to wait for day.

He sat very still indeed.

A great stillness came over the world, a velvet silence that wrapped about him, as the velvet shadows wrapped about him. The corncrakes had ceased, all the sounds and stir of animal life had died away, the breeze had fallen. A drowsing comfort took possession of him. He grew more placid and more placid still. He was enormously content to find that fear had fled before him and was gone. He drifted into that state of mind when one thinks without ideas, when one's mind is like a starless sky, serene and empty.

§ 12

Some hours later Benham found that the trees and rocks were growing visible again, and he saw a very bright star he knew must be Lucifer rising amidst the black branches. He was sitting upon a rock at the foot of a slender-stemmed leafless tree. He had been asleep, and it was daybreak. Everything was coldly clear and colourless.

He must have slept soundly.

He heard a cock crow, and another answer—jungle fowl these must be, because there could be no village within earshot—and then far away and bringing back memories of terraced houses and ripe walled gardens, was the scream of peacocks. And some invisible bird was making a hollow beating sound among the trees near at hand. *Tunk. . . . Tunk*, and out of the dry grass came a twittering.

There was a green light in the east that grew stronger, and the stars after their magnitudes were dissolving in the blue; only a few remained faintly visible. The sound of birds increased. Through the trees he saw towering up a great mauve thing like the back of a monster—but that was nonsense, it was the crest of a steep hillside covered with woods of teak.

He stood up and stretched himself, and wondered whether he had dreamed of a tiger.

He tried to remember and retrace the course of his overnight wanderings.

A flight of emerald parakeets tore screaming through the trees, and then far away uphill he heard the creaking of a cart.

He followed the hint of a footmark, and went back up the glen slowly and thoughtfully.

Presently he came to a familiar place, a group of trees, a sheet of water, and the ruins of an old embankment. It was the ancient tank of his overnight encounter. The pool of his dream?

With doubt still in his mind, he walked round its margin to the sandy level beyond, and cast about and sought intently, and at last found, and then found clearly, imposed upon the tracks of several sorts of deer and the footprints of many biggish birds, first the great spoor of the tiger and then his own. Here the beast had halted, and here it had leapt aside. Here his own footmarks stopped. Here his heels had come together.

It had been no dream.

There was a white mist upon the water of the old tank like the bloom upon a plum, and the trees about it seemed smaller and the sand-space wider and rougher than they had seemed in the moonshine. Then the ground had looked like a floor of frosted silver.

And thence he went on upward through the fresh morning, until just as the east grew red with sunrise, he reached the cart-track from which he had strayed overnight. It was, he found, a longer way back to the camp than he remembered it to be. Perhaps he had struck the path farther along. It curved about and went up and down and crossed three ravines. At last he came to that trampled place of littered white blossom under great trees where he had seen the bears.

The sunlight went before him in a sheaf of golden spears, and his shadow, that was at first limitless, crept towards his feet. The dew had gone from the dead grass and the sand was hot to his dry boots before he came back into the open space about the great banyan and the tents. And Kepple, refreshed by a night's rest and coffee, was wondering loudly where the devil he had gone.

THE STORY

CHAPTER THE FIRST

THE BOY GROWS UP

§ 1

BENHAM was the son of a schoolmaster. His father was assistant first at Cheltenham, and subsequently at Minchinghampton, and then he became head and later on sole proprietor of Martindale House, a high-class preparatory school at Seagate. He was extremely successful for some years, as success goes in the scholastic profession, and then disaster overtook him in the shape of a divorce. His wife, William Porphyry's mother, made the acquaintance of a rich young man named Nolan, who was recuperating at Seagate from the sequelæ of snake-bite, malaria, and a gun accident in Brazil. She ran away with him, and she was divorced. She was, however, unable to marry him because he died at Wiesbaden only three days after the Reverend Harold Benham obtained his decree absolute. Instead, therefore, being a woman of great spirit, enterprise and sweetness, she married Godfrey Marayne, afterwards Sir Godfrey Marayne, the great London surgeon.

Nolan was a dark, rather melancholy and sentimental young man, and he left about a third of his very large fortune entirely to Mrs Benham and the rest to her in trust for her son, whom he deemed himself to have injured. With this and a husband already distinguished, she returned presently to London, and was on the whole fairly well received there.

It was upon the reverend gentleman at Seagate that the brunt of this divorce fell. There is perhaps a certain injustice in the fact that a schoolmaster who has lost his wife should also lose the more valuable proportion of his pupils, but the tone of thought in England is against any association of a schoolmaster with matrimonial irregularity. And also Mr Benham remarried. It would certainly have been better for him if he could have produced a sister.

His school declined and his efforts to resuscitate it only hastened its decay. Conceiving that he could now only appeal to the broader-minded, more progressive type of parent, he became an educational reformer, and wrote upon modernising the curriculum with increasing frequency to the *Times*, He expended a considerable fraction of his dwindling capital upon a science laboratory and a fives court; he added a London Bachelor of Science with a Teaching Diploma to the school staff, and a library of about a thousand volumes, including the Hundred Best Books as selected by the late Lord Avebury, to the school equipment. None of these things did anything but enhance the suspicion of laxity his wife's escapade had created in the limited opulent and discreet class to which his establishment appealed. One boy who, under the influence of the Hundred Best Books, had quoted the *Zend-Avesta* to an irascible but influential grandfather, was withdrawn without notice or compensation in the middle of the term. It intensifies the tragedy of the Reverend Harold Benham's failure that in no essential respect did his school depart from the pattern of all other properly-conducted preparatory schools.

In appearance he was near the average of scholastic English gentlemen. He displayed a manifest handsomeness somewhat weakened by disregard and disuse, a large moustache and a narrow high forehead. His rather tired brown eyes were magnified by glasses. He was an active man in unimportant things, with a love for the phrase 'ship-shape,' and he played cricket better than any one else on the staff. He walked in wide strides, and would sometimes use the tail of his gown on the blackboard. Like so many clergymen and schoolmasters, he had early distrusted his natural impulse in conversation, and had adopted the defensive precaution of a rather formal and sonorous speech, which habit had made a part of him. His general effect was of one who is earnestly keeping up things that might otherwise give way, keeping them up by act and voice, keeping up an atmosphere of vigour and success in a school that was only too manifestly attenuated, keeping up a pretentious economy of administration in a school that must not be too manifestly impoverished, keeping up a claim to be in the scientific van and rather a flutterer of dovecots—with its method of manual training for example—keeping up *esprit de corps* and the manliness of himself and every one about him, keeping up his affection

for his faithful second wife and his complete forgetfulness
of and indifference to that spirit of distracting impulse
and insubordination away there in London, who had once
been his delight and insurmountable difficulty. 'After
my visits to her,' wrote Benham, 'he would show by a
hundred little expressions and poses and acts how intensely
he wasn't noting that anything of the sort had occurred.'

But one thing that from the outset the father seemed
to have failed to keep up thoroughly was his intention to
mould and dominate his son.

The advent of his boy had been a tremendous event in
the reverend gentleman's life. It is not improbable that
his disposition to monopolise the pride of this event contributed to the ultimate disruption of his family. It left
so few initiatives within the home to his wife. He had been
an early victim to that wave of philoprogenitive and
educational enthusiasm which distinguished the closing
decade of the nineteenth century. He was full of plans
in those days for the education of his boy, and the thought
of the youngster played a large part in the series of complicated emotional crises with which he celebrated the
departure of his wife, crises in which a number of old school
and college friends very generously assisted—spending
week-ends at Seagate for this purpose, and mingling
tobacco, impassioned hand-clasps and suchlike consolation
with much patient sympathetic listening to his carefully
balanced analysis of his feelings. He declared that his son
was now his one living purpose in life, and he sketched out
a scheme of moral and intellectual training that he
subsequently embodied in five very stimulating and intimate
articles for the *School World*, but never put into more than
partial operation.

'I have read my father's articles upon this subject,'
wrote Benham, 'and I am still perplexed to measure just
what I owe to him. Did he ever attempt this moral training
he contemplated so freely? I don't think he did. I know
now, I knew then, that he had something in his mind. . . .
There were one or two special walks we had together, he
invited me to accompany him with a certain portentousness,
and we would go out pregnantly making superficial remarks
about the school cricket and return, discussing botany,
with nothing said.

'His heart failed him.

'Once or twice, too, he seemed to be reaching out at me
from the school pulpit.

'I think that my father did manage to convey to me his belief that there were these fine things, honour, high aims, nobilities. If I did not get this belief from him then I do not know how I got it. But it was as if he hinted at a treasure that had got very dusty in an attic, a treasure which he hadn't himself been able to spend. . . .'

The father who had intended to mould his son ended by watching him grow, not always with sympathy or understanding. He was an overworked man assailed by many futile anxieties. One sees him striding about the establishment with his gown streaming out behind him, urging on the groundsman or the gardener, or, dignified, expounding the particular advantages of Seagate to inquiring parents; one sees him unnaturally cheerful and facetious at the midday dinner-table; one imagines him keeping up high aspirations in a rather too hastily scribbled sermon in the school pulpit, or keeping up an enthusiasm for beautiful language in a badly-prepared lesson on Virgil, or expressing unreal indignation and unjustifiably exalted sentiments to evil doers; and one realises his disadvantage against the quiet youngster whose retentive memory was storing up all these impressions for an ultimate judgment; and one understands, too, a certain relief that mingled with his undeniable emotion when at last the time came for young Benham, 'the one living purpose' of his life, to be off to Minchinghampton and the next step in the mysterious ascent of the English educational system.

Three times at least, and with an increased interval, the father wrote fine fatherly letters that would have stood the test of publication. Then his communications became comparatively hurried and matter-of-fact. His boy's return home for the holidays was always rather a stirring time for his private feelings, but he became more and more inexpressive. He would sometimes lay a hand on those growing shoulders and then withdraw it. They felt braced-up shoulders, stiffly inflexible or—they would wince. And when one has let the habit of indefinite feelings grow upon one, what is there left to say? If one did say anything one might be asked questions. . . .

One or two of the long vacations they spent abroad together. The last of these occasions followed Benham's convalescence at Montana and his struggle with the Bisse; the two went to Zermatt and did several peaks and crossed the Theodule, and it was clear that their joint expeditions were a strain upon both of them. The father thought the son reckless, unskilful, and impatient; the son found the father's insistence upon guides, ropes, precautions, the recognised way, the highest point and back again before you get a chill, and talk about it sagely but very, very modestly over pipes, tiresome. He wanted to wander in deserts of ice and see over the mountains, and discover what it is to be benighted on a precipice. And gradually he was becoming familiar with his father's repertory of Greek quotations. There was no breach between them, but each knew that holiday was the last they would ever spend together. . . .

The court had given the custody of young William Porphyry into his father's hands, but by a generous concession it was arranged that his mother should have him to see her for an hour or so five times a year. The Nolan legacy, however, coming upon the top of this, introduced a peculiar complication that provided much work for tactful intermediaries, and gave great and increasing scope for painful delicacies on the part of Mr Benham as the boy grew up.

'I see,' said the father over his study pipe and with his glasses fixed on remote distances above the head of the current sympathiser, 'I see more and more clearly that the tale of my sacrifices is not yet at an end. . . . In many respects he is like her. . . . Quick. Too quick. . . . He must choose. But I know his choice. Yes, yes—I'm not blind. She's worked upon him. . . . I have done what I could to bring out the manhood in him. Perhaps it will bear the strain. . . . It will be a wrench, old man—God knows.'

He did his very best to make it a wrench.

§ 2

Benham's mother, whom he saw quarterly and also on the first of May, because it was her birthday, touched and coloured his imagination far more than his father did. She was now Lady Marayne, and a prominent, successful, and happy little lady. Her dereliction had been forgiven quite soon, and whatever whisper of it remained was very completely forgotten during the brief period of moral kindliness which followed the accession of King Edward the Seventh. It no doubt contributed to her social reinstatement that her former husband was entirely devoid of social importance, while, on the other hand, Sir Godfrey

Marayne's temporary monopoly of the cæcal operation which became so fashionable in the last decade of Queen Victoria's reign as to be practically epidemic, created a strong feeling in her favour.

She was blue-eyed and very delicately complexioned, quick-moving, witty, given to little storms of clean enthusiasm; she loved handsome things, brave things, successful things, and the respect and affection of all the world. She did quite what she liked upon impulse, and nobody ever thought ill of her.

Her family were the Mantons of Blent, quite good west-country people. She had broken away from them before she was twenty to marry Benham, whom she had idealised at a tennis party. He had talked of his work and she had seen it in a flash, the noblest work in the world, him at his daily divine toil and herself a Madonna surrounded by a troupe of Blessed Boys—all of good family, some of quite the best. For a time she had kept it up even more than he had, and then Nolan had distracted her with a realisation of the heroism that goes to the ends of the earth. She became sick with desire for the forests of Brazil, and the Pacific, and—a peak in Darien. Immediately the school was frowsty beyond endurance, and for the first time she let herself perceive how dreadfully a gentleman and a scholar can smell of pipes and tobacco. Only one course lay open to a woman of spirit. . . .

For a year she did indeed live like a woman of spirit; and it was at Nolan's bedside that Marayne was first moved to admiration. She was plucky. All men love a plucky woman.

Sir Godfrey Marayne smelt a good deal of antiseptic soap, but he talked in a way that amused her, and he trusted as well as adored her. She did what she liked with his money, her own money, and her son's trust money, and she did very well. From the earliest Benham's visits were to a gracious presence amidst wealthy surroundings. The transit from the moral blamelessness of Seagate had an entirely misleading effect of ascent.

Their earlier encounters became rather misty in his memory; they occurred at various hotels in Seagate. Afterwards he would go, first taken by a governess, and later going alone, to Charing Cross, where he would be met, in earlier times by a maid and afterwards by a deferential manservant who called him 'Sir,' and conveyed, sometimes in a hansom cab and later in a smart brougham, by

Trafalgar Square, Lower Regent Street, Piccadilly, and streets of increasing wealth and sublimity to Sir Godfrey's house in Desborough Street. Very naturally he fell into thinking of these discreet and well-governed West End streets as a part of his mother's atmosphere.

The house had a dignified portico, and always before he had got down to the pavement the door opened agreeably and a second respectful manservant stood ready. Then came the large hall, with its noiseless carpets and great Chinese jars, its lacquered cabinets and the wide staircase, and floating down the wide staircase, inpatient to greet him, light and shining as a flower petal, sweet and welcoming, radiating a joyfulness as cool and clear as a dewy morning, came his mother. ' *Well*, little man, my son,' she would cry in her happy singing voice, ' *Well ?* '

So he thought she must always be, but indeed these meetings meant very much to her, she dressed for them and staged them, she perceived the bright advantages of her rarity and she was quite determined to have her son when the time came to possess him. She kissed him, but not oppressively, she caressed him cleverly; it was only on these rare occasions that he was ever kissed or caressed, and she talked to his shy boyishness until it felt a more spirited variety of manhood. 'What have you been doing,' she asked, 'since I saw you last?'

She never said he had grown, but she told him he looked tall; and though the tea was a marvellous display it was never an obtrusive tea, it wasn't poked at a fellow; a various plenty flowed well within reach of one's arm, like an agreeable accompaniment to their conversation.

'What have you done? All sorts of brave things? Do you swim now? I can swim. Oh! I can swim half a mile. Some day we will swim races together. Why not? And you ride? . . .

'The horse bolted—and you stuck on? Did you squeak? I stick on, but I *have* to squeak. But you—of course, no! you mustn't. I'm just a little woman. And I ride big horses. . . .'

And for the end she had invented a characteristic little ceremony.

She would stand up in front of him and put her hands on his shoulders and look into his face.

'Clean eyes?' she would say. '——still?'

Then she would take his ears in her little firm hands and kiss very methodically his eyes and his forehead and his cheeks and at last his lips.   Her own eyes would suddenly brim bright with tears.

'*Go*,' she would say.

That was the end.

It seemed to Benham as though he was being let down out of a sunlit fairyland to this gray world again.

§ 3

The contrast between Lady Marayne's pretty amenities and the good woman at Seagate who urged herself almost hourly to forget that William Porphyry was not her own son, was entirely unfair.   The second Mrs Benham's conscientious spirit and a certain handsome ability about her fitted her far more than her predecessor for the onerous duties of a schoolmaster's wife, but whatever natural buoyancy she possessed was outweighed by an irrepressible conviction derived from an episcopal grandparent that the remarriage of divorced persons is sinful, and by a secret but well-founded doubt whether her husband loved her with a truly romantic passion.   She might perhaps have borne either of these troubles singly, but the two crushed her spirit.

Her temperament was not one that goes out to meet happiness.   She had reluctant affections and suspected rather than welcomed the facility of other people's.   Her susceptibility to disagreeable impressions was however very ample, and life was fenced about with protections for her 'feelings.'   It filled young Benham with inexpressible indignations that his sweet own mother, so gay, so brightly cheerful that even her tears were stars, was never to be mentioned in his stepmother's presence, and it was not until he had fully come to years of reflection that he began to realise with what honesty, kindness and patience this naturally not very happy lady had nursed, protected, mended for and generally mothered him.

§ 4

As Benham grew to look manly and bear himself with pride, his mother's affection for him blossomed into a passion.   She made him come down to London from Cambridge as often as she could;   she went about with him;   she made him squire her to theatres and take her out to dinners and sup with her at the Carlton, and in the summer she had him with her at Chexington Manor, the Hertford-shire house Sir Godfrey had given her. And always when they parted she looked into his eyes to see if they were still clean—whatever she meant by that—and she kissed his forehead and cheeks and eyes and lips. She began to make schemes for his career, she contrived introductions she judged would be useful to him later.

Everybody found the relationship charming. Some of the more conscientious people, it is true, pretended to think that the Reverend Harold Benham was a first husband and long since dead, but that was all. As a matter of fact, in his increasingly futile way he wasn't, either at Seagate or in the Educational Supplement of the *Times*. But even the most conscientious of us are not obliged to go to Seagate or read the Educational Supplement of the *Times*.

Lady Marayne's plans for her son's future varied very pleasantly. She was an industrious reader of biographies, and more particularly of the large fair biographies of the recently contemporary; they mentioned people she knew, they recalled scenes, each sowed its imaginative crop upon her mind, a crop that flourished and flowered until a newer growth came to oust it. She saw her son a diplomat, a prancing pro-consul, an empire builder, a trusted friend of the august, the bold leader of new movements, the saviour of ancient institutions, the youngest, brightest, modernest of prime ministers—or a tremendously popular poet. As a rule she saw him unmarried—with a wonderful little mother at his elbow. Sometimes in romantic flashes he was adored by German princesses or eloped with Russian grand-duchesses. But such fancies were *hors d'œuvre*. The modern biography deals with the career. Every project was bright, every project had *go*—tremendous go. And they all demanded a hero, debonair and balanced. And Benham, as she began to perceive, wasn't balanced. Some-thing of his father had crept into him, a touch of moral stiffness, She knew the flavour of that moral stiffness so well. It was a stumbling, an elaboration, a spoil-sport and weakness. She tried not to admit to herself that even in the faintest degree it was there. But it was there.

'Tell me all that you are doing *now*,' she said to him one afternoon when she had got him to herself during his first visit to Chexington Manor. 'How do you like Cambridge? Are you making friends? Have you joined that thing— the Union is it?—and delivered your maiden speech?

If you're for politics, Poff, that's your game.   Have you
begun it?'

She lay among splashes of sunshine on the red cushions
in the punt, a little curled-up figure of white, with her
sweet pale animated face warmed by the reflection of her
red sunshade, and her eyes like little friendly heavens.
And he, lean, and unconsciously graceful, sat at her feet
and admired her beyond measure, and rejoiced that now
at last they were going to be ever so much together, and
doubted if it would be possible ever to love any other
woman so much as he did her.

He tried to tell her of Cambridge and his friends and the
undergraduate life he was leading, but he found it difficult.
All sorts of things that seemed right and good at Trinity
seemed out of drawing in the peculiar atmosphere she
created about her.   All sorts of clumsiness and youthfulness
in himself and his associates he felt she wouldn't accept,
couldn't accept, that it would be wrong of her to accept.
Before they could come before her they must wear a
bravery.   He couldn't, for instance, tell her how Billy
Prothero, renouncing vanity and all social pretension, had
worn a straw hat into November and the last stages of
decay, and how it had been burnt by a special commission
ceremonially in the great court.   He couldn't convey to
her the long sessions of beer and tobacco and high thinking
that went on in Prothero's rooms into the small hours.   A
certain Gothic grayness and flatness and muddiness through
which the Cambridge spirit struggles to its destiny, he
concealed from her.   What remained to tell was—attenuated.
He could not romance.   So she tried to fill in his jejune
outlines.   She tried to inspire a son who seemed most
unaccountably up to nothing.

'You must make good friends,' she said.   'Isn't young
Lord Breeze at your college?   His mother the other day
told me he was.   And Sir Freddy Quenton's boy.   And
there are both the young Baptons at Cambridge.'

He knew one of the Baptons.

'Poff,' she said suddenly, 'has it ever occurred to you
what you are going to do afterwards?   Do you know you
are going to be quite well off?'

Benham looked up with a faint embarrassment.   'My
father said something.   He was rather vague.   It wasn't
his affair—that kind of thing.'

'You will be quite well off,' she repeated, without any
complicating particulars.   'You will be so well off that it

will be possible for you to do anything almost that you like in the world. Nothing will tie you. Nothing . . .'

'But—*how* well off?'

'You will have several thousands a year.'

'Thousands?'

'Yes. Why not?'

'But—— Mother, this is rather astounding. . . . Does this mean there are estates somewhere, responsibilities'

'It is just money. Investments.'

'You know, I've imagined—— I've thought always I should have to *do* something.'

'You *must* do something, Poff. But it needn't be for a living. The world is yours without that. And so you see you've got to make plans. You've got to know the sort of people who'll have things in their hands. You've got to keep out of—holes and corners. You've got to think of Parliament and abroad. There's the army, there's diplomacy. There's the Empire. You can be a Cecil Rhodes if you like. You can be a Winston. . . .'

§ 5

Perhaps it was only the innate eagerness of Lady Marayne which made her feel disappointed in her son's outlook upon life. He did not choose among his glittering possibilities, he did not say what he was going to be, pro-consul, ambassador, statesman, for days. And he talked *vaguely* of wanting to do something fine, but all in a fog. A boy of nearly nineteen ought to have at least the beginnings of *savoir faire*.

Was he in the right set? Was he indeed in the right college? Trinity, by his account, seemed a huge featureless place—and might he not conceivably be *lost* in it? In those big crowds one had to insist upon oneself. Poff never insisted upon himself—except quite at the wrong moment. And there was this Billy Prothero. *Billy!* Like a goat or something. People called William don't get their Christian name insisted upon unless they are vulnerable somewhere. Any form of William stamps a weakness, Willie, Willy, Will, Billy, Bill; it's a fearful handle for one's friends. At any rate Poff had escaped that. But this Prothero!

'But who *is* this Billy Prothero?' she asked one evening in the walled garden.

'He was at Minchinghampton.'

'But who *is* he? Who is his father? Where does he come from?'

Benham sought in his mind for a space. 'I don't know,' he said at last. Billy had always been rather reticent about his people. She demanded descriptions. She demanded an account of Billy's furniture, Billy's clothes, Billy's form of exercise. It dawned upon Benham that for some inexplicable reason she was hostile to Billy. It was like the unmasking of an ambuscade. He had talked a lot about Prothero's ideas and the discussions of social reform and social service that went on in his rooms, for Billy read at unknown times, and was open at all hours to any argumentative caller. To Lady Marayne all ideas were obnoxious, a form of fogging; all ideas, she held, were queer ideas. 'And does he call himself a Socialist?' she asked. 'I *thought* he would.'

'Poff,' she cried suddenly, 'you're not a *Socialist*?'

'Such a vague term.'

'But these friends of yours—they seem to be *all* Socialists. Red ties and everything complete.'

'They have ideas,' he evaded. He tried to express it better. 'They give one something to take hold of.'

She sat up stiffly on the garden-seat. She lifted her finger at him, very seriously. 'I hope,' she said with all her heart, 'that you will have nothing to do with such ideas. Nothing. *Socialism!*'

'They make a case.'

'Pooh! Any one can make a case.'

'But——'

'There's no sense in them. What is the good of talking about upsetting everything? Just disorder. How can one do anything then? You mustn't. You mustn't. No. It's nonsense, little Poff. It's absurd. And you may spoil so much. . . . I *hate* the way you talk of it. . . . As if it wasn't all—absolutely—*rubbish*. . . .'

She was earnest almost to the intonation of tears.

Why couldn't her son go straight for his ends, clear tangible ends, as she had always done? This thinking about everything! She had never thought about anything in all her life for more than half an hour—and it had always turned out remarkably well.

Benham felt baffled. There was a pause. How on earth could he go on telling her his ideas if this was how they were to be taken?

'I wish sometimes,' his mother said abruptly, with an

unusually sharp note in her voice, 'that you wouldn't look quite so like your father.'

'But I'm *not* like my father!' said Benham, puzzled.

'No,' she insisted, and with an air of appealing to his soberer reason, 'so why should you go *looking* like him? That *concerned* expression. . . .'

She jumped to her feet. 'Poff,' she said, 'I want to go and see the evening primroses pop. You and I are talking nonsense. *They* don't have ideas anyhow. They just pop —as God meant them to do. What stupid things we human beings are!'

Her philosophical moments were perhaps the most baffling of all.

§ 6

Billy Prothero became the symbol in the mind of Lady Marayne for all that disappointed her in Benham. He had to become the symbol, because she could not think of complicated or abstract things, she had to make things personal, and he was the only personality available. She fretted over his existence for some days therefore (once she awakened and thought about him in the night), and then suddenly she determined to grasp her nettle. She decided to seize and obliterate this Prothero. He must come to Chexington and be thoroughly and conclusively led on, examined, ransacked, shown up, and disposed of for ever. At once. She was not quite clear how she meant to do this, but she was quite resolved that it had to be done. Anything is better than inaction.

There was a little difficulty about dates and engagements, but he came, and through the season of expectation Benham, who was now for the first time in contact with the feminine nature, was delighted at the apparent change to cordiality. So that he talked of Billy to his mother much more than he had ever done before.

Billy had been his particular friend at Minchinghampton, at least during the closing two years of his school life. Billy had fallen into friendship with Benham, as some of us fall in love, quite suddenly, when he saw Benham get down from the fence and be sick after his encounter with the bull. Already Billy was excited by admiration, but it was the incongruity of the sickness conquered him. He went back to the school with his hands more than usually in his pockets, and no eyes for anything but this remarkable strung-up fellow creature. He felt he had never observed Benham before, and he was astonished that he had not done so.

Billy Prothero was a sturdy sort of boy, generously wanting in good looks. His hair was rough, and his complexion muddy, and he walked about with his hands in his pockets, long flexible lips protruded in a whistle, and a rather shapeless nose well up to show he didn't care. Providence had sought to console him by giving him a keen eye for the absurdity of other people. He had a suggestive tongue, and he professed and practised cowardice to the scandal of all his acquaintances. He was said never to wash behind his ears, but this report wronged him. There had been a time when he did not do so, but his mother had won him to a promise, and now that operation was often the sum of his simple hasty toilet. His desire to associate himself with Benham was so strong that it triumphed over a defensive reserve. It enabled him to detect accessible moments, do inobtrusive friendly services, and above all amuse his quarry He not only amused Benham, he stimulated him. They came to do quite a number of things together. In the language of schoolboy stories they became ' inseparables.'

Prothero's first desire, so soon as they were on a footing that enabled him to formulate desires, was to know exactly what Benham thought he was up to in crossing a field with a bull in it instead of going round, and by the time he began to understand that, he had conceived an affection for him that was to last a lifetime.

' I wasn't going to be bullied by a beast,' said Benham.

' Suppose it had been an elephant ? ' Prothero cried. . . . ' A mad elephant ? . . . A pack of wolves ? '

Benham was too honest not to see that he was entangled. ' Well, suppose in *your* case it had been a wild cat ? . . . A fierce mastiff ? . . . A mastiff ? . . . A terrier ? . . . A lap dog ? '

' Yes, but my case is that there are limits.'

Benham was impatient at the idea of limits. With a faintly malicious pleasure Prothero lugged him back to that idea.

' We both admit there are limits,' Prothero concluded. ' But between the absolutely impossible and the altogether possible there's the region of risk. You think a man ought to take that risk——' He reflected. ' I think—no—I think *not*.'

'If he feels afraid,' cried Benham, seeing his one point. 'If he feels afraid. Then he ought to take it. . . .

After a digestive interval, Prothero asked, '*Why?* Why should he?'

The discussion of that momentous question, that Why? which Benham perhaps might never have dared ask himself, and which Prothero perhaps might never have attempted to answer if it had not been for the clash of their minds, was the chief topic of their conversation for many months. From Why be brave? it spread readily enough to Why be honest? Why be clean?—all the great whys of life. . . . Because one believes. . . . But why believe it? Left to himself Benham would have felt the mere asking of this question was a thing ignoble, not to be tolerated. It was, as it were, treason to nobility. But Prothero put it one afternoon in a way that permitted no high dismissal of their doubts. 'You can't build your honour on fudge, Benham. Like committing sacrilege—in order to buy a cloth for the altar.'

By that Benham was slipped from the recognised code and launched upon speculations which became the magnificent research.

It was not only in complexion and stature and ways of thinking that Billy and Benham contrasted. Benham inclined a little to eloquence, he liked very clean hands, he had a dread of ridiculous outlines. Prothero lapsed readily into ostentatious slovenliness, when his hands were dirty he pitied them sooner than scrubbed them, he would have worn an overcoat with one tail torn off rather than have gone cold. Moreover, Prothero had an earthy liking for animals, he could stroke and tickle strange cats until they wanted to leave father and mother and all earthly possessions and follow after him, and he mortgaged a term's pocket money and bought and kept a small terrier in the school house against all law and tradition, under the baseless pretence that it was a stray animal of unknown origin. Benham, on the other hand, was shy with small animals and faintly hostile to big ones. Beasts he thought were just beasts. And Prothero had a gift for caricature, while Benham's aptitude was for music.

It was Prothero's eyes and pencil that first directed Benham to the poor indolences and evasions and insincerities of the masters. It was Prothero's wicked pictures that made him see the shrivelled absurdity of the vulgar theology. But it was Benham who stood between Prothero and that

rather coarsely conceived epicureanism that seemed his
logical destiny. When quite early in their Cambridge
days Prothero's revolt against foppery reached a nadir of
personal neglect, and two philanthropists from the rooms
below him, goaded beyond the normal tolerance of Trinity,
and assisted by two sportsmen from Trinity Hall, burnt
his misshapen straw hat (after partly filling it with gun-
powder and iron filings) and sought to duck him in the
fountain in the court, it was Benham, in a state between
distress and madness, and armed with a hornhandled cane
of exceptional size, who intervened, turned the business
into a blend of wrangle and scuffle, introduced the degrading
topic of duelling into a simple wholesome rag of four against
one, carried him off under the cloud of horror created by
this impropriety and so saved him, still only slightly wetted,
not only from this indignity but from the experiment in
rationalism that had provoked it.

Because Benham made it perfectly clear what he had
thought and felt about this hat.

Such was the illuminating young man whom Lady
Marayne decided to invite to Chexington, into the neighbourhood of herself, Sir Godfrey, and her circle of friends.

§ 7

He was quite anxious to satisfy the requirements of
Benham's people and to do his friend credit. He was still
in the phase of being a penitent pig, and he inquired carefully into the needs and duties of a summer guest in a
country house. He knew it was quite a considerable
country house, and that Sir Godfrey wasn't Benham's
father, but like most people, he was persuaded that Lady
Marayne had divorced the parental Benham. He arrived
dressed very neatly in a brown suit that had only one fault,
it had not the remotest suggestion of having been made
for him. It fitted his body fairly well, it did annex his
body with only a few slight incompatibilities, but it repudiated his hands and face. He had a conspicuously old
Gladstone bag and a conspicuously new despatch case, and
he had forgotten black ties and dress socks and a hair
brush. He arrived in the late afternoon, was met by
Benham, in tennis flannels, looking smartened up and a
little unfamiliar, and taken off in a spirited dog-cart driven
by a typical groom. He met his host and hostess at dinner.

Sir Godfrey was a rationalist and a residuum. Very

much of him, too much perhaps, had gone into the acquire-
ment and perfect performance of the cæcal operation; the
man one met in the social world was what was left over.
It had the effect of being quiet, but in its unobtrusive way
knobby. He had a knobby brow, with an air about it of
having recently been intent, and his conversation was
curiously spotted with little knobby arrested anecdotes.
If any one of any distinction was named, he would reflect
and say, 'Of course—ah, yes, I know him, I know him.
Yes, I did him a little service—in '96.'

And something in his manner would suggest a satisfaction,
or a dissatisfaction, with confidential mysteries.

He welcomed Billy Prothero in a colourless manner,
and made conversation about Cambridge. He had known
one or two of the higher dons. One he had done at Cambridge quite recently. 'The inns are better than they are
at Oxford, which is not saying very much, but the place
struck me as being changed. The men seemed younger. . .'

The burden of the conversation fell upon Lady Marayne.
She looked extraordinarily like a flower to Billy; a little
diamond buckle on a black velvet band glittered between
the two masses of butter-coloured hair that flowed back
from her forehead, her head was poised on the prettiest
neck conceivable, and her shapely little shoulders and her
shapely little arms came decidedly but pleasantly out of a
softness and sparkle of white and silver and old rose. She
talked what sounded like innocent commonplaces a little
spiced by whim, though indeed each remark had an ex-
ploratory quality and her soft blue eyes rested ever and
again upon Billy's white tie. It seemed she did so by the
merest inadvertency, but it made the young man wish he
had after all borrowed a black one from Benham. But the
manservant who had put his things out had put it out,
and he hadn't been quite sure. Also she noted all the little
things he did with fork and spoon and glass. She gave
him an unusual sense of being brightly, accurately, and
completely visible.

Chexington, it seemed to Billy, was done with a large
and costly and easy completeness. The table with its
silver and flowers was much more beautifully done than
any table he had sat at before, and in the dimness beyond
the brightness there were two men to wait on the four of
them. The old gray butler was really wonderfully good. . . .

'You shoot, Mr Prothero?'

'You hunt, Mr Prothero?'

'You know Scotland well, Mr Prothero?'

These questions disturbed Prothero. He did not shoot, he did not hunt, he did not go to Scotland for the grouse, he did not belong, and Lady Marayne ought to have seen that he did not belong, to the class that does these things.

'You ride much, Mr Prothero?'

Billy conceived a suspicion that these innocent inquiries were designed to emphasise a contrast in his social quality. But he could not be sure. One never could be sure with Lady Marayne. It might be just that she did not understand the sort of man he was. And in that case ought he to maintain the smooth social surface unbroken by pretending as far as possible to be this kind of person, or ought he to make a sudden gap in it by telling his realities? He evaded the shooting question anyhow. He left it open for Lady Marayne and the venerable butler and Sir Godfrey and every one to suppose he just happened to be the sort of gentleman of leisure who doesn't shoot. He disavowed hunting, he made it appear he travelled when he travelled in directions other than Scotland. But the fourth question brought him to bay. He regarded his questioner with his small rufous eye.

'I have never been across a horse in my life, Lady Marayne.'

'Tut, tut,' said Sir Godfrey. 'Why!—it's the best of exercise. Every man ought to ride. Good for the health. Keeps him fit. Prevents lodgments. Most trouble due to lodgments.'

'I've never had a chance of riding. And I think I'm afraid of horses.'

'That's only an excuse,' said Lady Marayne. 'Everybody's afraid of horses and nobody's really afraid of horses.'

'But I'm not used to horses. You see—I live on my mother. And she can't afford to keep a stable.'

His hostess did not see his expression of discomfort. Her pretty eyes were intent upon the peas with which she was being served.

'Does your mother live in the country?' she asked, and took her peas with fastidious exactness.

Prothero coloured brightly. 'She lives in London.'

'All the year?'

'All the year.'

'But isn't it dreadfully hot in town in the summer?'

Prothero had an uncomfortable sense of being very red

in the face. This kept him red. 'We're suburban people,' he said.

'But I thought—isn't there the seaside?'

'My mother has a business,' said Prothero, redder than ever.

'O-oh:' said Lady Marayne. 'What fun that must be for her?'

'It's a real business, and she has to live by it. Sometimes it's a worry.'

'But a business of her own!' She surveyed the confusion of his visage with a sweet intelligence. 'Is it an amusing sort of business, Mr Prothero?'

Prothero looked mulish. 'My mother is a dressmaker,' he said. 'In Brixton. She doesn't do particularly badly—or well. I live on my scholarship. I have lived on scholarships since I was thirteen. And you see, Lady Marayne, Brixton is a poor hunting country.'

Lady Marayne felt she had unmasked Prothero almost indecently. Whatever happened there must be no pause. There must be no sign of a hitch.

'But it's good at tennis,' she said. 'You *do* play tennis, Mr Prothero?'

'I—I gesticulate,' said Prothero.

Lady Marayne, still in flight from that pause, went off at a tangent.

'Poff, my dear,' she said, 'I've had a diving-board put at the deep end of the pond.'

The remark hung unanswered for a moment. The transition had been too quick for Benham's state of mind.

'Do you swim, Mr Prothero?' the lady asked, though a moment before she had determined that she would never ask him a question again. But this time it was a lucky question.

'Prothero mopped up the lot of us at Minchinghampton with his diving and swimming,' Benham explained, and the tension was relaxed.

Lady Marayne spoke of her own swimming, and became daring and amusing at her difficulties with local feeling when first she swam in the pond. The high-road ran along the far side of the pond—'And it didn't wear a hedge or anything,' said Lady Marayne. 'That was what they didn't quite like. Swimming in an undraped pond. . . .'

Prothero had been examined enough. Now he must be entertained. She told stories about the village people in her brightest manner. The third story she regretted as soon as she was fairly launched upon it; it was how she had interviewed the village dressmaker, when Sir Godfrey insisted upon her supporting local industries. It was very amusing but technical. The devil had put it into her head. She had to go through with it. She infused an extreme innocence into her eyes and fixed them on Prothero, although she felt a certain deepening pinkness in her cheeks was betraying her, and she did not look at Benham until her unhappy but otherwise quite amusing anecdote, was dead and gone and safely buried under another. . . .

But people ought not to go about having dressmakers for mothers. . . .

And coming into other people's houses and influencing their sons. . . .

§ 8

That night when everything was over Billy sat at the writing-table of his sumptuous bedroom—the bed was gilt wood, the curtains of the three great windows were tremendous, and there was a cheval glass that showed the full length of him and seemed to look over his head for more— and meditated upon this visit of his. It was more than he had been prepared for. It was going to be a great strain. The sleek young manservant in an alpaca jacket, who said 'Sir' whenever you looked at him, and who had seized upon and unpacked Billy's most private Gladstone bag without even asking if he might do so, and put away and displayed Billy's things in a way that struck Billy as faintly ironical, was unexpected. And it was unexpected that the brown suit, with its pockets stuffed with Billy's personal and confidential sundries, had vanished. And apparently a bath in a bathroom far down the corridor was prescribed for him in the morning; he hadn't thought of a dressing-gown. And after one had dressed, what did one do? Did one go down and wander about the house looking for the breakfast-room or wait for a gong? Would Sir Godfrey read Family Prayers? And afterwards did one go out or hang about to be entertained? He knew now quite clearly that those wicked blue eyes would mark his every slip. She did not like him. She did not like him, he supposed, because he was common stuff. He didn't play up to her world and her. He was a discord in this rich, cleverly elaborate household. You could see it in the servants' attitudes. And he was committed to a week of this.

Billy puffed out his cheeks to blow a sigh, and then decided to be angry and say 'Damn !'

This way of living which made him uncomfortable was clearly an irrational and objectionable way of living. It was, in a cumbersome way, luxurious. But the waste of life of it, the servants, the observances, all concentrated on the mere detail of existence ! There came a rap at the door. Benham appeared, wearing an expensive-looking dressing-jacket which Lady Marayne had bought for him. He asked if he might talk for a bit and smoke. He sat down in a capacious chintz-covered easy-chair beside Prothero, lit a cigarette, and came to the point after only a trivial hesitation.

'Prothero,' he said, 'you know what my father is.'

'I thought he ran a preparatory school.'

There was the profoundest resentment in Prothero's voice.

'And, all the same, I'm going to be a rich man.'

'I don't understand,' said Prothero, without any shadow of congratulation.

Benham told Prothero as much as his mother had conveyed to him of the resources of his wealth. Her version had been adapted to his tender years and the delicacies of her position. The departed Nolan had become an eccentric godfather. Benham's manner was apologetic and he made it clear that only recently had these facts come to him. He had never suspected that he had had this eccentric godfather. It altered the outlook tremendously. It was one of the reasons that made Benham glad to have Prothero there; one wanted a man of one's own age, who understood things a little, to try over one's new ideas. Prothero listened with an unamiable expression.

'What would you do, Prothero, if you found yourself saddled with some thousands a year ?'

'Godfathers don't grow in Brixton,' said Prothero concisely.

'Well, what am I to do, Prothero ?'

'Does all *this* belong to you ?'

'No, this is my mother's.'

'Godfather too ?'

'I've not thought. . . . I suppose so. Or her own.'

Prothero meditated.

'*This* life,' he said at last, 'this large expensiveness— . . .'

He left his criticism unfinished.

'I agree. It suits my mother somehow. I can't understand her living in any other way. But—-for me. . . .'

'What can one do with several thousands a year?'

Prothero's interest in this question presently swamped his petty personal resentments. 'I suppose,' he said, 'one might have rather a lark with money like that. One would be free to go anywhere. To set all sorts of things going. . . . It's clear you can't sell all you have and give it to the poor. That is pauperisation nowadays. You might run a tremendously revolutionary paper. A real upsetting paper. How many thousands is it?'

'I don't know. *Some.*'

Prothero's interest was growing as he faced the possibilities.

'I've dreamt of a paper,' he said, 'a paper that should tell the brute truth about things.'

'I don't know that I'm particularly built to be a journalist,' Benham objected.

'You're not,' said Billy. . . . 'You might go into Parliament as a perfectly independent member. . . . Only you wouldn't get in. . . .'

'I'm not a speaker,' said Benham.

'Of course,' said Billy, 'if you don't decide on a game, you'll just go on like this. You'll fall into a groove, you'll —you'll hunt. You'll go to Scotland for the grouse.'

For the moment Prothero had no further suggestions.

Benham waited for a second or so before he broached his own idea.

'Why, first of all, at any rate, Billy, shouldn't one use one's money to make the best of oneself? To learn things that men without money and leisure find it difficult to learn? By an accident, however unjust it is, one is in the position of a leader and a privileged person. Why not do one's best to give value as that?'

'Benham, that's the thin end of aristocracy!'

'Why not?'

'I hate aristocracy. For you it means doing what you like. While you are energetic you will kick about and then you will come back to this.'

'That's one's own look-out,' said Benham, after reflection.

'No, it's bound to happen.'

Benham retreated a little from the immediate question.

'Well, we can't suddenly at a blow change the world. If it isn't to be plutocracy to-day it has to be aristocracy.'

Prothero frowned over this, and then he made a sweeping proposition.

'*You cannot have aristocracy,*' he said, '*because, you see—*

all men are ridiculous. Democracy has to fight its way out from under plutocracy. There is nothing else to be done.'

'But a man in my position——?'

'It's a ridiculous position. You may try to escape being ridiculous. You won't succeed.'

It seemed to Benham for a moment as though Prothero had got to the bottom of the question, and then he perceived that he had only got to the bottom of himself. Benham was pacing the floor.

He turned at the open window, held out a long forefinger, and uttered his countervailing faith.

'Even if he is ridiculous, Prothero, a man may still be an aristocrat. A man may anyhow be as much of an aristocrat as he can be.'

Prothero reflected. 'No,' he said, 'it sounds all right, but it's wrong. I hate all these advantages and differences and distinctions. A man's a man. What you say sounds well, but it's the beginning of pretension, of pride——'

He stopped short.

'Better pride than dishonour,' said Benham, 'better the pretentious life than the sordid life. What else is there?'

'A life isn't necessarily sordid because it isn't pretentious,' said Prothero, his voice betraying a defensive disposition.

'But a life with a large income *must* be sordid unless it makes some sort of attempt to be fine. . . .'

§ 9

By transitions that were as natural as they were complicated and untraceable Prothero found his visit to Chexington developing into a tangle of discussions that all ultimately resolved themselves into an antagonism of the democratic and the aristocratic idea. And his part was, he found, to be the exponent of the democratic idea. The next day he came down early, his talk with Benham still running through his head, and after a turn or so in the garden he was attracted to the front door by a sound of voices, and found Lady Marayne had been up still earlier and was dismounting from a large effective black horse. This extorted an unwilling admiration from him. She greeted him very pleasantly and made a kind of introduction of her steed. There had been trouble at a gate, he was a young horse and fidgeted at gates; the dispute was still bright in her. Benham she declared was still in bed

'Wait till I have a mount for him.' She reappeared fitfully in the breakfast-room, and then he was left to Benham until just before lunch. They read and afterwards, as the summer day grew hot, they swam in the nude pond. She joined them in the water, splashing about in a costume of some elaboration and being very careful not to wet her hair. Then she came and sat with them on the seat under the big cedar and talked with them in a wrap that was pretty rather than prudish and entirely unmotherly. And she began a fresh attack upon him by asking him if he wasn't a Socialist and whether he didn't want to pull down Chexington and grow potatoes all over the park.

This struck Prothero as an inadequate statement of the Socialist project, and he made an unsuccessful attempt to get it amended.

The engagement thus opened was renewed with great energy at lunch. Sir Godfrey had returned to London and the inmost aspect of his fellow-creatures, but the party of three was supplemented by a vague young lady from the village and an alert agent from the neighbouring Tentington estate who had intentions about a cottage. Lady Marayne insisted upon regarding Socialism as a proposal to re-inaugurate the first French Revolution, as an inversion of society so that it would be bottom upward, as an attack upon rule, order, direction. 'And what good are all these proposals? If you had the poor dear king beheaded, you'd only get a Napoleon. If you divided all the property up between everybody, you'd have rich and poor again in a year.'

Billy perceived no way of explaining away this version of his Socialism that would not involve uncivil contradictions—and nobody ever contradicted Lady Marayne.

'But, Lady Marayne, don't you think there is a lot of disorder and injustice in the world?' he protested.

'There would be ever so much more if your Socialists had their way.'

'But still don't you think—— . . .'

It is unnecessary even to recapitulate these universal controversies of our time. The lunch-table and the dinner-table and the general talk of the house drifted more and more definitely at its own level in the same direction as the private talk of Prothero and Benham, towards the antagonism of the privileged few and the many, of the trained and traditioned against the natural and un-disciplined, of aristocracy against democracy. At the week-end Sir Godfrey returned to bring fresh elements. He said that democracy was unscientific. 'To deny aristocracy is to deny the existence of the fittest. It is on the existence of the fittest that progress depends.'

'But do our social conditions exalt the fittest?' asked Prothero.

'That is another question,' said Benham.

'Exactly,' said Sir Godfrey. 'That is another question. But speaking with some special knowledge, I should say that on the whole the people who are on the top of things *ought* to be on the top of things. I agree with Aristotle that there is such a thing as a natural inferior.'

'So far as I can understand Mr Prothero,' said Lady Marayne, 'he thinks that all the inferiors are the superiors and all the superiors inferior. It's quite simple. . . .'

It made Prothero none the less indignant with this, that there was indeed a grain of truth in it. He hated superiors, he felt for inferiors.

§ 10

At last came the hour of tipping. An embarrassed and miserable Prothero went slinking about the house distributing unexpected gold.

It was stupid, it was damnable; he had had to borrow the money from his mother. . . .

Lady Marayne felt he had escaped her. The controversy that should have split these two young men apart had given them a new interest in each other. When afterwards she sounded her son, very delicately, to see if indeed he was aware of the clumsiness, the social ignorance and uneasiness, the complete unsuitability of his friend, she could get no more from him than that exasperating phrase, 'He has ideas !'

What are ideas? England may yet be ruined by ideas. He ought never to have gone to Trinity, that monster packet of everything. He ought to have gone to some little *good* college, good all through. She ought to have asked some one who *knew*.

§ 11

One glowing afternoon in October, as these two young men came over Magdalen Bridge after a long, disputatious and rather tiring walk to Drayton—they had been talking of Eugenics and the 'family'—Benham was almost knocked

down by an American trotter driven by Lord Breeze.
'Whup there !' said Lord Breeze in a voice deliberately
brutal, and Benham, roused from that abstraction which
is partly fatigue, had to jump aside and stumbled against
the parapet as the gaunt pacer went pounding by.

Lord Breeze grinned the sort of grin a man remembers.
And passed.

'Damnation !' said Benham with a face that had become
suddenly very white.

Then presently. 'Any fool can do that who cares to go
to the trouble.'

'That,' said Prothero, taking up their unquenchable
issue, 'that is the feeling of democracy.'

'I walk because I choose to,' said Benham.

The thing rankled.

'This equestrianism,' he began, 'is a matter of time and
money—time even more than money. I want to read.
I want to deal with ideas. . . .'

'Any fool can drive. . . .'

'Exactly,' said Prothero.

'As for riding, it means no more than the elaborate study
and cultivation of your horse. You have to know him.
All horses are individuals. A made horse perhaps goes its
round like an omnibus, but for the rest. . . .'

Prothero made a noise of sympathetic assent.

'In a country where equestrianism is assertion I suppose
one must be equestrian. . . .'

That night some malignant spirit kept Benham awake,
and great American trotters with vast wide-striding feet
and long yellow teeth, uncontrollable, hard-mouthed
American trotters, pounded over his angry soul.

'Prothero,' he said in hall next day, 'we are going to
drive to-morrow.'

Next day, so soon as they had lunched, he led the way
towards Maltby's, in Crosshampton Lane. Something in
his bearing put a question into Prothero's mind. 'Benham,'
he asked, 'have you ever driven before?'

'*Never*,' said Benham.

'Well?'

'I'm going to now.'

Something between pleasure and alarm came into
Prothero's eyes. He quickened his pace so as to get along-
side his friend and scrutinise his pale determination.
'Why are you doing this?' he asked.

'I want to do it.'

' Benham, is it—*equestrian ?* '

Benham made no audible reply. They proceeded resolutely in silence.

An air of expectation prevailed in Maltby's yard. In the shafts of a high, bleak-looking vehicle with vast side wheels, a throne-like vehicle that impressed Billy Prothero as being a gig, a very large angular black horse was being harnessed.

' This is mine,' said Benham compactly.

' This is yours, sir,' said an ostler.

' He looks—*quiet.*'

' You'll find him fresh enough, sir.'

Benham made a complicated ascent to the driver's seat and was handed the reins. ' Come on,' he said, and Prothero followed to a less exalted seat at Benham's side. They seemed to be at a very great height indeed. The horse was then led out into Crosshampton Lane, faced towards Trinity Street and discharged. ' Check,' said Benham, and touched the steed with his whip. They started quite well, and the ostlers went back into the yard, visibly unanxious. It struck Prothero that perhaps driving was less difficult than he had supposed.

They went along Crosshampton Lane, that high-walled gulley, with dignity, with only a slight suggestion of the inaccuracy that was presently to become apparent, until they met a little old bearded don on a bicycle. Then some misunderstanding arose between Benham and the horse, and the little bearded don was driven into the narrow pavement and had to get off hastily. He made no comment, but his face became like a gargoyle. ' Sorry,' said Benham, and gave his mind to the corner. There was some difficulty about whether they were to turn to the right or the left, but at last Benham, it seemed, carried his point, and they went along the narrow street, past the gray splendours of King's, and rather in the middle of the way.

Prothero considered the beast in front of him, and how proud and disrespectful a horse in a dog-cart can seem to those behind it ! Moreover, unaccustomed as he was to horses, he was struck by the strong resemblance a bird's-eye view of a horse bears to a fiddle, a fiddle with devil's ears.

' Of course,' said Prothero, ' this isn't a trotter.'

' I couldn't get a trotter,' said Benham.

' I thought I would try this sort of thing before I tried a trotter,' he added.

And then suddenly came disaster.

There was a butcher's cart on the right, and Benham, mistrusting the intelligence of his steed, insisted upon an excessive amplitude of clearance. He did not reckon with the hand-barrow on his left, piled up with dirty plates from the lunch of Trinity Hall. It had been left there; its custodian was away upon some mysterious errand. Heaven knows why Trinity Hall exhibited the treasures of its crockery thus stained and defiled in the Cambridge streets. But it did—for Benham's and Prothero's undoing. Prothero saw the great wheel over which he was poised entangle itself with the little wheel of the barrow. 'God!' he whispered, and craned, fascinated. The little wheel was manifestly intrigued beyond all self-control by the great wheel; it clung to it, it went before it, heedless of the barrow, of which it was an inseparable part. The barrow came about with an appearance of unwillingness, it locked against the great wheel; it reared itself towards Prothero and began, smash, smash, smash, to shed its higher plates. It was clear that Benham was grappling with a crisis upon a basis of inadequate experience. A number of people shouted haphazard things. Then, too late, the barrow had persuaded the little wheel to give up its fancy for the great wheel, and there was an enormous crash.

'Whoa!' cried Benham. 'Whoa!' but also, unfortunately, he sawed hard at the horse's mouth.

The animal being in some perplexity, danced a little in the narrow street, and then it had come about and it was backing, backing, on the narrow pavement and towards the plate-glass window of a book and newspaper shop. Benham tugged at its mouth much harder than ever. Prothero saw the window bending under the pressure of the wheel. A sense of the profound seriousness of life and of the folly of this expedition came upon him. With extreme nimbleness he got down just as the window burst. It went with an explosion like a pistol shot, and then a clatter of falling glass. People sprang, it seemed, from nowhere, and jostled about Prothero, so that he became a peripheral figure in the discussion. He perceived that a man in a green apron was holding the horse, and that various people were engaged in simultaneous conversation with Benham, who with a pale serenity of face and an awful calm of manner, dealt with each of them in turn.

'I'm sorry,' he was saying. 'Somebody ought to have been in charge of the barrow. Here are my cards. I am ready to pay for any damage. . . .

'The barrow ought not to have been there. . . .

'Yes, I am going on. Of course I'm going on. Thank you.'

He beckoned to the man who had held the horse and handed him half-a-crown. He glanced at Prothero as one might glance at a stranger. 'Check!' he said. The horse went on gravely. Benham lifted out his whip. He appeared to have clean forgotten Prothero. Perhaps presently he would miss him. He went on past Trinity, past the ruddy brick of St John's. The curve of the street hid him from Prothero's eyes.

Prothero started in pursuit. He glimpsed the dogcart turning into Bridge Street. He had an impression that Benham used the whip at the corner, and that the dog-cart went forward out of sight with a startled jerk. Prothero quickened his pace.

But when he got to the fork between the Huntingdon Road and the Cottenham Road, both roads were clear.

He spent some time in hesitation. Then he went along the Huntingdon Road until he came upon a road-mender, and learnt that Benham had passed that way. 'Going pretty fast 'e was,' said the road-mender, 'and whipping 'is 'orse. Else you might 'a thought 'e was a boltin' with 'im.' Prothero decided that if Benham came back at all he would return by way of Cottenham, and it was on the Cottenham Road that at last he encountered his friend again.

Benham was coming along at that good pace which all experienced horses when they are fairly turned back towards Cambridge display. And there was something odd about Benham, as though he had a large circular halo with a thick rim. This, it seemed, had replaced his hat. He was certainly hatless. The warm light of the sinking sun shone upon the horse and upon Benham's erect figure and upon his face, and gleams of fire kept flashing from his head to this rim, like the gleam of drawn swords seen from afar. As he drew nearer this halo detached itself from him and became a wheel sticking up behind him. A large, clumsy-looking bicycle was attached to the dog-cart behind. The expression of Benham's golden face was still a stony expression; he regarded his friend with hard eyes.

'You all right, Benham?' cried Prothero, advancing into the road.

His eye examined the horse. It looked all right, if anything it was a trifle subdued; there was a little foam about its mouth, but not very much.

'Whoa!' said Benham, and the horse stopped. 'Are you coming up, Prothero?'

Prothero clambered up beside him. 'I was anxious,' he said.

'There was no need to be.'

'You've broken your whip.'

'Yes. It broke. . . . *Get* up!'

They proceeded on their way to Cambridge.

'Something has happened to the wheel,' said Prothero, trying to be at his ease.

'Merely a splinter or so. And a spoke perhaps.'

'And what is this behind?'

Benham made a half-turn of the head. 'It's a motor-bicycle.'

Prothero took in details.

'Some of it is missing.'

'No, the front wheel is under the seat.'

'Oh!'

'Did you find it?' Prothero asked, after an interval.

'No.'

'You mean?'

'He ran into a motor-car—as I was passing. I was perhaps a little to blame. He asked me to bring his machine to Cambridge. He went on in the car. . . . It is all perfectly simple.'

Prothero glanced at the splinters in the wheel with a renewed interest.

'Did your wheel get into it?' he asked.

Benham affected not to hear. He was evidently in no mood for story-telling.

'Why did you get down, Prothero?' he asked abruptly, with the note of suppressed anger thickening his voice.

Prothero became vividly red. 'I don't know,' he said, after an interval.

'I *do*,' said Benham, and they went on in a rich and active silence to Cambridge, and the bicycle repair shop in Bridge Street, and Trinity College. At the gate of Trinity Benham stopped, and conveyed rather by acts than words that Prothero was to descend. He got down meekly enough, although he felt that the return to Maltby's yard might have many points of interest. But the spirit had gone out of him.

§ 12

For three days the two friends avoided each other, and then Prothero went to Benham's room. Benham was smoking cigarettes—Lady Marayne, in the first warmth of his filial devotion, had prohibited his pipe—and reading Webb's *Industrial Democracy*. 'Hallo!' he said coldly, scarcely looking up, and continued to read that absorbing work.

'I keep on thinking how I jumped down from that damned dog-cart,' said Prothero, without any preface.

'It didn't matter in the least,' said Benham distantly.

'Oh! *Rot*,' said Prothero. 'I behaved like a coward.'

Benham shut the book.

'Benham,' said Prothero, 'you are right about aristocracy, and I am wrong. I've been thinking about it night and day.'

Benham betrayed no emotion. But his tone changed. 'Billy,' he said, 'there are cigarettes and whisky in the corner. Don't make a fuss about a trifle.'

'No whisky,' said Billy, and lit a cigarette. 'And it isn't a trifle.'

He came to Benham's hearthrug. 'That business,' he said, 'has changed all my views. No—don't say something polite! I see that if one hasn't the habit of pride one is bound to get off a dog-cart when it seems likely to smash. You have the habit of pride, and I haven't. So far as the habit of pride goes, I come over to the theory of aristocracy.'

Benham said nothing, but he put down Sidney and Beatrice Webb, and reached out for and got and lit a cigarette.

'I give up "Go as you please." I give up the natural man. I admit training. I perceive I am lax and flabby, unguarded, I funk too much, I eat too much, and I drink too much. And, yet, what I have always liked in you, Benham, is just this—that you don't.'

'I do,' said Benham.

'Do what?'

'Funk.'

'Benham, I believe that naturally you funk as much as I do. You're more a thing of nerves than I am, far more. But you keep yourself up to the mark, and I have let myself get flabby. You're so right. You're so utterly right. These last nights I've confessed it—aloud. I had an inkling of it—after that rag. But now it's as clear as daylight. I don't know if you mean to go on with me, after what's happened, but anyhow I want you to know, whether you end our friendship or not——'

'Billy, don't be an old ass,' said Benham.

Both young men paused for a moment. They made no demonstrations. But the strain was at an end between them.

'I've thought it all out,' Billy went on with a sudden buoyancy. 'We two are both of the same kind of men. Only you see, Benham, you have a natural pride and I haven't. You have pride. But we are both intellectuals· We both belong to what the Russians call the Intelligentsia. We have ideas, we have imagination, that is our strength. And that is our weakness. That makes us moral lightweights. We are flimsy and uncertain people. All intellectuals are flimsy and uncertain people. It's not only that they are critical and fastidious; they are weak-handed. They look about them; their attention wanders. Unless they have got a habit of controlling themselves and forcing themselves and holding themselves together.'

'The habit of pride.'

'Yes. And then—then we are lords of the world.'

'All this, Billy,' said Benham, 'I steadfastly believe.'

'I've seen it all now,' said Prothero. 'Lord ! how clearly I see it ! The intellectual is either a prince or he is a Greek slave in a Roman household. He's got to hold his chin up or else he becomes—even as these dons we see about us— a thing that talks appointments, a toady, a port-wine bibber, a mass of detail, a conscious maker of neat sayings, a growing belly under a dwindling brain. Their gladness is drink or gratified vanity or gratified malice, their sorrow is indigestion or—old maid's melancholy. They are the lords of the world who will not take the sceptre. . . . And what I want to say to you, Benham, more than anything else is, *you* go on—*you* make yourself equestrian. You drive your horse against Breeze's, and go through the fire and swim in the ice-cold water and climb the precipice and drink little and sleep hard. And—I wish I could do so too.'

'But why not?'

'Because I can't. Now, I admit, I've got shame in my heart and pride in my head, and I'm strung up. I might do something—this afternoon. But it won't last. *You*— you have pride in your bones. My pride will vanish at a laugh. My honour will go at a laugh. I'm just exalted by a crisis. That's all. I'm an animal of intelligence. Soul and pride are weak in me. My mouth waters, my cheek brightens, at the sight of good things. And I've got a lickerish tail, Benham. You don't know. You don't begin to imagine. I'm secretive. But I quiver with hot and stirring desires. And I'm indolent—dirty indolent. Benham, there are days when I splash my bath about without getting into it. There are days when I turn back from a walk because there's a cow in the field. . . . But, I spare you the viler details. . . . And it's that makes me hate fine people and try so earnestly to persuade myself that any man is as good as any man, if not a trifle better. Because I know it isn't so. . . .'

'Billy,' said Benham, 'you've the boldest mind that ever I met.'

Prothero's face lit with satisfaction. Then his countenance fell again. 'I know I'm better there,' he said, 'and yet, see how I let in a whole system of lies to cover my secret humiliations. There, at least, I will cling to pride. I will at least *think* free and clean and high. But you can climb higher than I can. You've got the grit to try to *live* high. There you are, Benham.'

Benham stuck one leg over the arm of his chair.

'Billy,' he said, 'come and be—equestrian, and stop this nonsense.'

'No.'

'Damn it—you *dive* !'

'You'd go in before me if a woman was drowning.'

'Nonsense. I'm going to ride. Come and ride too. You've a cleverer way with animals than I have. Why ! that horse I was driving the other day would have gone better alone. I didn't drive it. I just fussed it. I interfered. If I ride for ever, I shall never have decent hands, I shall always hang on my horse's mouth at a gallop, I shall never be sure at a jump. But at any rate I shall get hard. Come and get hard too.'

'You can,' said Billy, 'you can. But not I ! Heavens, the *trouble* of it ! The riding-school ! The getting up early ! No !—for me the Trumpington Road on foot in the afternoon. Four miles an hour and panting. And my fellowship and the combination-room port. And, besides, Benham, there's the expense. I can't afford the equestrian order.'

'It's not so great.'

'Not so great ! I don't mean the essential expense. But—the incidentals. I don't know whether any one can realise how a poor man is hampered by the dread of minor catastrophes. It isn't so much that he is afraid of breaking his neck, Benham, as that he is afraid of breaking something he will have to pay for. For instance—— Benham ! how much did your little expedition the other day——?'

He stopped short and regarded his friend with round eyes and raised eyebrows.

A reluctant grin overspread Benham's face. He was beginning to see the humour of the affair.

'The claim for the motor-bicycle isn't sent in yet. The repair of the mudguards of the car is in dispute. Trinity Hall's crockery, the plate-glass window, the whip-lash and wheel and so forth, the hire of the horse and trap, sundry gratuities. . . . I doubt if the total will come very much under fifty pounds. And I seem to have lost a hat somewhere.'

Billy regarded his toes and cleared his throat.

'Depending as I do on a widowed mother in Brixton for all the expenditure that isn't covered by my pot-hunting——'

'Of course,' said Benham, 'it wasn't a fair sample afternoon.'

'Still——'

'There's footer,' said Benham, 'we might both play footer.'

'Or boxing.'

'And, anyhow, you must come with me when I drive again. I'm going to start a trotter.'

'If I miss another drive may I be—lost for ever,' said Billy, with the utmost sincerity. 'Never more will I get down, Benham, wherever you may take me. Short of muffing my fellowship I'm with you always. . . . Will it be an American trotter?'

'It will be the rawest, gauntest, ungainliest brute that ever scared the motor-bicycles on the Northampton Road. It will have the legs and stride of an ostrich. It will throw its feet out like dealing cards. It will lift its head and look the sun in the eye like a vulture. It will have teeth like the English spinster in a French comic paper. . . . And we will fly. . . .'

'I shall enjoy it very much,' said Prothero in a small voice after an interval for reflection. 'I wonder where we shall fly? It will do us both a lot of good. And I shall insure my life for a small amount in my mother's interest. . . . Benham, I think I will, after all, take a whisky. . . . Life is short. . . .'

He did so, and Benham strolled to the window and stood looking out upon the great court.

'We might do something this afternoon,' said Benham.

'Splendid idea,' reflected Billy over his whisky. 'Living hard and thinking hard. A sort of Intelligentsia that is *blooded*. . . . I shall, of course, come as far as I can with you.'

§ 13

In one of the bureau drawers that White in his capacity of literary executor was examining, there were two documents that carried back right to these early days. They were both products of this long wide undergraduate argumentation that had played so large a part in the making of Benham. One recorded the phase of maximum opposition, and one was the outcome of the concluding approach of the antagonists. They were debating club essays. One had been read to a club in Pembroke, a club called the *Enquirers*, of which White also had been a member, and as he turned it over he found the circumstances of its reading coming back to his memory. He had been present, and Carnac's share in the discussion with his shrill voice and stumpy gestures would alone have sufficed to have made it a memorable occasion. The later one had been read to the daughter club of the *Enquirers*, the *Social Enquirers*, in the year after White had gone down, and it was new to him.

Both these papers were folded flat and neatly docketed; they were rather yellow and a little dog-eared, and with the outer sheet pencilled over with puzzling or illegible scribblings, Benham's memoranda for his reply. White took the earlier essay in his hand. At the head of the first page was written in large letters, 'Go slowly, speak to the man at the back.' It brought up memories of his own experiences, of rows of gaslit faces, and of a friendly helpful voice that said, 'Speak up !'

Of course this was what happened to every intelligent contemporary, this encounter with ideas, this restatement and ventilation of the old truths and the old heresies. Only in this way does a man make a view his own, only so does he incorporate it. These are our real turning points. The insignificant, the essential moments in the life of any one worth consideration are surely these moments when for the first time he faces towards certain broad ideas and certain broad facts. Life nowadays consists of adventures among generalisations. In class-rooms after the lecture, in studies in the small hours, among books or during solitary walks, the drama of the modern career begins. Suddenly a man sees his line, his intention. Yet though we are all of us writing long novels—White's world was the literary world, and that is how it looked to him—which profess to set out the lives of men, this part of the journey, this crucial passage among the Sphinxes, is still done—when it is done at all—slightly, evasively. Why?

White fell back on his professionalism. 'It does not make a book. It makes a novel into a treatise, it turns it into a dissertation.'

But even as White said this to himself he knew it was wrong, and it slid out of his thoughts again. Was not this objection to the play of ideas merely the expression of that conservative instinct which fights for every old convention? The traditional novel is a love story and takes ideas for granted, it professes a hero but presents a heroine. And to begin with at least, novels were written for the reading of heroines. Miss Lydia Languish sets no great store upon the contents of a man's head. That is just the stuffing of the doll. Eyes and heart are her game. And so there is never any more sphinx in the story than a lady may impersonate. And as inevitably the heroine meets a man. In his own first success, White reflected, the hero, before he had gone a dozen pages, met a very pleasant young woman very pleasantly in a sunlit thicket; the second opened at once with a bicycle accident that brought two young people together so that they were never afterwards disentangled; the third, failing to produce its heroine in thirty pages, had to be rearranged. The next——

White returned from an unprofitable digression to the matter before him'

§ 14

The first of Benham's early essays was written in an almost boyish hand, it was youthfully amateurish in its nervous disposition to definitions and distinctions, and in the elaborate linking of part to part. It was called *True Democracy*. Manifestly it was written before the incident of the Trinity Hall plates, and most of it had been done after Prothero's visit to Chexington. White could feel that now inaudible interlocutor. And there were even traces of Sir Godfrey Marayne's assertion that democracy was contrary to biology. From the outset it was clear that whatever else it meant, True Democracy, following the analogy of True Politeness, True Courage, True Honesty, and True Marriage, did not mean democracy at all. Benham was, in fact, taking Prothero's word, and trying to impose upon it his own solidifying and crystallising opinion of life.

They were not as yet very large or well-formed crystals. The proposition he struggled to develop was this, that True Democracy did not mean an equal share in the government, it meant an equal opportunity to share in the government. Men were by nature and in the most various ways unequal. True Democracy aimed only at the removal of artificial inequalities. . . .

It was on the truth of this statement, that men were by nature unequal, that the debate had turned, Prothero was passionately against the idea at that time. It was, he felt, separating himself from Benham more and more. He spoke with a personal bitterness. And he found his chief ally in a rigorous and voluble Frenchman named Carnac, an aggressive Roman Catholic, who opened his speech by saying that the first aristocrat was the devil, and shocked Prothero by claiming him as probably the only other sound Christian in the room. Several biologists were present, and one tall, fair youth with a wearisome forefinger tried to pin Carnac with questions.

'But you must admit some men are taller than others?'

'Then the others are broader.'

'Some are smaller altogether.'

'Nimbler—it's notorious.'

'Some of the smaller are less nimble than the others.'

'Then they have better nightmares. How can you tell?'

The biologist was temporarily incapacitated, and the talk went on over his prostrate attempts to rally and protest.

A second biologist seemed to Benham to come nearer the gist of the dispute when he said that they were not discussing the importance of men, but their relative inequalities. Nobody was denying the equal importance of everybody. But there was a virtue of this man and a virtue of that. Nobody could dispute the equal importance of every wheel in a machine, of every atom in the universe. Prothero and Carnac were angry because they thought the denial of absolute equality was a denial of equal importance. That was not so. Every man mattered in his place. But politically, or economically, or intellectually that might be a lowly place. . . .

At this point Carnac interrupted with a whooping and great violence, and a volley of obscure French colloquialisms.

He was understood to convey that the speaker was a Jew, and did not in the least mean what he was saying. . . .

§ 15

The second paper was an altogether maturer and more characteristic production. It was no longer necessary to answer Prothero. Prothero had been incorporated. And Benham had fairly got away with his great idea. It was evident to White that this paper had been worked over on several occasions since its first composition, and that Benham had intended to make it a part of his book. There were corrections in pencil and corrections in a different shade of ink, and there was an unfinished new peroration that was clearly the latest addition of all. Yet its substance had been there always. It gave the youth just grown to manhood, but anyhow fully grown. It presented the far-dreaming intellectualist shaped.

Benham had called it *Aristocracy*. But he was far away by now from political aristocracy.

This time he had not begun with definitions and generalisations, but with a curiously subjective appeal. He had not pretended to be theorising at large any longer, he was manifestly thinking of his own life and as manifestly he was thinking of life as a matter of difficulty and unexpected thwartings.

'We see life,' he wrote, 'not only life in the world outside us, but life in our own selves, as an immense choice of possibilities; indeed, for us in particular who have come up here, who are not under any urgent necessity to take this line or that, life is apparently pure choice. It is quite easy to think we are all going to choose the pattern of life we like best and work it out in our own way. . . . And, meanwhile, there is no great hurry. . . .

'I want to begin by saying that choice isn't so easy and so necessary as it seems. We think we are going to choose presently, and in the end we may never choose at all. Choice needs perhaps more energy than we think. The great multitude of older people we can observe in the world outside there, haven't chosen either in the matter of the world outside, where they shall go, what they shall do, what part they shall play, or in the matter of the world within, what they will be and what they are determined

they will never be. They are still in much the same state
of suspended choice as we seem to be in, but in the meanwhile *things happen to them*. And things are happening
to us, things will happen to us, while we still suppose ourselves in the wings waiting to be consulted about the casting
of the piece. . . .

'Nevertheless this immense appearance of choice which
we get in the undergraduate community here, is not
altogether illusion; it is more reality than illusion even if
it has not the stable and complete reality it appears to
have. And it is more a reality for us than it was for our
fathers, and much more a reality now than it was a few
centuries ago. The world is more confused and multitudinous than ever it was, the practicable world far wider,
and ourselves far less under the pressure of inflexible
moulding forces and inevitable necessities than any preceding generations. I want to put very clearly how I see
the new world, the present world, the world of novel choice
to which our youth and inexperience faces, and I want to
define to you a certain selection of choices which I am
going to call aristocratic, and to which it is our manifest
duty and destiny as the elect and favoured sons of our race
to direct ourselves.

'It isn't any choice of Hercules I mean, any mere alternative whether we will be—how shall I put it?—the
bridegrooms of pleasure or the bridegrooms of duty. It is
infinitely vaster and more subtly moral than that. There
are a thousand good lives possible, of which we may have
one, lives which are soundly good, or a thousand bad lives,
if you like, lives which are thoroughly bad—that's the old
and perpetual choice, that has always been—but what is
more evident to me and more remarkable and disconcerting
is that there are nowadays ten thousand muddled lives
lacking even so much moral definition, even so much
consistency as is necessary for us to call them either good
or bad; there are planless indeterminate lives, more and
more of them, opening out as the possible lives before us,
a perfect wilderness between salvation and damnation, a
wilderness so vast and crowded that at last it seems as
though the way to either hell or heaven would be lost in
its interminable futility. Such planless indeterminate lives,
plebeian lives, mere lives, fill the world; and the spectacle
of whole nations, our whole civilisation, seems to me to
re-echo this planlessness, this indeterminate confusion of
purpose. Plain issues are harder and harder to find; it is

as if they had disappeared. Simple living is the countryman
come to town. We are deafened and jostled and perplexed.
There are so many things afoot that we get nothing. . . .

'That is what is in my mind when I tell you that we
have to gather ourselves together much more than we
think. We have to clench ourselves upon a chosen end.
We have to gather ourselves together out of the swill of
this brimming world.

'Or—we are lost. . . .'

('Swill of this brimming world,' said White. 'Some of
this sounds uncommonly like Prothero.' He mused for a
moment and then resumed his reading.)

'That is what I was getting at when, three years ago,
I made an attack upon Democracy to the mother society
of this society, an attack that I expressed ill and failed to
drive home. That is what I have come down now to do
my best to make plainer. This age of confusion is Democracy; it is all that Democracy can ever give us. Democracy,
if it means anything, means the rule of the planless man,
the rule of the unkempt mind. It means as a necessary
consequence this vast boiling up of collectively meaningless
things.

'What is the quality of the common man, I mean of the
man that is common to all of us, the man who is the Standard
for such men as Carnac, the man who seems to be the ideal
of the Catholic Democrat? He is the creature of a few
fundamental impulses. He begins in blind imitation of the
life about him. He lusts and takes a wife, he hungers and
tills a field or toils in some other way to earn a living, a
mere aimless living, he fears and so he does not wander,
he is jealous and stays by his wife and his job, is fiercely
yet often stupidly and injuriously defensive of his children
and his possessions, and so until he wearies. Then he dies
and needs a cemetery. He needs a cemetery because he is
so afraid of dissolution that even when he has ceased to be,
he still wants a place and a grave to hold him together and
prevent his returning to the All that made him. Our chief
impression of long ages of mankind comes from its cemeteries.
And this is the life of man, as the common man conceives
and lives it. Beyond that he does not go, he never com-
prehends himself collectively at all; the state happens
about him; his passion for security, his gregarious self-
defensiveness, makes him accumulate upon himself until
he congests in cities that have no sense of citizenship and
states that have no structure; the clumsy, inconsecutive

lying and chatter of his newspapers, his hoardings and music-halls give the measure of his congested intelligences; the confusion of ugly, half empty churches and chapels and meeting-halls gauges the intensity of his congested souls; the tricks and slow blundering dishonesties of Diet and Congress and Parliament are his statecraft and his wisdom. . . .

'I do not care if this instant I am stricken dead for pride. I say here now to you and to High Heaven that *this life is not good enough for me*. I know there is a better life than this muddle about us, a better life possible now. I know it. A better individual life and a better public life. If I had no other assurances, if I were blind to the glorious intimations of art, to the perpetually widening promise of science, to the mysterious beckonings of beauty in form and colour and the inaccessible mockery of the stars, I should still know this from the insurgent spirit within me. . . .

'Now this better life is what I mean when I talk of Aristocracy. This idea of a life breaking away from the common life to something better, is the consuming idea in my mind.

'Constantly, recurringly, struggling out of the life of the farm and the shop, the inn and the market, the street and the crowd, is something that is not of the common life. Its way of thinking is Science, its dreaming is Art, its will is the purpose of mankind. It is not the common thing. But also it is not an unnatural thing. It is not as common as a rat, but it is no less natural than a panther.

'For it is as natural to be an explorer as it is to be a potato grower, it is rarer but it is as natural; it is as natural to seek explanations and arrange facts as it is to make love, or adorn a hut, or show kindness to a child. It is a folly I will not even dispute about, that man's only natural implement is the spade. Imagination, pride, exalted desire are just as much Man, as are hunger and thirst and sexual curiosities and the panic dread of unknown things. . . .

'Now you see better what I mean about choice. Now you see what I am driving at. We have to choose each one for himself and also each one for the race, whether we will accept the muddle of the common life, whether we ourselves will be muddled, weakly nothings, children of luck, steering our artful courses for mean success and tawdry honours, or whether we will be aristocrats, for that is what it amounts to, each one in the measure of his personal quality an aristocrat, refusing to be restrained by fear, refusing to be restrained by pain, resolved to know and understand up to the hilt of his understanding, resolved to sacrifice all the common stuff of his life to the perfection of his peculiar gift, a purged man, a trained, selected, artificial man not simply free, but lordly free, filled and sustained by pride. Whether you or I make that choice and whether you or I succeed in realising ourselves, though a great matter to ourselves, is, I admit, a small matter to the world. But the great matter is this, that *the choice is being made*, that it will continue to be made, and that all around us, so that it can never be arrested and darkened again, is the dawn of human possibility. . . .'

(White could also see his dead friend's face with its enthusiastic paleness, its disordered hair and the glowing darknesses in the eyes. On such occasions Benham always had an expression of *escape*. Temporary escape. And thus would his hand have clutched the reading-desk; thus would his long fingers have rustled these dry papers.)

'Man has reached a point when a new life opens before him. . . .

'The old habitual life of man is breaking up all about us, and for the new life our minds, our imaginations, our habits and customs are all unprepared. . . .

'It is only now, after some years of study and living that I begin to realise what this tremendous beginning we call Science means to mankind. Every condition that once justified the rules and imperatives, the manners and customs, the sentiments, the morality, the laws and limitations which make up the common life, has been or is being destroyed. . . . Two or three hundred years more and all that life will be as much a thing past and done with as the life that was lived in the age of unpolished stone. . . .

'Man is leaving his ancestral shelters and going out upon the greatest adventure that ever was in space or time, he is doing it now, he is doing it in us as I stand here and read to you.'

CHAPTER THE SECOND

THE YOUNG MAN ABOUT TOWN

§ 1

THE oldest novel in the world at any rate, White reflected, was a story with a hero and no love interest worth talking about. It was the story of Tobias and how he came out from the shelters of his youth into this magic and intricate world. Its heroine was incidental, part of the spoil, a seven times relict. . . .

White had not read the book of Tobit for many years, and what he was really thinking of was not that ancient story at all, but Botticelli's picture, that picture of the sunlit morning of life. When you say 'Tobias' that is what most intelligent people will recall. Perhaps you will remember how gaily and confidently the young man strides along with the armoured angel by his side. Absurdly enough, Benham and his dream of high aristocracy reminded White of that. . . .

'We have all been Tobias in our time,' said White.

If White had been writing this chapter he would have in all probability called it *The Tobias Stage*, forgetful that there was no Tobit behind Benham and an entirely different Sara in front of him.

§ 2

From Cambridge Benham came to London. For the first time he was to live in London. Never before had he been in London for more than a few days at a time. But now, guided by his mother's advice, he was to have a flat in Finacue Street, just round the corner from Desborough Street, a flat very completely and delightfully furnished under her supervision. It had an admirable study, in which she had arranged not only his books, but a number of others in beautiful old leather bindings that it had amused her extremely to buy; it had a splendid bureau and business-like letter-filing cabinets, a neat little drawing-room and a dining-room, well placed abundant electric lights, and a man called Merkle whom she had selected very carefully and who she felt would not only see to Benham's comfort but keep him, if necessary, up to the mark.

This man Merkle seemed quite unaware that humanity 'here and now'—even as he was engaged in meticulously putting out Benham's clothes—was 'leaving its ancestral shelters and going out upon the greatest adventure that ever was in space or time.' If we had been told as much by Benham he would probably have said, 'Indeed, sir,' and proceeded accurately with his duties. And if Benham's voice had seemed to call for any additional remark, he would probably have added, 'It's 'igh time, sir, something of the sort was done. Will you have the white wesket as before, sir, or a fresh one this evening? . . . Unless it's a very special occasion, sir. . . . Exactly, sir. *Thank* you, sir.'

And when her son was properly installed in his apartments Lady Marayne came round one morning with a large experienced-looking portfolio and rendered an account of her stewardship of his estate that was already some months overdue. It was all very confused and confusing, and there were inexplicable incidents, a heavy overdraft at the bank for example, but this was Sir Godfrey's fault, she explained. 'He never would help me with any of this business,' she said. 'I've had to add sometimes for *hours*. But, of course, you are a man, and when you've looked through it all, I know you'll understand.'

He did look through it enough to see that it was undesirable that he should understand too explicitly, and, anyhow, he was manifestly very well off indeed, and the circumstances of the case, even as he understood them, would have made any business-like book-keeping ungracious. The bankers submitted the corroborating account of securities, and he found himself possessed of his unconditional six thousand a year, with, as she put it, 'the world at his feet.' On the whole it seemed more wonderful to him now than when he had first heard of it. He kissed her and thanked her, and left the portfolio open for Merkle's entirely honest and respectful but very exact inspection, and walked back with her to Desborough Street, and all the while he was craving to ask the one tremendous question he knew he would never ask, which was just how exactly this beneficent Nolan came in. . . .

Once or twice in the small hours, and on a number of other occasions, this unspeakable riddle assumed a portentous predominance in his mind. He was forced back upon his inner consciousness for its consideration. He could discuss it with nobody else, because that would have been discussing his mother.

Probably most young men who find themselves with riches at large in the world have some such perplexity as this mixed in with the gift. Such men as the Cecils perhaps not, because they are in the order of things, the rich young Jews perhaps not, because acquisition is their principle, but for most other intelligent inheritors there must be this twinge of conscientious doubt. 'Why particularly am *I* picked out for so tremendous an advantage?' If the riddle is not Nolan, then it is rent, or it is the social mischief of the business, or the particular speculative *coup* that established their fortune.

'*Pecunia non olet*,' Benham wrote, 'and it is just as well. Or the west-ends of the world would reek with deodorisers. Restitution is inconceivable; how and to whom? And in the meanwhile here we are lifted up by our advantage to a fantastic appearance of opportunity. Whether the world looks to us or not to do tremendous things, it ought to look to us. And above all we ought to look to ourselves. *Richesse oblige*.'

§ 3

It is not to be supposed that Benham came to town only with a general theory of aristocracy. He had made plans for a career. Indeed, he had plans for several careers. None of them when brought into contrast with the great spectacle of London retained all the attractiveness that had saturated them at their inception.

They were all more or less political careers. Whatever a democratic man may be, Prothero and he had decided that an aristocratic man is a public man. He is made and protected in what he is by laws and the state and his honour goes out to the state. The aristocrat has no right to be a voluptuary or a mere artist or a respectable nonentity or any such purely personal things. Responsibility for the aim and ordering of the world is demanded from him as imperatively as courage.

Benham's deliberate assumption of the equestrian rôle brought him into contact with a new set of acquaintances, conscious of political destinies. They were amiable, hard young men, almost affectedly unaffected; they breakfasted before dawn to get in a day's hunting, and they saw to it that Benham's manifest determination not to discredit himself did not lead to his breaking his neck. Their bodies were beautifully tempered, and their minds were as flabby as Prothero's body. Among them were such men as Lord

Breeze and Peter Westerton, and that current set of Corinthians who supposed themselves to be resuscitating the Young England movement and Tory Democracy. Poor movements which indeed have never so much lived as suffered chronic resuscitation. These were days when Tariff Reform was only an inglorious possibility for the Tory Party, and Young England had yet to demonstrate its mental quality in an anti-socialist campaign. Seen from the perspectives of Cambridge and Chexington, the Tory party was still a credible basis for the adventure of a young man with an aristocratic theory in his mind.

These were the days when the strain and extremity of a dangerous colonial war were fresh in people's minds, when the quality of the public consciousness was braced up by its recent response to unanticipated demands. The conflict of stupidities that had caused the war was overlaid and forgotten by a hundred thousand devotions, by countless heroic deaths and sufferings, by a pacification largely conceived and broadly handled. The nation had displayed a belated regard for its honour and a sustained passion for great unities. It was still possible for Benham to regard the empire as a splendid opportunity, and London as the conceivable heart of the world He could think of Parliament as a career and of a mingling of aristocratic socialism based on universal service with a civilising imperialism as a purpose. . . .

But his thoughts had gone wider and deeper than that. . .

Already when Benham came to London he had begun to dream of possibilities that went beyond the accidental states and empires of to-day. Prothero's mind, replete with historical detail, could find nothing but absurdity in the alliances and dynasties and loyalties of our time. 'Patched-up things, Benham, temporary, pretentious. All very well for the undignified man, the democratic man, to take shelter under, all very well for the humorist to grin and bear, all very well for the crowd and the quack, but not for the aristocrat—No !—his mind cuts like steel and burns like fire. Lousy sheds they are, plastered hoardings . . . and such a damned nuisance too ! For any one who wants to do honourable things ! With their wars and their diplomacies, their tariffs and their encroachments; all their humbugging struggles, their bloody and monstrous struggles, that finally work out to no end at all. . . . If you are going for the handsome thing in life then the world has to be a united world, Benham, as a

matter of course. That was settled when the railways and
the telegraph came. Telephones, wireless telegraphy,
aeroplanes insist on it. We've got to mediatise all this
stuff, all these little crowns and boundaries and creeds,
and so on, that stand in the way. Just as Italy had to
be united in spite of all the rotten little dukes and princes
and republics, just as Germany had to be united in spite
of its scores of kingdoms and duchies and liberties, so now
the world. Things as they are may be fun for lawyers and
politicians and court people and—douaniers, they may suit
the loan-mongers and the armaments shareholders, they
may even be more comfortable for the middle-aged, but
what, except as an inconvenience, does that matter to you
or me?'

Prothero always pleased Benham when he swept away
empires. There was always a point when the rhetoric
broke into gesture.

'We've got to sweep them away, Benham,' he said, with
a wide gesture of his arm. 'We've got to sweep them all
away.'

Prothero helped himself to some more whisky, and spoke
hastily, because he was afraid some one else might begin.
He was never safe from interruption in his own room.
The other young men present sucked at their pipes and
regarded him doubtfully. They were never quite certain
whether Prothero was a prophet or a fool. They could not
understand a mixed type, and he was so manifestly both.

'The only sane political work for an intelligent man is
to get the world-state ready. For that we have to prepare
an aristocracy——'

'Your world-state will be aristocratic?' some one interpolated.

'Of course it will be aristocratic. How can uninformed
men think all round the globe? Democracy dies five miles
from the parish pump. It will be an aristocratic republic
of all the capable men in the world. . . .'

'Of course,' he added, pipe in mouth, as he poured out
his whisky, 'it's a big undertaking. It's an affair of
centuries. . . .'

And then, as a further afterthought: 'All the more
reason for getting to work at it. . . .'

In his moods of inspiration Prothero would discourse
through the tobacco smoke until that great world-state
seemed imminent—and Part Two in the Tripos a thing
relatively remote. He would talk until the dimly-lit

room about him became impalpable, and the young men squatting about it in elaborately careless attitudes caught glimpses of cities that are still to be, bridges in wild places, deserts tamed and oceans conquered, mankind no longer wasted by bickerings, going forward to the conquest of the stars. . . .

An aristocratic world state; this political dream had already taken hold of Benham's imagination when he came to town. But it was a dream, something that had never existed, something that indeed may never materialise, and such dreams, though they are vivid enough in a study at night, fade and vanish at the rustle of a daily newspaper or the sound of a passing band. To come back again. . . . So it was with Benham. Sometimes he was set clearly towards this world-state that Prothero had talked into possibility. Sometimes he was simply abreast of the patriotic and socially constructive British Imperialism of Breeze and Westerton. And there were moods when the two things were confused in his mind, and the glamour of world dominion rested wonderfully on the slack and straggling British Empire of Edward the Seventh—and Mr Rudyard Kipling and Mr Chamberlain. He did go on for a time honestly entertaining both these projects in his mind, each at its different level, the greater impalpable one and the lesser concrete one within it. In some unimaginable way he could suppose that the one by some miracle of ennoblement—and neglecting the Frenchman, the Russian, the German, the American, the Indian, the Chinaman, and, indeed, the greater part of mankind from the problem—might become the other. . . .

All of which is recorded here, without excess of comment, as it happened, and as, in a mood of astonished reminiscences, he came finally to perceive it, and set it down for White's meditative perusal.

§ 4

But to the enthusiasm of the young, dreams have something of the substance of reality, and realities something of the magic of dreams, The London to which Benham came from Cambridge and the disquisitions of Prothero was not the London of a mature and disillusioned vision. It was London seen magnified and distorted through the young man's crystalline intentions. It had for him a quality of multitudinous, unquenchable activity. Himself filled with an immense appetite for life, he was unable to conceive of London as fatigued. He could not suspect these statesmen he now began to meet and watch, of jaded wills and petty spites; he imagined that all the important and influential persons in this large world of affairs were as frank in their private lives and as unembarrassed in their financial relationships as his untainted self. And he had still to reckon with stupidity. He believed in the statecraft of leader-writers and the sincerity of political programmes. And so regarded, what an avenue to Empire was Whitehall! How momentous was the sunrise in St James's Park, and how significant the clustering knot of listeners and speakers beneath the tall column that lifts our Nelson to the windy sky!

For a time Benham was in love with the idea of London. He got maps of London and books about London. He made plans to explore its various regions. He tried to grasp it all, from the conscious picturesqueness of its garden suburbs to the factories of Croydon, from the clerk-villadoms of Ealing to the inky streams of Bow. In those days there were passenger steamboats that would take one from the meadows of Hampton Court past the whole spectacle of London out to the shipping at Greenwich and the towed liners, the incessant tugs, the heaving portals of the sea. . . . His time was far too occupied for him to carry out a tithe of these expeditions he had planned, but he had many walks that bristled with impressions. Northward and southward, eastward and westward a dreaming young man could wander into a wilderness of population, polite or sombre, poor, rich, or middle-class, but all ceaselessly active, all urgently pressing, as it seemed, to their part in the drama of the coming years. He loved the late afternoon, when every artery is injected and gorged with the multitudinous home-going of the daily workers, he loved the time of lighting up, and the clustering excitements of the late hours. And he went out southward and eastward into gaunt regions of reeking toil. As yet he knew nothing of the realities of industrialism. He saw only the beauty of the great chimneys that rose against the sullen smoke-barred sunsets, and he felt only the romance of the lurid shuddering flares that burst out from squat stacks of brickwork and lit the emptiness of strange and slovenly streets. . . .

And this London was only the foreground of the great scene upon which he, as a prosperous, well-befriended young

Englishman, was free to play whatever part he could. This narrow turbid tidal river by which he walked ran out under the bridges eastward beneath the gray-blue clouds towards Germany, towards Russia, and towards Asia, which still seemed in those days so largely the Englishman's Asia. And when you turned about at Blackfriars Bridge this sense of the round world was so upon you that you faced not merely Westminster, but the icy Atlantic and America, which one could yet fancy was a land of English-men—Englishmen a little estranged. At any rate they assimilated, they kept the tongue. The shipping in the lower reaches below the Tower there carried the flags of every country under the sky. . . . As he went along the riverside he met a group of dusky students, Chinese or Japanese. Cambridge had abounded in Indians, and beneath that tall clock tower at Westminster it seemed as though the world might centre. The background of the Englishman's world reached indeed to either pole, it went about the earth, his background it was—for all that he was capable of doing. All this had awaited him. . . .

Is it any wonder if a young man with an excitable imagination came at times to the pitch of audible threats? If the extreme indulgence of his opportunity and his sense of ability and vigour lifted his vanity at moments to the kingly pitch? If he ejaculated and made a gesture or so as he went along the Embankment?

§ 5

In the disquisition upon choice that opened Benham's paper on *Aristocracy*, he showed himself momentarily wiser than his day-dreams. For in these day-dreams he did seem to himself to be choosing among unlimited possi-bilities. Yet while he dreamt other influences were directing his movements. There were, for instance, his mother, Lady Marayne, who saw a very different London from what he did, and his mother Dame Nature, who cannot see London at all. She was busy in his blood as she is busy in the blood of most healthy young men; common experience must fill the gaps for us; and patiently and thoroughly she was preparing for the entrance of that heroine whom not the most self-centred of heroes can altogether avoid. . . .

And then there was the power of every day. Benham imagined himself at large on his liberating steed of property while indeed he was mounted on the made horse of Civilisation; while he was speculating whither he should go, he was already starting out upon the round. One hesitates upon the magnificent plan and devotion of one's lifetime and meanwhile there is usage, there are engagements. Every morning came Merkle, the embodiment of the established routine, the herald of all that the world expected and required Benham to be and do. Usually he awakened Benham with the opening of his door and the soft tinkle of the curtain rings as he let in the morning light. He moved softly about the room, gathering up and removing the crumpled hulls of yesterday; that done he reappeared at the bedside with a cup of admirable tea and one thin slice of bread-and-butter, reported on the day's weather, stood deferential for instructions. 'You will be going out for lunch, sir. Very good, sir. White slips of course, sir. You will go down into the country in the afternoon. Will that be the serge suit, sir, or the brown?'

These matters settled, the new aristocrat could yawn and stretch like any aristocrat under the old dispensation, and then, as the sound of running water from the bathroom ceased, stick his toes out of bed.

The day was tremendously indicated. World-states and aristocracies of steel and fire, things that were as real as coal-scuttles in Billy's rooms away there at Cambridge, were now remoter than Sirius.

He was expected to shave, expected to bath, expected to go in to the bright warmth and white linen and silver and china of his breakfast-table. And there he found letters and invitations, loaded with expectation. And beyond the coffee-pot, neatly folded, lay the *Times*, and the *Daily News* and the *Telegraph* all with an air of requiring his attention. There had been more fighting in Thibet and Mr Ritchie had made a Free Trade speech at Croydon. The Japanese had torpedoed another Russian ironclad and a British cruiser was ashore in the East Indies. A man had been found murdered in an empty house in Hoxton and the King had had a conversation with General Booth. Tadpole was in for North Winchelsea, beating Taper by nine votes, and there had been a new cut in the Atlantic passenger rates. He was expected to be interested and excited by these things.

Presently the telephone bell would ring and he would hear the clear little voice of his mother full of imperative expectations. He would be round for lunch? Yes, he would be round to lunch. And the afternoon, had he arranged to do anything with his afternoon? No!—put off Chexington until to-morrow. There was this new pianist, it was really an *experience,* and one might not get tickets again. And then tea at Panton's. It was rather fun at Panton's. . . Oh!—Weston Massinghay was coming to lunch. He was a useful man to know. So *clever.* . . . So long, my dear little Son, till I see you. . . .

So life puts out its Merkle threads, as the poacher puts his hair noose about the pheasant's neck, and while we theorise takes hold of us. . . .

It came presently home to Benham that he had been down from Cambridge for ten months, and that he was still not a step forward with the realisation of the new aristocracy. His political career waited. He had done a quantity of things, but their net effect was incoherence. He had not been merely passive, but his efforts to break away into creative realities had added to rather than diminished his accumulating sense of futility.

The natural development of his position under the influence of Lady Marayne had enormously enlarged the circle of his acquaintances. He had taken part in all sorts of social occasions, and sat and listened to a representative selection of political and literary and social personages, he had been several times to the opera and to a great number and variety of plays, he had been attentively inconspicuous in several really good week-end parties. He had spent a golden October in North Italy with his mother, and escaped from the glowing lassitude of Venice for some days of climbing in the Eastern Alps. In January in an outbreak of inquiry, he had gone with Lionel Maxim to Petrograd and had eaten zakuska, brightened his eyes with vodka, talked with a number of charming people of the war that was then imminent, listened to gipsy singers until dawn, careered in sledges about the most silent and stately of capitals, and returned with Lionel, discoursing upon autocracy and assassination, Japan, the Russian destiny, and the government of Peter the Great. That excursion was the most after his heart of all the dispersed employments of his first year. Through the rest of the winter he kept himself very fit, and still further qualified that nervous dislike for the horse that he had acquired from Prothero by hunting once a week in Essex. He was incurably a bad horseman; he rode without sympathy, he was unready and convulsive at hedges and ditches, and he judged distances badly. His white face and rigid seat and a certain joylessness of bearing in the saddle earned him the singular nickname, which never reached his ears, of the 'Galvanised Corpse.' He got through, however, at the cost of four quite trifling spills and without damaging either of the horses he rode. And his physical self-respect increased.

On his writing-desk appeared a few sheets of manuscript that increased only very slowly. He was trying to express his Cambridge view of aristocracy in terms of Finacue Street, West.

The artistic and intellectual movements of London had made their various demands upon his time and energies. Art came to him with a noble assumption of his interest and an intention that presently became unpleasantly obvious to sell him pictures that he did not want to buy and explain away pictures that he did. He bought one or two modern achievements, and began to doubt if art and aristocracy had any necessary connection. At first he had accepted the assumption that they had. After all, he reflected, one lives rather for life and things than for pictures of life and things or pictures arising out of life and things. This Art had an air of saying something, but when one came to grips with it what had it to say? Unless it was Yah! The drama, and more particularly the intellectual drama, challenged his attention. In the hands of Shaw, Barker, Masefield, Galsworthy, and Hankin, it, too, had an air of saying something, but he found it extremely difficult to join on to his own demands upon life anything whatever that the intellectual drama had the air of having said. He would sit forward in the front row of the dress-circle with his cheek on his hand and his brow slightly knit. His intentness amused observant people. The drama that did not profess to be intellectual he went to with Lady Marayne, and usually on first nights. Lady Marayne loved a big first night at St James's Theatre or His Majesty's. Afterwards, perhaps, Sir Godfrey would join them at a supper party, and all sorts of clever and amusing people would be there saying keen intimate things about each other. He met Yeats, who told amusing stories about George Moore, and afterwards he met George Moore, who told amusing stories about Yeats, and it was all, he felt, great fun for the people who were in it. But he was not in it, and he had no very keen desire to be in it. It wasn't his stuff. He had, though they were nowadays rather at the back of his mind, quite other intentions. In the meanwhile all these things took up his time and distracted his attention.

There was, as yet, no practicable aviation to beguile a young man of spirit, but there were times when Benham found himself wondering whether there might not be something rather creditable in the possession and control of a motor-car of exceptional power. Only one might smash people up. Should an aristocrat be deterred by the fear of smashing people up? If it is a selfish fear of smashing people up, if it is nerves rather than pity? At any rate it did not come to the car.

§ 6

Among other things that delayed Benham very greatly in the development of his aristocratic experiments was the advice that was coming to him fron every quarter. It came in extraordinary variety and volume, but always it had one unvarying feature. It ignored and tacitly contradicted his private intentions.

We are all of us disposed to be propagandists of our way of living, and the spectacle of a wealthy young man quite at large is enough to excite the most temperate of us without distinction of age or sex. 'If I were you,' came to be a familiar phrase in his ear. This was particularly the case with political people; and they did it not only from the natural infirmity of humanity, but because, when they seemed reluctant or satisfied with him as he was, Lady Marayne egged them on.

There was a general assumption that he was to go into Parliament, and most of his counsellors assumed further that on the whole his natural sympathies would take him into the Conservative party. But it was pointed out to him that just at present the Liberal party was the party of a young man's opportunity; sooner or later the swing of the pendulum which would weed the Conservatives and proliferate Liberals was bound to come, there was always more demand and opportunity for candidates on the Liberal side, the Tariff Reformers were straining their ministerial majority to the splitting point, and most of the old Liberal leaders had died off during the years of exile. The party was no longer dominated; it would tolerate ideas. A young man who took a distinctive line— provided it was not from the party point of view a vexatious or impossible line—might go very rapidly far and high. On the other hand, it was urged upon him that the Tariff Reform adventure called also for youth and energy. But there, perhaps, there was less scope for the distinctive line—and already they had Garvin. Quite a number of Benham's friends pointed out to him the value of working out some special aspect of our national political interests. A very useful speciality was the Balkans. Mr Pope, the well-known publicist, whose very sound and considerable reputation was based on the East Purblow Labour Experiment, met Benham at lunch and proposed to go with him in a spirit of instructive association to the Balkans, rub up their Greek together, and settle the problem of Albania. He wanted, he said, a foreign speciality to balance his East Purblow interest. But Lady Beach Mandarin warned Benham against the Balkans; the Balkans were getting to be too handy for Easter and summer holidays, and now that there were several good hotels in Serbia and Montenegro and Sofia, they were being over-done. Everybody went to the Balkans and came back with a pet nationality. She loathed pet nationalities. She believed most people loathed them nowadays. It was stale; it was *Gladstonian*. She was all for specialisation in social reform. She thought Benham ought to join the Fabian Society and consult the Webbs. Quite a number of able young men had been placed with the assistance of the Webbs. They were, she said, 'a perfect fount. . . .' Two other people, independently of each other, pointed out to Benham the helpfulness of a few articles in the half-crown monthlies. . . .

'What are the assumptions underlying all this?' Benham asked himself in a phase of lucidity.

And after reflection : 'Good God ! The assumptions ! What do they think will satisfy me? . . .'

Everybody, however, did not point to Parliament. Several people seemed to think Travel, with a large T, was indicated. One distant cousin of Sir Godfrey's, the kind of man of the world who has long moustaches, was for big game shooting. 'Get right out of all this while you are young,' he said. 'There's nothing to compare with stopping a charging lion at twenty yards. I've done it, my boy. You can come back for all this pow-wow afterwards.' He gave the diplomatic service as a second choice. 'There you are,' he said, 'first-rate social position, nothing to do, theatres, operas, pretty women, colour, life. The best of good times. Barring Washington, that is. But Washington, they say, isn't as bad as it used to be—since Teddy has Europeanised 'em. . . .'

Even the Reverend Harold Benham took a subdued but thoughtful share in his son's admonition. He came up to the flat—due precautions were taken to prevent a painful encounter—he lunched at his son's new club, and he was visibly oppressed by the contrast between the young man's youthful fortunes and his own. As visibly he bore up bravely. 'There are few men, Poff, who would not envy you your opportunities,' he said. 'You have the Feast of Life spread out at your feet. . . . I hope you have had yourself put up for the Athenæum. They say it takes years. When I was a young man—and ambitious—I thought that some day I might belong to the Athenæum. . . . One has to learn. . . .'

§ 7

And with an effect of detachment, just as though it didn't belong to the rest of him at all, there was beginning a sort of backstairs and underside to Benham's life. There is no need to discuss how inevitable that may or may not be in the case of a young man of spirit and large means, nor to embark upon the discussion of the temptations and opportunities of large cities. Several ladies, of various positions and qualities, had reflected upon his manifest need of education. There was in particular Mrs Skelmersdale, a very pretty little widow with hazel eyes, black hair, a mobile mouth, and a pathetic history, who talked of old music to him and took him to a Dolmetsch concert in Clifford's Inn, and expanded that common interest to a general participation in his indefinite outlook. She advised him about his probable politics—everybody did that—but when he broke through his usual reserve and suggested views of his own, she was extraordinarily sympathetic. She was so sympathetic, and in such a caressing way, that she created a temporary belief in her understanding, and it was quite imperceptibly that he was drawn into the discussion of modern ethical problems. She herself was a rather stimulating instance of modern ethical problems. She told him something of her own story, and then their common topics narrowed down very abruptly. He found he could help her in several ways. There is, unhappily, a disposition on the part of many people, who ought to know better, to regard a rôle played by Joseph during his

earlier days in Egypt as a ridiculous one. This point of
view became very inopportunely dominant in Benham's
mind when he was lunching *tête à tête* with Mrs Skelmersdale
at her flat. . . .

The ensuing intimacy was of an entirely concealed and
respectable nature, but a certain increased preoccupation
in his manner set Lady Marayne thinking. He had as a
matter of fact been taken by surprise.

Still he perceived that it is no excuse for a man that he
has been taken by surprise. Surprises in one's own conduct
ought not to happen. When they do happen then an
aristocrat ought to stick to what he has done. He was now
in a subtle and complicated relationship to Mrs Skelmersdale, a relationship in which her pride had become suddenly
a matter of tremendous importance. Once he had launched
himself upon this affair, it was clear to him that he owed
it to her never to humiliate her. And to go back upon
himself now would be a tremendous humiliation for her.
You see, he had helped her a little financially. And she
looked to him, she wanted him. . . .

She wasn't, he knew, altogether respectable. Indeed,
poor dear, her ethical problems, already a little worn,
made her seem at times anything but respectable. He had
met her first one evening at Jimmy Gluckstein's when he
was forming his opinion of Art. Her manifest want of
interest in pictures had attracted him. And that had led
to music. And to the mention of a Clementi piano, that
short, gentle, sad, old, little sort of piano people will
insist upon calling a spinet, in her flat.

And so to this. . . .

It was very wonderful and delicious, this first indulgence
of sense.

It was shabby and underhand.

The great god Pan is a glorious god. (And so was Swin-
burne.) And what can compare with the warmth of blood
and the sheen of sunlit limbs?

But Priapus. . . .

She was the most subtle, delightful and tender of created
beings.

She had amazing streaks of vulgarity.

And some astonishing friends.

Once she had seemed to lead the talk deliberately to
money matters.

She loved him and desired him. There was no doubt of it.

There was a curious effect about her as though when she

R.M.   G went round the corner she would become somebody else. And a curious recurrent feeling that round the corner there was somebody else.

He had an extraordinary feeling that his mother knew about this business. This feeling came from nothing in her words or acts, but from some indefinable change in her eyes and bearing towards him. But how could she know?

It was unlikely that she and Mrs Skelmersdale would ever meet, and it seemed to him that it would be a particularly offensive incident for them to meet.

There were times now when life took on a gray and boring quality such as it had never had before he met Mrs Skelmersdale, and the only remedy was to go to her. She could restore his nervous tranquillity, his feeling of solidity and reality, his pride in himself. For a time that is.

Nevertheless his mind was as a whole pervaded by the feeling that he ought not to have been taken by surprise.

And he had the clearest conviction in his mind that if now he could be put back again to the day before that lunch. . . .

No ! he should not have gone there to lunch.

He had gone there to see her Clementi piano.

Had he or had he not thought beforehand of any other possibility?

On a point so vital his memory was curiously unsure.

§ 8

The worry and disorganisation of Benham's life and thoughts increased as the spring advanced. His need in some way to pull things together became overpowering. He began to think of Billy Prothero, more and more did it seem desirable to have a big talk with Billy and place everything that had got disturbed. Benham thought of going to Cambridge for a week of exhaustive evenings. Small engagements delayed that expedition. . . .

Then came a day in April when all the world seemed wrong to Benham. He was irritable; his will was unstable; whatever presented itself to be done presented itself as undesirable; he could settle to nothing. He had been keeping away from Mrs Skelmersdale, and in the morning there came a little note from her designed to correct this abstention. She understood the art of the attractive note. But he would not decide to go to her. He left the note unanswered.

Then came his mother at the telephone and it became

instantly certain to Benham that he could not play the dutiful son that evening. He answered her that he could not come to dinner. He had engaged himself. 'Where?'
'With some men.'

There was a pause and then his mother's voice came, flattened by disappointment. 'Very well then, little Poff. Perhaps I shall see you to-morrow.'

He replaced the receiver and fretted back into his study where the notes on aristocracy lay upon his desk, the notes he had been pretending to work over all the morning.

'Damned liar!' he said, and then, 'Dirty liar!'

He decided to lunch at the club, and in the afternoon he was moved to telephone an appointment with his siren. And having done that he was bound to keep it.

About one o'clock in the morning he found himself walking back to Finacue Street. He was no longer a fretful conflict of nerves, but if anything he was less happy than he had been before. It seemed to him that London was a desolate and inglorious growth.

London ten years ago was much less nocturnal than it is now. And not so brightly lit. Down the long streets came no traffic but an occasional hansom. Here and there a cat halted or bolted in the road. Near Piccadilly a policeman hovered artfully in a doorway, and then came a few belated prostitutes waylaying the passers-by, and a few youths and men, wearily lust driven.

As he turned up New Bond Street he saw a figure that struck him as familiar. Surely!—it was Billy Prothero! Or at any rate it was astonishingly like Billy Prothero. He glanced again and the likeness was more doubtful. The man had his back to Benham; he was halting and looking back at a woman.

By some queer flash of intuition it came to Benham that even if this was not Prothero, still Prothero did these things. It might very well be Prothero even though, as he now saw, it wasn't. Everybody did these things. . . .

It came into Benham's head for the first time that life could be tiresome.

This Bond Street was a tiresome place; with its shops all shut and muffled, its shops where in the crowded daytime one bought costly furniture, costly clothes, costly scent, sweets, bibelots, pictures, jewellery, presents of all sorts, clothes for Mrs Skelmersdale, sweets for Mrs Skelmersdale, presents for Mrs Skelmersdale, all the elaborate fittings and equipage of—*that!*

'Good-night, dear,' a woman drifted by him.

'I've *said* good-night,' he cried, 'I've *said* good night,' and so went on to his flat. The unquenchable demand, the wearisome insatiability of sex! When everything else has gone, then it shows itself bare in the bleak small hours. And at first it had seemed so light a matter! He went to bed, feeling dog-tired—he went to bed at an hour and with a finished completeness that Merkle would have regarded as entirely becoming in a young gentleman of his position.

And a little past three o'clock in the morning he awoke to a mood of indescribable desolation. He awoke with a start to an agony of remorse and self-reproach.

§ 9

For a time he lay quite still staring at the darkness, then he groaned and turned over. Then, suddenly, like one who fancies he hears a strange noise, he sat up in bed and listened.

'Oh, God!' he said at last.

And then: 'Oh! The *dirtiness* of life! The dirty muddle of life!

'What are we doing with life? What are we all doing with life?

'It isn't only this poor Milly business. This only brings it to a head. Of course she wants money. . . .'

His thoughts came on again.

'But the ugliness!

'Why did I begin it?'

He put his hands upon his knees and pressed his eyes against the backs of his hands and so remained very still, a blankness beneath his own question.

After a long interval his mind moved again.

And now it was as if he looked upon his whole existence; he seemed to see in a large, clear, cold comprehensiveness all the wasted days, the fruitless activities, the futilities, the perpetual postponements that had followed his coming to London. He saw it all as a joyless indulgence, as a confusion of playthings and undisciplined desires, as a succession of days that began amiably and weakly, that became steadily more crowded with ignoble and trivial occupations, that had sunken now to indignity and uncleanness. He was overwhelmed by that persuasion, which only freshly soiled youth can feel in its extreme intensity, that life was slipping away from him, that the sands were running out, that in a little while his existence would be irretrievably lost.

By some trick of the imagination he saw life as an interminable Bond Street, lit up by night lamps, desolate, full of rubbish, full of the very best rubbish, trappings, temptations, and down it all he drove, as the damned drive, wearily, inexplicably.

What are we up to with life ? What are we making of life ?

But hadn't he intended to make something tremendous of life? Hadn't he come to London trailing a glory? . . .

He began to remember it as a project. It was the project of a great World-State sustained by an aristocracy of noble men. He was to have been one of those men, too fine and far-reaching for the dull manœuvres of such politics as rule the world to-day. The project seemed still large, still whitely noble, but now it was unlit and dead, and in the foreground he sat in the flat of Mrs Skelmersdale, feeling dissipated and fumbling with his white tie. And she was looking tired. 'God !' he said. 'How did I get there?'

And then suddenly he reached out his arms in the darkness and prayed aloud to the silences.

'Oh, God ! Give me back my visions ! Give me back my visions !'

He could have imagined he heard a voice calling upon him to come out into life, to escape from the body of this death. But it was his own voice that called to him. . . .

§ 10

The need for action became so urgent in him, that he got right out of his bed and sat on the edge of it. Something had to be done at once. He did not know what it was, but he felt that there could be no more sleep, no more rest, no dressing nor eating nor going forth before he came to decisions. Christian before his pilgrimage began was not more certain of this need of flight from the life of routine and vanities.

What was to be done?

In the first place he must get away and think about it all, think himself clear of all these—these immediacies, these associations and relations and holds and habits. He must get back his vision, get back to the God in his vision. And to do that he must go alone.

He was clear he must go alone. It was useless to go to

Prothero, one weak man going to a weaker. Prothero he was convinced could help him not at all, and the strange thing is that this conviction had come to him and had established itself incontestably because of that figure at the street corner, which had for just one moment resembled Prothero. By some fantastic intuition Benham knew that Prothero would not only participate but excuse. And he knew that he himself could endure no excuses. He must cut clear of any possibility of qualification. This thing had to be stopped. He must get away, he must get free, he must get clean. In the extravagance of his reaction Benham felt that he could endure nothing but solitary places and to sleep under the open sky.

He wanted to get right away from London and everybody and lie in the quiet darkness and stare up at the stars.

His plans grew so definite that presently he was in his dressing-gown and turning out the maps in the lower drawer of his study bureau. He would go down into Surrey with a knapsack, wander along the North Downs until the Guilford gap was reached, strike across the Weald country to the South Downs and then beat eastward. The very thought of it brought a coolness to his mind. He knew that over those southern hills one could be as lonely as in the wilderness and as free to talk to God. And there he would settle something. He would make a plan for his life and end this torment.

When Merkle came in to him in the morning he was fast asleep.

The familiar curtain rings awakened Benham. He turned his head over, stared for a moment and then remembered.

'Merkle,' he said, 'I am going for a walking tour. I am going off this morning. Haven't I a rücksack?'

'You 'ave a sort of canvas bag, sir, with pockets to it,' said Merkle. 'Will you be needing the *very* 'eavy boots with 'obnails—Swiss, I fancy, sir—or your ordinary shooting boots?'

'And when may I expect you back, sir?' asked Merkle as the moment for departure drew near.

'God knows,' said Benham, 'I don't.'

'Then will there be any address for forwarding letters, sir?'

Benham hadn't thought of that. For a moment he regarded Merkle's scrupulous respect with a transient perplexity.

'I'll let you know, Merkle,' he said. 'I'll let you know.' For some days at least, notes, telephone messages, engagements, all this fuss and clamour about nothing, should clamour for him in vain. . . .

§ 11

'But how closely,' cried White, in a mood of cultivated enthusiasm; 'how closely must all the poor little stories that we tell to-day follow in the footsteps of the Great Exemplars ! A little while ago and the springtime freshness of Tobias irradiated the page. Now, see ! it is Christian——'

Indeed it looked extremely like Christian as Benham went up across the springy turf from Epsom Downs station towards the crest of the hill. Was he not also fleeing in the morning sunlight from the City of Destruction? Was he not also seeking that better city whose name is Peace? And there was a bundle on his back. It was the bundle, I think, that seized most firmly upon the too literary imagination of White.

But the analogy of the bundle was a superficial one. Benham had not the slightest desire to lose it from his shoulders. It would have inconvenienced him very greatly if he had done so. It did not contain his sins. Our sins nowadays are not so easily separated. It contained a light, warm cape-coat he had bought in Switzerland and which he intended to wrap about him when he slept under the stars, and in addition Merkle had packed it with his silk pyjamas, an extra pair of stockings, tooth-brush, brush and comb, a safety razor. . . . And there were several sheets of the Ordnance map.

§ 12

The urgency of getting away from something dominated Benham to the exclusion of any thought of what he might be getting to. That muddle of his London life had to be left behind. First, escape. . . .

Over the downs great numbers of larks were singing. It was warm April that year, and early. All the cloud stuff in the sky was gathered into great towering, slow-sailing masses, and the rest was blue of the intensest. The air was so clean that Benham felt it clean in the substance of his body. The chestnuts down the hill to the right were flowering, the beeches were luminously green, and the oaks in the valley foaming gold. And sometimes it was one lark filled his ears, and sometimes he seemed to be hearing all the larks for miles about him. Presently over the crest he would be out of sight of the grand stand and the men exercising horses, and that brace of red-jacketed golfers. . . .

What was he to do?

For a time he could think of nothing to do except to keep up and out of the valley. His whole being seemed to have come to his surfaces to look out at the budding of the year and hear the noise of the birds. And then he got into a long road from which he had to escape, and trespassing southward through plantations he reached the steep edge of the hills and sat down over above a great chalk pit somewhere near Dorking and surveyed all the tumbled wooded spaces of the Weald. . . . It is after all not so great a country this Sussex, nor so hilly, from deepest valley to highest crest is not six hundred feet, yet what a greatness of effect it can achieve ! There is something in those downland views which, like sea views, lifts a mind out to the skies. All England it seemed was there to Benham's vision, and the purpose of the English, and his own purpose in the world. For a long time he surveyed the large delicacy of the detail before him, the crests, the tree-protected houses, the fields and the farmsteads, the distant gleams of water. And then he became interested in the men who were working in the chalk pit down below.

They at any rate were not troubled with the problem of what to do with their lives.

§ 13

Benham found his mind was now running clear, and so abundantly that he could scarcely, he felt, keep pace with it. As he thought his flow of ideas was tinged with a fear that he might forget what he was thinking. In an instant, for the first time in his mental existence, he could have imagined he had discovered Labour and seen it plain. A little while ago and he had seemed a lonely man among the hills, but indeed he was not lonely, these men had been with him all the time, and he was free to wander, to sit here, to think and choose simply because those men down there were not free. *He was spending their leisure.* . . . Not once but many times with Prothero had he used the phrase *Richesse oblige.* Now he remembered it. He began to remember a mass of ideas that had been overlaid and stifling within him. This was what Merkle and the club servants and the entertainments and engagements and his mother and the artistic touts and the theatrical touts and the hunting and the elaboration of games and—Mrs Skelmersdale and all that had clustered thickly round him in London had been hiding from him. Those men below there had not been trusted to choose their work; they had been given it. And he had been trusted. . . .

And now to grapple with it! Now to get it clear! What work was he going to do? That settled, he would deal with his distractions rapidly enough. Until that was settled he was lax and exposed to every passing breeze of invitation.

'What work am I going to do? What work am I going to do?' He repeated it.

It is the only question for the aristocrat. What amusement? That for a footman on holiday. That for a silly child, for any creature that is kept or led or driven. That perhaps for a tired invalid, for a toiler worked to a rag. But able-bodied amusement! The arms of Mrs Skelmersdale were no worse than the solemn aimlessness of hunting, and an evening of dalliance not an atom more reprehensible than an evening of chatter. It was the waste of him that made the sin. His life in London had been of a piece together. It was well that his intrigue had set a light on it, put a point to it, given him this saving crisis of the nerves. That, indeed, is the chief superiority of idle love-making over other more prevalent forms of idleness and self-indulgence; it does at least bear its proper label. It is reprehensible. It brings your careless honour to the challenge of concealment and shabby evasions and lies. . . .

But in this pellucid air things took their proper proportions again.

And now what was he to do?

'Politics,' he said aloud to the turf and the sky.

Is there any other work for an aristocratic man? . . . Science? One could admit science in that larger sense that sweeps in History, or Philosophy. Beyond that whatever work there is is work for which men are paid. Art? Art is nothing aristocratic except when it is a means of scientific or philosophical expression. Art that does not argue nor demonstrate nor discover is merely the craftsman's impudence.

He pulled up at this and reflected for a time with some distinguished instances in his mind. They were so distinguished, so dignified, they took their various arts with so admirable a gravity that the soul of this young man recoiled from the verdicts to which his reasoning drove him. 'It's not for me to judge them,' he decided, 'except in relation to myself. For them there may be tremendous significances in Art. But if these do not appear to me, then so far as I am concerned they do not exist for me. They are not in my world. So far as they attempt to invade me and control my attitudes or my outlook, or to judge me in any way, there is no question of their impudence. Impudence is the word for it. My world is real. I want to be really aristocratic, really brave, really paying for the privilege of not being a driven worker. The things the artist makes are like the things my private dream-artist makes, relaxing, distracting. What can Art at its greatest be, pure Art that is, but a more splendid, more permanent, transmissible reverie? The very essence of what I am after is *not* to be an artist. . . .'

After a large and serious movement through his mind he came back to Science, Philosophy or Politics as the sole three justifications for the usurpation of leisure.

So far as devotion to science went, he knew he had no specific aptitude for any departmentalised subject, and equally he felt no natural call to philosophy. He was left with politics. . . .

'Or else, why shouldn't I go down there and pick up a shovel and set to work? To make leisure for my betters. . . .'

And now it was that he could take up the real trouble that more than anything else had been keeping him ineffective and the prey of every chance demand and temptation during the last ten months. He had not been able to get himself into politics, and the reason why he had not been able to do so was that he could not induce himself to fit in. Statecraft was a remote and faded thing in the political life of the time; politics was a choice of two sides in a game, and either side he found equally unattractive. Since he had come down from Cambridge the Tariff Reform people had gone far to capture the Conservative party. There was little chance of a candidature for him without an adhesion to that. And he could find nothing he could imagine himself working for in the declarations of the Tariff Reform people. He distrusted them, he disliked them. They took all the light and pride out of imperialism, they reduced it to a shabby conspiracy of the British and their colonies against foreign industrialism. They were violent for armaments and hostile to education. They could give him no assurance of any scheme of growth and

unification, and no guarantees against the manifest dangers
of economic disturbance and political corruption a tariff
involves. Imperialism without noble imaginations, it
seemed to him, was simply nationalism with megalomania.
It was swaggering, it was greed, it was German; its enthusiasm was forced, its nobility a vulgar lie. No. And
when he turned to the opposite party he found little that
was more attractive. They were prepared, it seemed, if
they came into office, to pull the legislature of the British
Isles to pieces in obedience to the Irish demand for Home
Rule, and they were totally unprepared with any scheme
for doing this that had even a chance of success. In the
twenty years that had elapsed since Gladstone's hasty
and disastrous essay in political surgery they had studied
nothing, learnt nothing, produced no ideas whatever in the
matter. They had not had the time. They had just
negotiated, like the mere politicians they were, for the
Nationalist vote. They seemed to hope that by a marvel
God would pacify Ulster. Lord Dunraven, Plunkett, were
voices crying in the wilderness. The sides in the party
game would as soon have heeded a poet. . . . But unless
Benham was prepared to subscribe either to Home Rule
or Tariff Reform there was no way whatever open to him
into public life. He had had some decisive conversations.
He had no illusions left upon that score. . . .

Here was the real barrier that had kept him inactive
for ten months. Here was the problem he had to solve.
This was how he had been left out of active things, a prey
to distractions, excitements, idle temptations—and Mrs
Skelmersdale.

Running away to shoot big game or explore wildernesses
was no remedy. That was just running away. Aristocrats
do not run away. What of his debt to those men down
there in the quarry? What of his debt to the unseen men
in the mines away in the north? What of his debt to the
stokers on the liners, and to the clerks in the city? He
reiterated the cardinal article of his creed. The aristocrat
is a privileged man in order that he may be a public and
political man.

But how is one to be a political man when one is not in
politics?

Benham frowned at the Weald. His ideas were running
thin.

He might hammer at politics from the outside. And
then again how? He would make a list of all the things

that he might do. For example, he might write. He rested one hand on his knee and lifted one finger and regarded it. *Could* he write? There were one or two men who ran papers and seemed to have a sort of independent influence. Strachey, for example, with his *Spectator*; Maxse, with his *National Review*. But they were grown up, they had formed their ideas. He had to learn first.

He lifted a second finger. How to learn? For it was learning that he had to do.

When one comes down from Oxford or Cambridge one falls into the mistake of thinking that learning is over and action must begin. But until one perceives clearly just where one stands action is impossible.

How is one with no experience of affairs to get an experience of affairs when the door of affairs is closed to one by one's own convictions? Outside of affairs how can one escape being flimsy? How can one escape becoming merely an intellectual like those wordy Fabians, those writers, poseurs, and sham publicists whose wrangles he had attended? And, moreover, there is danger in the leisure of your intellectual. One cannot be always reading and thinking and discussing and inquiring. . . . *Would it not be better after all to make a concession, swallow Home Rule or Tariff Reform, and so at least get his hands on things?*

And then in a little while the party conflict would swallow him up !

Still it would engage him, it would hold him. If, perhaps, he did not let it swallow him up. If he worked with an eye open for opportunities of self-assertion. . . .

The party game had not altogether swallowed 'Mr Arthur' . . .

But every one is not a Balfour. . . .

He reflected profoundly. On his left knee his left hand rested with two fingers held up. By some rapid mental alchemy these fingers had now become Home Rule and Tariff Reform. His right hand, which had hitherto taken no part in the controversy, had raised its index finger by imperceptible degrees. It had been raised almost subconsciously. And by still obscurer processes this finger had become Mrs Skelmersdale. He recognised her sudden reappearance above the threshold of consciousness with mild surprise. He had almost forgotten her share in these problems. He had supposed her dismissed to an entirely subordinate position. . . .

Then he perceived that the workmen in the chalk pit

far below had knocked off and were engaged upon their midday meal. He understood why his mind was no longer moving forward with any alacrity.

Food?

The question where he should eat arose abruptly and dismissed all other problems from his mind. He unfolded a map.

Here must be the chalk pit, here was Dorking. That village was Brockham Green. Should he go down to Dorking, or this way over Box Hill to the little inn at Burford Bridge? He would try the latter.

§ 14

The April sunset found our young man talking to himself for greater emphasis, and wandering along a turfy cart-track through a wilderness mysteriously planted with great bushes of rhododendra on the Downs above Shere. He had eaten a belated lunch at Burford Bridge, he had got some tea at a little inn near a church with a splendid yew tree, and for the rest of the time he had wandered and thought. He had travelled perhaps a dozen or fifteen miles, and a good way from his first meditations above the Dorking chalk pit.

He had recovered long ago from that remarkable conception of an active if dishonest political career as a means of escaping Mrs Skelmersdale and all that Mrs Skelmersdale symbolised. That would be just louting from one bad thing to another. He had to settle Mrs Skelmersdale clean and right, and he had to do as exquisitely right in politics as he could devise. If the public life of the country had got itself into a stupid antagonism of two undesirable things, the only course for a sane man of honour was to stand out from the parties and try to get them back to sound issues again. There must be endless people of a mind with himself in this matter. And even if there were not, if he was the only man in the world, he still had to follow his lights and do the right. And his business was to find out the right. . . .

He came back from these imaginative excursions into contemporary politics with one idea confirmed in his mind, an idea that had been indeed already in his mind during his Cambridge days. This was the idea of working out for himself, thoroughly and completely, a political scheme, a theory of his work and duty in the world, a plan of the world's future that should give a rule for his life. The Research Magnificent was emerging. It was an alarmingly vast proposal, but he could see no alternative but submission, a plebeian's submission to the currents of life about him.

Little pictures began to flit before his imagination of the way in which he might build up this tremendous inquiry. He would begin by hunting up people; everybody who seemed to have ideas and promise ideas he would get at. He would travel far—and exhaustively. He would, so soon as the ideas seemed to indicate it, hunt out facts. He would learn how the world was governed. He would learn how it did its thinking. He would live sparingly. ('Not *too* sparingly,' something interpolated.) He would work ten or twelve hours a day. Such a course of investigation must pass almost of its own accord into action and realisation. He need not trouble now how it would bring him into politics. Inevitably somewhere it would bring him into politics. And he would travel. Almost at once he would travel. It is the manifest duty of every young aristocrat to travel. Here he was, ruling India. At any rate, passively, through the mere fact of being English, he was ruling India. And he knew nothing of India. He knew nothing indeed of Asia. So soon as he returned to London his preparations for this travel must begin, he must plot out the men to whom he would go, and so contrive that also he would go round the world. Perhaps he would get Lionel Maxim to go with him. Or if Maxim could not come, then possibly Prothero. Some one surely could be found, some one thinking and talking of state-craft and the larger idea of life. All the world is not swallowed up in every day. . . .

§ 15

His mind shifted very suddenly from these large proposals to an entirely different theme. These mental landslips are not unusual when men are thinking hard and wandering. He found himself holding a trial upon himself for Presumptuousness, for setting himself up against the wisdom of the ages, and the decisions of all the established men in the world, for being in short a Presumptuous Sort of Ass. He was judge and jury and prosecutor, but rather inexplicably the defence was conducted in an irregular and undignified way by some inferior stratum of his being.

At first the defence contented itself with arguments that did at least aim to rebut the indictment. The decisions of all the established men in the world were notoriously in conflict. However great was the gross wisdom of the ages the nett wisdom was remarkably small. Was it after all so very immodest to believe that the Liberals were right in what they said about Tariff Reform, and the Tories right in their criticism of Home Rule?

And then suddenly the defence threw aside its mask and insisted that Benham had to take this presumptuous line because there was no other tolerable line possible for him.

'Better die with the Excelsior chap up the mountains,' the defence interjected.

Than what?

Consider the quality Benham had already betrayed. He was manifestly incapable of a decent modest mediocre existence. Already he had ceased to be—if one may use so fine a word for genteel abstinence—virtuous. He didn't ride well, he hadn't good hands, and he hadn't good hands for life. He must go hard and harsh, high or low. He was a man who needed *bite* in his life. He was exceptionally capable of boredom. He had been bored by London. Social occasions irritated him, several times he had come near to gross incivilities; art annoyed him; sport was an effort, wholesome perhaps, but unattractive; music he loved, but it excited him. The defendant broke the sunset calm by uttering amazing and improper phrases.

'I can't smug about in a state of falsified righteousness like these Crampton chaps.

'I shall roll in women. I shall rollick in women. If, that is, I stay in London with nothing more to do than I have had this year past.

'I've been sliding fast to it. . . .

'*No! I'm damned if I do! . . .*'

§ 16

For some time he had been bothered by a sense of something, something else, awaiting his attention. Now it came swimming up into his consciousness. He had forgotten. He was, of course, going to sleep out under the stars.

He had settled that overnight, that was why he had this cloak in his rücksack, but he had settled none of the details.

Now he must find some place where he could lie down. Here, perhaps, in this strange forgotten wilderness of rhododendra.

He turned off from the track and wandered among the bushes. One might lie down anywhere here. But not yet; it was as yet barely twilight. He consulted his watch. *Half-past seven.*

Nearly dinner-time. . . .

No doubt Christian during the earlier stages of his pilgrimage noticed the recurrence of the old familiar hours of his life of emptiness and vanity. Or rather of vanity—simply. Why drag in the thought of emptiness just at this point? . . .

It was very early to go to bed.

He might perhaps sit and think for a time. Here for example was a mossy bank, a seat, and presently a bed. So far there were only three stars visible, but more would come. He dropped into a reclining attitude. *Damp!*

When one thinks of sleeping out under the stars one is apt to forget the dew.

He spread his Swiss cloak out on the soft thick carpeting of herbs and moss, and arranged his knapsack as a pillow. Here he would lie and recapitulate the thoughts of the day. (That squealing might be a young fox.) At the club at present men would be sitting about holding themselves back from dinner. Excellent the clear soup always was at the club! Then perhaps a Chateaubriand. That—what was that? Soft and large and quite near and noiseless. An owl!

The damp feeling was coming through his cloak. And this April night air had a knife-edge. Early ice coming down the Atlantic perhaps. It was wonderful to be here on the top of the round world and feel the icebergs away there. Or did this wind come from Russia? He wasn't quite clear just how he was oriented, he had turned about so much. Which was east? Anyhow it was an extremely cold wind.

What had he been thinking? Suppose after all that ending with Mrs Skelmersdale was simply a beginning. So far he had never looked sex in the face. . . .

He sat up and sneezed violently.

It would be ridiculous to start out seeking the clue to one's life and be driven home by rheumatic fever. One should not therefore incur the risk of rheumatic fever.

Something squealed in the bushes.

It was impossible to collect one's thoughts in this place. He stood up. The night was going to be bitterly cold, savagely, cruelly cold. . . .

No. There was no thinking to be done here, no thinking at all. He would go on along the track and presently he would strike a road and so come to an inn. One can solve no problems when one is engaged in a struggle with the elements. The thing to do now was to find that track again. . . .

It took Benham two hours of stumbling and walking, with a little fence climbing and some barbed wire thrown in, before he got down into Shere to the shelter of a friendly little inn. And then he negotiated a satisfying meal, with beef-steak as its central fact, and stipulated for a fire in his bedroom.

The landlord was a pleasant-faced man; he attended to Benham himself and displayed a fine sense of comfort. He could produce wine, a half-bottle of Australian hock, Big Tree brand No. 8, a virile wine; he thought of sardines to precede the meal, he provided a substantial Welsh rarebit by way of a savoury, he did not mind in the least that it was nearly ten o'clock. He ended by suggesting coffee. 'And a liqueur?'

Benham had some Benedictine!

One could not slight such sympathetic helpfulness. The Benedictine was genuine. And then came the coffee.

The cup of coffee was generously conceived and honestly made.

A night of clear melancholy ensued. . . .

§ 17

Hitherto Benham had not faced in any detail the problem of how to break with Mrs Skelmersdale. Now he faced it pessimistically. She would, he knew, be difficult to break with. (He ought never to have gone there to lunch.) There would be something ridiculous in breaking off. In all sorts of ways she might resist. And face to face with her he might find himself a man divided against himself. That opened preposterous possibilities. On the other hand it was out of the question to do the business by letter. A letter hits too hard; it lies too heavy on the wound it has made. And in money matters he could be generous. He must be generous. At least financial worries need not complicate her distresses of desertion. But to suggest such generosities on paper, in cold ink, would be outrageous. And, in brief—he ought not to have gone there to lunch. After that he began composing letters at a great rate. Delicate—explanatory. Was it on the whole best to be explanatory? . . .

It was going to be a tremendous job, this breaking with her. And it had begun so easily. . . .

There was, he remembered with amazing vividness, a little hollow he had found under her ear, and how when he kissed her there it always made her forget her worries and ethical problems for a time and turn to him. . . .

'No,' he said grimly, 'it must end,' and rolled over and stared at the black. . . .

Like an insidious pedlar that old rascal whom young literary gentlemen call the Great God Pan, began to spread his wares in the young man's memory. . . .

After long and feverish wanderings of the mind, and some talking to himself and walking about the room, he did at last get a little away from Mrs Skelmersdale.

He perceived that when he came to tell his mother about this journey round the world there would be great difficulties. She would object very strongly, and if that did not do then she would become extremely abusive, compare him to his father, cry bitterly, and banish him suddenly and heart-brokenly from her presence for ever. She had done that twice already—once about going to the opera instead of listening to a lecture on Indian ethnology, and once about a week-end in Kent. . . . He hated hurting his mother, and he was beginning to know now how easily she was hurt. It is an abominable thing to hurt one's mother—whether one has a justification or whether one hasn't.

Recoiling from this, he was at once resumed by Mrs Skelmersdale; who had in fact an effect of really never having been out of the room. But now he became penitent about her. His penitence expanded until it was on a nightmare scale. At last it blotted out the heavens. He felt like one of those unfortunate victims of religious mania who are convinced they have committed the Sin against the Holy Ghost. (Why had he gone there to lunch? That was the key to it. *Why* had he gone there to lunch?) . . . He began to have remorse for everything, for everything he had ever done, for everything he had ever not done, for everything in the world. In a moment of lucidity he even had remorse for drinking that stout honest cup of black coffee. . . .

And so on and so on and so on.

When daylight came it found Benham still wide awake. Things crept mournfully out of the darkness into a reproachful clearness. The sound of birds that had been so delightful on the yesterday was no longer agreeable. The thrushes, he thought, repeated themselves a great deal.

He fell asleep as it seemed only a few minutes before the landlord, accompanied by a great smell of frying bacon, came to call him.

§ 18

The second day opened rather dully for Benham. There was not an idea left in his head about anything in the world. It was—*solid*. He walked through Bramley and Godalming and Witley and so came out upon the purple waste of Hindhead. He strayed away from the road and found a sunny place of turf amidst the heather and lay down and slept for an hour or so. He arose refreshed. He got some food at the Huts Inn on the Hindhead crest and went on across sunlit heathery wildernesses variegated by patches of spruce and fir and silver birch. And then suddenly his mental inanition was at an end and his thoughts were wide and brave again. He was astonished that for a moment he could have forgotten that he was vowed to the splendid life.

'Continence by preoccupation'; he tried the phrase. . . .

'A man must not give in to fear; neither must he give in to sex. It's the same thing really. The misleading of instinct.'

This set the key of his thought throughout the afternoon —until Amanda happened to him.

CHAPTER THE THIRD

AMANDA

§ 1

AMANDA happened to Benham very suddenly.

From Haslemere he had gone on to further heaths and gorse beyond Liphook, and thence he had wandered into a pretty district beset with Hartings. He had found himself upon a sandy ridge looking very beautifully into a sudden steep valley that he learnt was Harting Coombe; he had been through a West Harting and a South Harting and read finger-posts pointing to others of the clan; and in the evening, at the foot of a steep hill where two roads met, he sat down to consider whether he should go back and spend the night in one of the two kindly-looking inns of the latter place or push on over the South Downs towards the unknown luck of Singleton or Chichester. As he sat down two big retrievers, black and brown, came headlong down the road. The black carried a stick, the brown disputed and pursued. As they came abreast of him the foremost a little relaxed his hold, the pursuer grabbed at it, and in an instant the rivalry had flared to rage and a first-class dog-fight was in progress.

Benham detested dog-fights. He stood up, pale and distressed. 'Lie down!' he cried. 'Shut up, you brutes!' and was at a loss for further action.

Then it was Amanda leapt into his world, a light, tall figure of a girl, fluttering a short petticoat. Hatless she was, brown, flushed, and her dark hair tossing loose, and in a moment she had the snarling furious dogs apart, each gripped firmly by its collar. Then with a wriggle black was loose and had closed again. Inspired by the best traditions of chivalry Benham came to her assistance. He was not expert with dogs. He grasped the black dog under its ear. He was bitten in the wrist, rather in excitement than malice, and with a certain excess of zeal he was strangling the brute before you could count ten.

Amanda seized the fallen stick and whacked the dog she held, reasonably but effectively until its yelps satisfied her. 'There!' she said pitching her victim from her, and stood erect again. She surveyed the proceedings of her helper for the first time.

'You needn't,' she said, 'choke Sultan any more.'

'Ugh!' she said, as though that was enough for Sultan. And peace was restored.

'I'm obliged to you. But—— . . . I say! He didn't bite you, did he? Oh, *Sultan!*'

Sultan tried to express his disgust at the affair. Rotten business. When a fellow is fighting one can't be meticulous. And if people come interfering. Still—*sorry!* So Sultan by his code of eye and tail.

'May I see? . . . Something ought to be done to this. . .'

She took his wrist in her hand, and her cheek and eyelashes came within a foot of his face.

Some observant element in his composition guessed, and guessed quite accurately, that she was nineteen. . . .

§ 2

She had an eyebrow like a quick stroke of a camel's-hair brush, she had a glowing face, half childish imp, half-woman, she had honest hazel eyes, a voice all music, a manifest decision of character. And he must have this bite seen to at once. She lived not five minutes away. He must come with her.

She had an aunt who behaved like a mother and a mother who behaved like a genteel visitor, and they both agreed with Amanda that although Mr Walter Long and his dreadful muzzles and everything did seem to have stamped out rabies, yet you couldn't be too careful with a dog bite. A dog bite might be injurious in all sorts of ways—particularly Sultan's bite. He was, they had to confess, a dog without refinement, a coarse-minded omnivorous dog. Both the elder ladies insisted upon regarding Benham's wound as clear evidence of some gallant rescue of Amanda from imminent danger—'she's always so *reckless* with those dogs,' as though Amanda was not manifestly capable of taking care of herself; and when he had been Listerined and bandaged, they would have it that he should join them at their supper-dinner, which was already prepared and waiting. They treated him as if he were still an under-graduate, they took his arrangements in hand as though he was a favourite nephew. He must stay in Harting that night. Both the Ship and the Coach and Horses were excellent inns, and over the Downs there would be nothing for miles and miles. . . .

The house was a little long house with a veranda and a garden in front of it with flint-edged paths; the room in which they sat and ate was long and low and equipped with pieces of misfitting good furniture, an accidental-looking gilt tarnished mirror, and a sprinkling of old and middle-aged books. Some one had lit a fire, which cracked and spurted about cheerfully in a motherly fireplace, and a lamp and some candles got lit. Mrs Wilder, Amanda's aunt, a comfortable dark broad-browed woman, directed things, and sat at the end of the table and placed Benham on her right hand between herself and Amanda. Amanda's mother remained undeveloped, a watchful little woman with at least an eyebrow like her daughter's. Her name, it seemed, was Morris. No servant appeared, but two cousins of a vague dark picturesqueness and with a stamp of thirty upon them, the first young women Benham had ever seen dressed in djibbahs, sat at the table or moved about and attended to the simple needs of the service. The reconciled dogs were in the room and shifted inquiring noses from one human being to another.

Amanda's people were so easy and intelligent and friendly, and Benham after his thirty hours of silence so freshly ready for human association, that in a very little while he could have imagined he had known and trusted this household for years. He had never met such people before, and yet there was something about them that seemed familiar—and then it occurred to him that something of their easy-going freedom was to be found in Russian novels. A photographic enlargement of somebody with a vegetarian expression of face and a special kind of slouch hat gave the atmosphere a flavour of Socialism, and a press and tools and stamps and pigments on an oak table in the corner, suggested some such socialistic art as bookbinding. They were clearly 'advanced' people. And Amanda was tremendously important to them, she was their light, their pride, their most living thing. They focused on her. When he talked to them all in general he talked to her in particular. He felt that some introduction of himself was due to these welcoming people. He tried to give it mixed with an itinerary and a sketch of his experiences. He praised the heather country and Harting Coombe and the Hartings. He told them that London had suddenly become intolerable—'In the spring sunshine.'

'You live in London?' said Mrs Wilder.

Yes. And he had wanted to think things out. In London one could do no thinking——

'Here we could do nothing else,' said Amanda.

'Except dog-fights,' said the elder cousin.

'I thought I would just wander and think and sleep in the open air. Have you ever tried to sleep in the open air?'

'In the summer we all do,' said the younger cousin. 'Amanda makes us. We go out on to the little lawn at the back.'

'You see Amanda has some friends at Limpsfield. And there they all go out and camp and sleep in the woods.'

'Of course,' reflected Mrs Wilder, 'in April it must be different.'

'It *is* different,' said Benham with feeling; 'the night comes five hours too soon. And it comes wet,' He described his experiences and his flight to Shere and the kindly

landlord and the cup of coffee. 'And after that I thought
with a vengeance.'

'Do you write things?' asked Amanda abruptly, and it
seemed to him with a note of hope.

'No. No, it was just a private puzzle. It was something
I couldn't get straight.'

'And you have got it straight?' asked Amanda.

'I think so.'

'You were making up your mind about something?'

'Amanda *dear*!' cried her mother.

'Oh! I don't mind telling you,' said Benham.

They seemed such unusual people that he was moved to
unusual confidences. They had that effect one gets at
times with strangers freshly met as though they were not
really in the world. And there was something about
Amanda that made him want to explain himself to her
completely.

'What I wanted to think about was what I should do
with my life.'

'Haven't you any *work*——?' asked the elder cousin.

'None that I'm obliged to do.'

'That's where a man has the advantage,' said Amanda
with the tone of profound reflection. 'You can choose.
And what are you going to do with your life?'

'Amanda,' her mother protested, 'really you mustn't!'

'I'm going round the world to think about it,' Benham
told her.

'I'd give my soul to travel,' said Amanda.

She addressed her remark to the salad in front of her.

'But have you no ties?' asked Mrs Wilder.

'None that hold me,' said Benham. 'I'm one of those
unfortunates who needn't do anything at all. I'm independent. You see my riddles. East and west and
north and south, it's all my way for the taking. There's
not an indication.'

'If I were you,' said Amanda, and reflected. Then she
half turned herself to him. 'I should go first to India,'
she said, 'and I should shoot, one, two, three, yes, three
tigers. And then I would see Farukhabad Sikri—I was
reading in a book about it yesterday—where the jungle
grows in the palaces; and then I would go right up the
Himalayas; and then, then I would have a walking tour in
Japan; and then I would sail in a sailing ship down to
Borneo and Java and set myself up as a Ranee—— . . .
And then I would think what I would do next.'

'All alone, Amanda?' asked Mrs Wilder.

'Only when I shoot tigers. You and mother should certainly come to Japan.'

'But Mr Benham perhaps doesn't intend to shoot tigers, Amanda,' said Amanda's mother.

'Not at once. My way will be a little different. I think I shall go first through Germany. And then down to Constantinople. And then I've some idea of getting across Asia Minor and Persia to India. That would take some time. One must ride.'

'Asia Minor ought to be fun,' said Amanda. 'But I should prefer India because of the tigers. It would be so jolly to begin with the tigers right away.'

'It is the towns and governments and peoples I want to see rather than tigers,' said Benham. 'Tigers if they are in the programme. But I want to find out about—other things.'

'Don't you think there's something to be found out at home?' said the elder cousin, blushing very brightly and speaking with the effort of one who speaks for conscience' sake.

'Betty's a Socialist,' Amanda said to Benham with a suspicion of apology.

'Well, we're all rather that,' Mrs Wilder protested.

'If you are free, if you are independent, then don't you owe something to the workers?' Betty went on, getting graver and redder with each word.

'It's just because of that,' said Benham, 'that I am going round the world.'

§ 3

He was as free with these odd people as if he had been talking to Prothero. They were—alert. And he had been alone and silent and full of thinking for two clear days. He tried to explain why he found Socialism at once obvious and inadequate. . . .

Presently the supper things got themselves put away and the talk moved into a smaller room with several arm-chairs and a fire. Mrs Wilder and the cousins and Amanda each smoked a cigarette as if it were symbolical; and they were joined by a grave gray-bearded man with a hyphenated name and slightly Socratic manner, dressed in a very blue linen shirt and collar, a very woolly mustard-coloured suit and loose tie, and manifestly devoted to one of those branches of exemplary domestic decoration that grow upon

Socialist soil in England. He joined Betty in the opinion
that the duty of a free and wealthy young man was to
remain in England and give himself to democratic Socialism
and the abolition of 'profiteering.' 'Consider that chair,'
he said. But Benham had little feeling for the craftsman-
ship of chairs.

Under cross-examination Mr Rathbone-Sanders became
entangled and prophetic. It was evident he had never
thought out his 'democratic,' he had rested in some vague
tangle of idealism from which Benham now set himself
with the zeal of a specialist to rout him. Such an argument
sprang up as one meets with rarely beyond the happy undergraduate's range. Everybody lived in the discussion, even
Amanda's mother listened visibly. Betty said she herself
was certainly democratic and Mrs Wilder had always
thought herself to be so, and outside the circle round the
fire Amanda hovered impatiently, not quite sure of her
side as yet, but eager to come down with emphasis at the
first flash of intimation.

She came down vehemently on Benham's.

And being a very clear-cutting personality with an
instinct for the material rendering of things, she also came
and sat beside him on the little square cornered sofa.

'Of course, Mr Rathbone-Sanders,' she said, 'of course
the world must belong to the people who dare. Of course
people aren't all alike, and dull people, as Mr Benham says,
and spiteful people, and narrow people have no right to
any voice at all in things. . . .'

§ 4

In saying this she did but echo Benham's very words,
and all she said and did that evening was in quick response
to Benham's earnest expression of his views. She found
Benham a delightful novelty. She liked to argue because
there was no other talk so lively, and she had perhaps a
lurking intellectual grudge against Mr Rathbone-Sanders
that made her welcome an ally. Everything from her that
night that even verges upon the notable has been told, and
yet it sufficed, together with something in the clear, long
line of her limbs, in her voice, in her general physical
quality, to convince Benham that she was the freest, finest,
bravest spirit that he had ever encountered.

In the papers he left behind him was to be found his
perplexed endeavours to explain this mental leap, that

after all his efforts still remained unexplained. He had been vividly impressed by the decision and courage of her treatment of the dogs; it was just the sort of thing he could not do. And there was a certain contagiousness in the petting admiration with which her family treated her. But she was young and healthy and so was he, and in a second mystery lies the key of the first. He had fallen in love with her, and that being so whatever he needed that instantly she was. He needed a companion, clean and brave and understanding. . . .

In his bed in the Ship that night he thought of nothing but her before he went to sleep, and when next morning he walked on his way over the South Downs to Chichester his mind was full of her image and of a hundred pleasant things about her. In his confessions he wrote, 'I felt there was a sword in her spirit. I felt she was as clean as the wind.'

Love is the most chastening of powers, and he did not even remember now that two days before he had told the wind and the twilight that he would certainly 'roll and rollick in women' unless there was work for him to do. She had a peculiarly swift and easy stride that went with him in his thoughts along the turf by the wayside halfway and more to Chichester. He thought always of the two of them as being side by side. His imagination became childishly romantic. The open down about him with its scrub of thorn and yew became the wilderness of the world, and through it they went—in armour, weightless armour— and they wore long swords. There was a breeze blowing and larks were singing, and something, something dark and tortuous, dashed suddenly in headlong flight from before their feet. It was an ethical problem such as those Mrs Skelmersdale nursed in her bosom. But at the sight of Amanda it had straightened out—and fled. . . .

And interweaving with such imaginings, he was some day to record, there were others. She had brought back to his memory the fancies that had been aroused in his first reading of Plato's *Republic*; she made him think of those women Guardians, who were the friends and mates of men. He wanted now to re-read that book and the *Laws*. He could not remember if the Guardians were done in the *Laws* as well as in the *Republic*. He wished he had both these books in his rücksack, but as he had not, he decided he would hunt for them in Chichester. When would he see Amanda again? He would ask his mother to make the acquaintance of these very interesting people, but as they did not come to London very much it might be some time before he had a chance of seeing her again. And besides, he was going to America and India. The prospect of an exploration of the world was still noble and attractive; but he realised it would stand very much in the way of his seeing more of Amanda. Would it be a startling and unforgivable thing if presently he began to write to her? Girls of that age and spirit living in out-of-the-way villages have been known to marry. . . .

Marriage didn't at this stage strike Benham as an agreeable aspect of Amanda's possibilities; it was an inconvenience; his mind was running in the direction of pedestrian tours in armour of no particular weight, amidst scenery of a romantic wildness. . . .

When he had gone to the house and taken his leave that morning it had seemed quite in the vein of the establishment that he should be received by Amanda alone and taken up the long garden before anybody else appeared, to see the daffodils and the early apple-trees in blossom and the pear-trees white and delicious.

Then he had taken his leave of them all and made his social tentatives. Did they ever come to London? When they did they must let his people know. He would so like them to know his mother, Lady Marayne. And so on with much gratitude.

Amanda had said that she and the dogs would come with him up the hill, she had said it exactly as a boy might have said it; she had brought him up to the corner of Up Park and had sat down there on a heap of stones and watched him until he was out of sight, waving to him when he looked back. 'Come back again,' she had cried.

In Chichester he found a little green-bound *Republic* in a second-hand bookshop near the Cathedral, but there was no copy of the *Laws* to be found in the place. Then he was taken with the brilliant idea of sleeping the night in Chichester and going back next day via Harting to Petersfield station and London. He carried out this scheme and got to South Harting neatly about four o'clock in the afternoon. He found Mrs Wilder and Mrs Morris and Amanda and the dogs entertaining Mr Rathbone-Sanders at tea, and they all seemed a little surprised, and, except Mr Rathbone-Sanders, they all seemed pleased to see him again so soon. His explanation of why he hadn't gone back to London from Chichester struck him as a little unconvincing in the cold light of Mr Rathbone-Sanders's

eye. But Amanda was manifestly excited by his return'
and he told them his impressions of Chichester and described
the entertainment of the evening guest at a country inn
and suddenly produced his copy of the *Republic*. 'I found
this in a bookshop,' he said, 'and I brought it for you,
because it describes one of the best dreams of aristocracy
there has ever been dreamt.'

At first she praised it as a pretty book in the dearest
little binding, and then realised that there were deeper
implications, and became grave and said she would read it
through and through, she loved such speculative reading.

She came to the door with the others and stayed at the
door after they had gone in again. When he looked back
at the corner of the road to Petersfield she was still at the
door and waved farewell to him.

He only saw a light slender figure, but when she came back
into the sitting-room Mr Rathbone-Sanders noted the faint
flush in her cheek and an unwonted abstraction in her eye.

And in the evening she tucked her feet up in the arm-
chair by the lamp and read the *Republic* very intently and
very thoughtfully, occasionally turning over a page.

§ 5

When Benham got back to London he experienced an
unwonted desire to perform his social obligations to the
utmost.

So soon as he had had some dinner at his club he wrote
his South Harting friends a most agreeable letter of thanks
for their kindness to him. In a little while he hoped he
should see them again. His mother, too, was most desirous
to meet them. . . . That done, he went on to his flat and
to various aspects of life for which he was quite unprepared.

But here we may note that Amanda answered him. Her
reply came some four days later. It was written in a square
schoolgirl hand, it covered three sheets of notepaper, and
it was a very intelligent essay upon the *Republic* of Plato.
'Of course,' she wrote, 'the Guardians are inhuman, but it
was a glorious sort of inhumanity. They had a spirit—like
sharp knives cutting through life.'

It was her best bit of phrasing and it pleased Benham
very much. But, indeed, it was not her own phrasing;
she had culled it from a disquisition into which she had led
Mr Rathbone-Sanders, and she had sent it to Benham as
she might have sent him a flower.

§ 6

Benham re-entered the flat from which he had fled so precipitately with three very definite plans in his mind. The first was to set out upon his grand tour of the world with as little delay as possible, to shut up this Finacue Street establishment for a long time, and get rid of the soul-destroying perfections of Merkle. The second was to end his ill-advised intimacy with little Mrs Skelmersdale as generously and cheerfully as possible. The third was to bring Lady Marayne into social relations with the Wilder and Morris *ménage* at South Harting. It did not strike him that there was any incompatibility among these projects or any insurmountable difficulty in any of them until he was back in his flat.

The accumulation of letters, packages, and telephone memoranda upon his desk included a number of notes and slips to remind him that both Mrs Skelmersdale and his mother were ladies of some determination. Even as he stood turning over the pile of documents the mechanical vehemence of the telephone filled him with a restored sense of the adverse will in things. 'Yes, mam,' he heard Merkle's voice, 'yes, mam. I will tell him, mam. Will you keep possession, mam.' And then in the doorway of the study, 'Mrs Skelmersdale, sir. Upon the telephone, sir.'

Benham reflected with various notes in his hand. Then went to the telephone.

'You Wicked Boy, where have you been hiding?'

'I've been away. I may have to go away again.'

'Not before you have seen me. Come round and tell me all about it.'

Benham lied about an engagement.

'Then to-morrow in the morning.' . . . Impossible.

'In the afternoon. You don't *want* to see me.' Benham did want to see her.

'Come round and have a jolly little evening to-morrow night. I've got some more of that harpsichord music. And I'm dying to see you. Don't you understand?'

Further lies. 'Look here,' said Benham, 'can you come and have a talk in Kensington Gardens? You know the place, near that Chinese garden. Paddington Gate. . . .'

The lady's voice fell to flatness. She agreed. 'But why not come to see me *here*?' she asked.

Benham hung up the receiver abruptly.

He walked slowly back to his study. 'Phew!' he whispered to himself. It was like hitting her in the face. He didn't want to be a brute, but short of being a brute there was no way out for him from this entanglement. Why, oh! why the devil had he gone there to lunch? . . .

He resumed his examination of the waiting letters with a ruffled mind. The most urgent thing about them was the clear evidence of gathering anger on the part of his mother. He had missed a lunch party at Sir Godfrey's on Tuesday and a dinner engagement at Philip Magnet's, quite an important dinner in its way, with various promising young Liberals, on Wednesday evening. And she was furious at 'this stupid mystery. Of course you're bound to be found out, and of course there will be a scandal.' . . . He perceived that this last note was written on his own paper. 'Merkle!' he cried sharply.

'Yessir!'

Merkle had been just outside, on call.

'Did my mother write any of these notes here?' he asked.

'Two, sir. Her ladyship was round here three times, sir.'

'Did she see all these letters?'

'Not the telephone calls, sir. I 'ad put them on one side. But . . . It's a little thing, sir.'

He paused and came a step nearer. 'You see, sir,' he explained with the faintest flavour of the confidential softening his mechnical respect, 'yesterday, when 'er ladyship was 'ere, sir, some one rang up on the telephone——'

'But you, Merkle——'

'Exactly, sir. But 'er ladyship said, "*I'll* go to that, Merkle," and just for a moment I couldn't exactly think 'ow I could manage it, sir, and there 'er ladyship was, at the telephone. What passed, sir, I couldn't 'ear. I 'eard her say, "Any message?" And I *fancy*, sir, I 'eard 'er say, "I'm the 'ousemaid," but that, sir, I think must have been a mistake, sir.'

'Must have been,' said Benham. 'Certainly—must have been. And the call you think came from——?'

'There again, sir, I'm quite in the dark. But of course, sir, it's usually Mrs Skelmersdale, sir. Just about her time in the afternoon. On an average, sir. . . .'

§ 7

'I went out of London to think about my life.'

It was manifest that Lady Marayne did not believe him.

'Alone?' she asked.

'Of course alone.'

'*Stuff!*' said Lady Marayne.

She had taken him into her own little sitting-room, she had thrown aside gloves and fan and theatre wrap, curled herself comfortably into the abundantly cushioned corner by the fire, and proceeded to a mixture of cross-examination and tirade that he found it difficult to make head against. She was vibrating between distressed solicitude and resentful anger. She was infuriated at his going away and deeply concerned at what could have taken him away.

'I was worried,' he said. 'London is too crowded to think in. I wanted to get myself alone.'

'And there I was while you were getting yourself alone, as you call it, wearing my poor little brains out to think of some story to tell people. I had to stuff them up you had a sprained knee at Chexington, and for all I knew any of them might have been seeing you that morning. Besides, what has a boy like you to worry about? It's all nonsense, Poff.'

She awaited his explanations. Benham looked for a moment like his father.

'I'm not getting on, mother,' he said. 'I'm scattering myself. I'm getting no grip. I want to get a better hold upon life, or else I do not see what is to keep me from going to pieces—and wasting existence. It's rather difficult sometimes to tell what one thinks and feels——'

She had not really listened to him.

'Who is that woman,' she interrupted suddenly, 'Mrs Fly-by-Night or some such name, who rings you up on the telephone?'

Benham hesitated, blushed, and regretted it.

'Mrs Skelmersdale,' he said after a little pause.

'It's all the same. Who is she?'

'She's a woman I met at a studio somewhere, and I went with her to one of those Dolmetsch concerts.'

He stopped.

Lady Marayne considered him in silence for a little while. 'All men,' she said at last, 'are alike. Husbands, sons, and brothers, they are all alike. Sons! One expects them to be different. They aren't different. Why should they be? I suppose I ought to be shocked, Poff. But I'm not. She seems to be very fond of you.'

'She's—she's very good—in her way. She's had a difficult life. . . .'

'You can't leave a man about for a moment,' Lady Marayne reflected. 'Poff, I wish you'd fetch me a glass of water.'

When he returned she was looking very fixedly into the fire. 'Put it down,' she said, 'anywhere. Poff! is this Mrs Helter-Skelter a discreet sort of woman? Do you like her?' She asked a few additional particulars and Benham made his grudging admission of facts. 'What I still don't understand, Poff, is why you have been away.'

'I went away,' said Benham, 'because I want to clear things up.'

'But why? Is there some one else?'

'No.'

'You went alone? All the time?'

'I've told you I went alone. Do you think I tell you lies, mother?'

'Everybody tells lies somehow,' said Lady Marayne. 'Easy lies or stiff ones. Don't *flourish*, Poff. Don't start saying things like a moral windmill in a whirlwind. It's all a muddle. I suppose every one in London is getting in or out of these entanglements—or something of the sort. And this seems a comparatively slight one. I wish it hadn't happened. They do happen.'

An expression of perplexity came into her face. She looked at him. 'Why do you want to throw her over?'

'I *want* to throw her over,' said Benham.

He stood up and went to the hearthrug, and his mother reflected that this was exactly what all men did at just this phase of a discussion. Then things ceased to be sensible.

From overhead he said to her: 'I want to get away from this complication, this servitude. I want to do some —some work. I want to get my mind clear and my hands clear. I want to study government and the big business of the world.'

'And she's in the way?'

He assented.

'You men!' said Lady Marayne after a little pause. 'What queer beasts you are! Here is a woman who is kind to you. She's fond of you. I could tell she's fond of you directly I heard her. And you amuse yourself with her.

And then its Gobble, Gobble, Gobble, Great Work, Hands Clear, Big Business of the World. Why couldn't you think of that before, Poff? Why did you begin with her?'

'It was unexpected. . . .'

'*Stuff!*' said Lady Marayne for a second time.

'Well,' she said, 'well. Your Mrs Fly-by-Night—oh, it doesn't matter!—whatever she calls herself, must look after herself. I can't do anything for her. I'm not supposed even to know about her. I dare say she'll find her consolations. I suppose you want to go out of London and get away from it all. I can help you there perhaps. I'm tired of London, too. It's been a tiresome season. Oh! tiresome and disappointing! I want to go over to Ireland and travel about a little. The Pothercareys want us to come. They've asked us twice. . . .'

Benham braced himself to face fresh difficulties. It was amazing how different the world could look from his mother's little parlour and from the crest of the North Downs.

'But I want to start round the world,' he cried with a note of acute distress. 'I want to go to Egypt and India and see what is happening in the East, all this wonderful waking up of the East; I know nothing of the way the world is going—— . . .'

'India!' cried Lady Marayne. 'The East. Poff, what is the *matter* with you? Has something happened—something else? Have you been having a love affair?—a *real* love affair?'

'Oh, *damn* love affairs!' cried Benham. 'Mother!—I'm sorry, mother! But don't you see there's other things in the world for a man than having a good time and making love. I'm for something else than that. You've given me the splendidest time—— . . .'

'I see,' cried Lady Marayne, 'I see. I've bored you. I might have known I should have bored you.'

'You've *not* bored me!' cried Benham.

He threw himself on the rug at her feet. 'Oh, mother!' he said, 'little, dear, gallant mother, don't make life too hard for me. I've got to do my job, I've got to find my job.'

'I've bored you,' she wept.

Suddenly she was weeping with all the unconcealed distressing grief of a disappointed child. She put her pretty be-ringed little hands in front of her face and recited the accumulation of her woes.

R.M.

I

'I've done all I can for you, planned for you, given all my time for you and I've *bored* you.'

'Mother!'

'Don't come near me, Poff! Don't *touch* me! All my plans. All my ambitions. Friends—every one. You don't know all I've given up for you. . . .'

He had never seen his mother weep before. Her self-abandonment amazed him. Her words were distorted by her tears. It was the most terrible and distressing of crises. . . .

'Go away from me! How can you help me? All I've done has been a failure! Failure! Failure!'

§ 8

That night the silences of Finacue Street heard Benham's voice again. 'I must do my job,' he was repeating, 'I must do my job. Anyhow. . . .'

And then after a long pause, like a watchword and just a little unsurely; 'Aristocracy. . . .'

The next day his resolution had to bear the brunt of a second ordeal. Mrs Skelmersdale behaved beautifully and this made everything tormentingly touching and difficult. She convinced him she was really in love with him, and indeed if he could have seen his freshness and simplicity through her experienced eyes he would have known there was sound reason why she should have found him exceptional. And when his clumsy hints of compensation could no longer be ignored she treated him with a soft indignation, a tender resentment, that left him soft and tender. She looked at him with pained eyes and a quiver of the lips. What did he think she was? And then a little less credibly, did he think she would have given herself to him if she hadn't been in love with him? Perhaps that was not altogether true, but at any rate it was altogether true to her when she said it, and it was manifest that she did not for a moment intend him to have the cheap consolation of giving her money. But, and that seemed odd to Benham, she would not believe, just as Lady Marayne would not believe, that there was not some other woman in the case. He assured her and she seemed reassured, and then presently she was back at exactly the same question. Would no woman ever understand the call of Asia, the pride of duty, the desire for the world?

One sort of woman perhaps. . . .

It was odd that for the first time now, in the sunshine of Kensington Gardens, he saw the little gossamer lines that tell that thirty years and more have passed over a face, a little wrinkling of the eyelids, a little hardening of the mouth. How slight it is, how invisible it has been, how suddenly it appears ! And the sunshine of the warm April afternoon, heightened it may be by her determined un-mercenary pose, betrayed too the faintest hint of shabbiness in her dress. He had never noticed these shadows upon her or her setting before, and their effect was to fill him with a strange regretful tenderness. . . .

Perhaps men only begin to love when they cease to be dazzled and admire. He had thought she might reproach him, he had felt and feared she might set herself to stir his senses, and both these expectations had been unjust to her he saw, now that he saw her beside him, a brave, rather ill-advised and unlucky little struggler, stung and shamed. He forgot the particulars of that first lunch of theirs together and he remembered his mother's second contemptuous ' *Stuff !* '

Indeed he knew now it had not been unexpected.

Why hadn't he left this little sensitive soul and this little sensitive body alone ? And since he hadn't done so, what right had he now to back out of their common adventure ? He felt a sudden wild impulse to marry Mrs Skelmersdale, in a mood between remorse and love and self-immolation, and then a sunlit young woman with a leaping stride in her paces, passed across his heavens, pointing to Asia and Utopia and forbidding even another thought of the banns. . . .

' You will kiss me good-bye, dear, won't you ? ' said Mrs Skelmersdale, brimming over. ' You will do that.'

He couldn't keep his arm from her little shoulders. And as their lips touched he suddenly found himself weeping also. . . .

His spirit went limping from that interview. She chose to stay behind in her chair and think, she said, and each time he turned back she was sitting in the same attitude looking at him as he receded, and she had one hand on the chair back and her arm drawn up to it. The third time he waved his hat clumsily, and she started and then answered with her hand. Then the trees hid her. . . .

This sex business was a damnable business. If only because it made one hurt women. . . .

He had trampled on Mrs Skelmersdale, he had hurt

and disappointed his mother. Was he a brute? Was he a cold-blooded prig? What was this aristocracy? Was his belief anything more than a theory? Was he only dreaming of a debt to the men in the quarry, to the miners, to the men in the stokeholes, to the drudges on the fields? And while he dreamt he wounded and distressed real living creatures in the sleep-walk of his dreaming. . . .

So long as he stuck to his dream he must at any rate set his face absolutely against the establishment of any further relations with women.

Unless they were women of an entirely different type, women hardened and tempered, who would understand.

§ 9

So Benham was able to convert the unfortunate Mrs Skelmersdale into a tender but for a long time an entirely painful memory. But mothers are not so easily disposed of, and more particularly a mother whose conduct is coloured deeply by an extraordinary persuasion of having paid for her offspring twice over. Nolan was inexplicable; he was, Benham understood quite clearly, never to be mentioned again; but somehow from the past his shadow and his legacy cast a peculiar and perplexing shadow of undefined obligation upon Benham's outlook. His resolution to go round the world carried on his preparations rapidly and steadily, but at the same time his mother's thwarted and angry bearing produced a torture of remorse in him. It was constantly in his mind, like the suit of the importunate widow, that he ought to devote his life to the little lady's happiness and pride, and his reason told him that even if he wanted to make this sacrifice he couldn't; the mere act of making it would produce so entirely catastrophic a revulsion. He could as soon have become a croquet champion or the curate of Chexington church, lines of endeavour which for him would have led straightly and simply to sacrilegious scandal or manslaughter with a mallet.

There is so little measure in the wild atonements of the young that it was perhaps as well for the Research Magnificent that the remorses of this period of Benham's life were too complicated and scattered for a cumulative effect. In the background of his mind and less subdued than its importance could seem to warrant was his promise to bring the Wilder-Morris people into relations with Lady Marayne. They had been so delightful to him that he felt quite

acutely the slight he was putting upon them by this delay.
Lady Marayne's moods, however, had been so uncertain
that he had found no occasion to broach this trifling matter,
and when at last the occasion came he perceived in the
same instant the fullest reasons for regretting it.

'Ah!' she said, hanging only for a moment, and then:
'you told me you were alone!' . . .

Her mind leapt at once to the personification of these
people as all that had puzzled and baffled her in her son
since his flight from London. They were the enemy, they
had got hold of him.

'When I asked you if you were alone you pretended to
be angry,' she remembered with a flash. 'You said,
"Do I tell lies?"'

'I *was* alone. Until—— It was an accident. On my
walk I was alone.'

But he flinched before her accusing, her almost triumphant forefinger.

From the instant she heard of them she hated these
South Harting people unrestrainedly. She made no
attempt to conceal it. Her valiant bantam spirit caught
at this quarrel as a refuge from the rare and uncongenial
ache of his secession. 'And who are they? What are they?
What sort of people can they be to drag in a passing young
man? I suppose this girl of theirs goes out every evening—
Was she painted, Poff?'

She whipped him with her questions as though she was
slashing his face. He became dead-white and grimly civil,
answering every question as though it was the sanest,
most justifiable inquiry.

'Of course I don't know who they are. How should I
know? What need is there to know?'

'There are ways of finding out,' she insisted. 'If I am
to go down and make myself pleasant to these people
because of you.'

'But I implore you not to.'

'And five minutes ago you were imploring me to! Of
course I shall.'

'Oh, well!—well!'

'One has to know *something* of the people to whom one
commits oneself, surely.'

'They are decent people; they are well-behaved people.'

'Oh!—I'll behave well. Don't think I'll disgrace your
casual acquaintances. But who they are, what they are,
I *will* know. . . .'

On that point Lady Marayne was to score beyond her utmost expectations.

'Come round,' she said over the telephone, two mornings later. 'I've something to tell you.'

She was so triumphant that she was sorry for him. When it came to telling him, she failed from her fierceness.

'Poff, my little son,' she said, 'I'm so sorry I hardly know how to tell you. Poff, I'm sorry. I have to tell you —and it's utterly beastly.'

'But what?' he asked.

'These people are dreadful people.'

'But how?'

'You've heard of the great Kent and Eastern Bank smash and the Marlborough Building Society frauds eight or nine years ago?'

'Vaguely. But what has that to do with them?'

'That man Morris.'

She stopped short, and Benham nodded for her to go on.

'Her father,' said Lady Marayne.

'But who was Morris? Really, mother, I don't remember.'

'He was sentenced to seven years—ten years—I forget. He had done all sorts of dreadful things. He was a swindler. And when he went out of the dock into the waiting-room— He had a signet-ring with prussic acid in it—— . . .'

'I remember now,' he said.

A silence fell between them.

Benham stood quite motionless on the hearthrug and stared very hard at the little volume of Henley's poetry that lay upon the table.

He cleared his throat presently.

'You can't go and see them then,' he said. 'After all ——since I am going abroad so soon—— . . . It doesn't so very much matter.'

§ 10

To Benham it did not seem to be of the slightest importance that Amanda's father was a convicted swindler who had committed suicide. Never was a resolved and conscious aristocrat so free from the hereditary delusion. Good parents, he was convinced, are only an advantage in so far as they have made you good stuff, and bad parents are no discredit to a son or daughter of good quality. Conceivably he had a bias against too close an examination of origins, and he held that the honour of the children should atone for the sins of the fathers and the questionable achievements of any intervening testator. Not half a dozen rich and established families in all England could stand even the most conventional inquiry into the foundations of their pride, and only a universal amnesty could prevent ridiculous distinctions. But he brought no accusation of inconsistency against his mother. She looked at things with a lighter logic and a kind of genius for the acceptance of superficial values. She was condoned and forgiven, a rescued lamb, re-established, notoriously bright and nice, and the Morrises were damned. That was their status, exclusion, damnation, as fixed as colour in Georgia or caste in Bengal. But if his mother's mind worked in that way there was no reason why his should. So far as he was concerned, he told himself, it did not matter whether Amanda was the daughter of a swindler or the daughter of a god. He had no doubt that she herself had the spirit and quality of divinity. He had seen it.

So there was nothing for it in the failure of his mother's civilities but to increase his own. He would go down to Harting and take his leave of these amiable outcasts himself. With a certain effusion. He would do this soon because he was now within sight of the beginning of his world tour. He had made his plans and prepared most of his equipment. Little remained to do but the release of Merkle, the wrappering and locking up of Finacue Street, which could await him indefinitely, and the buying of tickets. He decided to take the opportunity afforded by a visit of Sir Godfrey and Lady Marayne to the Blights, big iron people in the North of England of so austere a morality that even Benham was ignored by it. He announced his invasion in a little note to Mrs Wilder. He parted from his mother on Friday afternoon; she was already, he perceived, a little reconciled to his project of going abroad; and contrived his arrival at South Harting for that sunset hour which was for his imagination the natural halo of Amanda.

'I'm going round the world,' he told them simply. 'I may be away for two years, and I thought I would like to see you all again before I started.'

That was quite the way they did things.

The supper-party included Mr Rathbone-Sanders, who displayed a curious tendency to drift in between Benham and Amanda; a literary youth with a Byronic visage, dark very curly hair, and a number of extraordinarily mature chins; a girl-friend of Betty's who had cycled down from

London, and who it appeared maintained herself at large in London by drawing for advertisements; and a silent colourless friend of Mr Rathbone-Sanders.   The talk lit by Amanda's enthusiasm circled actively round Benham's expedition.   It was clear that the idea of giving some years to thinking out one's possible work in the world was for some reason that remained obscure highly irritating to both Mr Rathbone-Sanders and the Byronic youth.   Betty too regarded it as levity when there was 'so much to be done,' and the topic whacked about and rose to something like a wrangle, and sat down and rested and got up again reinvigorated, with a continuity of interest that Benham had never yet encountered in any London gathering.   He made a good case for his modern version of the Grand Tour, and he gave them something of his intellectual enthusiasm for the distances and views, the cities and seas, the multitudinous wide spectacle of the world he was to experience. He had been reading about Benares and North China. As he talked Amanda, who had been animated at first, fell thoughtful and silent.   And then it was discovered that the night was wonderfully warm and the moon shining. They drifted out into the garden, but Mr Rathbone-Sanders was suddenly entangled and drawn back by Mrs Wilder and the young woman from London upon some technical point, and taken to the work-table in the corner of the dining-room to explain.   He was never able to get to the garden.

Benham found himself with Amanda upon a side path, a little isolated by some swaggering artichokes and a couple of apple trees and so forth from the general conversation. They cut themselves off from the continuation of that by a little silence, and then she spoke abruptly and with the quickness of a speaker who has thought out something to say and fears interruption : 'Why did you come down here?'

'I wanted to see you before I went.'

'You disturb me.   You fill me with envy.'

'I didn't think of that.   I wanted to see you again.'

'And then you will go off round the world, you will see the Tropics, you will see India, you will go into Chinese cities all hung with vermilion, you will climb mountains. Oh! men can do all the splendid things.   Why do you come here to remind me of it?   I have never been anywhere, anywhere at all.   I never shall go anywhere.   Never in my life have I seen a mountain.   Those Downs there—look at them !—are my highest.   And while you are travelling I shall think of you—and think of you. . . .'

'Would *you* like to travel?' he asked as though that was an extraordinary idea.

'Do you think *every* girl wants to sit at home and rock a cradle?'

'I never thought *you* did.'

'Then what did you think I wanted?'

'What *do* you want?'

She held her arms out widely, and the moonlight shone in her eyes as she turned her face to him.

'Just what you want,' she said; '—*the whole World!*'

'Life is like a feast,' she went on; 'it is spread before everybody and nobody must touch it. What am I? Just a prisoner. In a cottage garden. Looking for ever over a hedge. I should be happier if I couldn't look. I remember once, only a little time ago, there was a cheap excursion to London. Our only servant went. She had to get up at an unearthly hour, and I—I got up too. I helped her to get off. And when she was gone I went up to my bedroom again and cried. I cried with envy for any one, any one who could go away. I've been nowhere—except to school at Chichester and three or four times to Emsworth and Bognor—for eight years. When you go'—the tears glittered in the moonlight—'I shall cry. It will be worse than the excursion to London. . . . Ever since you were here I've been thinking of it.'

It seemed to Benham that here indeed was the very sister of his spirit. His words sprang into his mind as one thinks of a repartee. 'But why shouldn't you come too?' he said.

She stared at him in silence. The two white-lit faces examined each other. Both she and Benham were trembling.

'*Come too?*' she repeated.

'Yes, with me.'

'But—*how?*'

Then suddenly she was weeping like a child that is teased; her troubled eyes looked out from under puckered brows. 'You don't mean it,' she said. 'You don't mean it.'

And then indeed he meant it.

'Marry me,' he said very quickly, glancing towards the dark group at the end of the garden. 'And we will go together.'

He seized her arm and drew her to him. 'I love you,' he said. 'I love your spirit. You are not like any one else.'

There was a moment's hesitation.

Both he and she looked to see how far they were still alone.

Then they turned their dusky faces to each other. He drew her still closer.

'Oh !' she said, and yielded herself to be kissed.

Their lips touched, and for a moment he held her lithe body against his own.

'I want you,' he whispered close to her. 'You are my mate. From the first sight of you I knew that. . . .'

They embraced—alertly furtive.

Then they stood a little apart. Some one was coming towards them. Amanda's bearing changed swiftly. She put up her little face to his, confidently and intimately.

'Don't *tell* any one,' she whispered eagerly, shaking his arm to emphasis her words. 'Don't tell any one—not yet. Not for a few days. . . .'

She pushed him from her quickly as the shadowy form of Betty appeared in a little path between the artichokes and raspberry canes.

'Listening to the nightingales?' cried Betty.

'Yes, aren't they?' said Amanda inconsecutively.

'That's our very own nightingale!' cried Betty, advancing. 'Do you hear it, Mr Benham? No, not that one. That is a quite inferior bird that performs in the vicarage trees. . . .'

§ 11

When a man has found and won his mate then the best traditions demand a lyrical interlude. It should be possible to tell, in that ecstatic manner which melts words into moonshine, makes prose almost uncomfortably rhythmic, and brings all the freshness of every spring that ever was across the page, of the joyous exaltation of the happy lover. This at any rate was what White had always done in his novels hitherto, and what he would certainly have done at this point had he had the telling of Benham's story uncontrolledly in his hands. But, indeed, indeed, in real life, in very truth, the heart has not this simplicity. Only the heroes of romance, and a few strong simple clean-shaven Americans have that much emotional integrity. (And even the Americans do at times seem to an observant eye to be putting in work at the job and keeping up their gladness.) Benham was excited that night, but not in the proper bright-eyed, red-cheeked way; he did not dance

down the village street of Harting to his harbour at the
Ship, and the expression in his eyes as he sat on the edge
of his bed was not the deep elemental wonder one could
have wished there, but amazement. Do not suppose that
he did not love Amanda, that a rich majority of his being
was not triumphantly glad to have won her, that the
image of the two armour-clad lovers was not still striding
and flourishing through the lit wilderness of his imagination.
For three weeks things had pointed him to this. They
would do everything together now, he and his mate, they
would scale mountains together and ride side by side
towards ruined cities across the deserts of the World. He
could have wished no better thing. But at the same time,
even as he felt and admitted this and rejoiced at it, the sky
of his mind was black with consternation. . . .

It is remarkable, White reflected, as he turned over the
abundant but confused notes upon this perplexing phase of
Benham's development that lay in the third drawer devoted
to the Second Limitation, how dependent human beings
are upon statement. Man is the animal that states a case.
He lives not in things but in expressed ideas, and what
was troubling Benham inordinately that night, a night
that should have been devoted to purely blissful and
exalted expectations, was the sheer impossibility of stating
what had happened in any terms that would be tolerable
either to Mrs Skelmersdale or Lady Marayne. The thing
had happened with the suddenness of a revelation. Whatever had been going on in the less illuminated parts of his
mind, his manifest resolution had been merely to bid South
Harting good-bye—— And in short they would never
understand. They would accuse him of the meanest
treachery. He could see his mother's face, he could hear
her voice saying, 'And so because of this sudden infatuation
for a swindler's daughter, a girl who runs about the roads
with a couple of retrievers hunting for a man, you must
spoil all my plans, ruin my year, tell me a lot of pretentious
stuffy lies. . . .' And Mrs Skelmersdale too would say,
'Of course he just talked of the world and duty and all
that rubbish to save my face. . . .'

It wasn't so at all.

But it looked so frightfully like it !

Couldn't they realise that he had fled out of London
before ever he had seen Amanda? They might be able to
do it perhaps, but they never would. It just happened that
in the very moment when the edifice of his noble resolutions

had been ready, she had stepped into it—out of nothingness
and nowhere. She wasn't an accident; that was just the
point upon which they were bound to misjudge her; she
was an embodiment. If only he could show her to them
as she had first shown herself to him, swift, light, a little
flushed from running but not in the least out of breath,
quick as a leopard upon the dogs. . . . But even if the
improbable opportunity arose, he perceived it might still
be impossible to produce the Amanda he loved, the Amanda
of the fluttering short skirt and the clear enthusiastic voice.
Because, already he knew she was not the only Amanda.
There was another, there might be others, there was this
perplexing person who had flashed into being at the very
moment of their mutual confession, who had produced the
entirely disconcerting demand that nobody must be told.
Then Betty had intervened. But that sub-Amanda and her
carneying note had to be dealt with on the first occasion,
because when aristocrats love they don't care a rap who is
told and who is not told. They just step out into the light
side by side. . . .

'Don't tell any one,' she had said, 'not for a few days. . .'

This sub-Amanda was perceptible next morning again,
flitting about in the background of a glad and loving
adventuress, a pre-occupied Amanda who had put her
head down while the real Amanda flung her chin up and
contemplated things on the Asiatic scale, and who was
apparently engaged in disentangling something obscure
connected with Mr Rathbone-Sanders that ought never
to have been entangled. . . .

'A human being,' White read, 'the simplest human
being, is a clustering mass of aspects. No man will judge
another justly who judges everything about him. And of
love in particular is this true. We love not persons but
revelations. The woman one loves is like a goddess hidden
in a shrine; for her sake we live on hope and suffer the
kindred priestesses that make up herself. The art of love
is patience till the gleam returns. . . .'

Sunday and Monday did much to develop this idea of
the intricate complexity of humanity in Benham's mind.
On Monday morning he went up from the Ship again to get
Amanda alone and deliver his ultimatum against a further
secrecy, so that he could own her openly and have no more
of the interventions and separations that had barred him
from any intimate talk with her throughout the whole of
Sunday. The front door stood open, the passage hall was

empty, but as he hesitated whether he should proclaim himself with the knocker or walk through, the door of the little drawing-room flew open and a black-clad cylindrical clerical person entirely unknown to Benham stumbled over the threshold, blundered blindly against him, made a sound like ' *Moo* ' and a pitiful gesture with his arm, and fled forth. . . .

It was a curate and he was weeping bitterly. . . .

Benham stood in the doorway and watched a clumsy broken-hearted flight down the village street.

He had been partly told and partly left to infer, and anyhow he was beginning to understand about Mr Rathbone-Sanders. That he could dismiss. But—why was the curate in tears?

§ 12

He found Amanda standing alone in the room from which this young man had fled. She had a handful of daffodils in her hand, and others were scattered over the table. She had been arranging the big bowl of flowers in the centre. He left the door open behind him and stopped short with the table between them. She looked up at him—intelligently and calmly. Her pose had a divine dignity.

'I want to tell them now,' said Benham without a word of greeting.

'Yes,' she said, 'tell them now.'

They heard steps in the passage outside. 'Betty !' cried Amanda.

Her mother's voice answered, 'Do you want Betty?'

'We want you all,' answered Amanda. 'We have something to tell you. . . .'

'Carrie !' they heard Mrs Morris call her sister after an interval, and her voice sounded faint and flat and unusual. There was the soft hissing of some whispered words outside and a muffled exclamation. Then Mrs Wilder and Mrs Morris and Betty came into the room. Mrs Wilder came first, and Mrs Morris with an alarmed face as if sheltering behind her. 'We want to tell you something,' said Amanda.

'Amanda and I are going to marry each other,' said Benham, standing in front of her.

For an instant the others made no answer; they looked at each other.

'*But does he know ?*' Mrs Morris said in a low voice.

Amanda turned her eyes to her lover. She was about to speak, she seemed to gather herself for an effort, and

then he knew that he did not want to hear her explanation·
He checked her by a gesture.

'*I know,*' he said, and then, 'I do not see that it matters
to us in the least. '

He went to her holding out both his hands to her.

She took them and stood shyly for a moment, and then
the watchful gravity of her face broke into soft emotion.
'Oh !' she cried and seized his face between her hands in a
passion of triumphant love and kissed him.

And then he found himself being kissed by Mrs Morris.

She kissed him thrice, with solemnity, with thankfulness,
with relief, as if in the act of kissing she transferred to him
precious and entirely incalculable treasures.

CHAPTER THE FOURTH

THE SPIRITED HONEYMOON

§ 1

IT was a little after sunrise one bright morning in September
that Benham came up on to the deck of the sturdy Austrian
steamboat that was churning its way with a sedulous
deliberation from Spalato to Cattaro, and lit himself a
cigarette and seated himself upon a deck chair. Save for
a yawning Greek sailor busy with a mop the first-class
deck was empty.

Benham surveyed the haggard beauty of the Illyrian
coast. The mountains rose gaunt and enormous and
barren to a jagged fantastic silhouette against the sun;
their almost vertical slopes, still plunged in blue shadow,
broke only into a little cold green and white edge of olive
terraces and vegetation and houses before they touched
the clear blue water. An occasional church or a house
perched high upon some seemingly inaccessible ledge did
but accentuate the vast barrenness of the land. It was a
land desolated and destroyed. At Ragusa, at Salona, at
Spalato and Zara and Pola Benham had seen only variations
upon one persistent theme, a dwindled and uncreative
human life living amidst the giant ruins of preceding times,
as worms live in the sockets of a skull. Forward an un-
savoury group of passengers still slumbered amidst fruit-
peel and expectorations, a few soldiers, some squalid
brigands armed with preposterous red umbrellas, a group
of curled-up human lumps brooded over by an aquiline

individual caparisoned with brass like a horse, his head wrapped picturesquely in a shawl. Benham surveyed these last products of the 'life force' and resumed his pensive survey of the coast. The sea was deserted save for a couple of little lateen craft with suns painted on their gaudy sails, sea butterflies that hung motionless as if unawakened close inshore. . . .

The travel of the last few weeks had impressed Benham's imagination profoundly. For the first time in his life he had come face to face with civilisation in defeat. From Venice hitherward he had marked with cumulative effect the clustering evidences of effort spent and power crumbled to nothingness. He had landed upon the marble quay of Pola and visited its deserted amphitheatre; he had seen a weak provincial life going about ignoble ends under the walls of the great Venetian fortress and the still more magnificent cathedral of Zara; he had visited Spalato, clustered in sweltering grime within the ample compass of the walls of Diocletian's villa, and a few troublesome sellers of coins and iridescent glass and fragments of tessellated pavement and such-like loot was all the population he had found amidst the fallen walls and broken friezes and columns of Salona. Down this coast there ebbed and flowed a mean residual life, a life of violence and dishonesty, peddling trades, vendettas and war. For a while the unstable Austrian ruled this land and made a sort of order that the incalculable chances of international politics might at any time shatter. Benham was drawing near now to the utmost limit of that extended peace. Ahead beyond the mountain capes was Montenegro and, further, Albania and Macedonia, lands of lawlessness and confusion. Amanda and he had been warned of the impossibility of decent travel beyond Cattaro and Cettinjé, but this had but whetted her adventurousness and challenged his spirit. They were going to see Albania for themselves.

The three months of honeymoon they had been spending together had developed many remarkable divergences of their minds that had not been in the least apparent to Benham before their marriage. Then their common resolve to be as spirited as possible had obliterated all minor considerations. But that was the limit of their unanimity. Amanda loved wild and picturesque things, and Benham strong and clear things; the vines and brush-wood amidst the ruins of Salona that had delighted her had filled him with a sense of tragic retrogression. Salona had revived again in the acutest form a dispute that had been smouldering between them throughout a fitful and lengthy exploration of north and central Italy. She could not understand his disgust with the mediæval colour and confusion that had swamped the pride and state of the Roman Empire, and he could not make her feel the ambition of the ruler, the essential discipline and responsibilities of his aristocratic idea. While his adventurousness was conquest, hers, it was only too manifest, was brigandage. His thoughts ran now into the form of an imaginary discourse, that he would never deliver to her, on the decay of states, on the triumphs of barbarians over rulers who will not rule, on the relaxation of patrician orders and the return of the robber and assassin as lordship decays. This coast was no theatrical scenery for him; it was a shattered empire. And it was shattered because no men had been found, united enough, magnificent and steadfast enough, to hold the cities and maintain the roads, keep the peace and subdue the brutish hates and suspicions and cruelties that devastated the world.

And as these thoughts came back into his mind, Amanda flickered up from below, light and noiseless as a sunbeam, and stood behind his chair.

Freedom and the sight of the world had if possible brightened and invigorated her. Her costume and bearing were subtly touched by the romance of the Adriatic. There was a flavour of the pirate in the cloak about her shoulders and the light knitted cap of scarlet she had stuck upon her head. She surveyed his preoccupation for a moment, glanced forward, and then covered his eyes with her hands. In almost the same movement she had bent down and nipped the tip of his ear between her teeth.

'Confound you, Amanda!'

'You'd forgotten my existence, you star-gazing Cheetah. And then, you see, these things happen to you!'

'I was thinking.'

'Well—*don't* . . . I distrust your thinking. . . . This coast is wilder and grimmer than yesterday. It's glorious.'

She sat down on the chair he unfolded for her.

'Is there nothing to eat?' she asked abruptly.

'It is too early.'

§ 2

'This coast is magnificent,' she said presently.

'It's hideous,' he answered. 'It's as ugly as a heap of slag.'

'It's nature at its wildest.'

'That's Amanda at her wildest.'

'Well, isn't it?'

'No! This land isn't nature. It's waste. Not wilderness. It's the other end. Those hills were covered with forests; this was a busy civilised coast just a little thousand years ago. The Venetians wasted it. They cut down the forests; they filled the cities with a mixed mud of population, *that* stuff. Look at it!'—he indicated the sleepers forward by a movement of his head.

'I suppose they *were* rather feeble people, said Amanda.

'Who?'

'The Venetians.'

'They were traders—and nothing more. Just as we are. And when they were rich they got splendid clothes and feasted and rested. Much as we do.'

Amanda surveyed him. 'We don't rest.'

'We idle.'

'We are seeing things.'

'Don't be a humbug, Amanda. We are making love. Just as they did. And it has been—ripping. In Salona they made love tremendously. They did nothing else until the barbarians came over the mountains. . . '

'Well,' said Amanda virtuously, 'we will do something else.'

He made no answer, and her expression became profoundly thoughtful. Of course this wandering must end. He had been growing impatient for some time. But it was difficult, she perceived, to decide just what to do with him. . . .

Benham picked up the thread of his musing.

He was seeing more and more clearly that all civilisation was an effort, and so far always an inadequate and very partially successful effort. Always it had been aristocratic, aristocratic in the sense that it was the work of minorities, who took power, who had a common resolution against the inertia, the indifference, the insubordination and instinctive hostility of the mass of mankind. And always the set-backs, the disasters of civilisation, had been failures of the aristocratic spirit. Why had the Roman purpose faltered and shrivelled? Every order, every brotherhood, every organisation carried with it the seeds of its own destruction. Must the idea of statecraft and rule perpetually reappear, reclothe itself in new forms, age, die, even as life does—making each time its almost infinitesimal addition to human achievement? Now the world is crying aloud for a renascence of the spirit that orders and controls. Human affairs sway at a dizzy height of opportunity. Will they keep their footing there, or stagger? We have got back at last to a time as big with opportunity as the early empire. Given only the will in men and it would be possible now to turn the dazzling accidents of science, the chancy attainments of the nineteenth century, into a sane and permanent possession, a new starting-point. . . . What a magnificence might be made of life !

He was aroused by Amanda's voice.

'When we go back to London, old Cheetah,' she said, 'we must take a house.'

For some moments he stared at her, trying to get back to their point of divergence.

'Why?' he asked at length.

'We must have a house,' she said.

He looked at her face. Her expression was profoundly thoughtful, her eyes were fixed on the slumbering ships poised upon the transparent water under the mountain shadows.

'You see,' she thought it out, 'you've got to *tell* in London. You can't just sneak back there. You've got to strike a note of your own. With all these things of yours.'

'But how?'

'There's a sort of little house, I used to see them when I was a girl and my father lived in London, about Brook Street and that part. Not too far north. . . . You see, going back to London for us is just another adventure. We've got to capture London. We've got to scale it. We've got advantages of all sorts. But at present we're outside. We've got to march in.'

Her clear hazel eyes contemplated conflicts and triumphs. She was roused by Benham's voice.

'What the deuce are you thinking of, Amanda?'

She turned her level eyes to his. 'London,' she said. 'For you.'

'I don't want London,' he said.

'I thought you did. You ought to. I do.'

'But to take a house ! Make an invasion of London !'

'You dear old Cheetah, you can't be always frisking about in the wilderness, staring at the stars.'

'But I'm not going back to live in London in the old way, theatres, dinner-parties, chatter——'

'Oh no ! We aren't going to do that sort of thing. We aren't going to join the ruck. We'll go about in holiday times all over the world. I want to see Fusiyama. I mean to swim in the South Seas. With you. We'll dodge the sharks. But all the same we shall have to have a house in London. We have to be *felt* there.'

She met his consternation fairly. She lifted her fine eyebrows. Her little face conveyed a protesting reasonableness.

'Well, *mustn't* we ?'

She added, 'If we want to alter the world we ought to live in the world.'

Since last they had disputed the question she had thought out these new phrases.

'Amanda,' he said. 'I think sometimes you haven't the remotest idea of what I am after. I don't believe you begin to suspect what I am up to.'

She put her elbows on her knees, dropped her chin between her hands and regarded him impudently. She had a characteristic trick of looking up with her face downcast that never failed to soften his regard.

'Look here, Cheetah, don't you give way to your early morning habit of calling your own true love a fool,' she said.

'Simply I tell you I will not go back to London.'

'You will go back with me, Cheetah.'

'I will go back as far as my work calls me there.'

'It calls you through the voice of your mate and slave and doormat to just exactly the sort of house you ought to have. . . . It is the privilege and duty of the female to choose the lair.'

For a space Benham made no reply. This controversy had been gathering for some time, and he wanted to state his view as vividly as possible. The Benham style of connubial conversation had long since decided for emphasis rather than delicacy.

'I think,' he said slowly, 'that this wanting to take London by storm is a beastly *vulgar* thing to want to do.'

Amanda compressed her lips.

'I want to work out things in my mind,' he went on.

'I do not want to be distracted by social things, and I do not want to be distracted by picturesque things. This life—it's all very well on the surface, but it isn't real. I'm not getting hold of reality. Things slip away from me. God! but how they slip away from me!'

He got up and walked to the side of the boat.

She surveyed his back for some moments. Then she went and leant over the rail beside him.

'I want to go to London,' she said.

'I don't.'

'Where do you want to go?'

'Where I can see into the things that hold the world together.'

'I have loved this wandering—I could wander always. But . . . Cheetah! I tell you I *want* to go to London.'

He looked over his shoulder into her warm face. '*No,*' he said.

'But, I ask you.'

He shook his head.

She put her face closer and whispered. 'Cheetah! big beast of my heart. Do you hear your mate asking for something?'

He turned his eyes back to the mountains. 'I must go my own way.'

'Haven't I, so far, invented things, made life amusing, Cheetah? Can't you trust the leopard's wisdom?'

He stared at the coast inexorably.

'I wonder,' she whispered.

'What?'

'You *are* that Cheetah, that lank, long, *eager* beast——'

Suddenly with a nimble hand she had unbuttoned and rolled up the sleeve of her blouse. She stuck her pretty blue-veined arm before his eyes. 'Look here, sir, it was you, wasn't it? It was your powerful jaw inflicted this bite upon the arm of a defenceless young leopardess——'

'Amanda!'

'Well.' She wrinkled her brows.

He turned about and stood over her, he shook a finger in her face, and there was a restrained intensity in his voice as he spoke.

'Look here, Amanda!' he said, 'if you think that you are going to make me agree to any sort of project about London, to any sort of complication of our lives with houses in smart streets and a campaign of social assertion—by *that*, then may I be damned for an uxorious fool!'

Her eyes met his and there was mockery in her eyes.

'This, Cheetah, is the morning mood,' she remarked.

'This is the essential mood. Listen, Amanda——'

He stopped short. He looked towards the gangway, they both looked. The magic word 'Breakfast' came simultaneously from them.

'Eggs,' she said ravenously, and led the way.

A smell of coffee as insistent as a herald's trumpet had called a truce between them.

§ 3

Their marriage had been a comparatively inconspicuous one, but since that time they had been engaged upon a honeymoon of great extent and variety. Their wedding had taken place at South Harting church in the marked absence of Lady Marayne, and it had been marred by only one untoward event. The Reverend Amos Pugh, who in spite of the earnest advice of several friends had insisted upon sharing in the ceremony, had suddenly covered his face with the sleeves of his surplice and fled with a swift rustle to the vestry, whence an uproar of inadequately smothered sorrow came as an obligato accompaniment to the more crucial passages of the service. Amanda appeared unaware of the incident at the time, but afterwards she explained things to Benham. 'Curates,' she said, 'are such pent-up men. One ought, I suppose, to remember that. But he never had anything to go upon at all—not anything—except his own imaginations.'

'I suppose when you met him you were nice to him.'

'I was nice to him, of course. . . .'

They drove away from Harting, as it were, over the weeping remains of this infatuated divine. His sorrow made them thoughtful for a time, and then Amanda nestled closer to her lover and they forgot about him, and their honeymoon became so active and entertaining that only very rarely and transitorily did they ever think of him again.

The original conception of their honeymoon had been identical with the plans Benham had made for the survey and study of the world, and it was through a series of modifications, replacements, and additions that it became at last a prolonged and very picturesque tour in Switzerland, the Austrian Tyrol, North Italy, and down the Adriatic coast. Amanda had never seen mountains, and longed, she said, to climb. This took them first to Switzerland. Then, in spite of their exalted aims, the devotion of their lives to noble purposes, it was evident that Amanda had no intention of scamping the detail of love, and for that what background is so richly beautiful as Italy? An important aspect of the grand tour round the world as Benham had planned it, had been interviews, inquiries and conversations with every sort of representative and understanding person he could reach. An unembarrassed young man who wants to know and does not promise to bore may reach almost any one in that way, he is as impersonal as pure reason and as mobile as a letter, but the presence of a lady in his train leaves him no longer unembarrassed. His approach has become a social event. The wife of a great or significant personage must take notice or decide not to take notice. Of course, Amanda was prepared to go anywhere, just as Benham's shadow; it was the world that was unprepared. And a second leading aspect of his original scheme had been the examination of the ways of government in cities and the shifting and mixture of nations and races. It would have led to back streets, and involved and complicated details, and there was something in the fine flame of girlhood beside him that he felt was incompatible with those shadows and that dust. And also they were lovers, and very deeply in love. It was amazing how swiftly that draggled shameful London sparrow-gamin, Eros, took heart from Amanda, and became wonderful, beautiful, glowing, life-giving, confident, clear-eyed; how he changed from flesh to sweet fire, and grew until he filled the sky. So that you see they went to Switzerland and Italy at last very like two ordinary young people who were not aristocrats at all, had no theory about the world or their destiny, but were simply just ardently delighted with the discovery of one another.

Nevertheless Benham was for some time under a vague impression that in a sort of way still he was going round the world and working out his destinies.

It was part of the fascination of Amanda that she was never what he had supposed her to be, and that nothing that he set out to do with her ever turned out as they had planned it. Her appreciations marched before her achievement, and when it came to climbing it seemed foolish to toil to summits over which her spirit had flitted days before. Their Swiss expeditions which she had foreseen as glorious wanderings amidst the blue ice of crevasses and nights of exalted hardihood became a walking tour of fitful vigour and abundant fun and delight. They spent a long day on the ice of the Aletsch glacier, but they reached the inn on its eastward side with magnificent appetites a little late for dinner.

Amanda had revealed an unexpected gift for nicknames and pretty fancies. She named herself the Leopard, the spotless Leopard; in some obscure way she intimated that the colour was black, but that was never to be admitted openly, there was supposed to be some lurking traces of a rusty brown, but the word was spotless and the implication white, a dazzling white; she would play a thousand variations on the theme; in moments of despondency she was only a black cat, a common lean black cat, and sacks and half-bricks almost too good for her. But Benham was always a Cheetah. That had come to her as a revelation from heaven. But so clearly he was a Cheetah. He was a Hunting Leopard; the only beast that has an up-cast face and dreams and looks at you with absent-minded eyes like a man. She laced their journeys with a fantastic monologue telling in the third person what the Leopard and the Cheetah were thinking and seeing and doing. And so they walked up mountains and over passes and swam in the warm clear water of romantic lakes and loved each other mightily always, in chestnut woods and olive orchards and flower-starred alps and pine forests and awning-covered boats, and by sunset and moonlight and starshine; and out of these agreeable solitudes they came brown and dusty, striding side by side into sunlit entertaining fruit-piled market-places and envious hotels. For days and weeks together it did not seem to Benham that there was anything that mattered in life but Amanda and the elemental joys of living. And then the Research Magnificent began to stir in him again. He perceived that Italy was not India, that the clue to the questions he must answer lay in the crowded new towns that they avoided, in the packed bookshops and the talk of men, and not in the picturesque and flowery solitudes to which their love-making carried them.

Moods began in which he seemed to forget Amanda altogether.

This happened first in the Certosa di Pavia, whither they had gone one afternoon from Milan. That was quite soon after they were married. They had a bumping journey thither in a motor-car, a little doubtful if the excursion was worth while, and they found a great amazement in the lavish beauty and decorative wealth of that vast church and its associated cloisters, set far away from any population as it seemed in a flat wilderness of reedy ditches and patchy cultivation. The distilleries and outbuildings were deserted—their white walls were covered by one monstrously great and old wisteria in flower—the soaring marvellous church was in possession of a knot of un-attractive guides. One of these conducted them through the painted treasures of the gold and marble chapels; he was an elderly but animated person who evidently found Amanda more wonderful than any church. He poured out great accumulations of information and compliments before her. Benham dropped behind, went astray and was presently recovered dreaming in the great cloister. The guide showed them over two of the cells that opened thereupon, each a delightful house for a solitary, bookish and clean, and each with a little secret walled garden of its own. He was covertly tipped, against all regulations, and departed regretfully with a beaming dismissal from Amanda. She found Benham wondering why the Carthusians had failed to produce anything better in the world than a liqueur. 'One might have imagined that men would have done something in this beautiful quiet; that there would have come thought from here or will from there.'

'In these dear little nests they ought to have put lovers,' said Amanda.

'Oh, of course, *you* would have made the place Thelema.'

But as they went shaking and bumping back along the evil road to Milan, he fell into a deep musing. Suddenly he said, 'Work has to be done. Because this order or that has failed, there is no reason why we should fail. And look at those ragged children in the road ahead of us, and those dirty women sitting in the doorways, and the foul ugliness of these gaunt nameless towns through which we go! They are what they are, because we are what we are—idlers, excursionists. In a world we ought to rule. . . .

'Amanda, we've got to get to work. . . .'

That was his first display of this new mood, which presently became a common one. He was less and less content to let the happy hours slip by, more and more sensitive to the reminders in giant ruin and deserted cell, in a chance encounter with a string of guns and soldiers on their way to manœuvres or in the sight of a stale news-paper, of a great world process going on in which he was now playing no part at all. And a curious irritability manifested itself more and more plainly, whenever human pettiness obtruded upon his attention, whenever some trivial dishonesty, some manifest slovenliness, some spiritless failure, a cheating waiter or a wayside beggar brought before him the shiftless, selfish, aimless elements in that war against the great dream of life made glorious. 'Accursed things,' he would say, as he flung some importunate cripple at a church door a ten-centime piece; 'why were they born? Why do they consent to live? They are no better than some chance fungus that is because it must.'

'It takes all sorts to make a world,' said Amanda.

'Nonsense,' said Benham. 'Where is the megatherium? That sort of creature has to go. Our sort of creature has to end it.'

'Then why did you give it money?'

'Because—— I don't want the thing to be more wretched than it is. But if I could prevent more of them—. . . . What am I doing to prevent them?'

'These beggars annoy you,' said Amanda after a pause. 'They do me. Let us go back into the mountains.'

But he fretted in the mountains.

They made a ten days' tour from Macugnaga over the Monte Moro to Sass, and thence to Zermatt and back by the Theodule to Macugnaga. The sudden apparition of douaniers upon the Monteo Moro annoyed Benham, and he was also irritated by the solemn English mountain climbers at Saas Fee. They were as bad as golfers, he said, and reflected momentarily upon his father. Amanda fell in love with Monte Rosa, she wanted to kiss its snowy forehead, she danced like a young goat down the path to Mattmark, and rolled on the turf when she came to gentians and purple primulas. Benham was tremendously in love with her most of the time, but one day when they were sitting over the Findelen glacier his perceptions blundered for the first time upon the fundamental antagonism of their quality. She was sketching out jolly things that they were to do together, expeditions, entertainments, amusements, and adventures, with a voluble swiftness, and suddenly in a flash his eyes were opened, and he saw that she would never for a moment feel the quality that made life worth while for him. He saw it in a flash, and in that flash he made his urgent resolve not to see it. From that moment forth his bearing was poisoned by his secret determination not to think of this, not to admit it to his mind. And, forbidden to come into his presence in its proper form, this conflict of intellectual temperaments took on strange disguises, and the gathering tension of his mind sought to relieve itself along grotesque irrelevant channels.

There was, for example, the remarkable affair of the drive from Macugnaga to Piedimulera.

They had decided to walk down in a leisurely fashion, but with the fatigues of the precipitous clamber down from Switzerland still upon them they found the white road between rock above and gorge below wearisome, and the valley hot in the late morning sunshine, and already before they reached the inn they had marked for lunch Amanda had suggested driving the rest of the way. The inn had a number of brigand-like customers consuming such sustenance as garlic and salami and wine; it received them with an indifference that bordered on disrespect, until the landlord, who seemed to be something of a beauty himself, discovered the merits of Amanda. Then he became markedly attentive. He was a large, fat, curly-headed person with beautiful eyes, a cherished moustache, and an air of great gentility, and when he had welcomed his guests and driven off the slatternly waiting-maid, and given them his best table, and consented, at Amanda's request, to open a window, he went away and put on a tie and collar. It was an attention so conspicuous that even the group of men in the far corner noticed and commented on it, and then they commented on Amanda and Benham, assuming an ignorance of Italian in the visitors that was only partly justifiable. 'Bellissima,' 'bravissima,' 'signorina,' 'Inglesa,' one need not be born in Italy to understand such words as these. Also they addressed sly comments and encouragements to the landlord as he went to and fro.

Benham was rather still and stiff during the meal, but it ill becomes an English aristocrat to discuss the manners of an alien population, and Amanda was amused by the effusion of the landlord and a little disposed to experiment upon him. She sat radiating light amidst the shadows.

The question of the vehicle was broached. The landlord was doubtful; then an idea, it was manifestly a questionable idea, occurred to him. He went to consult an obscure brown-faced individual in the corner, disappeared, and the world without became eloquent. Presently he returned and announced that a carozza was practicable. It had been difficult, but he had contrived it. And he remained hovering over the conclusion of their meal, asking questions about Amanda's mountaineering and expressing incredulous admiration.

His bill, which he presented with an uneasy flourish, was large and included the carozza.

He ushered them out to the carriage with civilities and compliments. It had manifestly been difficult and contrived. It was dusty and blistered, there had been a hasty effort to conceal its recent use as a hen-roost, the harness was mended with string. The horse was gaunt and scandalous, a dirty white, and it carried its head apprehensively. The driver had but one eye, through which there gleamed a concentrated hatred of God and man.

'No wonder he charged for it before we saw it,' said Benham.

'It's better than walking,' said Amanda.

The company in the inn gathered behind the landlord and scrutinised Amanda and Benham intelligently. The young couple got in. 'Avanti,' said Benham, and Amanda bestowed one last ineradicable memory on the bowing landlord.

Benham did not speak until just after they turned the first corner, and then something portentous happened, considering the precipitous position of the road they were upon. A small boy appeared sitting in the grass by the wayside, and at the sight of him the white horse shied extravagantly. The driver rose in his seat ready to jump. But the crisis passed without a smash. 'Cheetah!' cried Amanda suddenly. 'This isn't safe.' 'Ah!' said Benham, and began to act with the vigour of one who has long accumulated force. He rose in his place and gripped the one-eyed driver by the collar. '*Aspetto*,' he said, but he meant 'Stop!' The driver understood that he meant 'Stop,' and obeyed.

Benham wasted no time in parleying with the driver. He indicated to him and to Amanda by a comprehensive gesture that he had business with the landlord, and with a gleaming appetite upon his face went running back towards the inn.

The landlord was sitting down to a little game of dominoes with his friends when Benham reappeared in the sunlight of the doorway. There was no misunderstanding Benham's expression.

For a moment the landlord was disposed to be defiant. Then he changed his mind. Benham's earnest face was within a yard of his own, and a threatening forefinger was almost touching his nose.

'Albergo cattivissimo,' said Benham. 'Cattivissimo! Pranzo cattivissimo 'orrido. Cavallo cattivissimo, dangerousissimo. Gioco abominablissimo, damnissimo. Capisce. Eh?'[1]

The landlord made deprecatory gestures.

'*You* understand all right,' said Benham. 'Da me il argento per il carozza. Subito?'[2]

The landlord was understood to ask whether the signor no longer wished for the carriage.

'*Subito!*' cried Benham, and giving way to a long-restrained impulse seized the padrone by the collar of his coat and shook him vigorously.

There were dissuasive noises from the company, but no attempt at rescue. Benham released his hold.

'Adesso!'[3] said Benham.

The landlord decided to disgorge. It was at any rate a comfort that the beautiful lady was not seeing anything of this. And he could explain afterwards to his friends that the Englishman was clearly a lunatic, deserving pity rather than punishment. He made some sound of protest, but attempted no delay in refunding the money Benham had prepaid.

Outside sounded the wheels of the returning carriage. They stopped. Amanda appeared in the doorway and discovered Benham dominant.

He was a little short of breath, and as she came in he was addressing the landlord with much earnestness in the following compact sentences.

'Attendez! Ecco! Adesso noi andiamo con questa cattivissimo cavallo a Piedimulera. Si noi arrivero in safety, securo, that is, pagaremo. Non altro. Si noi abbiamo accidento Dio—Dio have mercy on your sinful soul. See! Capisce? That's all.'[4]

He turned to Amanda. 'Get back into the thing,' he said. 'We won't have these stinking beasts think we are afraid of the job. I've just made sure we won't have a profit by it if we smash up. That's all. I might have

---

[1] This is vile Italian. It may—with a certain charity to Benham—be rendered: 'The beastliest inn! The beastliest! The beastliest, most awful lunch! The vilest horse! Most dangerous! Abominable trick! Understand?'
[2] 'Give me back the money for the carriage. *Quickly!*'
[3] '*Now!*'
[4] 'Now we will go with this beastly horse to Piedimulera. If we get there safely I will pay. If we have an accident then——'

known what he was up to when he wanted the money beforehand.' He came to the doorway and with a magnificent gesture commanded the perplexed driver to turn the carriage.

While that was being done he discoursed upon his adjacent fellow-creatures. 'A man who pays beforehand for anything in this filthy sort of life is a fool. You see the standards of the beasts. They think of nothing but their dirty little tricks to get profit, their garlic, their sour wine, their games of dominoes, their moments of lust. They crawl in this place like cockroaches in a warm corner of the fireplace until they die. Look at the scabby frontage of the house. Look at the men's faces. . . . Yes. So! Adequato. Aspettate. . . . Get back into the carriage, Amanda.'

'You know it's dangerous, Cheetah. The horse is a shier. That man is blind in one eye.'

'Get back into the carriage,' said Benham, whitely angry. *'I am going to drive !'*

'But——!'

Just for a moment Amanda looked scared. Then with a queer little laugh she jumped in again.

Amanda was never a coward when there was excitement afoot. 'We'll smash !' she cried, by no means woefully.

'Get up beside me,' said Benham speaking in English to the driver, but with a gesture that translated him. Power over men radiated from Benham in this angry mood. He took the driver's seat. The little driver ascended, and then with a grim calmness that brooked no resistance Benham reached over, took and fastened the apron over their knees to prevent any repetition of the jumping-out tactics.

The recovering landlord became voluble in the doorway.

'In Piedimulera pagaro,' said Benham over his shoulder and brought the whip across the white outstanding ribs. 'Get up !' said Benham.

Amanda gripped the sides of the seat as the carriage started into motion.

He laid the whip on again with such vigour that the horse forgot altogether to shy at the urchin that had scared it before.

'Amanda,' said Benham, leaning back. 'If we do happen to go over on *that* side, jump out. It's all clear and wide for you. This side won't matter so——'

'*Mind !*' screamed Amanda and recalled him to his

duties. He was off the road and he had narrowly missed an outstanding chestnut tree.

'No you don't,' said Benham presently, and again their career became erratic for a time as after a slight struggle he replaced the apron over the knees of the deposed driver. It had been furtively released. After that Benham kept an eye on it that might have been better devoted to the road.

The road went down in a series of curves and corners. Now and then there were pacific interludes when it might have been almost any road. Then, again, it became specifically an Italian mountain road. Now and then only a row of all too infrequent granite stumps separated them from a sheer precipice. Some of the corners were miraculous, and once they had a wheel in a ditch for a time, they shaved the parapet of a bridge over a gorge and they drove a cyclist into a patch of maize, they narrowly missed a goat and jumped three gullies, thrice the horse stumbled and was jerked up in time, there were sickening moments, and withal they got down to Piedimulera unbroken and unspilt. It helped perhaps that the brake, with its handle like a barrel organ, had been screwed up before Benham took control. And when they were fairly on the level outside the town Benham suddenly pulled up, relinquished the driving into the proper hands and came into the carriage with Amanda.

'Safe now,' he said compactly.

The driver appeared to be murmuring prayers very softly as he examined the brake.

Amanda was struggling with profound problems. 'Why didn't you drive down in the first place,' she asked, 'without going back?'

'The landlord annoyed me,' he said. 'I had to go back. . . . I wish I had kicked him. Hairy beast ! If anything had happened, you see, he would have had his mean money. I couldn't bear to leave him.'

'And why didn't you let *him* drive?' She indicated the driver by a motion of the head.

'I was angry,' said Benham. 'I was angry at the whole thing.'

'Still——'

'You see, I think I did that because he might have jumped off if I hadn't been up there to prevent him—I mean if we had had a smash. I didn't want him to get out of it.'

'But you too——'

'You see I was angry. . . .'

'It's been as good as a switchback,' said Amanda after reflection. 'But weren't you a little careless about me, Cheetah?'

'I never thought of you,' said Benham, and then as if he felt that inadequate : 'You see—I was so annoyed. It's odd at times how annoyed one gets. Suddenly when that horse shied I realised what a beastly business life was —as those brutes up there live it. I want to clear out the whole hot, dirty, little aimless nest of them. . . .

'No, I'm sure,' he repeated after a pause as though he had been digesting something, 'I wasn't thinking about you at all.'

§ 4

The suppression of his discovery that his honeymoon was not in the least the great journey of world exploration he had intended, but merely an impulsive pleasure hunt, was by no means the only obscured and repudiated conflict that disturbed the mind and broke out upon the behaviour of Benham. Beneath that issue he was keeping down a far more intimate conflict. It was in those lower, still less recognised depths that the volcanic fire arose and the earthquakes gathered strength. The Amanda he had loved, the Amanda of the gallant stride and fluttering skirt, was with him still; she marched rejoicing over the passes, and a dearer Amanda, a soft whispering creature with dusky hair, who took possession of him when she chose, a soft creature who was nevertheless a fierce creature, was also interwoven with his life. But—— But there was now also a multitude of other Amandas who had this in common —that they roused him to opposition, that they crossed his moods and jarred upon his spirit. And particularly there was the Conquering Amanda, not so much proud of her beauty as eager to test it, so that she was not unmindful of the stir she made in hotel lounges, nor of the magic that may shine memorably through the most commonplace incidental conversation. This Amanda was only too manifestly pleased to think that she made peasant lovers discontented and hotel porters unmercenary; she let her light shine before men. We lovers, who had deemed our own subjugation a profound privilege, love not this further expansiveness of our lady's empire. But Benham knew that no aristocrat can be jealous; jealousy he held to be the vice of the hovel and farmstead and suburban villa, and at an enormous expenditure of will he ignored Amanda's waving flags and roving glances. So, too, he denied that Amanda who was sharp and shrewd about money matters, that flash of an Amanda who was greedy for presents and possessions, that restless Amanda who fretted at any cessation of excitement, and that darkly thoughtful Amanda whom chance observations and questions showed to be still considering an account she had to settle with Lady Marayne. He resisted these impressions, he shut them out of his mind, but still they worked into his thoughts, and presently he could find himself asking, even as he and she went in step striding side by side through the red-scarred pinewoods in the most perfect outward harmony, whether after all he was so happily mated as he declared himself to be a score of times a day, whether he wasn't catching glimpses of reality through a veil of delusion that grew thinner and thinner and might leave him disillusioned in the face of a relationship——

Sometimes a man may be struck by a thought as though he had been struck in the face, and when the name of Mrs Skelmersdale came into his head, he glanced at his wife by his side as if it were something that she might well have heard. Was this indeed the same thing as that? Wonderful, fresh as the day of Creation, clean as flame, yet the same! Was Amanda indeed the sister of Mrs Skelmersdale—wrought of clean fire, but her sister? . . .

But also beside the inimical aspects which could set such doubts afoot there were in her infinite variety yet other Amandas neither very dear nor very annoying, but for the most part delightful, who entertained him as strangers might, Amandas with an odd twist which made them amusing to watch, jolly Amandas who were simply irrevelant. There was, for example, Amanda the Dog Mistress, with an astonishing tact and understanding of dogs, who could explain dogs and the cock of their ears and the droop of their tails and their vanity and their fidelity, and why they looked up and why they suddenly went off round the corner, and their pride in the sound of their voices and their dastardly thoughts and sniffing satisfactions, so that for the first time dogs had souls for Benham to see; and there was an Amanda with a striking passion for the sleekness and soft noses of horses. And there was an Amanda extremely garrulous who was a biographical dictionary and critical handbook to all the girls in the school she had attended at Chichester—they seemed a very girlish lot of girls—and an Amanda who was very knowing—knowing was the only word for it—about pictures and architecture. And these and all the other Amandas agreed together to develop and share this one quality in common—that altogether they pointed to no end, they converged on nothing. She was, it grew more and more apparent, a miscellany bound in a body. She was an animated discursiveness. That passion to get all things together into one aristocratic aim, that restraint of purpose, that imperative to focus, which was the structural essential of Benham's spirit, was altogether foreign to her composition.

There were so many Amandas, they were as innumerable as the Venuses—Cytherea, Cypria, Paphia, Popularia, Euploea, Area, Verticordia, Etaira, Basilea, Myrtea, Libertina, Freya, Astarte, Philommedis, Telessigamma, Anadyomene, and a thousand others to whom men have bowed and built temples, a thousand and the same, and yet it seemed to Benham there was still one wanting.

The Amanda he had loved most wonderfully was that Amanda in armour who had walked with him through the wilderness of the world along the road to Chichester—and that Amanda came back to him no more.

§ 5

Amanda too was making her observations and discoveries.

These moods of his perplexed her; she was astonished to find he was becoming irritable; she felt that he needed a firm but gentle discipline in his deportment as a lover. At first he had been perfect. . . .

But Amanda was more prepared for human inconsecutiveness than Benham, because she herself was inconsecutive and her dissatisfaction with his irritations and preoccupation broadened to no general discontent. He had seemed perfect and he wasn't. So nothing was perfect. And he had to be managed, just as one must manage a dog or a cousin or a mother or a horse. Anyhow she had got him, she had no doubt that she held him by a thousand ties; the spotless leopard had him between her teeth, he was a prisoner in the dusk of her hair, and the world was all one vast promise of entertainment.

§ 6

But the raid into the Balkans was not the tremendous success she had expected it to be. They had adventures, but they were not the richly coloured, mediæval affairs she had anticipated. For the most part until Benham broke loose beyond Ochrida they were adventures in discomfort. In those remote parts of Europe inns die away and cease, and it had never occurred to Amanda that inns could die away anywhere. She had thought that they just became very simple and natural and quaint. And she had thought that when benighted people knocked at a door it would presently open hospitably. She had not expected shots at random from the window. And it is not usual in Albania generally for women, whether they are Christian or Moslem, to go about unveiled; when they do so it leads to singular manifestations. The moral sense of the men is shocked and staggered, and they show it in many homely ways. Small boys at that age when feminine beauty does not yet prevail with them, pelt. Also in Mahometan districts they pelt men who do not wear fezzes, while occasionally Christians of the shawl-headed or skull-cap persuasions will pelt a fez. Sketching is always a peltable or mobable offence, as being contrary to the Koran, and sitting down tempts the pelter. Generally they pelt. The dogs of Albania are numerous, big, dirty, white dogs, large and hostile, and they attack with little hesitation. The women of Albania are secluded and remote, and indisposed to be of service to an alien sister. Roads are infrequent and most bridges have broken down. No bridge has been repaired since the later seventeenth century, and no new bridge has been made since the decline and fall of the Roman Empire. There are no shops at all. The scenery is magnificent but precipitous, and many of the high-roads are difficult to trace. And there is rain. In Albania there is sometimes very heavy rain.

Yet in spite of these drawbacks they spent some splendid hours in their exploration of that wild lost country beyond the Adriatic headlands. There was the approach to Cattaro, for example, through an arm of the sea, amazingly beautiful on either shore, that wound its way into the wild mountains and ended in a deep blue bay under the tremendous declivity of Montenegro. The quay, with its trees and lateen craft, ran along under the towers and portcullised gate of the old Venetian wall; within clustered the town; and then the fortifications zigzagged up steeply to a monstrous fantastic fortress perched upon a great mountain headland that overhung the town. Behind it the rocks, slashed to and fro with the road to Cettinjé, continued to ascend into blue haze, upward and upward until they became a purple curtain that filled half the heavens. The paved still town was squalid by day, but in the evening it became theatrically incredible, with an outdoor café amidst flowers and creepers, a Hungarian military band, a rabble of promenaders like a stage chorus in gorgeous costumes, and a great gibbous yellow moon.

And there was Kroia, which Benham and Amanda saw first through the branches of the great trees that bordered the broad green track they were following. The town and its castle were poised at a tremendous height, sunlit and brilliant against a sombre mass of storm cloud, over vast cliffs and ravines. Kroia continued to be beautiful through a steep laborious approach up to the very place itself, a clustering group of houses and bazaars crowned with a tower and a minaret, and from a painted corridor upon this crest they had a wonderful view of the great seaward levels, and even far away the blue sea itself stretching between Scutari and Durazzo. The eye fell in succession down the stages of a vast and various descent, on the bazaars and tall minarets of the town, on jagged rocks and precipices, on slopes of oak forest and slopes of olive woods, on blue hills dropping away beyond blue hills to the coast. And behind them when they turned they saw great mountains, sullenly magnificent, cleft into vast irregular masses, dense with woods below and grim and desolate above.

These were unforgettable scenes, and so too was the wild lonely valley through which they rode to Ochrida amidst walnut and chestnut trees and scattered rocks, and the first vision of that place itself, with its fertile levels dotted with sheep and cattle, its castle and clustering mosques, its spacious blue lake and the great mountains rising up towards Olympus under the sun. And there was the first view of the blue Lake of Presba seen between silvery beech stems, and that too had Olympus in the far background, plain now and clear and unexpectedly snowy. And there were midday moments when they sat and ate under vines and heard voices singing very pleasantly, and there were forest glades and forest tracks in a great variety of beauty with mountains appearing through their parted branches, there were ilex woods, chestnut woods, beech woods, and there were strings of heavily-laden mules staggering up torrent-worn tracks, and strings of blue-swathed mysterious-eyed women with burdens on their heads passing silently, and white remote houses and ruins and deep gorges and precipices and ancient half-ruinous bridges over unruly streams. And if there was rain there was also the ending of rain, rainbows, and the piercing of clouds by the sun's incandescence, and sunsets and the moon, first full, then new, and then growing full again as the holiday wore on.

They found tolerable accommodation at Cattaro and at Cettinjé and at a place half-way between them. It was only when they had secured a guide and horses, and pushed on into the south-east of Montenegro that they began to realise the real difficulties of their journey. They aimed for a place called Podgoritza, which had a partially justifiable reputation for an inn, they missed the road and spent the night in the open beside a fire, rolled in the blankets they had very fortunately bought in Cettinjé. They supped on biscuits and Benham's brandy flask. It chanced to be a fine night, and, drawn like moths by the fire, four heavily-armed mountaineers came out of nowhere, sat down beside Benham and Amanda, rolled cigarettes, achieved conversation in bad Italian through the muleteer, and awaited refreshment. They approved of the brandy highly, they finished it, and towards dawn warmed to song. They did not sing badly, singing in chorus, but it appeared to Amanda that the hour might have been better chosen. In the morning they were agreeably surprised to find one of the Englishmen was an Englishwoman, and followed every accessible detail of her toilet with great interest. They were quite helpful about breakfast when the trouble was put to them; two vanished over a crest and reappeared with some sour milk, a slabby kind of bread, goat's cheese young but hardened, and coffee and the means of making coffee, and they joined spiritedly in the ensuing meal. It ought to have been extraordinarily good fun, this camp under the vast heavens and these wild visitors, but it was not such fun as it ought to have been because both Amanda and Benham were extremely cold, stiff, sleepy, grubby and cross, and when at last they were back in the way to Podgoritza and had parted, after some present-giving, from their chance friends, they halted in a sunlit grassy place, rolled themselves up in their blankets and recovered their arrears of sleep.

Podgoritza was their first experience of a khan, those

Oriental substitutes for hotels, and it was a deceptively good khan, indeed it was not a khan at all, it was an inn; it provided meals, it had a kind of bar, or at any rate a row of bottles and glasses, it possessed an upper floor with rooms, separate rooms, opening on to a gallery. The room had no beds, but it had a shelf about it on which Amanda and Benham rolled up in their blankets and slept. 'We can do this sort of thing all right,' said Amanda and Benham. 'But we mustn't lose the way again.'

'In Scutari,' said Benham, 'we will get an extra horse and a tent.'

The way presently became a lake and they reached Scutari by boat towards the dawn of the next day. . . .

The extra horse involved the addition of its owner, a small suspicious Latin Christian, to the company, and of another horse for him and an ugly almost hairless boy attendant. Moreover, the British consul prevailed with Benham to accept the services of a picturesque Arnaut cavasse, complete with a rifle, knives, and other implements and the name of Giorgio. And as they got up into the highlands beyond Scutari they began to realise the deceitfulness of Podgoritza and the real truth about khans. Their next one they reached after a rainy evening, and it was a cavernous room with a floor of indurated mud and full of eye-stinging wood-smoke and wind and the smell of beasts, unpartitioned, with a weakly hostile custodian from whom no food could be got but a little goat's flesh and bread. The meat Giorgio stuck upon a skewer in gobbets like cats-meat and cooked before the fire. For drink there was coffee and raw spirits. Against the wall in one corner was a slab of wood rather like the draining board in a scullery, and on this the guests were expected to sleep. The horses and the rest of the party camped loosely about the adjacent corner after a bitter dispute upon some unknown point between the horse owner and the custodian.

Amanda and Benham were already rolled up on their slanting board like a couple of chrysalids when other company began to arrive through the open door out of the moonlight, drawn thither by the report of a travelling Englishwoman.

They were sturdy men in light-coloured garments adorned ostentatiously with weapons ; they moved mysteriously about in the firelit darknesses and conversed in undertones with Giorgio. Giorgio seemed to have considerable powers of exposition and a gift for social organisation. Presently he came to Benham and explained that raki was available and that hospitality would do no harm; Benham and Amanda sat up and various romantic figures with splendid moustaches came forward and shook hands with him, modestly ignoring Amanda. There was drinking, in which Benham shared, incomprehensible compliments, much ineffective saying of '*Buona notte*,' and at last Amanda and Benham counterfeited sleep. This seemed to remove a check on the conversation and a heated discussion in tense undertones went on, it seemed interminably. . . . Probably very few aspects of Benham and Amanda were ignored. . . . Towards morning the twanging of a string proclaimed the arrival of a querulous-faced minstrel with a sort of embryonic one-stringed horse-headed fiddle, and after a brief parley singing began, a long high-pitched solo. The fiddle squealed pitifully under the persuasion of a semicircular bow. Two heads were lifted inquiringly.

The singer had taken up his position at their feet and faced them. It was a compliment.

'*Oh!*' said Amanda, rolling over.

The soloist obliged with three songs and then, just as day was breaking, stopped abruptly and sprawled suddenly on the floor as if he had been struck asleep. He was vocal even in his sleep. A cock in the far corner began crowing and was answered by another outside. . . .

But this does not give a full account of the animation of the khan. '*Oh!*' said Amanda, rolling over again with the suddenness of accumulated anger.

'They're worse than in Scutari,' said Benham, understanding her trouble instantly.

'It isn't days and nights we are having,' said Benham a few days later, 'it's days and nightmares.'

But both he and Amanda had one quality in common. The deeper their discomfort the less possible it was to speak of turning back from the itinerary they had planned. . . .

They met no robbers, though an excited little English Levantine in Scutari had assured them they would do so and told a vivid story of a ride to Ipek, a delay on the road due to a sudden inexplicable lameness of his horse after a halt for refreshment, a political discussion that delayed him, his hurry through the still twilight to make up for lost time, the coming on of night and the sudden silent apparition out of the darkness of the woods about the road of a dozen armed men each protruding a gun-barrel. 'Sometimes they will wait for you at a ford or a broken bridge,' he said. ' In the mountains they rob for arms. They assassinate the Turkish soldiers even. It is better to go unarmed unless you mean to fight for it. . . . Have you got arms?'

' Just a revolver,' said Benham.

But it was after that that he closed with Giorgio.

If they found no robbers in Albania they met soon enough with bloodshed. They came to a village where a friend of a friend of Giorgio's was discovered, and they slept at his house in preference to the unclean and crowded khan. Here for the first time Amanda made the acquaintance of Albanian women and was carried off to the woman's region at the top of the house, permitted to wash, closely examined, shown a baby, and confided in as generously as gesture and some fragments of Italian would permit. Benham slept on a rug on the first floor in a corner of honour beside the wood fire. There had been much confused conversation and some singing, he was dog-tired and slept heavily, and when presently he was awakened by piercing screams he sat up in a darkness that seemed to belong neither to time nor place. . . .

Near his feet was an ashen glow that gave no light.

His first perplexity gave way to dismay at finding no Amanda by his side. 'Amanda!' he cried. . . .

Her voice floated down through a chink in the floor above. 'What can it be, Cheetah?'

Then : 'It's coming nearer.'

The screaming continued, heart-rending, eviscerating shrieks. Benham, still confused, lit a match. All the men about him were stirring or sitting up and listening, their faces showing distorted and ugly in the flicker of his light. '*Che e ?*' he tried. No one answered. Then one by one they stood up and went softly to the ladder that led to the stable-room below. Benham struck a second match and a third.

'Giorgio!' he called.

The cavasse made an arresting gesture and followed discreetly and noiselessly after the others, leaving Benham alone in the dark.

Benham heard their shuffling patter, one after the other, down the ladder, the sounds of a door being unbarred softly, and then no other sound but that incessant shrieking in the darkness.

Had they gone out? Were they standing at the door looking out into the night and listening?

Amanda had found the chink and her voice sounded nearer. 'It's a woman,' she said.

The shrieking came nearer and nearer, long, repeated, throat-tearing shrieks. Far off there was a great clamour of dogs. And there was another sound, a whisper—?

'*Rain !*'

The shrieks seemed to turn into a side street and receded. The tension of listening relaxed. Men's voices sounded below in question and answer. Dogs close at hand barked shortly and then stopped inquiringly.

Benham seemed to himself to be sitting alone for an interminable time. He lit another match and consulted his watch. It was four o'clock and nearly dawn. . . .

Then slowly and stumbling up the ladder the men began to return to Benham's room.

'Ask them what it is,' urged Amanda.

But for a time not even Giorgio would understand Benham's questions. There seemed to be a doubt whether he ought to know. The shrieking approached again and then receded. Giorgio came and stood, a vague thoughtful figure, by the embers of the fire. Explanation dropped from him reluctantly. It was nothing. Some one had been killed : that was all. It was a vendetta. A man had been missing overnight, and this morning his brother who had been prowling and searching with some dogs had found him, or rather his head. It was on this side of the ravine, thrown over from the other bank on which the body sprawled stiffly, wet through, and now growing visible in the gathering daylight. Yes—the voice was the man's wife. It was raining hard. . . . There would be shrieking for nine days. Yes, nine days. Confirmation with the fingers when Benham still fought against the facts. Her friends and relatives would come and shriek too. Two of the dead man's aunts were among the best keeners in the whole land. They could keen marvellously. It was raining too hard to go on. . . . The road would be impossible in rain. . . . Yes, it was very melancholy. Her house was close at hand. Perhaps twenty or thirty women would join her. It was impossible to go on until it had stopped raining. It would be tiresome, but what could one do? . . .

§ 7

As they sat upon the parapet of a broken bridge on the road between Elbassan and Ochrida Benham was moved to a dissertation upon the condition of Albania and the politics of the Balkan peninsula.

'Here we are,' he said, 'not a week from London, and you see the sort of life that men live when the forces of civilisation fail. We have been close to two murders——'

'Two?'

'That little crowd in the square at Scutari—— That was a murder. I didn't tell you at the time.'

'But I knew it was,' said Amanda.

'And you see the filth of it all, the toiling discomfort of it all. There is scarcely a house here in all the land that is not filthier and viler than the worst slum in London. No man ventures far from his village without arms, everywhere there is fear. The hills are impassable because of the shepherds' dogs. Over those hills a little while ago a stranger was torn to pieces by dogs—and partially eaten. Amanda, these dogs madden me. I shall let fly at the beasts. The infernal indignity of it! But that is by the way. You see how all this magnificent country lies waste with nothing but this crawling, ugly mockery of human life.'

'They sing,' said Amanda.

'Yes,' said Benham and reflected, 'they do sing. I suppose singing is the last thing left to men. When there is nothing else you can still sit about and sing. Miners who have been buried in mines will sing, people going down in ships.'

'The Sussex labourers don't sing,' said Amanda. 'These people sing well.'

'They would probably sing as well if they were civilised. Even if they didn't I shouldn't care. All the rest of their lives is muddle and cruelty and misery. Look at the women. There was that party of bent creatures we met yesterday, carrying great bundles, carrying even the men's cloaks and pipes, while their rascal husbands and brothers swaggered behind. Look at the cripples we have seen and the mutilated men. If we have met one man without a nose we have met a dozen. And stunted people. All these people are like evil schoolboys; they do nothing but malicious mischief; there is nothing adult about them but their voices; they are like the heroic dreams of young ruffians in a penitentiary. You saw that man at Scutari in the corner of the bazaar, the gorgeous brute, you admired him——'

'The man with the gold inlaid pistols and the diamonds on his yataghan. He wanted to show them to us.'

'Yes. You let him see you admired him.'

'I liked the things on his stall.'

'Well, he has killed nearly thirty people.'

'In duels?'

'Good Lord! *No!* Assassinations. His shoemaker annoyed him by sending in a bill. He went to the man's stall, found him standing with his child in his arms and blew out his brains. He blundered against a passer-by in the road and shot him. Those are his feats. Sometimes his pistols go off in the bazaar just by accident.'

'Does nobody kill him?'

'I wanted to,' said Benham and became thoughtful for a time. 'I think I ought to have made some sort of quarrel. But then as I am an Englishman he might have hesitated. He would have funked a strange beast like me. And I couldn't have shot him if he had hesitated. And if he hadn't——'

'But doesn't a blood feud come down on him?'

'It only comes down on his family. The shoemaker's son thought the matter over and squared accounts by putting the muzzle of a gun into the small of the back of our bully's uncle. It was easier that way. . . . You see you're dealing with men of thirteen years old or thereabouts, the boy who doesn't grow up.'

'But doesn't the law——?'

'There's no law. Only custom and the Turkish tax collector.

'You see this is what men are where there is no power, no discipline, no ruler, no responsibility. This is a masterless world. This is pure democracy. This is the natural state of men. This is the world of the bully and the brigand and assassin, the world of the mud-pelter and brawler, the world of the bent woman, the world of the flea and the fly, the open drain and the baying dog. This is what the British sentimentalist thinks a noble state for men.'

'They fight for freedom.'

'They fight among each other. There are their private feuds and their village feuds and above all that great feud religion. In Albania there is only one religion and that is hate. But there are three churches for the better cultivation of hate and cruelty, the Latin, the Greek and the Mahometan.'

'But no one has ever conquered these people.'

'Any one could, the Serbians, the Bulgarians, the Greeks, the Italians, the Austrians. Why, they can't even shoot! It's just the balance of power and all that foolery keeps this country a roadless wilderness. Good God, how I tire of it ! These men who swagger and stink, their brawling dogs, their greasy priests and dervishes, the down-at-heel soldiers, the bribery and robbery, the cheating over the money. . . .'

He slipped off the parapet, too impatient to sit any longer, and began to pace up and down in the road.

'One marvels that no one comes to clear up this country, one itches to be at the job, and then one realises that before one can begin here, one must get to work back there, where the fools and pedants of *Welt Politik* scheme mischief one against another. This country frets me. I can't see any fun in it, can't see the humour of it. And the people away there know no better than to play off tribe against tribe, sect against sect, one peasant prejudice against another. Over this pass the foolery grows grimmer and viler. We shall come to where the Serbian plots against the Bulgarian and the Greek against both, and the Turk, with spasmodic massacres and indulgences, broods over the brew. Every division is subdivided. There are two sorts of Greek church, Exarchic, Patriarchic, both teaching by threat and massacre. And there is no one, no one, with the sense to over-ride all these squalid hostilities. All those fools away there in London and Vienna and St Petersburg and Rome take sides as though these beastly tribes and leagues and superstitions meant anything but blank, black, damnable ignorance. One fool stands up for the Catholic Albanians, another finds heroes in the Serbians, another talks of Brave Little Montenegro, or the Sturdy Bulgarian, or the Heroic Turk. There isn't a religion in the whole Balkan peninsula, there isn't a tribal or national sentiment that deserves a moment's respect from a sane man. They're things like niggers' nose-rings and Chinese secret societies; childish things, idiot things that have to go. Yet there is no one who will preach the only possible peace, which is the peace of the world-state, the open conspiracy of all the sane men in the world against the things that break us up into wars and futilities. And here am I—who have the light—*wandering !* Just wandering !'

He shrugged his shoulders and came to stare at the torrent under the bridge.

'You're getting ripe for London, Cheetah,' said Amanda softly.

'I want somehow to get to work, to get my hands on definite things.'

'How can we get back?'

She had to repeat her question presently.

'We can go on. Over the hills is Ochrida and then over another pass is Presba, and from there we go down into Monastir and reach a railway and get back to the world of our own times again.'

§ 8

But before they reached the world of their own times Macedonia was to show them something grimmer than Albania.

They were riding through a sunlit walnut wood beyond Ochrida when they came upon the thing.

The first they saw of it looked like a man lying asleep on a grassy bank. But he lay very still indeed, he did not look up, he did not stir as they passed, the pose of his hand was stiff, and when Benham glanced back at him, he stifled a little cry of horror. For this man had no face and the flies had been busy upon him. . . .

Benham caught Amanda's bridle so that she had to give her attention to her steed.

'Ahead!' he said, 'ahead! Look, a village!'

(Why the devil didn't they bury the man? Why?

And that fool Giorgio and the others were pulling up and beginning to chatter. After all she might look back.)

Through the trees now they could see houses. He quickened his pace and jerked Amanda's horse forward. . . .

But the village was a still one. Not a dog barked.

Here was an incredible village without even a dog!

And then, then they saw some more people lying about. A woman lay in a doorway. Near her was something muddy that might have been a child, beyond were six men all spread out very neatly in a row with their faces to the sky.

'Cheetah!' cried Amanda, with her voice going up. 'They've been killed. Some one has killed them.'

Benham halted beside her and stared stupidly.

'It's a band,' he said. 'It's—propaganda. Greeks or Turks or Bulgarians.'

'But their feet and hands are fastened! And——. . . . *What have they been doing to them? . . .*'

'I want to kill,' cried Benham. 'Oh! I want to kill people. Come on, Amanda! It blisters one's eyes. Come away. Come away! Come!'

Her face was white and her eyes terror-stricken. She

obeyed him mechanically. She gave one last look at those
bodies. . . .

Down the deep-rutted soil of the village street they
clattered. They came to houses that had been set on
fire. . . .

'What is that hanging from a tree?' cried Amanda.
'Oh, Oh!'

'Come on. . . .'

Behind them rode the others scared and hurrying.

The sunlight had become the light of hell. There was
no air but horror. Across Benham's skies these fly-blown
trophies of devilry dangled mockingly in the place of God.
He had no thought but to get away.

Presently they encountered a detachment of Turkish
soldiers, very greasy and ragged, with worn-out boots and
yellow faces, toiling up the stony road belatedly to the
village. Amanda and Benham riding one behind the other
in a stricken silence passed this labouring column without
a gesture, but presently they heard the commander stopping
and questioning Giorgio. . . .

Then Giorgio and the others came clattering to overtake
them.

Giorgio was too full to wait for questions. He talked
eagerly to Benham's silence.

It must have happened yesterday, he explained. They
were Bulgarians—traitors. They had been converted to
the Patriarchists by the Greeks—by a Greek band, that is
to say. They had betrayed one of their own people. Now
a Bulgarian band had descended upon them. Bulgarian
bands it seemed were always particularly rough on
Bulgarian speaking Patriarchists. . . .

§ 9

That night they slept in a dirty little room in a peasant's
house in Resnia, and in the middle of the night Amanda
woke up with a start and heard Benham talking. He
seemed to be sitting up as he talked. But he was not
talking to her and his voice sounded strange.

'Flies,' he said, 'in the sunlight!'

He was silent for a time, and then he repeated the same
words.

Then suddenly he began to declaim. 'Oh! Brutes
together. Apes. Apes with knives. Have they no lord,
no master, to save them from such things? This is the life

of men when no man rules. . . . When no man rules. . . .
Not even himself. . . . It is because we are idle, because
we keep our wits slack and our wills weak that these poor
devils live in hell. These things happen here and everywhere when the hand that rules grows weak. Away in
China now they are happening. Persia. Africa. . . .
Russia staggers. And I who should serve the law, I who
should keep order, wander and make love. . . . My God!
May I never forget! May I never forget! Flies in the
sunlight! That man's face. And those six men!

'Grip the savage by the throat.

'The weak savage in the Foreign Office, the weak savage
at the party headquarters, feud and indolence and folly.
It is all one world. This and that are all one thing. The
spites of London and the mutilations of Macedonia. The
maggots that eat men's faces and the maggots that rot
their minds. Rot their minds. Rot their minds. Rot their
minds. . . .'

To Amanda it sounded like delirium.

'Cheetah!' she said suddenly between remonstrance and
a cry of terror.

The darkness suddenly became quite still. He did not
move.

She was afraid. 'Cheetah!' she said again.

'What is it, Amanda?'

'I thought—— Are you all right?'

'Quite.'

'But do you feel well?'

'I've got this cold I caught in Ochrida. I suppose I'm
feverish. But—yes, I'm well.'

'You were talking.'

Silence for a time.

'I was thinking,' he said.

'You talked.'

'I'm sorry,' he said after another long pause.

§ 10

The next morning Benham had a pink spot on either
cheek, his eyes were feverishly bright, he would touch no
food and instead of coffee he wanted water. 'In Monastir
there will be a doctor,' he said. 'Monastir is a big place.
In Monastir I will see a doctor. I want a doctor.'

They rode out of the village in the freshness before
sunrise and up long hills, and sometimes they went in the

shade of woods and sometimes in a flooding sunshine. Benham now rode in front, preoccupied, intent, regardless of Amanda, a stranger, and she rode close behind him wondering.

'When you get to Monastir, young man,' she told him, inaudibly, 'you will go straight to bed and we'll see what has to be done with you.'

'*Ammalato*,' said Giorgio, confidentially coming abreast of her.

'*Medico in Monastir*,' said Amanda.

'*Si—molti medici, Monastir*,' Giorgio agreed.

Then came the inevitable dogs, big white brutes, three in full cry charging hard at Benham and a younger less enterprising beast running along the high bank above yapping and making feints to descend.

The goatherd reclining under the shadow of a rock, awaited Benham's embarrassment with an indolent malice.

'You *uncivilised* Beasts!' cried Benham, and before Amanda could realise what he was up to, she heard the crack of his revolver and saw a puff of blue smoke drift away above his right shoulder. The foremost beast rolled over and the goatherd had sprung to his feet. He shouted with something between anger and dismay as Benham, regardless of the fact that the other dogs had turned and were running back, let fly a second time. Then the goatherd had clutched at the gun that lay on the grass near at hand, Giorgio was bawling in noisy remonstrance and also getting ready to shoot, and the horse-owner and his boy were clattering back to a position of neutrality up the stony road. '*Bang!*' came a flight of lead within a yard of Benham, and then the goatherd was in retreat behind a rock and Giorgio was shouting '*Avanti, Avanti!*' to Amanda.

She grasped his intention and in another moment she had Benham's horse by the bridle and was leading the retreat. Giorgio followed close driving the two baggage mules before him.

'I am tired of dogs,' Benham said. 'Tired to death of dogs. All savage dogs must be shot. All through the world. I am tired——'

Their road carried them down through the rocky pass and then up a long slope in the open. Far away on the left they saw the goatherd running and shouting and other armed goatherds appearing among the rocks. Behind them the horse-owner and his boy came riding headlong across the zone of danger.

'Dogs must be shot,' said Benham, exalted. 'Dogs must be shot.'

'Unless they are *good* dogs,' said Amanda, keeping beside him with an eye on his revolver.

'Unless they are good dogs to every one,' said Benham.

They rushed along the road in a turbulent dusty huddle of horses and mules and riders. The horse-owner, voluble in Albanian, was trying to get past them. His boy pressed behind him. Giorgio in the rear had unslung his rifle and got it across the front of his saddle. Far away they heard the sound of a shot and a kind of shudder in the air overhead witnessed to the flight of the bullet. They crested a rise and suddenly between the tree boughs Monastir was in view, a wide stretch of white town, with many cypress and plane trees, a winding river with many wooden bridges, clustering minarets of pink and white, a hilly cemetery, and scattered patches of soldiers' tents like some queer white crop to supplement its extensive barracks.

As they hurried down towards this city of refuge a long string of mules burdened with great bales of green stuff appeared upon a convergent track to the left. Besides the customary muleteers there were, by way of an escort, a couple of tattered Turkish soldiers. All these men watched the headlong approach of Benham's party with apprehensive inquiry. Giorgio shouted some sort of information that made the soldiers brighten up and stare up the hill, and set the muleteers whacking and shouting at their convoy. It struck Amanda that Giorgio must be telling lies about a Bulgarian band. In another moment Benham and Amanda found themselves swimming in a torrent of mules. Presently they overtook a small flock of fortunately nimble sheep, and picked up several dogs, dogs that happily disregarded Benham in the general confusion. They also comprehended a small springless cart, two old women with bundles and an elderly Greek priest, before their dusty, barking, shouting cavalcade reached the outskirts of Monastir. The two soldiers had halted behind to cover the retreat.

Benham's ghastly face was now bedewed with sweat and he swayed in his saddle as he rode. 'This is *not* civilisation, Amanda,' he said, 'this is *not* civilisation.'

And then suddenly with extraordinary pathos: Oh! I want to go to *bed*! I want to go to *bed*! A bed with sheets. . . .'

To ride into Monastir is to ride into a maze. The streets

go nowhere in particular. At least that was the effect on Amanda and Benham. It was as if Monastir too had a temperature and was slightly delirious. But at last they found an hotel—quite a civilised hotel. . . .

The doctor in Monastir was an Armenian with an ambition that outran his capacity to speak English. He had evidently studied the language chiefly from books. He thought *these* was pronounced 'theser' and *those* was pronounced 'thoser,' and that every English sentence should be taken at a rush. He diagnosed Benham's complaint in various languages and failed to make his meaning clear to Amanda. One combination of words he clung to obstinately, having clearly the utmost faith in its expressiveness. To Amanda it sounded like, 'May Ah! Slays,' and it seemed to her that he sought to intimate a probable fatal termination of Benham's fever. But it was clear that the doctor was not satisfied that she understood. He came again with a queer little worn book, a parallel vocabulary of half-a-dozen European languages.

He turned over the pages and pointed to a word. 'May! Ah! Slays!' he repeated, reproachfully, almost bitterly. 'Oh, *measles* !' cried Amanda. . . .

So the spirited honeymoon passed its zenith.

§ 11

The Benhams went as soon as possible down to Smyrna and thence by way of Uskub tortuously back to Italy. They recuperated at the best hotel of Locarno in golden November weather, and just before Christmas they turned their faces back to England.

Benham's plans were comprehensive but entirely vague; Amanda had not so much plans as intentions. . . .

CHAPTER THE FIFTH

THE ASSIZE OF JEALOUSY

§ 1

It was very manifest from the disorder of papers amidst which White spent so many evenings of interested perplexity before his novel began to be written that Benham had never made any systematic attempt at editing or revising his accumulation at all. There were not only overlapping documents, in which he had returned again to old ideas and re-stated them in the light of fresh facts and an apparent unconsciousness of his earlier effort, but there were mutually destructive papers; new views quite ousting the old had been tossed in upon the old, and the very definition of the second limitation, as it had first presented itself to the writer, had been abandoned. To begin with, this second division had been labelled 'Sex,' in places the heading remained; no effective substitute had been chosen for some time, but there was a closely-written memorandum, very much erased and written over and amended, which showed Benham's early dissatisfaction with that crude rendering of what he had in mind. This memorandum was tacked to an interrupted fragment of autobiography, a manuscript soliloquy in which Benham had been discussing his married life.

'It was not until I had been married for the better part of a year, and had spent more than six months in London, that I faced the plain issue between the aims I had set before myself and the claims and immediate necessities of my personal life. For all that time I struggled not so much to reconcile them as to serve them simultaneously. . . .'

At that the autobiography stopped short, and the intercalary note began.

This intercalary note runs as follows:—

'I suppose a mind of my sort cannot help but tend towards simplification, towards making all life turn upon some one dominant idea, complex perhaps in its reality but reducible at last to one consistent simple statement, a dominant idea which is essential as nothing else is essential, which makes and sustains and justifies. This is perhaps the innate disposition of the human mind, at least of the European mind—for I have some doubts about the Chinese. Theology drives obstinately towards an ultimate unity in God, science towards an ultimate unity in law, towards a fundamental element and a universal material truth from which all material truths evolve, and in matters of conduct there is the same tendency to refer to a universal moral law. Now this may be a simplification due to the need of the human mind to comprehend, and its inability to do so until the load is lightened by neglecting factors. William James has suggested that on account of this, theology may be obstinately working away from the truth, that the truth may be that there are several or many incompatible and incommensurable gods; science, in the same search for unity, may follow divergent methods of inquiry into ultimately uninterchangeable generalisations; and there may be not only not one universal moral law, but no effective reconciliation of the various rights and duties of a single individual. At any rate I find myself doubtful to this day about my own personal systems of right and wrong. I can never get all my life into one focus. It is exactly like examining a rather thick section with a microscope of small penetration; sometimes one level is clear and the rest foggy and monstrous, and sometimes another.

'Now the ruling *me*, I do not doubt, is the man who has set his face to this research after aristocracy, and from the standpoint of this research it is my duty to subordinate all other considerations to this work of clearing up the conception of rule and nobility in human affairs. This is my aristocratic self. What I did not grasp for a long time, and which now grows clearer and clearer to me, is firstly that this aristocratic self is not the whole of me, it has absolutely nothing to do with a pain in my ear or in my heart, with a scar on my hand or my memory; and secondly that it is not altogether mine. Whatever knowledge I have of the quality of science, whatever will I have towards right, is of it; but if from without, from the reasoning or demonstration or reproof of some one else, there comes to me clear knowledge, clarified will, that also is as it were a part of my aristocratic self coming home to me from the outside. How often have I not found my own mind in Prothero after I have failed to find it in myself? It is, to be paradoxical, my impersonal personality, this Being that I have in common with all scientific-spirited and aristocratic-spirited men. This it is that I am trying to get clear from the great limitations of humanity. When I assert a truth for the sake of truth to my own discomfort or injury, there again is this incompatibility of the aristocratic self and the accepted, confused, conglomerate self of the unanalysed man. The two have a separate system of obligations. One's affections, compounded as they are in the strangest way of physical reactions and emotional associations, one's implicit pledges to particular people, one's involuntary reactions, one's pride and jealousy, all that one might call the dramatic side of one's life, may be in conflict with the definitely seen rightnesses of one's higher use. . . .'

The writing changed at this point.

'All this seems to me at once as old as the hills and too

new to be true. This is like the conflict of the Superior Man of Confucius to control himself, it is like the Christian battle of the spirit with the flesh, it savours of that eternal wrangle between the general and the particular which is metaphysics; it was for this aristocratic self, for righteousness' sake, that men have hungered and thirsted, and on this point men have left father and mother and child and wife and followed after salvation. This world-wide, ever-returning antagonism has filled the world in every age with hermits and lamas, recluses and teachers, devoted and segregated lives. It is a perpetual effort to get above the simplicity of barbarism. Whenever men have emerged from the primitive barbarism of the farm and the tribe, then straightway there has emerged this conception of a specialised life a little lifted off the earth; often, for the sake of freedom, celibate, usually disciplined, sometimes directed, having a generalised aim beyond personal successes and bodily desires. So it is that the philosopher, the scientifically concentrated man, has appeared, often, I admit, quite ridiculously at first, setting out upon the long journey that will end only when the philosopher is king. . . .

'At first I called my Second Limitation, Sex. But from the outset I meant more than mere sexual desire, lust and lustful imaginings, more than personal reactions to beauty and spirited living, more even than what is called love. On the one hand I had in mind many appetites that are not sexual yet turn to bodily pleasure, and on the other there are elements of pride arising out of sex and passing into other regions, all the elements of rivalry, for example, that have strained my first definition to the utmost. And I see now that this Second Limitation as I first imagined it spreads out without any definite boundary, to include one's rivalries with old schoolfellows, for example, one's generosities to beggars and dependents, one's desire to avenge an injured friend, one's point of honour, one's regard for the good opinion of an aunt, and one's concern for the health of a pet cat. All these things may enrich, but they may also impede and limit the aristocratic scheme. I thought for a time I would call this ill-defined and miscellaneous wilderness of limitation the Personal Life. But at last I have decided to divide this vast territory of difficulties into two sub-divisions and make one of these Indulgence, meaning thereby pleasurable indulgence of sense or feeling, and the other a great mass of self-regarding motives that will go with a little stretching under the heading of Jealousy.

I admit motives are continually playing across the boundary of these two divisions, I should find it difficult to argue a case for my classification, but in practice these two group-ings have a quite definite meaning for me, There is pride in the latter group of impulses and not in the former; the former are always a little apologetic. Fear, Indulgence, Jealousy, these are the First Three Limitations of the soul of man. And the greatest of these is Jealousy because it can use pride. Over them the Life Aristocratic, as I con-ceive it, marches to its end. It saves itself for the truth rather than sacrifices itself romantically for a friend. It justifies vivisection if thereby knowledge is won for ever. It upholds that Brutus who killed his sons. It forbids devotion to women, courts of love, and all such decay of the chivalrous idea. And it resigns—so many things that no common Man of Spirit will resign. Its intention tran-scends these things. Over all the world it would maintain justice, order, a noble peace, and it would do this without indignation, without resentment, without mawkish tender-ness or individualised enthusiasm or any queen of beauty. It is of a cold austere quality, commanding sometimes admiration but having small hold upon the affections of men. So that it is among its foremost distinctions that its heart is steeled. . . .'

There this odd fragment ended and White was left to resume the interrupted autobiography.

§ 2

What moods, what passions, what nights of despair and gathering storms of anger, what sudden cruelties and amazing tendernesses are buried and hidden and implied in every love story ! What a waste is there of exquisite things ! So each spring sees a million glorious beginnings, a sunlit heaven in every opening leaf, warm perfection in every stirring egg, hope and fear and beauty beyond com-putation in every forest tree; and in the autumn before the snows come they have all gone—of all that incalculable abundance of life, of all that hope and adventure, excite-ment and deliciousness there is scarcely more to be found than a soiled twig, a dirty seed, a dead leaf, black mould or a rotting feather. . . .

White held the ten or twelve pencilled pages that told how Benham and Amanda drifted into antagonism and estrangement, and as he held it he thought of the laughter and delight they must have had together, the exquisite excitement of her eye, the racing colour of her cheek, the gleams of light upon her skin, the flashes of wit between them, the sense of discovery, the high rare paths they had followed, the pools in which they had swum together. And now it was all gone into nothingness, there was nothing left of it, nothing at all, but just those sheets of statement, and it may be, stored away in one single mind, like things forgotten in an attic, a few neglected faded memories. . . .

And even those few sheets of statement were more than most love leaves behind it. For a time White would not read them. They lay neglected on his knee as he sat back in Benham's most comfortable chair and enjoyed an entirely beautiful melancholy.

White too had seen and mourned the spring.

Indeed, poor dear ! he had seen and mourned several springs. . . .

With a sigh he took up the manuscript and read Benham's dessicated story of intellectual estrangement, and how in the end he had decided to leave his wife and go out alone upon that journey of inquiry he had been planning when first he met her.

§ 3

Amanda had come back to England in a state of extravagantly vigorous womanhood. Benham's illness, though it lasted only two or three weeks, gave her a sense of power and leadership for which she had been struggling instinctively ever since they came together. For a time at Locarno he was lax-minded and indolent, and in that time she formed her bright and limited plans for London. Benham had no plans as yet, but only a sense of divergence, as though he was being pulled in opposite directions by two irresistible forces. To her it was plain that he needed occupation, some distinguished occupation, and she could imagine nothing better for him than a political career. She perceived he had personality, that he stood out among men so that his very silences were effective. She loved him immensely, and she had tremendous ambitions for him and through him.

And also London, the very thought of London filled her with appetite. Her soul thirsted for London. It was like some enormous juicy fruit waiting for her pretty white teeth, a place almost large enough to give her avidity the sense of enough. She felt it waiting for her, household servants, a carriage, shops and the jolly delight of buying and possessing things, the opera, first-nights, picture exhibitions, great dinner-parties, brilliant lunch parties, crowds seen from a point of vantage, the carriage in a long string of fine carriages with the lamp-lit multitude peering, Amanda in a thousand bright settings, in a thousand various dresses. She had had love; it had been glorious, it was still glorious, but her love-making became now at times almost perfunctory in the contemplation of these approaching delights and splendours and excitements.

She knew, indeed, that ideas were at work in Benham's head; but she was a realist. She did not see why ideas should stand in the way of a career. Ideas are a brightness, the good looks of the mind. One talks ideas, but *the thing that is, is the thing that is*. And though she believed that Benham had a certain strength of character of his own, she had that sort of confidence in his love for her and in the power of her endearments that has in it the assurance of a faint contempt. She had mingled pride and sense in the glorious realisation of the power over him that her wit and beauty gave her. She had held him faint with her divinity, intoxicated with the pride of her complete possession, and she did not dream that the moment when he should see clearly that she would deliberately use these ultimate delights to rule and influence him, would be the end of their splendour and her power. Her nature, which was just a nest of vigorous appetites, was incapable of suspecting his gathering disillusionment until it burst upon her.

Now with her attention set upon London ahead he could observe her. In the beginning he had never seemed to be observing her at all, they dazzled one another; it seemed extraordinary now to him to note how much he had been able to disregard. There were countless times still when he would have dropped his observation and resumed that mutual exaltation very gladly, but always now other things possessed her mind. . . .

There was still an immense pleasure for him in her vigour; there was something delightful in her pounce, even when she was pouncing on things superficial, vulgar or destructive. She made him understand and share the excitement of a big night at the opera, the glitter and prettiness of a smart restaurant, the clustering little acute adventures of a great reception of gay people, just as she had already made him understand and sympathise with dogs. She picked up the art world where he had laid it down, and she forced him to feel dense and slow before he rebelled against her multitudinous enthusiasms and admirations. South Harting had had its little group of artistic people; it is not one of your sleepy villages, and she slipped back at once into the movement. Those were the great days of John, the days before the Post-Impressionist outbreak. John, Orpen, Tonks, she bought them with vigour. Artistic circles began to revolve about her. Very rapidly she was in possession. . . . And among other desirable things she had, it seemed, pounced upon and captured Lady Marayne.

At any rate, it was clear that that awful hostile silence and aloofness were to end. Benham never quite mastered how it was done. But Amanda had gone in one morning to Desborough Street, very sweetly and chastely dressed, had abased herself and announced a possible (though subsequently disproved) grandchild. And she had appreciated the little lady so highly and openly, she had so instantly caught and reproduced her tone, that her success, though only temporary in its completeness, was immediate. In the afternoon Benham was amazed by the apparition of his mother amidst the scattered unsettled furnishings of the new home Amanda had chosen in Lancaster Gate. He was in the hall, the door stood open awaiting packing-cases from a van without. In the open doorway she shone, looking the smallest of dainty things. There was no effect of her coming but only of her having arrived there, as a little blue butterfly will suddenly alight on a flower.

'Well, Poff!' said Lady Marayne, ignoring abysses, 'What are you up to now, Poff? Come and embrace me. . . .

'No, not so,' she said, 'stiffest of sons. . . .'

She laid hold of his ears in the old fashion and kissed one eye.

'Congratulations, dear little Poff. Oh! congratulations! In heaps. I'm so *glad*.'

Now what was that for?

And then Amanda came out upon the landing upstairs, saw the encounter with an involuntary cry of joy, and came downstairs with arms wide open. It was the first intimation he had of their previous meeting. He was for some minutes a stunned, entirely inadequate Benham. . . .

§ 4

At first Amanda knew nobody in London, except a few people in the Hampstead Garden suburb that she had not the slightest wish to know, and then very quickly she seemed to know quite a lot of people. The artistic circle brought in people, Lady Marayne brought in people; they spread. It was manifest the Benhams were a very bright young couple; he would certainly do something considerable presently, and she was bright and daring, jolly to look at and excellent fun, and, when you came to talk to her, astonishingly well informed. They passed from one hostess's hand to another : they reciprocated. The Clynes people and the Rushtones took her up; Mr Evesham was amused by her, Lady Beach Mandarin proclaimed her charm like a trumpet, the Young Liberal people made jealous advances, Lord Moggeridge found she listened well, she lit one of the brightest week-end parties Lady Marayne had ever gathered at Chexington. And her descriptions of recent danger and adventure in Albania not only entertained her hearers, but gave her just that flavour of personal courage which completes the fascination of a young woman. People in the gaps of a halting dinner-table conversation would ask : 'Have you met Mrs Benham?'

Meanwhile Benham appeared to be talking. A smiling and successful young woman, who a year ago had been nothing more than a leggy girl with a good lot of miscellaneous reading in her head, and vaguely engaged, or at least friendly to the pitch of engagement, to Mr Rathbone-Sanders, may be forgiven if in the full tide of her success she does not altogether grasp the intention of her husband's discourse. It seemed to her that he was obsessed by a responsibility for civilisation and the idea that he was aristocratic. (Secretly she was inclined to doubt whether he was justified in calling himself aristocratic; at the best his mother was county-stuff; but still if he did there was no great harm in it nowadays.) Clearly his line was Tory-Democracy, social reform through the House of Lords and friendly intimacy with the more spirited young peers. And it was only very slowly and reluctantly that she was forced to abandon this satisfactory solution of his problem. She reproduced all the equipment and comforts of his Finacue Street study in their new home, she declared constantly that she would rather forgo any old social thing than interfere with his work, she never made him go anywhere with her without first asking if his work permitted it. To relieve him of the burden of such social attentions she even made a fag or so. The making of fags out of manifestly stricken men, the keeping of tamed and hopeless admirers, seemed to her to be the most natural and reasonable of feminine privileges. They did their useful little services until it pleased the Lord Cheetah to come to his own. That was how she put it. . . .

But at last he was talking to her in tones that could no longer be ignored. He was manifestly losing his temper with her. There was a novel austerity in his voice and a peculiar whiteness about his face on certain occasions that lingered in her memory.

He was indeed making elaborate explanations. He said that what he wanted to do was to understand 'the collective life of the world,' and that this was not to be done in a West-End study. He had an extraordinary contempt, it seemed, for both sides in the drama of British politics. He had extravagant ideas of beginning in some much more fundamental way. He wanted to understand this 'collective life of the world,' because ultimately he wanted to help control it. (Was there ever such nonsense?) The practical side of this was serious enough, however; he was back at his old idea of going round the earth. Later on that might be rather a jolly thing to do, but not until they had struck root a little more surely in London.

And then with amazement, with incredulity, with indignation, she began to realise that he was proposing to go off by himself upon this vague extravagant research, that all this work she had been doing to make a social place for him in London was as nothing to him, that he was thinking of himself as separable from her. . . .

'But Cheetah ! How can you leave your spotless leopard ? You would howl in the lonely jungle !'

'Possibly I shall. But I am going.'

'Then I shall come.'

'No.' He considered her reasons. 'You see you are not interested.'

'But I am.'

'Not as I am. You would turn it all into a jolly holiday. You don't want to see things as I want to do. You want romance. All the world is a show for you. As a show I can't endure it. I want to lay hands on it.'

'But, Cheetah !' she said, 'this is separation.'

'You will have your life here. And I shall come back.'

'But, Cheetah! How can we be separated?'

'We are separated,' he said.

Her eyes became round with astonishment. Then her face puckered.

'Cheetah!' she cried in a voice of soft distress, 'I love you. What do you mean?'

And she staggered forward, tear-blinded, and felt for his neck and shoulders so that she might weep in his arms. . . .

§ 5

'Don't say we are separated,' she whispered, putting her still wet face close to his.

'No. We're mates,' he answered softly, with his arm about her.

'How could we ever keep away from each uvver?' she whispered.

He was silent.

'How *could* we?'

He answered aloud. 'Amanda,' he said, 'I mean to go round the world.'

She disentangled herself from his arm and sat up beside him.

'What is to become of me,' she asked suddenly in a voice of despair, 'while you go round the world? If you desert me in London,' she said, 'if you shame me by deserting me in London—— If you leave me, I will never forgive you, Cheetah! Never.' Then in an almost breath-less voice, and as if she spoke to herself, 'Never in all my days.'

§ 6

It was after that that Amanda began to talk about children. There was nothing involuntary about Amanda. 'Soon,' she said, 'we must begin to think of children. Not just now, but a little later. It's good to travel and have our fun, but life is unreal until there are children in the background. No woman is really content until she is a mother. . . .' And for nearly a fortnight nothing more was said about that solitary journey round the world.

But children were not the only new topic in Amanda's talk. She set herself with an ingenious subtlety to remind her husband that there were other men in the world. The convenient fags, sometimes a little embarrassed, found their inobtrusive services being brought into the light before Benham's eyes. Most of them were much older men than himself, elderly philanderers of whom it seemed to him no sane man need be jealous, men often of forty or more, but one was a contemporary, Sir Philip Easton, a man with a touch of Spanish blood and a suggestion of Spanish fire, who quite manifestly was very much in love with Amanda, and of whom she spoke with a slight perceptible difference of manner that made Benham faintly uneasy. He was ashamed of the feeling. Easton it seemed was a man of a peculiarly fine honour, so that Amanda could trust herself with him to an extent that would have been inadvisable with men of a commoner substance, and he had a gift of understanding and sympathy that was almost feminine; he could cheer one up when one was lonely and despondent. For Amanda was so methodical in the arrangement of her time that even in the full rush of a London season she could find an hour now and then for being lonely and despondent. And he was a liberal and understanding purchaser of the ascendant painters; he understood that side of Amanda's interests, a side upon which Benham was notably deficient. . . .

'Amanda seems to like that dark boy, Poff; what is his name?—Sir Philip Easton?' said Lady Marayne.

Benham looked at her with a slightly hostile intelligence, and said nothing.

'When a man takes a wife, he has to keep her,' said Lady Marayne.

'No,' said Benham after consideration. 'I don't intend to be a wife-herd.'

'What?'

'Wife-herd—same as goat-herd.'

'Coarse, you are sometimes, Poff—nowadays.'

'It's exactly what I mean. I can understand the kind of curator's interest an Oriental finds in shepherding a large establishment, but to spend my days looking after one person who ought to be able to look after herself——'

'She's very young.'

'She's quite grown up. Anyhow I'm not a moral nurse-maid.'

'If you leave her about and go abroad——'

'Has she been talking to you, mother?'

'The thing shows.'

'But about my going abroad?'

'She said something, my little Poff.'

Lady Marayne suddenly perceived that beneath Benham's

indifference was something strung very tight, as though he had been thinking inordinately. He weighed his words before he spoke again. 'If Amanda chooses to threaten me with a sort of conditional infidelity, I don't see that it ought to change the plans I have made for my life. . . .'

§ 7

'No aristocrat has any right to be jealous,' Benham wrote. 'If he chances to be mated with a woman who does not see his vision or naturally go his way, he has no right to expect her, much less to compel her, to go his way. What is the use of dragging an unwilling companion through morasses of uncongenial thought to unsought ends? What is the use of dragging even a willing pretender, who has no inherent will to seek and live the aristocratic life?

'But that does not excuse him from obedience to his own call. . . .'

He wrote that very early in his examination of the Third Limitation. Already he had thought out and judged Amanda. The very charm of her, the sweetness, the nearness and magic of her, was making him more grimly resolute to break away. All the elaborate process of thinking her over had gone on behind the mask of his silences while she had been preoccupied with her housing and establishment in London; it was with a sense of extraordinary injustice, of having had a march stolen upon her, of being unfairly trapped, that Amanda found herself faced by foregone conclusions. He was ready now even with the details of his project. She should go on with her life in London exactly as she had planned it. He would take fifteen hundred a year for himself, and all the rest she might spend without check or stint as it pleased her. He was going round the world for one or two years. It was even possible he would not go alone. There was a man at Cambridge he might persuade to come with him, a don called Prothero who was peculiarly useful in helping him to hammer out his ideas. . . .

To her it became commandingly necessary that none of these things should happen.

She tried to play upon his jealousy, but her quick instinct speedily told her that this only hardened his heart. She perceived that she must make a softer appeal. Now of a set intention she began to revive and imitate the spontaneous passion of the honeymoon; she perceived for the first time clearly how wise and righteous a thing it is for a woman to bear a child. 'He cannot go if I am going to have a child,' she told herself. But that would mean illness, and for illness in herself or others Amanda had the intense disgust natural to her youth. Yet even illness would be better than this intolerable publication of her husband's ability to leave her side. . . .

She had a wonderful facility of enthusiasm, and she set herself forthwith to cultivate a philoprogenitive ambition, to communicate it to him. Her dread of illness disappeared; her desire for offspring grew.

'Yes,' he said, 'I want to have children, but I must go round the world none the less.'

She argued with all the concentrated subtlety of her fine keen mind. She argued with persistence and repetition. And then suddenly, so that she was astonished at herself, there came a moment when she ceased to argue.

She stood in the dusk in a window that looked out upon the park, and she was now so intent upon her purpose as to be still and self-forgetful; she was dressed in a dinner-dress of white and pale green, that set off her slim erect body and the strong clear lines of her neck and shoulders very beautifully; some greenish stones caught a light from without and flashed soft whispering gleams from amidst the misty darkness of her hair. She was going to Lady Marayne and the opera, and he was bound for a dinner at the House with some young Liberals at which he was to meet two representative Indians with a grievance from Bengal. Husband and wife had but a few moments together. She asked about his company, and he told her.

'They will tell you about India.'

'Yes.'

She stood for a moment looking out across the lights and the dark green trees, and then she turned to him.

'Why cannot I come with you?' she asked with sudden passion. 'Why cannot I see the things you want to see?'

'I tell you you are not interested. You would only be interested through me. That would not help me. I should just be dealing out my premature ideas to you. If you cared as I care, if you wanted to know as I want to know, it would be different. But you don't. It isn't your fault that you don't. It happens so. And there is no good in forced interest, in prescribed discovery.'

'Cheetah,' she asked, 'what is it that you want to know —that I don't care for?'

'I want to know about the world. I want to rule the world.'

'So do I.'

'No, you want to have the world.'

'Isn't it the same?'

'No. You're a greedier thing than I am, you Black Leopard you—standing there in the dusk. You're a stronger thing. Don't you know you're stronger? When I am with you, you carry your point, because you are more concentrated, more definite, less scrupulous. When you run beside me you push me out of my path. . . . You've made me afraid of you. . . . And so I won't go with you, Leopard. I go alone. It isn't because I don't love you. I love you too well. It isn't because you aren't beautiful and wonderful. . . .'

'But, Cheetah! nevertheless you care more for this that you want than you care for me.'

Benham thought of it. 'I suppose I do,' he said.

'What is it that you want? Still I don't understand.'

Her voice had the break of one who would keep reasonable in spite of pain.

'I ought to tell you.'

'Yes, you ought to tell me.'

'I wonder if I can tell you,' he said very thoughtfully, and rested his hands on his hips. 'I shall seem ridiculous to you.'

'You ought to tell me.'

'I think what I want is to be king of the world.'

She stood quite still staring at him.

'I do not know how I can tell you of it. Amanda, do you remember those bodies—you saw those bodies—those mutilated men?'

'I saw them,' said Amanda.

'Well. Is it nothing to you that those things happen?'

'They must happen.'

'No. They happen because there are no kings but pitiful kings. They happen because the kings love their Amandas and do not care.'

'But what can *you* do, Cheetah?'

'Very little. But I can give my life and all my strength. I can give all I can give.'

'But how? How can you help it—help things like that massacre?'

'I can do my utmost to find out what is wrong with my world and rule it and set it right.'

'*You!* Alone.'

'Other men do as much. Every one who does so, helps others to do so. You see—— . . . In this world one may wake in the night and one may resolve to be a king, and directly one has resolved one is a king. Does that sound foolishness to you? Anyhow, it's fair that I should tell you, though you count me a fool. This—this kingship— this dream of the night—is my life. It is the very core of me. Much more than you are. More than anything else can be. I mean to be a king in this earth. *King.* I'm not mad. . . . I see the world staggering from misery to misery and there is little wisdom, less rule, folly, prejudice, limitation, the good things come by chance and the evil things recover and slay them, and it is my world and I am responsible. Every man to whom this light has come is responsible. As soon as this light comes to you, as soon as your kingship is plain to you, there is no more rest, no peace, no delight, except in work, in service, in utmost effort. As far as I can do it I will rule my world. I cannot abide in this smug city, I cannot endure its self-complacency, its routine, its gloss of success, its rottenness. . . . I shall do little, perhaps I shall do nothing, but what I can understand and what I can do I will do. Think of that wild beautiful country we saw, and the mean misery, the filth and the warring cruelty of the life that lives there, tragedy, tragedy without dignity; and think, too, of the limitless ugliness here, and of Russia slipping from disorder to massacre, and China, that sea of human beings, sliding steadily to disaster. Do you think these are only things in the newspapers? To me at any rate they are not things in newspapers; they are pain and failure, they are torment, they are blood and dust and misery. They haunt me day and night. Even if it is utterly absurd I will still do my utmost. It *is* absurd. I'm a madman, and you and my mother are sensible people. . . . And I will go my way. . . . I don't care for the absurdity. I don't care a rap.'

He stopped abruptly.

'There you have it, Amanda. It's rant, perhaps. Sometimes I feel it's rant. And yet it's the breath of life to me. . . . There you are. . . . At last I've been able to break silence and tell you. . . .'

He stopped with something like a sob and stood regarding the dusky mystery of her face. She stood quite still, she was just a beautiful outline in the twilight, her face was an indistinctness under the black shadow of her hair, with eyes that were two patches of darkness.

He looked at his watch, lifting it close to his face to see the time. His voice changed. 'Well—if you provoke a man enough, you see he makes speeches. Let it be a lesson to you, Amanda. Here we are talking instead of going to our dinners. The car has been waiting ten minutes.'

Amanda, so still, was the most disconcerting of all Amandas. . . .

A strange exaltation seized upon her very suddenly. In an instant she had ceased to plot against him. A vast wave of emotion swept her forward to a resolution that astonished her.

'Cheetah!' she said, and the very quality of her voice had changed, 'give me one thing. Stay until June with me.'

'Why?' he asked.

Her answer came in a voice so low that it was almost a whisper.

'Because—now—no, I don't want to keep you any more—I am not trying to hold you any more. . . . I want. . . .'

She came forward to him and looked up closely at his face.

'Cheetah,' she whispered almost inaudibly, 'Cheetah— I didn't understand. But now—— I want to bear your child.'

He was astonished. 'Old Leopard!' he said.

'No,' she answered putting her hands upon his shoulders and drawing very close to him, 'Queen—if I can be—to your King.'

'You want to bear me a child!' he whispered, profoundly moved.

§ 8

The Hindu agitators at the cavernous dinner under the House of Commons came to the conclusion that Benham was a dreamer. And over against Amanda at her dinner-party sat Sir Sidney Umber, one of those men who know that their judgments are quoted.

'Who is the beautiful young woman who is seeing visions?' he asked of his neighbour in confidential undertones. . . .

He tittered. 'I think, you know, she ought to seem just *slightly* aware that the man to her left is talking to her. . . .'

§ 9

A few days later Benham went down to Cambridge, where Prothero was now a Fellow of Trinity and Brissenden Trust Lecturer. . . .

All through Benham's writing there was manifest a persuasion that in some way Prothero was necessary to his mind. It was as if he looked to Prothero to keep him real. He suspected, even while he obeyed, that upward flourish which was his own essential characteristic. He had a peculiar feeling that somehow that upward bias would betray him; that from exaltation he might presently float off, into the higher, the better, and so to complete unreality. He fled from priggishness and the terror of such sublimity alike to Prothero. Moreover, in relation to so many things Prothero in a peculiar distinctive manner *saw*. He had less self-control than Benham, less integrity of purpose, less concentration, and things that were before his eyes were by the very virtue of these defects invariably visible to him. Things were able to insist upon themselves with him. Benham on the other hand, when facts contradicted his purpose too stoutly, had a way of becoming blind to them. He repudiated inconvenient facts. He mastered and made his world; Prothero accepted and recorded his. Benham was a will towards the universe where Prothero was a perception and Amanda a confusing responsive activity. And it was because of his realisation of this profound difference between them that he was possessed by the idea of taking Prothero with him about the world, as a detachable kind of vision—rather like that eye the Graiae used to hand one another. . . .

After the busy sunlit streets of Maytime Cambridge Prothero's rooms in Trinity, their windows full of Gothic perspectives and light-soaked blue sky, seemed cool and quiet. A flavour of scholarship pervaded them—a little blended with the flavour of innumerable breakfasts nearly but not completely forgotten. Prothero's door had been locked against the world, and he had appeared after a slight delay looking a little puffy and only apprehending who his visitor was after a resentful stare for the better part of a second. He might have been asleep, he might have been doing anything but the examination papers he appeared to be doing. The two men exchanged personal details; they had not met since some months before Benham's marriage, and the visitor's eye went meanwhile from his host to the room and back to his host's face as though they were all aspects of the thing he was after, the Prothero humour, the earthly touch, the distinctive Prothero flavour. Then his eye was caught by a large red, incongruous, meretricious looking volume upon the couch that had an air of having been flung aside, *Venus in Gem and Marble*, its cover proclaimed. . . .

His host followed that glance and blushed. 'They send me all sorts of inappropriate stuff to review,' he remarked.

And then he was denouncing celibacy.

The transition wasn't very clear to Benham. His mind had been pre-occupied by the problem of how to open his own large project. Meanwhile Prothero got, as it were, the conversational bit between his teeth and bolted. He began to say the most shocking things right away, so that Benham's attention was caught in spite of himself.

'Inflammatory classics.'

'What's that?'

'Celibacy, my dear Benham, is maddening me,' said Prothero. 'I can't stand it any longer.'

It seemed to Benham that somewhere, very far away, in another world, such a statement might have been credible. Even in his own life—it was now indeed a remote, forgotten stage—there had been something distantly akin. . . .

'You're going to marry?'

'I must.'

'Who's the lady, Billy?'

'I don't know. Venus.'

His little red-brown eye met his friend's defiantly.

'So far as I know, it is Venus Anadyomene.' A flash of laughter passed across his face and left it still angrier, still more indecorously defiant. 'I like her best, anyhow. I do indeed. But, Lord! I feel that almost any of them——'

'Tut, tut!' said Benham.

Prothero flushed deeply but stuck to his discourse.

'Wasn't it always your principle, Benham, to look facts in the face? I am not pronouncing an immoral principle. Your manner suggests I am. I am telling you exactly how I feel. That is how I feel. I want—Venus. I don't want her to talk to or anything of that sort. . . . I have been studying that book, yes, that large, vulgar, red book, all the morning, instead of doing any work. Would you like to see it? . . . *No!* . . .

'This spring, Benham, I tell you, is driving me mad.

It is a peculiarly erotic spring. I cannot sleep, I cannot fix my mind, I cannot attend to ordinary conversation. These feelings, I understand, are by no means peculiar to myself. . . . No, don't interrupt me, Benham; let me talk now that the spirit of speech is upon me. When you came in you said, "How are you?" I am telling you how I am. You brought it on yourself. Well—I am—inflamed. I have no strong moral or religious convictions to assist me either to endure or deny this—this urgency. And so why should I deny it? It's one of our chief problems here. The majority of my fellow dons who look at me with secretive faces in hall and court and combination-room are in just the same case as myself. The fever in oneself detects the fever in others. I know their hidden thoughts. Their fishy eyes defy me to challenge their hidden thoughts. Each covers his miserable secret under the cloak of a wholesome manly indifference. A tattered cloak. . . . Each tries to hide his abandonment to this horrible vice of continence——'

'Billy, what's the matter with you?'

Prothero grimaced impatience. 'Shall I *never* teach you not to be a humbug, Benham?' he screamed, and in screaming became calmer. 'Nature taunts me, maddens me. My life is becoming a hell of shame. "Get out from all these books," says Nature, "and serve the Flesh." The Flesh, Benham. Yes—I insist—the Flesh. Do I look like a pure spirit? Is any man a pure spirit? And here am I at Cambridge like a lark in a cage, with too much port and no Aspasia. Not that I should have liked Aspasia.'

'Mutual, perhaps. Billy.'

'Oh! you can sneer!'

'Well, clearly—Saint Paul is my authority—it's marriage, Billy.'

Prothero had walked to the window. He turned round. 'I *can't* marry,' he said. 'The trouble has gone too far. I've lost my nerve in the presence of women. I don't like them any more. They come at one—done up in a lot of ridiculous clothes, and chattering about all sorts of things that don't matter. . . .'

He surveyed his friend's thoughtful attitude.

'I'm getting to hate women, Benham. I'm beginning now to understand the bitterness of spinsters against men. I'm beginning to grasp the unkindliness of priests. The perpetual denial. To you, happily married, a woman is just a human being. You can talk to her, like her, you can even admire her calmly; you've got, you see, no grudge against her. . . .'

He sat down abruptly.

Benham, upon the hearthrug before the empty fireplace, considered him.

'Billy! this is delusion,' he said. 'What's come over you?'

'I'm telling you,' said Prothero.

'No,' said Benham.

Prothero awaited some further utterance.

'I'm looking for the cause of it. It's feeding, Billy. It's port and stimulants where there is no scope for action. It's idleness. I begin to see now how much fatter you are, how much coarser.'

'Idleness! Look at this pile of examination answers. Look at that filing system like an arsenal of wisdom. Useless wisdom, I admit, but anyhow not idleness.'

'There's still bodily idleness. No. That's your trouble. You're stuffy. You've enlarged your liver. You sit in this room of a warm morning after an extravagant breakfast——And peep and covet.'

'Just eggs and bacon!'

'Think of it! Coffee and toast, it ought to be. Come out of it, Billy, and get aired.'

'How can one?'

'Easily. Come out of it now. Come for a walk, you Pig!'

'It's an infernally warm morning.'

'Walk with me to Grantchester.'

'We might go by boat. You could row.'

'*Walk.*'

'I ought to do these papers.'

'You weren't doing them.'

'No . . .'

'Walk with me to Grantchester. All this affliction of yours is—horrid—and just nothing at all. Come out of it! I want you to come with me to Russia and about the world. I'm going to leave my wife——'

'Leave your wife!'

'Why not? And I came here hoping to find you clear-headed, and instead you are in this disgusting state. I've never met anything in my life so hot and red and shiny and shameless. Come out of it, man! How can one talk to you?'

§ 10

'You pull things down to your own level,' said Benham as they went through the heat of Grantchester.

'I pull them down to truth,' panted Prothero.

'Truth! As though being full of gross appetites was truth, and discipline and training some sort of falsity!'

'Artificiality. And begetting pride, Benham, begetting a prig's pride.'

For a time there was more than the heat of the day between them. . . .

The things that Benham had come down to discuss were thrust into the background by the impassioned materialism of Prothero.

'I'm not talking of Love,' he said, remaining persistently outrageous. 'I'm talking of physical needs. That first. What is the good of arranging systems of morality and sentiment before you know what is physically possible? . . .'

'But how can one disentangle physical and moral necessities?'

'Then why don't we up and find out?' said Billy.

He had no patience with the secrecy, the ignorance, the emotion that surrounded these questions. We didn't worship our ancestors when it came to building bridges or working metals or curing disease or studying our indigestion, and why should we become breathless or wordless with awe and terror when it came to this fundamental affair. Why here in particular should we give way to Holy Fear and stifled submission to traditional suppressions and the wisdom of the ages? 'What is the wisdom of the ages?' said Prothero. 'Think of the corners where that wisdom was born. . . . Flea-bitten sages in stone-age hovels. . . . Wandering wise man with a rolling eye, a fakir under a tree, a Jewish sheik, an Arab epileptic. . . .'

'Would you sweep away the experience of mankind?' protested Benham.

The experience of mankind in these matters had always been bitter experience. Most of it was better forgotten. It didn't convince. It had never worked things out. In this matter just as in every other matter that really signified things had still to be worked out. Nothing had been worked out hitherto. The wisdom of the ages was a Cant. People had been too busy quarrelling, fighting, and running away. There wasn't any digested experience of the ages at all. Only the mis-remembered hankey-pankey of the Dead Old Man.

'Is this love-making a physical necessity for most men and women or isn't it?' Prothero demanded. 'There's a simple question enough, and is there anything whatever in your confounded wisdom of the ages to tell me yes or no? Can an ordinary celibate be as healthy and vigorous as a mated man? Is a spinster of thirty-eight a healthy human being? Can she be? I don't believe so. Then why in thunder do we let her be? Here am I at a centre of learning and wisdom and I don't believe so; and there is nothing in all our colleges, libraries, and rooms full of wise-acres here, to settle that plain question for me, plainly and finally. My life is a grubby torment of cravings because it isn't settled. If sexual activity *is* a part of the balance of life, if it *is* a necessity, well let's set about making it accessible and harmless and have done with it. Swedish exercises. That sort of thing. If it isn't, if it can be reduced and done without, then let us set about teaching people *how* to control themselves and reduce and get rid of this vehement passion. But all this muffled mystery, this pompous sneak's way we take with it!'

'But, Billy! How can one settle these things? It's a matter of idiosyncrasy. What is true for one man isn't true for another. There's infinite difference of temperaments.

'Then why haven't we a classification of temperaments and a moral code for each sort? Why am I ruled by the way of life that is convenient for Rigdon the vegetarian and fits Bowler the saint like a glove? It isn't convenient for me. It fits me like a hair-shirt. Of course there are temperaments, but why can't we formulate them and exercise the elementary charity of recognising that one man's health in these matters is another man's death? Some want love and gratification and some don't. There are people who want children and people who don't want to be bothered by children but who are full of vivid desires. There are people whose only happiness is chastity, and women who would rather be courtesans than mothers. Some of us would concentrate upon a single passion or a single idea; others overflow with a miscellaneous—tenderness. Yes—and you smile! Why spit upon and insult a miscellaneous tenderness, Benham? Why grin at it? Why try every one by the standards that suit oneself? We're savages, Benham, shamefaced savages, still. Shame-faced and persecuting.

'I was angry about sex by seventeen,' he went on. 'Every year I live I grow angrier.'

His voice rose to a squeal of indignation as he talked.

'Think,' he said, 'of the amount of thinking and feeling about sex that is going on in Cambridge this morning. The hundreds out of these thousands full of it. A vast tank of cerebration. And we put none of it together; we work nothing out from that but poor little couplings and casual stories, patchings up of situations, misbehaviours, blunders, disease, trouble, escapes; and the next generation will start, and the next generation after that will start with nothing but your wisdom of the ages, which isn't wisdom at all, which is just awe and funk, taboos and mystery and the secretive cunning of the savage. . . .

'What I really want to do is my work,' said Prothero, going off quite unexpectedly again. 'That is why all this business, this incessant craving and the shame of it and all makes me so infernally angry. . . .'

§ 11

'There I'm with you,' cried Benham, struggling out of the thick torrent of Prothero's prepossessions. 'What we want to do is our work.'

He clung to his idea. He raised his voice to prevent Prothero getting the word again.

'It's this, that you call Work, that I call—what do I call it?—living the aristocratic life, which takes all the coarse simplicity out of this business. If it was only submission. . . . *You* think it is only submission—giving way. . . . It isn't only submission. We'd manage sex all right, we'd be the happy swine our senses would make us, if we didn't know all the time that there was something else to live for, something far more important. And different. Absolutely different and contradictory. So different that it cuts right across all these considerations. It won't fit in. . . . I don't know what this other thing is; it's what I want to talk about with you. But I know that it *is*, in all my bones. . . . *You* know. . . . It demands control, it demands continence, it insists upon disregard.'

But the ideas of continence and disregard were unpleasant ideas to Prothero that day.

'Mankind,' said Benham, 'is overcharged with this sex. It suffocates us. It gives life only to consume it. We struggle out of the urgent necessities of a mere animal existence. We are not so much living as being married

and given in marriage. All life is swamped in the love
story. . . .'

'Man is only overcharged because he is unsatisfied,' said
Prothero, sticking stoutly to his own view.

§ 12

It was only as they sat at a little table in the orchard
at Grantchester after their lunch that Benham could make
head against Prothero and recover that largeness of outlook
which had so easily touched the imagination of Amanda.
And then he did not so much dispose of Prothero's troubles
as soar over them. It is the last triumph of the human
understanding to sympathise with desires we do not share,
and to Benham who now believed himself to be loved
beyond the chances of life, who was satisfied and tranquil
and austerely content, it was impossible that Prothero's
demands should seem anything more than the grotesque
and squalid squealings of the beast that has to be over-
ridden and rejected altogether. It is a freakish fact of our
composition that these most intense feelings in life are just
those that are most rapidly and completely forgotten;
hate one may recall for years, but the magic of love and the
flame of desire serve their purpose in our lives and vanish,
leaving no trace, like the snows of Venice. Benham was
still not a year and a half from the meretricious delights of
Mrs Skelmersdale, and he looked at Prothero as a marble
angel might look at a swine in its sty. . . .

What he had now in mind was an expedition to Russia.
When at last he could sufficiently release Prothero's
attention, he unfolded the project that had been developing
steadily in him since his honeymoon experience.

He had discovered a new reason for travelling. The
last country we can see clearly, he had discovered, is our
own country. It is as hard to see one's own country as it
is to see the back of one's head. It is too much behind
us, too much ourselves. But Russia is like England with
everything larger, more vivid, cruder; one felt that directly
one walked about St Petersburg. St Petersburg upon its
Neva was like a savage untamed London on a larger
Thames; they were seagull-haunted tidal cities, like no
other capitals in Europe. The shipping and buildings
mingled in their effects. Like London it looked over the
heads of its own people to a limitless polyglot empire.
And Russia was an aristocratic land, with a middle-class

that had no pride in itself as a class; it had a British tough-
ness and incompetence, a British disregard of logic and
meticulous care. Russia, like England, was outside Catholic
Christendom; it had a state church and the opposition
to that church was not secularism but dissent. One could
draw a score of such contrasted parallels. And now it
was in a state of intolerable stress, that laid bare the
elemental facts of a great social organisation. It was having
its South Africa war, its war at the other end of the earth,
with a certain defeat instead of a dubious victory. . . .

'There is far more freedom for the personal life in Russia
than in England,' said Prothero, a little irrelevantly.

Benham went on with his discourse about Russia. . . .

'At the college of Troitzka,' said Prothero, 'which I
understand is a kind of monster Trinity unencumbered by
a University, Binns tells me that although there is a profession of celibacy within the walls, the arrangements of
the town and more particularly of the various hotels are
conceived in a spirit of extreme liberality.'

Benham hardly attended at all to these interruptions.

He went on to point out the elemental quality of the
Russian situation. He led up to the assertion that to go to
Russia, to see Russia, to try to grasp the broad outline of
the Russian process, was the manifest duty of every
responsible intelligence that was free to do as much. And
so he was going, and if Prothero cared to come too——

'Yes,' said Prothero, 'I should like to go to Russia.'

§ 13

But throughout all their travel together that summer
Benham was never able to lift Prothero away from his
obsession. It was the substance of their talk as the Holland
boat stood out past waiting destroyers and winking beacons
and the lights of Harwich, into the smoothly undulating
darkness of the North Sea; it rose upon them again as they
sat over the cakes and cheese of a Dutch breakfast in the
express for Berlin. Prothero filled the Sieges Allee with his
complaints against nature and society, and distracted
Benham in his contemplation of Polish agriculture from
the windows of the train with turgid sexual liberalism. So
that Benham during this period, until Prothero left him
and until the tragic enormous spectacle of Russia in
revolution took complete possession of him, was as it were
thinking upon two floors. Upon the one he was thinking

of the vast problems of a society of a hundred million people staggering on the verge of anarchy, and upon the other he was perplexed by the feverish inattention of Prothero to the tremendous things that were going on all about them. It was only presently when the serenity of his own private life began to be ruffled by disillusionment, that he began to realise the intimate connexion of these two systems of thought. Yet Prothero put it to him plainly enough.

'Inattentive,' said Prothero, 'of course I am inattentive. What is really the matter with all this—this social mess people are in here, is that nearly everybody is inattentive. These Big Things of yours, nobody is thinking of them really. Everybody is thinking about the Near Things that concern himself.'

'The bombs they threw yesterday? The Cossacks and the whips?'

'Nudges. Gestures of inattention. If everybody was thinking of the Res Publica would there be any need for bombs?'

He pursued his advantage. 'It's all nonsense to suppose people think of politics because they are in 'em. As well suppose that the passengers on a liner understand the engines, or soldiers a war. Before men can think of to-morrow, they must think of to-day. Before they can think of others, they must be sure about themselves. First of all, food; the private, the personal economic worry. Am I safe for food? Then sex, and until one is tranquil and not ashamed, not irritated and dissatisfied, how can one care for other people, or for next year or the Order of the World? How can one, Benham?'

He seized the illustration at hand. 'Here we are, in Warsaw—not a month after bomb-throwing and Cossack charging. Windows have still to be mended, smashed doors restored. There's bloodstains still on some of the houses. There are hundreds of people in the Citadel and in the Ochrana prison. This morning there were executions. Is it anything more than an eddy in the real life of the place? Watch the customers in the shops, the crowd in the streets, the men in the cafés who stare at the passing women. They are all swallowed up again in their own business. They just looked up as the Cossacks galloped past; they just shifted a bit when the bullets spat. . . .'

And when the streets of Moscow were agog with the grotesque amazing adventure of the Potemkin mutineers, Prothero was in the full tide of the private romance that

severed him from Benham and sent him back to Cambridge
—changed.

Before they reached Moscow, Benham was already
becoming accustomed to disregard Prothero. He was
looking over him at the vast heaving trouble of Russia,
which now was like a sea that tumbles under the hurrying
darknesses of an approaching storm. In those days it
looked as though it must be an overwhelming storm.
He was drinking in the wide and massive Russian effects,
the drifting crowds in the entangling streets, the houses
with their strange lettering in black and gold, the innumerable barbaric churches, the wildly driven droshkys, the
sombre red fortress of the Kremlin, with its bulbous
churches clustering up into the sky, the crosses, the innumerable gold crosses, the mad church of St Basil, carrying
the Russian note beyond the pitch of permissible caricature, and in this setting the obscure drama of clustering,
staring, sash-wearing peasants, long-haired students, sane-
eyed women, a thousand varieties of uniform, a running
and galloping to and fro of messengers, a flutter of little
papers, whispers, shouts, shots, a drama elusive and
portentous, a gathering of forces, an accumulation of tension
going on to a perpetual clash and clamour of bells. Benham
had brought letters of introduction to a variety of people;
some had vanished, it seemed. They were 'away,' the
porters said, and they continued to be 'away,'—it was the
formula, he learnt, for arrest—others were evasive, a few
showed themselves extraordinarily anxious to inform him
about things, to explain themselves and things about them
exhaustively. One young student took him to various
meetings and showed him in great detail the scene of the
recent murder of the Grand Duke Sergius. The buildings
opposite the old French cannons were still under repair.
'The assassin stood just there. The bomb fell there, look!
right down there towards the gate; that was where they
found his arm. He was torn to fragments. He was scraped
up. He was mixed with the horses. . . .'

Every one who talked spoke of the outbreak of revolution
as a matter of days or at the utmost weeks. And whatever
question Benham chose to ask these talkers were prepared
to answer . Except one. 'And after the revolution,' he
asked, 'what then? . . . .' Then they waved their hands,
and failed to convey meanings by reassuring gestures.

He was absorbed in his effort to understand this universal
ominous drift towards a conflict. He was trying to piece

together a process, if it was one and the same process, which involved riots in Lodz, fighting at Libau, wild disorder at Odessa, remote colossal battlings in Manchuria, the movements of a disastrous fleet lost somewhere now in the Indian seas, steaming clumsily to its fate, he was trying to rationalise it all in his mind, to comprehend its direction. He was struggling strenuously with the obscurities of the language in which these things were being discussed about him, a most difficult language demanding new sets of visual images because of its strange alphabet. Is it any wonder that for a time he failed to observe that Prothero was involved in some entirely disconnected affair?

They were staying at the big Cosmopolis Bazaar in the Theatre Square. Thither, through the doors that are opened by distraught-looking men with peacocks' feathers round their caps, came Benham's friends and guides to take him out and show him this and that. At first Prothero always accompanied Benham on these expeditions; then he began to make excuses. He would stay behind in the hotel. Then when Benham returned Prothero would have disappeared. When the porter was questioned about Prothero his nescience was profound.

One night no Prothero was discoverable at any hour, and Benham, who wanted to discuss a project for going on to Kieff and Odessa, was alarmed.

'Moscow is a late place,' said Benham's student friend. 'You need not be anxious until after four or five in the morning. It will be quite time—*quite* time to be anxious to-morrow. He may be—close at hand.'

When Benham hunted up Prothero in his room next morning he found him sleepy and irritable.

'I don't trouble if *you* are late,' said Prothero, sitting up in his bed with a red resentful face and crumpled hair. 'I wasn't born yesterday.'

'I wanted to talk about leaving Moscow.'

'I don't want to leave Moscow.'

'But Odessa——Odessa is the centre of interest just now.'

'I want to stay in Moscow.'

Benham looked baffled.

Prothero stuck up his knees and rested his night-shirted arms upon them. 'I don't want to leave Moscow,' he said, 'and I'm not going to do so.'

'But haven't we done——'

Prothero interrupted. 'You may. But I haven't.

We're not after the same things.   Things that interest you, Benham, don't interest me.   I've found—different things.'

His expression was extraordinarily defiant.

'I want,' he went on, 'to put our affairs on a different footing.   Now you've opened the matter we may as well go into it.   You were good enough to bring me here. . . . There was a sort of understanding we were working together. . . . We aren't. . . . The long and short of it is, Benham, I want to pay you for my journey here and go on my own —independently.'

His eye and voice achieved a fierceness that Benham found nearly incredible in him.

Something that had got itself overlooked in the press of other matters jerked back into Benham's memory.   It popped back so suddenly that for an instant he wanted to laugh.   He turned towards the window, picked his way among Prothero's carelessly dropped garments, and stood for a moment staring into the square, with its drifting, assembling and dispersing fleet of trams and its long line of blue-coated *izvoshtchiks*.   Then he turned.

'Billy,' he said, 'didn't I see you the other evening driving towards the Hermitage?'

'Yes,' said Prothero, and added, 'that's it.'

'You were with a lady.'

'And she *is* a lady,' said Prothero, so deeply moved that his face twitched as though he was going to weep.

'She's a Russian?'

'She had an English mother.   Oh, you needn't stand there and look so damned ironical!   She's—she's a woman. She's a thing of kindness. . . .'

He was too full to go on.

'Billy, old boy,' said Benham distressed, 'I don't want to be ironical——'

Prothero had got his voice again.

'You'd better know,' he said, 'you'd better know.   She's one of those women who live in this hotel.'

'Live in this hotel!'

'On the fourth floor.   Didn't you know?   It's the way in most of these big Russian hotels.   They come down and sit about after lunch and dinner.   A woman with a yellow ticket.   Oh!   I don't care.   I don't care a rap.   She's been kind to me; she's—she's dear to me.   How are you to understand?   I shall stop in Moscow.   I shall take her to England. I can't live without her, Benham.   And then—— And then you come worrying me to come to your damned Odessa!'

And suddenly this extraordinary young man put his hands to his face as though he feared to lose it and would hold it on, and after an apoplectic moment burst noisily into tears. They ran between his fingers. 'Get out of my room,' he shouted, suffocatingly. 'What business have you to come prying on me?'

Benham sat down on a chair in the middle of the room and stared round-eyed at his friend. His hands were in his pockets. For a time he said nothing.

'Billy,' he began at last, and stopped again. 'Billy, in this country somehow one wants to talk like a Russian. Billy, my dear—I'm not your father, I'm not your judge. I'm—unreasonably fond of you. It's not my business to settle what is right or wrong for you. If you want to stay in Moscow, stay in Moscow. Stay here, and stay as my guest. . . .'

He stopped and remained staring at his friend for a little space.

'I didn't know,' said Prothero brokenly; 'I didn't know it was possible to get so fond of a person. . . .'

Benham stood up. He had never found Prothero so attractive and so abominable in his life before.

'I shall go to Odessa alone, Billy. I'll make things all right here before I go. . . .'

He closed the door behind him and went in a state of profound thought to his own room. . . .

Presently Prothero came to him with a vague inopportune desire to explain what so evidently did not need explaining. He walked about the room trying ways of putting it, while Benham packed.

In an unaccountable way Prothero's bristling little mind seemed to have shrunken to something sleek and small.

'I wish,' he said, 'you could stay for a later train and have lunch and meet her. She's not the ordinary thing. She's—different.'

Benham plumbed depths of wisdom. 'Billy,' he said, 'no woman *is* the ordinary thing. They are all—different.' . . .

§ 14

For a time this affair of Prothero's seemed to be a matter as disconnected from the Research Magnificent as one could imagine any matter to be. While Benham went from Moscow and returned, and travelled hither and thither, and involved himself more and more in the endless tangled threads of the revolutionary movement in Russia, Prothero was lost to all those large issues in the development of his personal situation. He contributed nothing to Benham's thought except attempts at discouragement. He reiterated his declaration that all the vast stress and change of Russian national life was going on because it was universally disregarded. 'I tell you, as I told you before, that nobody is attending. You think because all Moscow, all Russia, is in the picture, that everybody is concerned. Nobody is concerned. Nobody cares what is happening. Even the men who write in newspapers and talk at meetings about it don't care. They are thinking of their dinners, of their clothes, of their money, of their wives. They hurry home. . . .'

That was his excuse.

Manifestly it was an excuse.

His situation developed into remarkable complications of jealousy and divided counsels that Benham found altogether incomprehensible. To Benham in those days everything was very simple in this business of love. The aristocrat had to love ideally; that was all. He had to love Amanda. He and Amanda were now very deeply in love again, more in love, he felt, then they had ever been before. They were now writing love-letters to each other and enjoying a separation that was almost voluptuous. She found in the epistolary treatment of her surrender to him and to the natural fate of women, a delightful exercise for her very considerable powers of expression. Life pointed now wonderfully to the great time ahead when there would be a Cheetah cub in the world, and meanwhile the Cheetah loped about the wild world upon a mighty quest. In such terms she put it. Such foolishness written in her invincibly square and youthful hand went daily from London to Russia and stacked up against his return in the porter's office at the Cosmopolis Bazaar or pursued him down through the jarring disorders of south-west Russia, or waited for him at ill-chosen post-offices that deflected his journeyings wastefully, or in several instances went altogether astray. Perhaps they supplied self-educating young strikers in the postal service with useful exercises in the deciphering of manuscript English. He wrote back five hundred different ways of saying that he loved her extravagantly. . . .

It seemed to Benham in those days that he had found

the remedy and solution of all those sexual perplexities
that distressed the world; Heroic Love to its highest note—
and then you go about your business. It seemed impossible
not to be happy and lift one's chin high and diffuse a
bracing kindliness among the unfortunate multitudes who
stewed in affliction and hate because they had failed as
yet to find this simple, culminating elucidation. And
Prothero—Prothero, too, was now achieving the same
grand elementariness; out of his lusts and protests and
general physical squalor he had flowered into love. For a
time it is true it made rather an ineffective companion of
him, but this was the mere goose-stepping for the triumphal
march; this way ultimately lay exaltation. Benham had
had as yet but a passing glimpse of this Anglo-Russian,
who was a lady and altogether unlike her fellows; he had
seen her for a doubtful second or so as she and Prothero
drove past him, and his impression was of a rather little
creature, white-faced with dusky hair under a red cap,
paler and smaller but with something in her, a quiet
alertness, that gave her a touch of kinship with Amanda.
And if she liked old Prothero—— And, indeed, she must
like old Prothero or could she possibly have made him so
deeply in love with her?

They must stick to each other, and then, presently,
Prothero's soul would wake up and face the world again.
What did it matter what she had been?

Through stray shots and red conflict, long tediums of
strained anxiety, and the physical dangers of a barbaric
country staggering towards revolution, Benham went with
his own love like a lamp within him and this affair of
Prothero's reflecting its light, and he was quite prepared
for the most sympathetic and liberal behaviour when he
came back to Moscow to make the lady's acquaintance.
He intended to help Prothero to marry and take her back
to Cambridge, and to assist by every possible means in
destroying and forgetting the official yellow ticket that
defined her status in Moscow. But he reckoned without
either Prothero or the young lady in this expectation.

It only got to him slowly through his political pre-
occupations that there were obscure obstacles to this manifest
course. Prothero hesitated; the lady expressed doubts.

On closer acquaintance her resemblance to Amanda
diminished. It was chiefly a similarity of complexion.
She had a more delicate face than Amanda, and its youthful
brightness was deadened; she had none of Amanda's

glow, and she spoke her mother's language with a pretty halting limp that was very different from Amanda's clear decisions.

She put her case compactly.

'I would not *do* in Cambridge,' she said, with an infinitesimal glance at Prothero.

'Mr Benham,' she said, and her manner had the gravity of a woman of affairs, 'now do you see me in Cambridge? Now do you see me? Kept outside the walls? In a little *datcha*? With no occupation? Just to amuse him.'

And on another occasion when Prothero was not with her she achieved still completer lucidity.

'I would come if I thought he wanted me to come,' she said. 'But you see if I came he would not want me to come. Because then he would have me and so he wouldn't want me. He would just have the trouble. And I am not sure if I should be happy in Cambridge. I am not sure I should be happy enough to make him happy. It is a very learned and intelligent and charming society, of course; but here, *things happen*. At Cambridge nothing happens— there is only education. There is no revolution in Cambridge; there are not even sinful people to be sorry for. . . . And he says himself that Cambridge people are particular. He says they are liberal but very, very particular, and perhaps I could not always act my part well. Sometimes I am not always well behaved. When there is music I behave badly sometimes, or when I am bored. He says the Cambridge people are so liberal that they do not mind what you are, but he says they are so particular that they mind dreadfully how you are what you are. . . . So that it comes to exactly the same thing. . . .'

'Anna Alexievna,' said Benham suddenly, 'are you in love with Prothero?'

Her manner became conscientiously scientific.

'He is very kind and very generous—too generous. He keeps sending for more money—hundreds of roubles. I try to prevent him.'

'Were you *ever* in love?'

'Of course. But it's all gone long ago. It was like being hungry. Only very fine hungry. Exquisite hungry. . . . And then being disgusted. . . .'

'He is in love with you.'

'What is love?' said Anna. 'He is grateful. He is by nature grateful.' She smiled a smile, like the smile of a pale Madonna who looks down on her bambino.

'And you love nothing?'

'I love Russia—and being alone, being completely alone. When I am dead perhaps I shall be alone. Not even my own body will touch me then.'

Then she added, 'But I shall be sorry when he goes.'

Afterwards Benham talked to Prothero alone. 'Your Anna,' he said, 'is rather wonderful. At first, I tell you now frankly I did not like her very much, I thought she looked "used"; she drank vodka at lunch, she was gay, uneasily; she seemed a sham thing—all that was prejudice. She thinks; she's generous, she's fine.'

'She's tragic,' said Prothero, as though it was the same thing.

He spoke as though he noted an objection. His next remark confirmed this impression. 'That's why I can't take her back to Cambridge,' he said.

'You see, Benham,' he went on. ''she's human. She's not really feminine. I mean, she's—unsexed. She isn't fitted to be a wife or a mother any more. We've talked about the possible life in England, very plainly. I've explained what a household in Cambridge would mean. . . . It doesn't attract her. . . . In a way she's been let out from womanhood, forced out of womanhood, and I see now that when women are let out from womanhood there's no putting them back. I could give a lecture on Anna. I see now that if women are going to be wives and mothers and homekeepers and ladies, they must be got ready for it from the beginning, sheltered, never really let out into the wild chances of life. She has been. Bitterly. She's *really* emancipated. And it's let her out into a sort of nothingness. She's no longer a woman, and she isn't a man. She ought to be able to go on her own—like a man. But I can't take her back to Cambridge. Even for her sake.'

His perplexed eyes regarded Benham.

'You won't be happy in Cambridge—alone,' said Benham.

'Oh, damnably not! But what can I do? I had at first some idea of coming to Moscow for good—teaching.'

He paused. 'Impossible. I'm worth nothing here. I couldn't have kept her.'

'Then what are you going to do, Billy?'

'I don't *know* what I'm going to do, I tell you. I live for the moment. To-morrow we are going out into the country.'

'I don't understand,' said Benham with a gesture of

resignation. 'It seems to me that if a man and woman love each other—well, they insist upon each other. What is to happen to her if you leave her in Moscow?'

'Damnation! Is there any need to ask that?'

'Take her to Cambridge, man. And if Cambridge objects, teach Cambridge better manners.'

Prothero's face was suddenly transfigured with rage.

'I tell you she won't come!' he said.

'Billy!' said Benham, 'you should make her!'

'I can't.'

'If a man loves a woman he can make her do anything—'

'But I don't love her like that,' said Prothero, shrill with anger. 'I tell you I don't love her like that.'

Then he lunged into further deeps. 'It's the other men,' he said, 'it's the things that have been. Don't you understand? Can't you understand? The memories—she must have memories—they come between us. It's something deeper than reason. It's in one's spine and under one's nails. One could do anything, I perceive, for one's very own woman. . . .'

'*Make* her your very own woman,' said the exponent of heroic love.

'I shirk deeds, Benham, but you shirk facts. How could any man make her his very own woman now? You—you don't seem to understand—*anything*. She's nobody's woman—for ever. That—that might-have-been has gone for ever. . . . It's nerves—a passion of the nerves. There's a cruelty in life and—— She's *kind* to me. She's so kind to me. . . .'

And then again Prothero was weeping like a vexed child.

§ 15

The end of Prothero's first love affair came to Benham in broken fragments in letters. When he looked for Anna Alexievna in December—he never learnt her surname—he found she had left the Cosmopolis Bazaar soon after Prothero's departure and he could not find whither she had gone. He never found her again. Moscow and Russia had swallowed her up.

Of course she and Prothero parted; that was a foregone conclusion. But Prothero's manner of parting succeeded in being at every phase a shock to Benham's ideas. It was clear he went off almost callously; it would seem there was very little crying. Towards the end it was evident that the two had quarrelled. The tears only came at the very end of all. It was almost as if he had got through the passion and was glad to go. Then came regret, a regret that increased in geometrical proportion with every mile of distance.

In Warsaw it was that grief really came to Prothero. He had some hours there and he prowled the crowded streets, seeing girls and women happy with their lovers, abroad upon bright expeditions and full of delicious secrets, girls and women who ever and again flashed out some instant resemblance to Anna. . . .

In Berlin he stopped a night and almost decided that he would go back. 'But now I had the damned frontier,' he wrote, 'between us.'

It was so entirely in the spirit of Prothero, Benham thought, to let the 'damned frontier' tip the balance against him.

Then came a scrawl of passionate confession, so passionate that it seemed as if Prothero had been transfigured. 'I can't stand this business,' he wrote. 'It has things in it, possibilities of emotional disturbance—you can have no idea ! In the train—luckily I was alone in the compartment —I sat and thought, and suddenly, I could not help it, I was weeping—noisy weeping, an uproar ! A beastly German came and stood in the corridor to stare. I had to get out of the train. It is disgraceful, it is monstrous we should be made like this. . . .

'Here I am stranded in Hanover with nothing to do but to write to you about my dismal feelings. . . .'

After that surely there was nothing before a broken-hearted Prothero but to go on with his trailing wing to Trinity and a life of unappeasable regrets; but again Benham reckoned without the invincible earthliness of his friend. Prothero stayed three nights in Paris.

'There is an extraordinary excitement about Paris,' he wrote. 'A levity. I suspect the gypsum in the subsoil— some as yet undescribed radiations. Suddenly the world looks brightly cynical. . . . None of those tear-compelling German emanations. . . .

'And, Benham, I have found a friend.

'A woman. Of course you will laugh, you will sneer. You do not understand these things. . . . Yet they are so simple. It was the strangest accident brought us together. There was something that drew us together. A sort of instinct. Near the Boulevard Poissonière. . . .'

'Good heavens !' said Benham. 'A sort of instinct !'

'I told her all about Anna !'

'Good Lord !' cried Benham.

'She understood. Perfectly. None of your so-called "respectable" women could have understood. . . . At first I intended merely to talk to her. . . .'

Benham crumpled the letter in his hand.

'Little Anna Alexievna !' he said, 'you were too clean for him.'

§ 16

Benham had a vision of Prothero returning from all this foreign travel meekly, pensively, a little sadly, and yet not without a kind of relief to the gray mildness of Trinity. He saw him, capped and gowned, and restored to academic dignity again, nodding greetings, resuming friendships.

The little man merged again into his rare company of discreet Benedicts and restrained celibates at the high tables. They ate on in their mature wisdom long after the undergraduates had fled. Presently they would withdraw processionally to the combination-room. . . .

There would be much to talk about over the wine.

Benham speculated what account Prothero would give of Moscow. . . .

He laughed abruptly.

And with that laugh Prothero dropped out of Benham's world for a space of years. There may have been other letters, but if so they were lost in the heaving troubles of a revolution-strained post-office. Perhaps to this day they linger sere and yellow in some forgotten pigeon-hole in Kishinev or Ekaterinoslav. . . .

§ 17

In November, after an adventure in the traders' quarter of Kieff which had brought him within an inch of death, and because an emotional wave had swept across him and across his correspondence with Amanda, Benham went back suddenly to England and her. He wanted very greatly to see her, and also he wanted to make certain arrangements about his property. He returned by way of Hungary, and sent telegrams like shouts of excitement whenever the train stopped for a sufficient time. 'Old Leopard, I am coming, I am coming,' he telegraphed, announcing his coming for the fourth time. It was to be the briefest of visits, very passionate, the mutual refreshment of two noble lovers, and then he was returning to Russia again.

Amanda was at Chexington, and there he found her installed in the utmost dignity of expectant maternity. Like many other people he had been a little disposed to regard the bearing of children as a common human experience; at Chexington he came to think of it as a rare and sacramental function. Amanda had become very beautiful in quiet, gray, dove-like tones; her sun-touched boy's complexion had given way to a soft glow of the utmost loveliness, her brisk little neck that had always reminded him of the stalk of a flower was now softened and rounded; her eyes were tender, and she moved about the place in the manner of one who is vowed to a great sacrifice. She dominated the scene, and Lady Marayne, with a certain astonishment in her eyes and a smouldering disposition to irony, was the half-sympathetic, half-resentful priestess of her daughter-in-law's unparalleled immolation. The *motif* of motherhood was everywhere, and at his bedside he found—it had been put there for him by Amanda—among much other exaltation of woman's mission, that most wonderful of all philoprogenitive stories, Hudson's *Crystal Age*.

Everybody at Chexington had an air of being grouped about the impending fact. An epidemic of internal troubles, it is true, kept Sir Godfrey in the depths of London society, but to make up for his absence Mrs Morris had taken a little cottage down by the river and the Wilder girls were with her, both afire with fine and subtle feelings, and both, it seemed, and more particularly Betty, prepared to be keenly critical of Benham's attitude.

He did a little miss his cue in these exaltations, because he had returned in a rather different vein of exaltation.

In missing it he was assisted by Amanda herself, who had at moments an effect upon him of a priestess confidentially disrobed. It was as if she put aside for him something official, something sincerely maintained, necessary, but at times a little irksome. It was as if she was glad to take him into her confidence and unbend. Within the pre-natal Amanda an impish Amanda still lingered.

There were aspects of Amanda that it was manifest dear Betty must never know. . . . .

But the real Amanda of that November visit even in her most unpontifical moods did not quite come up to the imagined Amanda who had drawn him home across Europe. At times she was extraordinarily jolly. They had two or three happy walks about the Chexington woods; that year the golden weather of October had flowed over into November, and except for a carpet of green and gold under the horse-chestnuts most of the leaves were still on the trees. Gleams of her old wanton humour shone on him. And then would come something else, something like a shadow across the world, something he had quite forgotten since his idea of heroic love had flooded him, something that reminded him of those long explanations with Mr Rathbone-Sanders that had never been explained, and of the curate in the doorway of the cottage and his unaccountable tears.

On the afternoon of his arrival at Chexington he was a little surprised to find Sir Philip Easton coming through the house into the garden, with an accustomed familiarity. Sir Philip perceived him with a start that was instantly controlled, and greeted him with unnatural ease.

Sir Philip, it seemed, was fishing and reading and playing cricket in the neighbourhood, which struck Benham as a poor way of spending the summer, the sort of soft holiday a man learns to take from scholars and literary men. A man like Sir Philip, he thought, ought to have been aviating or travelling.

Moreover, when Sir Philip greeted Amanda it seemed to Benham that there was a flavour of established association in their manner. But then Sir Philip was also very assiduous with Lady Marayne. She called him 'Pip,' and afterwards Amanda called across the tennis-court to him, 'Pip!' And then he called her 'Amanda.' When the Wilder girls came up to join the tennis he was just as brotherly. . . .

The next day he came to lunch.

During that meal Benham became more aware than he had ever been before of the peculiar deep expressiveness of this young man's eyes. They watched him and they watched Amanda with a solicitude that seemed at once pained and tender. And there was something about Amanda, a kind of hard brightness, an impartiality and an air of something undefinably suspended, that gave Benham an intuitive certitude that that afternoon Sir Philip would be spoken to privately, and that then he would pack up and go away in a state of illumination from Chexington. But before he could be spoken to he contrived to speak to Benham.

They were left to smoke after lunch, and then it was he

took advantage of a pause to commit his little indiscretion.

'Mrs Benham,' he said, 'looks amazingly well—extraordinarily well, don't you think?'

'Yes,' said Benham, startled. 'Yes. She certainly keeps very well.'

'She misses you terribly,' said Sir Philip; 'it is a time when a woman misses her husband. But, of course, she does not want to hamper your work. . . .'

Benham felt it was very kind of him to take so intimate an interest in these matters, but on the spur of the moment he could find no better expression for this than a grunt.

'You don't mind,' said the young man with a slight catch in the breath that might have been apprehensive, 'that I sometimes bring her books and flowers and things? Do what little I can to keep life interesting down here? It's not very congenial. . . . She's so wonderful. I think she is the most wonderful woman in the world.'

Benham perceived that so far from being a modern aristocrat he was really a primitive barbarian in these matters.

'I've no doubt,' he said, 'that my wife has every reason to be grateful for your attentions.'

In the little pause that followed Benham had a feeling that Sir Philip was engendering something still more personal. If so, he might be constrained to invert very gently but very firmly the bowl of chrysanthemums over Sir Philip's head, or kick him in an improving manner. He had a ridiculous belief that Sir Philip would probably take anything of the sort very touchingly. He scrambled in his mind for some remark that would avert this possibility.

'Have you ever been in Russia?' he asked hastily. 'It is the most wonderful country in Europe. I had an odd adventure near Kiev. During a pogrom.'

And he drowned the developing situation in a flood of description. . . .

But it was not so easy to drown the little things that were presently thrown out by Lady Marayne. They were so much more in the air. . . .

§ 18

Sir Philip suddenly got out of the picture even as Benham had foreseen.

'Easton has gone away,' he remarked three days later to Amanda.

'I told him to go. He is a bore with you about. . . .
But otherwise he is rather a comfort, Cheetah.' She
meditated upon Sir Philip. 'And he's an *honourable* man,'
she said. He's safe. . . .'

§ 19

After that visit it was that the notes upon love and sex
began in earnest. The scattered memoranda upon the
perfectness of heroic love for the modern aristocrat ended
abruptly. Instead there came the first draft for a study
of jealousy. The note was written in pencil on Chexington
notepaper and manifestly that had been supported on the
ribbed cover of a book. There was a little computation
in the corner, converting forty-five degrees Réaumur into
degrees Fahrenheit, which made White guess it had been
written in the Red Sea. But, indeed, it had been written
in a rather amateurishly stoked corridor-train on Benham's
journey to the gathering revolt in Moscow. . . .

'I think I have been disposed to underrate the force of
sexual jealousy. . . . I thought it was something essentially
contemptible, something that one dismissed and put
behind oneself in the mere effort to be aristocratic, but I
begin to realise that it is not quite so easily settled with. . . .

'One likes to know. . . Possibly one wants to know too
much. . . . In phases of fatigue, and particularly in
phases of sleeplessness, when one is leaving all that one
cares for behind, it becomes an irrational torment. . . .

'And it is not only in oneself that I am astonished by the
power of this base motive. I see, too, in the queer business
of Prothero how strongly jealousy, how strongly the sense
of proprietorship, weighs with a man. . . .

'There is no clear reason why one should insist upon
another human being being one's ownest own—utterly
one's own. . . .

'There is, of course, no clear reason for most human
motives. . . .

'One does. . . .

'There is something dishonouring in distrust—to both
the distrusted and the one who distrusts. . . .'

After that, apparently, it had been too hot and stuffy
to continue.

§ 20

Benham did not see Amanda again until after the birth of their child. He spent his Christmas in Moscow, watching the outbreak, the fitful fighting and the subsequent breakup, of the revolution, and taking care of a lost and helpless English family whose father had gone astray temporarily on the way home from Baku. Then he went southward to Rostov and thence to Astrakhan. Here he really began his travels. He determined to get to India by way of Herat, and for the first time in his life rode out into an altogether lawless wilderness. He went on obstinately because he found himself disposed to funk the journey, and because discouragements were put in his way. He was soon quite cut off from all the ways of living he had known. He learnt what it is to be flea-bitten, saddle-sore, hungry and, above all, thirsty. He was haunted by a dread of fever, and so contrived strange torments for himself with over-doses of quinine. He ceased to be traceable from Chexington in March, and he reappeared in the form of a telegram from Karachi demanding news in May. He learnt he was the father of a man-child and that all was well with Amanda.

He had not expected to be so long away from any communication with the outer world, and something in the nature of a stricken conscience took him back to England. He found a second William Porphyry in the world, dominating Chexington, and Amanda tenderly triumphant and passionate, the Madonna enthroned. For William Porphyry he could feel no emotion. William Porphyry was very red and ugly and protesting, feeble and aggressive, a matter for a skilled nurse. To see him was to ignore him and dispel a dream. It was to Amanda Benham turned again.

For some days he was content to adore his Madonna and listen to the familiar flatteries of her love. He was a leaner, riper man, Amanda said, and wiser, so that she was afraid of him. . . .

And then he became aware that she was requiring him to stay at her side. 'We have both had our adventures,' she said, which struck him as an odd phrase.

It forced itself upon his obstinate incredulity that all those conceptions of heroic love and faithfulness he had supposed to be so clearly understood between them had vanished from her mind. She had absolutely forgotten that twilight moment at the window which had seemed to him the crowning instant, the real marriage of their lives. It had gone, it had left no recoverable trace in her. And upon his interpretations of that he had loved her passionately for a year. She was back at exactly the ideas and intentions that ruled her during their first settlement in London. She wanted a joint life in the social world of London, she demanded his presence, his attention, the daily practical evidences of love. It was all very well for him to be away when the child was coming, but now everything was different. Now he must stay by her.

This time he argued no case. These issues he had settled for ever. Even an indignant dissertation from Lady Marayne, a dissertation that began with appeals and ended in taunts, did not move him. Behind these things now was India. The huge problems of India had laid an unshakeable hold upon his imagination. He had seen Russia, and he wanted to balance that picture by a vision of the East. . . .

He saw Easton only once during a week-end at Chexington. The young man displayed no further disposition to be confidentially sentimental. But he seemed to have something on his mind. And Amanda said not a word about him. He was a young man above suspicion, Benham felt. . . .

And from his departure the quality of the correspondence of these two larger carnivores began to change. Except for the repetition of accustomed endearments, they ceased to be love-letters in any sense of the word. They dealt chiefly with the 'Cub,' and even there Benham felt presently that the enthusiasm diminished. A new amazing quality for Amanda appeared—triteness. The very writing of her letters changed as though it had suddenly lost backbone. Her habitual liveliness of phrasing lost its point. Had she lost her animation? Was she ill unknowingly? Where had the light gone? It was as if her attention was distracted. . . . As if every day when she wrote her mind was busy about something else.

Abruptly at last he understood. A fact that had never been stated, never formulated, never in any way admitted, was suddenly pointed to convergently by a thousand indicating fingers, and beyond question perceived to be *there*. . . .

He left a record of that moment of realisation.

'Suddenly one night I woke up and lay still, and it was as if I had never seen Amanda before. Now I saw her plainly, I saw her with that same dreadful clearness that sometimes comes at dawn, a pitiless, a scientific distinctness that has neither light nor shadow. . . .

'Of course,' I said, and then presently I got up very softly. . . .

'I wanted to get out of my intolerable, close, personal cabin. I wanted to feel the largeness of the sky. I went out upon the deck. We were off the coast of Madras, and when I think of that moment, there comes back to me also the faint flavour of spice in the air, the low line of the coast, the cool flooding abundance of the Indian moonlight, the swish of the black water against the side of the ship. And a perception of infinite loss, as if the limitless heavens above this earth and below to the very uttermost star were just one boundless cavity from which delight had fled. . . . .

'Of course I had lost her. I knew it with absolute certainty. I knew it from her insecure temperament, her adventurousness, her needs. I knew it from every line she had written me in the last three months. I knew it intuitively. She had been unfaithful. She must have been unfaithful.

'What had I been dreaming about to think that it would not be so?'

§ 21

'Now let me write down plainly what I think of these matters. Let me be at least honest with myself, whatever self-contradictions I may have been led into by force of my passions. Always I have despised jealousy. . . .

'Only by the conquest of four natural limitations is the aristocratic life to be achieved. They come in a certain order, and in that order the spirit of man is armed against them less and less efficiently. Of fear and my struggle against fear I have told already. I am fearful. I am a physical coward until I can bring shame and anger to my assistance, but in overcoming fear I have been helped by the whole body of human tradition. Every one, the basest creatures, every Hottentot, every stunted creature that ever breathed poison in a slum, knows that the instinctive constitution of man is at fault here and that fear is shameful and must be subdued. The race is on one's side. And so there is a vast traditional support for a man against the Second Limitation, the limitation of physical indulgence. It is not so universal as the first; there is a grinning bawling humour on the side of grossness, but common pride is against it. And in this matter my temperament has been my help : I am fastidious, I eat little, drink little, and feel a shivering recoil from excess. It is no great virtue; it happens so; it is something in the nerves of my skin. I cannot endure myself unshaven or in any way unclean; I am tormented by dirty hands or dirty blood or dirty memories, and after I had once loved Amanda I could not—unless some irrational impulse to get equal with her had caught me—have broken my faith to her, whatever breach there was in her faith to me. . . .

'I see that in these matters I am cleaner than most men and more easily clean; and it may be that it is in the vein of just that distinctive virtue that I fell so readily into a passion of resentment and anger.

'I despised a jealous man. There is a traditional discredit of jealousy, not so strong as that against cowardice, but still very strong. But the general contempt of jealousy is curiously wrapped up with the supposition that there is no cause for jealousy, that it is unreasonable suspicion. Given a cause then tradition speaks with an uncertain voice. . . .

'I see now that I despised jealousy because I assumed that it was impossible for Amanda to love any one but me; it was intolerable to imagine anything else, I insisted upon believing that she was as fastidious as myself and as faithful as myself, made indeed after my image, and I went on disregarding the most obvious intimations that she was not, until that still moment in the Indian Ocean, when silently, gently as a drowned body might rise out of the depths of a pool, that knowledge of love dead and honour gone for ever floated up into my consciousness.

'And then I felt that Amanda had cheated me! Outrageously. Abominably.

'Now, so far as my intelligence goes, there is not a cloud upon this question. My demand upon Amanda was outrageous and I had no right whatever to her love or loyalty. I must have that very clear. . . .

'This aristocratic life, as I conceive it, must be, except accidentally here and there, incompatible with the domestic life. It means going hither and thither in the universe of thought as much as in the universe of matter, it means adventure, it means movement and adventure that must needs be hopelessly encumbered by an inseparable associate, it means self-imposed responsibilities that will not fit into the welfare of a family. In all ages, directly society had risen above the level of a barbaric tribal village, this need of a release from the family for certain necessary types of

people has been recognised. It was met sometimes in-
formally, sometimes formally, by the growth and establishment of special classes and orders, of priests, monks, nuns,
of pledged knights, of a great variety of non-family people,
whose concern was the larger collective life that opens out
beyond the simple necessities and duties and loyalties of
the steading and of the craftsman's house. Sometimes,
but not always, that release took the form of celibacy; but
besides that there have been a hundred institutional
variations of the common life to meet the need of the
special man, the man who must go deep and the man who
must go far. A vowed celibacy ceased to be a tolerable
rule for an aristocracy directly the eugenic idea entered
the mind of man, because a celibate aristocracy means the
abandonment of the racial future to a proletariat of base
unleaderly men. That was plain to Plato. It was plain to
Campanella. It was plain to the Protestant reformers.
But the world has never yet gone on to the next step beyond
that recognition, to the recognition of feminine aristocrats,
rulers and the mates of rulers, as untrammelled by domestic
servitudes and family relationships as the men of their
kind. That I see has always been my idea since in my
undergraduate days I came under the spell of Plato. It
was a matter of course that my first gift to Amanda should
be his *Republic*. I loved Amanda transfigured in that
dream. . . .

'There are no such women. . . .

'It is no excuse for me that I thought she was like-
minded with myself. I had no sound reason for supposing
that. I did suppose that, I did not perceive that not only
was she younger than myself, but that while I had been
going through a mill of steely education, kept close, severely
exercised, polished by discussion, she had but the weak
training of a not very good school, some scrappy reading,
the vague discussions of village artists, and the draped and
decorated novelties of the "advanced." It all went to
nothing on the impact of the world. . . . She showed
herself the woman the world has always known, no miracle,
and the alternative was for me to give myself to her in
the ancient way, to serve her happiness, to control her and
delight and companion her, or to let her go. . . .

'The normal woman centres upon herself; her mission
is her own charm and her own beauty and her own setting;
her place is her home. She demands the concentration
of a man. Not to be able to command that is her failure.

Not to give her that is to shame her. As I had shamed Amanda. . . .'

§ 22

'There are no such women.' He had written this in and struck it out, and then at some later time written it in again. There it stayed now as his last persuasion, but it set White thinking and doubting. And, indeed, there was another sheet of pencilled broken stuff that seemed to glance at quite another type of womanhood.

§ 23

'It is clear that the women aristocrats who must come to the remaking of the world will do so in spite of limitations at least as great as those from which the aristocratic spirit of man escapes. These women must become aristocratic through their own innate impulse, they must be self-called to their lives, exactly as men must be; there is no making an aristocrat without a predisposition for rule and nobility. And they have to discover and struggle against just exactly the limitations that we have to struggle against. They have to conquer not only fear but indulgence, indulgence of a softer, more insidious quality, and jealousy—proprietorship. . . .

'It is as natural to want a mate as to want bread, and a thousand times in my work and in my wanderings I have thought of a mate and desired a mate. A mate—not a possession. It is a need almost naïvely simple. If only one could have a woman who thought of one and with one ! Though she were on the other side of the world and busied about a thousand things. . . .

'"*With* one,'" I see it must be rather than "*of* one." That "of one" is just the unexpurgated egotistical demand coming back again. . . .

'Man is a mating creature. It is not good to be alone. But mating means a mate. . . .

'We should be lovers, of course; that goes without saying. . . .

'And yet not specialised lovers, not devoted, *attending* lovers. "Dancing attendance"—as they used to say. We should meet upon our ways as the great carnivores do. . . .

'That at any rate was a sound idea. Though we only played with it.

'But that mate desire is just a longing that can have no possible satisfaction now for me. What is the good of dreaming? Life and chance have played a trick upon my body and soul. I am mated, though I am mated to a phantom. I loved and I love Amanda, not Easton's Amanda, but Amanda in armour, the Amanda of my dreams. Sense, and particularly the sense of beauty, lies deeper than reason in us. There can be no mate for me now unless she comes with Amanda's voice and Amanda's face and Amanda's quick movements and her clever hands. . . .

§ 24

'Why am I so ungrateful to her still for all the happiness she gave me?

'There were things between us two as lovers—love, things more beautiful than anything else in the world, things that set the mind hunting among ineffectual images in a search for impossible expression, images of sunlight shining through blood-red petals, images of moonlight in a scented garden, of marble gleaming in the shade, of far-off wonderful music heard at dusk in a great stillness, of fairies dancing softly, of floating happiness and stirring delights, of joys as keen and sudden as the knife of an assassin, assassin's knives made out of tears, tears that are happiness; wordless things; and surprises, expectations, gratitudes, sudden moments of contemplation, the sight of a soft eyelid closed in sleep, shadowy tones in the sound of a voice heard unexpectedly; sweet, dear magical things that I can find no words for. . . .

'If she was a goddess to me, should it be any affair of mine that she was not a goddess to herself; that she could hold all this that has been between us more cheaply than I did? It does not change one jot of it for me. At the time she did not hold it cheaply. She forgets where I do not forget. . . .'

§ 25

Such were the things that Benham could think and set down.

Yet for whole days he was possessed by the thought of killing Amanda and himself.

He did not at once turn homeward. It was in Ceylon that he dropped his work and came home. At Colombo he found a heap of letters awaiting him, and there were two of these that had started at the same time. They had been posted in London on one eventful afternoon. Lady Marayne and Amanda had quarrelled violently. Two earnest, flushed, quick-breathing women, full of neat but belated repartee, separated to write their simultaneous letters. Each letter trailed the atmosphere of that truncated encounter. Lady Marayne told her story ruthlessly. Amanda, on the other hand, generalised, and explained. Sir Philip's adoration of her was a love-friendship, it was beautiful, it was pure. Was there no trust nor courage in the world? She would defy all jealous scandal. She would not even banish him from her side. Surely the Cheetah could trust her. But the pitiless facts of Lady Marayne went beyond Amanda's explaining. The little lady's dignity had been stricken. 'I have been used as a cloak,' she wrote.

Her phrases were vivid. She quoted the very words of Amanda, words she had overheard at Chexington in the twilight. They were no invention. They were the very essence of Amanda, the lover. It was as sure as if Benham had heard the sound of her voice, as if he had peeped and seen, as if she had crept by him, stooping and rustling softly. It brought back the living sense of her, excited, flushed, reckless; his wild-haired Amanda of infinite delight. . . .

All day those words of hers pursued him. All night they flared across the black universe. He buried his face in the pillows and they whispered softly in his ear.

He walked his room in the darkness longing to smash and tear.

He went out from the house and shook his ineffectual fists at the stirring quiet of the stars.

He sent no notice of his coming back. Nor did he come back with a definite plan. But he wanted to get at Amanda.

§ 26

It was with Amanda he had to reckon. Towards Easton he felt scarcely any anger at all. Easton he felt only existed for him because Amanda willed to have it so.

Such anger as Easton did arouse in him was a contemptuous anger. His devotion filled Benham with scorn. His determination to serve Amanda at any price, to bear the grossest humiliations and slights for her, his humility, his service and tenderness, his care for her moods and happiness, seemed to Benham a treachery to human nobility. That rage against Easton was like the rage of a trade-unionist against a blackleg. Are all the women to fall to the men who will be their master-slaves and keepers? But it was not simply that Benham felt men must be freed from this incessant attendance; women too must free themselves from their almost instinctive demand for an attendant. . . .

His innate disposition was to treat women as responsible beings. Never in his life had he thought of a woman as a pretty thing to be fooled and won and competed for and fought over. So that it was Amanda he wanted to reach and reckon with now, Amanda who had mated and ruled his senses only to fling him into this intolerable pit of shame and jealous fury. But the forces that were driving him home now were the forces below the level of reason and ideas, organic forces compounded of hate and desire, profound aboriginal urgencies. He thought, indeed, very little as he lay in his berth or sulked on deck; his mind lay waste under a pitiless invasion of exasperating images that ever and again would so wring him that his muscles would tighten and his hands clench or he would find himself restraining a snarl, the threat of the beast, in his throat.

Amanda grew upon his imagination until she over-shadowed the whole world. She filled the skies. She bent over him and mocked him. She became a mystery of passion and dark beauty. She was the sin of the world. One breathed her in the winds of the sea. She had taken to herself the greatness of elemental things. . . .

So that when at last he saw her he was amazed to see her, and see that she was just a creature of common size and quality, a rather tired and very frightened-looking white-faced young woman, in an evening-dress of un-familiar fashion, with little common trinkets of gold and colour about her wrists and neck.

In that instant's confrontation he forgot all that had brought him homeward. He stared at her as one stares at a stranger whom one has greeted in mistake for an intimate friend.

For he saw that she was no more the Amanda he hated and desired to kill than she had ever been the Amanda he had loved.

§ 27

He took them by surprise. It had been his intention to take them by surprise. Such is the inelegance of the jealous state.

He reached London in the afternoon and put up at a hotel near Charing Cross. In the evening about ten he appeared at the house in Lancaster Gate. The butler was deferentially amazed. Mrs Benham was, he said, at a theatre with Sir Philip Easton, and he thought some other people also. He did not know when she would be back. She might go on to supper. It was not the custom for the servants to wait up for her.

Benham went into the study that reduplicated his former rooms in Finacue Street and sat down before the fire the butler lit for him. He sent the man to bed, and fell into profound meditation.

It was nearly two o'clock when he heard the sound of her latchkey and went out at once upon the landing.

The half-door stood open and Easton's car was outside. She stood in the middle of the hall and relieved Easton of the gloves and fan he was carrying.

'Good-night,' she said, 'I am so tired.'

'My wonderful goddess,' he said.

She yielded herself to his accustomed embrace, then started, stared, and wrenched herself out of his arms.

Benham stood at the top of the stairs looking down upon them, white-faced and inexpressive. Easton dropped back a pace. For a moment no one moved nor spoke, and then very quietly Easton shut the half-door and shut out the noises of the road.

For some seconds Benham regarded them, and as he did so his spirit changed. . . .

Everything he had thought of saying and doing vanished out of his mind.

He stuck his hands into his pockets and descended the staircase. When he was five or six steps above them, he spoke. 'Just sit down here,' he said, with a gesture of one hand, and sat down himself upon the stairs. '*Do* sit down,' he said with a sudden testiness as they continued standing. 'I know all about this affair. Do please sit down and let us talk. . . . Everybody's gone to bed long ago.'

'Cheetah!' she said. 'Why have you come back like this?'

Then at his mute gesture she sat down at his feet.

'I wish you would sit down, Easton,' he said in a voice of subdued savagery.

'Why have you come back?' Sir Philip Easton found his voice to ask.

'*Sit* down,' Benham spat, and Easton obeyed unwillingly.

'I came back,' Benham went on, 'to see to all this. Why else? I don't—now I see you—feel very fierce about it. But it has distressed me. You look changed, Amanda, and fagged. And your hair is untidy. It's as if something had happened to you and made you a stranger. . . . You two people are lovers. Very natural and simple, but I want to get out of it. Yes, I want to get out of it. That wasn't quite my idea, but now I see it is. It's queer, but on the whole I feel sorry for you. All of us, poor humans—— There's reason to be sorry for all of us. We're full of lusts and uneasiness and resentments that we haven't the will to control. What do you two people want me to do to you? Would you like a divorce, Amanda? It's the clean, straight thing, isn't it? Or would the scandal hurt you?'

Amanda sat crouched together, with her eyes on Benham.

'Give us a divorce,' said Easton, looking to her to confirm him.

Amanda shook her head.

'I don't want a divorce,' she said.

'Then what do you want?' asked Benham with sudden asperity.

'I don't want a divorce,' she repeated. 'Why do you, after a long silence, come home like this, abruptly, with no notice?'

'It was the way it took me,' said Benham, after a little interval.

'You have left me for long months.'

'Yes. I was angry. And it was ridiculous to be angry. I thought I wanted to kill you, and now I see you I see that all I want to do is to help you out of this miserable mess—and then get away from you. You two would like to marry. You ought to be married.'

'I would die to make Amanda happy,' said Easton.

'Your business, it seems to me, is to live to make her happy. That you may find more of a strain. Less tragic and more tiresome. I, on the other hand, want neither to die nor live for her.' Amanda moved sharply. 'It's extraordinary what amazing vapours a lonely man may get into his head. If you don't want a divorce then I suppose things might go on as they are now.'

'I hate things as they are now,' said Easton.   'I hate this falsehood and deception.'

'You would hate the scandal just as much,' said Amanda.

'I would not care what the scandal was unless it hurt you.'

'It would be only a temporary inconvenience,' said Benham.   'Every one would sympathise with you. . . . The whole thi g is so natural. . . . People would be glad to forget very soon.   They did with my mother.'

'No,' said Amanda, 'it isn't so easy as that.'

She seemed to come to a decision.

'Pip,' she said.   'I want to talk to—*him*—alone.'

Easton's brown eyes were filled with distress and perplexity.   'But why?' he asked.

'I do,' she said.

'But this is a thing for *us*.'

'Pip, I want to talk to him alone.   There is something—something I can't say before you. . . .'

Sir Philip rose slowly to his feet.

'Shall I wait outside?'

'No, Pip.   Go home.   Yes—there are some things you must leave to me.'

She stood up too and turned so that she and Benham both faced the younger man.   The strangest uneasiness mingled with his resolve to be at any cost splendid.   He felt—and it was a most unexpected and disconcerting feeling—that he was no longer confederated with Amanda; that prior, more fundamental and greater associations prevailed over his little new grip upon her mind and senses. He stared at husband and wife aghast in this realisation. Then his resolute romanticism came to his help.   'I would trust you——' he began.   'If you tell me to go——'

Amanda seemed to measure her hold upon him.

She laid her hand upon his arm.   'Go, my dear Pip,' she said.   'Go.'

He had a moment of hesitation, of anguish, and it seemed to Benham as though he eked himself out with unreality, as though somewhen, somewhere, he had seen something of the sort in a play and filled in a gap that otherwise he could not have supplied.

Then the door had closed upon him, and Amanda, pale and darkly dishevelled, faced her husband, silently and intensely.

'*Well ?*' said Benham.

She held out her arms to him.

'Why did you leave me, Cheetah?   Why did you leave me?'

§ 28

Benham affected to ignore those proffered arms. But they recalled in a swift rush the animal anger that had brought him back to England. To remind him of desire now was to revive an anger stronger than any desire. He spoke seeking to hurt her.

'I am wondering now,' he said, 'why the devil I came back.'

'You had to come back to me.'

'I could have written just as well about these things.'

'*Cheetah*,' she said softly, and came towards him slowly, stooping forward and looking into his eyes, 'you had to come back to see your old Leopard. Your wretched Leopard. Who has rolled in the dirt. And is still yours.'

'Do you want a divorce? How are we to fix things, Amanda?'

'Cheetah, I will tell you how we will fix things.'

She dropped upon the step below him. She laid her hands with a deliberate softness upon him, she gave a toss so that her disordered hair was a little more disordered, and brought her soft chin down to touch his knees. Her eyes implored him.

'Cheetah,' she said. 'You are going to forgive.'

He sat rigid, meeting her eyes.

'Amanda,' he said at last, 'you would be astonished if I kicked you away from me and trampled over you to the door. That is what I want to do.'

'Do it,' she said, and the grip of her hands tightened. 'Cheetah dear! I would love you to kill me.'

'I don't want to kill you.'

Her eyes dilated. 'Beat me.'

'And I haven't the remotest intention of making love to you,' he said, and pushed her soft face and hands away from him as if he would stand up.

She caught hold of him again. 'Stay with me,' she said.

He made no effort to shake off her grip. He looked at the dark cloud of her hair that had ruled him so magically, and the memory of old delights made him grip a great handful almost inadvertently as he spoke. 'Dear Leopard,' he said, 'we humans are the most streaky of conceivable things. I thought I hated you. I do. I hate you like poison. And also I do not hate you at all.'

Then abruptly he was standing over her.

She rose to her knees.

'Stay here, old Cheetah!' she said. 'This is your house. I am your wife.'

He went towards the unfastened front door.

'Cheetah!' she cried with a note of despair.

He halted at the door.

'Amanda, I will come to-morrow. I will come in the morning, in the sober London daylight, and then we will settle things.'

He stared at her, and to her amazement he smiled. He spoke as one who remarks upon a quite unexpected fact. . .

'Never in my life, Amanda, have I seen a human being that I wanted so little to kill.'

§ 29

White found a fragment that might have been written within a week of those last encounters of Benham and Amanda.

'The thing that astonished me most in Amanda was the change in her mental quality.

'With me in the old days she had always been a sincere person; she had deceived me about facts, but she had never deceived me about herself. Her personal, stark frankness had been her essential strength. And it was gone. I came back to find Amanda an accomplished actress, a thing of poses and calculated effects. She was a surface, a sham, a Lorelei. Beneath that surface I could not discover anything individual at all. Fear and a grasping quality, such as God gave us all when He gave us hands; but the individual I knew, the humorous wilful Spotless Leopard was gone. Whither, I cannot imagine. An amazing disappearance. Clean out of space and time like a soul lost for ever.

'When I went to see her in the morning, she was made up for a scene, she acted an intricate part, never for a moment was she there in reality. . . .

'I have got a remarkable persuasion that she lost herself in this way, by cheapening love, by making base love to a lover she despised. . . . There can be no inequality in love. Give and take must balance. One must be one's natural self or the whole business is an indecent trick, a vile use of life! To use inferiors in love one must needs talk down to them, interpret oneself in their insufficient phrases, pretend, sentimentalise. And it is clear that unless oneself is to be lost, one must be content to leave alone all those people that one can reach only by sentimentalising. But Amanda—and yet somehow I love her for it still—could not leave any one alone. So she was always feverishly weaving nets of false relationship. Until her very self was forgotten. So she will go on until the end. With Easton it had been necessary for her to key herself to a simple exalted romanticism that was entirely insincere. She had so accustomed herself to these poses that her innate gestures were forgotten. She could not recover them; she could not even reinvent them. Between us there were momentary gleams as though presently we should be our frank former selves again. They were never more than momentary. . . .'

And that was all that this astonishing man had seen fit to tell of his last parting from his wife.

Perhaps he did Amanda injustice. Perhaps there was a stronger thread of reality in her desire to recover him than he supposed. Clearly he believed that under the circumstances Amanda would have tried to recover anybody.

She had dressed for that morning's encounter in a very becoming and intimate wrap of soft mauve and white silk, and she had washed and dried her dark hair so that it was a vapour about her face. She set herself with a single mind to persuade herself and Benham that they were inseparable lovers, and she would not be deflected by his grim determination to discuss the conditions of their separation. When he asked her whether she wanted a divorce, she offered to throw over Sir Philip and banish him for ever as lightly as a great lady might sacrifice an objectionable poodle to her connubial peace.

Benham passed through perplexing phases, so that she herself began to feel that her practice with Easton had spoilt her hands. His initial grimness she could understand and partially its breakdown into irritability. But she was puzzled by his laughter. For he laughed abruptly.

'You know, Amanda, I came home in a mood of tremendous tragedy. And really—you are a Lark.'

And then overriding her altogether, he told her what he meant to do about their future and the future of their little son.

'You don't want a divorce and a fuss. Then I'll leave things. I perceive I've no intention of marrying any more. But you'd better do the straight thing. People forget and forgive. Especially when there is no one about making a fuss against you.

'Perhaps, after all, there is something to be said for shirking it. We'll both be able to get at the boy then. You'll not hurt him, and I shall want to see him. It's better for the boy anyhow not to have a divorce.

'I'll not stand in your way. I'll get a little flat and I shan't come too much to London, and when I do, you can get out of town. You must be discreet about Easton, and if people say anything about him, send them to me. After all, this is our private affair.

'We'll go on about money matters as we have been going. I trust to you not to run me into overwhelming debts. And, of course, if at any time, you do want to marry—on account of children or anything—if nobody knows of this conversation we can be divorced then. . . .'

Benham threw out these decisions in little dry sentences while Amanda gathered her forces for her last appeal.

It was an unsuccessful appeal, and at the end she flung herself down before him and clung to his knees. He struggled ridiculously to get himself clear, and when at last he succeeded she dropped prostrate on the floor with her dishevelled hair about her.

She heard the door close behind him, and still she lay there, a dark Guinevere, until with a start she heard a step upon the thick carpet without. He had come back. The door reopened. There was a slight pause, and then she raised her face and met the blank stare of the second housemaid. There are moments, suspended fragments of time rather than links in its succession, when the human eye is more intelligible than any words.

The housemaid made a rapid apologetic noise and vanished with a click of the door.

'*Damn !*' said Amanda.

Then slowly she rose to her knees.

She meditated through vast moments.

'It's a cursed thing to be a woman,' said Amanda.

She stood up. She put her hand on the telephone in the corner and then she forgot about it. After another long interval of thought she spoke.

'Cheetah !' she said, 'old Cheetah ! . . .

'I didn't *think* it of you. . . .'

Then presently with the even joyless movements of one who does a reasonable business, with something indeed of the manner of one who packs a trunk, she rang up Sir Philip Easton.

§ 30

The head chambermaid on the first floor of the Westwood Hotel in Danebury Street had a curious and perplexing glimpse of Benham's private processes the morning after this affair.

Benham had taken Room 27 on the afternoon of his return to London. She had seen him twice or three times, and he had struck her as a coldly decorous person, tall, white-faced, slow speaking; the last man to behave violently or surprise a head chambermaid in any way. On the morning of his departure she was told by the first-floor waiter that the occupant of Room 26 had complained of an uproar in the night, and almost immediately she was summoned to see Benham.

He was standing facing the door and in a position which did a little obscure the condition of the room behind him. He was carefully dressed, and his manner was more cold and decorous than ever. But one of his hands was tied up in a white bandage.

'I am going this morning,' he said; 'I am going down now to breakfast. I have had a few little accidents with some of the things in the room and I have cut my hand. I want you to tell the manager and see that they are properly charged for on the bill. . . . Thank you.'

The head chambermaid was left to consider the accidents.

Benham's things were all packed up and the room had an air of having been straightened up neatly and methodically after a destructive cataclysm. One or two items that the chambermaid might possibly have overlooked in the normal course of things were carefully exhibited. For example, the sheet had been torn into half a dozen strips and they were lying side by side on the bed. The clock on the mantelpiece had been knocked into the fireplace and then pounded to pieces. All the looking-glasses in the room were smashed, apparently the electric lamp that stood on the night table by the bedside had been wrenched off and flung or hammered about amidst the other break-ables. And there was a considerable amount of blood splashed about the room. The head chambermaid felt unequal to the perplexities of the spectacle and summoned her most convenient friend, the head chambermaid on the third floor, to her aid. The first-floor waiter joined their deliberations and several housemaids displayed a respectful interest in the matter. Finally they invoked the manager.

He was still contemplating the scene of the disorder when the precipitate retreat of his subordinates warned him of Benham's return.

Benham was smoking a cigarette and his bearing was reassuringly tranquil.

'I had a kind of nightmare,' he said. 'I am fearfully sorry to have disarranged your room. You must charge me for the inconvenience as well as for the damage.'

§ 31

'An aristocrat cannot be a lover.

'One cannot serve at once the intricacies of the wider issues of life and the intricacies of another human being. I do not mean that one may not love. One loves the more because one does not concentrate one's love. One loves nations, the people passing in the street, beasts hurt by the wayside, troubled scoundrels and university dons in tears. . . .

'But if one does not give one's whole love and life into a woman's hands I do not think one can expect to be loved.

'An aristocrat must do without close personal love. . . .'

This much was written at the top of a sheet of paper. The writing ended halfway down the page. Manifestly it was an abandoned beginning. And it was, it seemed to White, the last page of all this confusion of matter that dealt with the Second and Third Limitations. Its incompleteness made its expression perfect. . . .

There Benham's love experience ended. He turned to the great business of the world. Desire and Jealousy should deflect his life no more; like Fear they were to be dismissed as far as possible and subdued when they could not be altogether dismissed. Whatever stirrings of blood or imagination there were in him after that parting, whatever failures from this resolution, they left no trace on the rest of his research, which was concerned with the hates of peoples and classes and war and peace and the possibilities science unveils and starry speculations of what mankind may do.

§ 32

But Benham did not leave England again until he had had an encounter with Lady Marayne.

The little lady came to her son in a state of extraordinary anger and distress. Never had she seemed quite so resolute nor quite so hopelessly dispersed and mixed. And when for a moment it seemed to him that she was not as a matter of fact dispersed and mixed at all, then with an instant eagerness he dismissed that one elucidatory gleam. 'What are you doing in England, Poff?' she demanded. 'And what are you going to do?

'Nothing! And you are going to leave her in your house, with your property and a lover. If that's it, Poff, why did you ever come back? And why did you ever marry her? You might have known; her father was a swindler. She's begotten of deceit. She'll tell her own story while you are away, and a pretty story she'll make of it.'

'Do you want me to divorce her and make a scandal?'

'I never wanted you to go away from her. If you'd stayed and watched her as a man should, as I begged you and implored you to do—— Didn't I tell you, Poff? Didn't I warn you?'

'But now what am I to do?'

'There you are! That's just a man's way. You get yourself into this trouble, you follow your passions and your fancies and fads and then you turn to me! How can I help you now, Poff? If you'd listened to me before!'

Her blue eyes were demonstratively round.

'Yes, but——'

'I warned you,' she interrupted. 'I warned you. I've done all I could for you. It isn't that I haven't seen through her. When she came to me at first with that made-up story of a baby! And all about loving me like her own mother. But I did what I could. I thought we might still make the best of a bad job. And then—— I might have known she couldn't leave Pip alone. . . . But for weeks I didn't dream. I wouldn't dream. Right under my nose. The impudence of it!'

Her voice broke. 'Such a horrid mess! Such a hopeless, horrid mess!'

She wiped away a bright little tear. . . .

'It's all alike. It's your way with us. All of you. There isn't a man in the world deserves to have a woman in the world. We do all we can for you. We do all we can to amuse you, we dress for you and we talk for you. All the sweet, warm little women there are! And then you go away from us! There never was a woman yet who pleased and satisfied a man, who did not lose him. Give you everything and off you must go! Lovers, mothers. . . .'

It dawned upon Benham dimly that his mother's troubles did not deal exclusively with himself.

'But Amanda,' he began.

'If you'd looked after her properly, it would have been right enough. Pip was as good as gold until she undermined him. . . . A woman can't wait about like an umbrella in a stand. . . . He was just a boy. . . . Only of course there she was—a novelty. It is perfectly easy to understand. She flattered him. . . Men are such fools.'

'Still—it's no good saying that now.'

'But she'll spend all your money, Poff! She'll break your back with debts. What's to prevent her? With him living on her! For that's what it comes to practically.'

'Well, what am I to do?'

'You aren't going back without tying her up, Poff? You ought to stop every farthing of her money—every farthing. It's your duty.'

'I can't do things like that.'

'But have you no Shame? To let that sort of thing go on!'

'If I don't feel the Shame of it—— And I don't.'

'And that money—— I got you that money, Poff! It was my money.'

Benham stared at her perplexed. 'What am I to do?' he asked.

'Cut her off, you silly boy! Tie her up! Pay her through a solicitor. Say that if she sees him *once* again——!'

He reflected. 'No,' he said at last.

'Poff!' she cried, 'every time I see you, you are more and more like your father. You're going off—just as he did. That baffled, *mulish* look—priggish—solemn! Oh! it's strange the stuff a poor woman has to bring into the world. But you'll do nothing. I know you'll do nothing. You'll stand everything, You—you Cuckold! And she'll drive by me, she'll pass me in theatres with the money that ought to have been mine! Oh! Oh!'

She dabbed her handkerchief from one swimming eye to the other. But she went on talking. Faster and faster, less and less coherently; more and more wildly abusive. Presently in a brief pause of the storm Benham sighed profoundly. . . .

It brought the scene to a painful end. . . .

For weeks her distress pursued and perplexed him.

He had an extraordinary persuasion that in some obscure way he was in default, that he was to blame for her distress, that he owed her—he could never define what he owed her.

And yet, what on earth was one to do?

And something his mother had said gave him the odd idea that he had misjudged his father, that he had missed depths of perplexed and kindred goodwill. He went down to see him before he returned to India. But if there was a hidden well of feeling in Mr Benham, senior, it had been very carefully boarded over. The parental mind and attention were entirely engaged in a dispute in the *School World* about the heuristic method. Somebody had been disrespectful to Martindale House, and the thing was rankling almost unendurably. It seemed to be a relief to him to show his son very fully the essentially illogical position of his assailant. He was entirely inattentive to Benham's carefully made conversational opportunities. He would be silent at times while Benham talked, and then he would break out suddenly with : ' What seems to me so unreasonable, so ridiculous, in the whole of that fellow's second argument—if one can call it an argument——. . . A man who reasons as he does is bound to get laughed at. If people will only see it. . . .'

CHAPTER THE SIXTH

THE NEW HAROUN AL RASCHID

§ 1

BENHAM corresponded with Amanda until the summer of 1913. Sometimes the two wrote coldly to one another, sometimes with warm affection, sometimes with great bitterness. When he met White in Johannesburg during the strike period of 1913, he was on his way to see her in London and to settle their relationship upon a new and more definite footing. It was her suggestion that they should meet.

About her he felt an enormous, inexorable dissatisfaction. He could not persuade himself that his treatment of her and that his relations to her squared with any of his pre-conceptions of nobility, and yet at no precise point could he detect where he had definitely taken an ignoble step. Through Amanda he was coming to the full experience of life. Like all of us he had been prepared, he had prepared himself, to take life in a certain way, and life had taken him, as it takes all of us, in an entirely different and unexpected way. . . . He had been ready for noble deeds and villainies, for achievements and failures, and here as the dominant fact of his personal life was a perplexing riddle. He could not hate and condemn her for ten minutes at a time without a flow of exoneration; he could not think of her tolerantly or lovingly without immediate shame and resentment, and with the utmost will in the world he could not banish her from his mind.

During the intervening years he had never ceased to have her in his mind; he would not think of her, it is true, if he could help it, but often he could not help it; and as a negative presence, as a thing denied, she was almost more potent than she had been as a thing accepted. Meanwhile he worked. His nervous irritability increased, but it did not hinder the steady development of his Research.

Long before his final parting from Amanda he had worked out his idea and method for all the more personal problems in life; the problems he put together under his headings of the first three 'Limitations.' He had resolved to emancipate himself from fear, indulgence, and that instinctive preoccupation with the interests and dignity of self which he chose to term Jealousy, and with the one tremendous exception of Amanda he had to a large extent succeeded. Amanda. Amanda. Amanda. He stuck the more grimly to his Research to drown that beating in his brain.

Emancipation from all these personal things he held now to be a mere prelude to the real work of a man's life, which was to serve this dream of a larger human purpose. The bulk of his work was to discover and define that purpose, that purpose which must be the directing and comprehending form of all the activities of the noble life. One cannot be noble, he had come to perceive, at large; one must be noble to an end. To make human life, collectively and in detail, a thing more comprehensive, more beautiful, more generous and coherent than it is to-day seemed to him the fundamental intention of all nobility. He believed more and more firmly that the impulses to make and help and subserve great purposes are abundantly present in the world, that they are inhibited by hasty thinking, limited thinking and bad thinking, and that the real ennoblement of human life was not so much a creation as a release. He lumped the preventive and destructive forces that keep men dispersed, unhappy and ignoble under the heading of Prejudice; and he made this Prejudice his fourth and greatest and most difficult limitation. In one place he had written it, 'Prejudice or Divisions.' That being subdued in oneself and in the world, then in the measure of its subjugation, the new life of our race, the great age, the noble age, would begin.

So he set himself to examine his own mind and the mind of the world about him for prejudice, for hampering follies, disguised disloyalties and mischievous distrusts; and the great bulk of the papers that White struggled with at Westhaven Street were devoted to various aspects of this search for 'Prejudice.' It seemed to White to be at once the most magnificent and the most preposterous of enterprises. It was indeed no less than an inquiry into all the preventible sources of human failure and disorder. . . . And it was all too manifest to White also that the last place in which Benham was capable of detecting a prejudice was at the back of his own head. . . .

Under this Fourth Limitation he put the most remarkable array of influences, race-hatred, national suspicion, the evil side of patriotism, religious and social intolerance, every social consequence of muddle-headedness, every dividing force indeed except the purely personal dissensions between man and man. And he developed a metaphysical interpretation of these troubles. 'No doubt,' he wrote in one place, 'much of the evil between different kinds of men is due to uncultivated feeling, to natural bad feeling, but far more is it due to bad thinking ' At times he seemed on the verge of the persuasion that most human trouble is really due to bad metaphysics. It was, one must remark, an extraordinary journey he had made; he had started from chivalry and arrived at metaphysics; every knight he held must be a logician, and ultimate bravery is courage of the mind. One thinks of his coming to this conclusion with knit brows and balancing intentness above whole gulfs of bathos—very much as he had once walked the Leysin Bisse. . . .

'Men do not know how to think,' he insisted—getting along the planks; 'and they will not realise that they do not know how to think. Nine-tenths of the wars in the world have arisen out of misconceptions. . . . Misconception is the sin and dishonour of the mind, and muddle thinking as ignoble as dirty conduct. . . . Infinitely more disastrous.'

And again he wrote: 'Man, I see, is an over-practical

creature, too eager to get into action. There is our deepest trouble. He takes conclusions ready-made, or he makes them in a hurry. Life is so short that he thinks it better to err than wait. He has no patience, no faith in anything but himself. He thinks he is a being when in reality he is only a link in a being, and so he is more anxious to be complete than right. The last devotion of which he is capable is that devotion of the mind which suffers partial performance, and before he is dead it is already being abandoned and begun all over again by some one else in the same egotistical haste. . . .'

It is, I suppose, a part of the general humour of life that these words should have been written by a man who walked the plank to fresh ideas with the dizziest difficulty unless he had Prothero to drag him forward, and who acted time after time with an altogether disastrous hastiness.

§ 2

Yet there was a kind of necessity in this journey of Benham's from the cocked hat and wooden sword of Seagate and his early shame at cowardice and baseness to the spiritual megalomania of his complete Research Magnificent. You can no more resolve to live a life of honour nowadays and abstain from social and political scheming on a world-wide scale, than you can profess religion and refuse to think about God. In the past it was possible to take all sorts of things for granted and be loyal to unexamined things. One could be loyal to unexamined things because they were unchallenged things. But now everything is challenged. By the time of his second visit to Russia, Benham's ideas of conscious and deliberate aristocracy reaching out to an idea of universal responsibility had already grown into the extraordinary fantasy that he was, as it were, an uncrowned king in the world. To be noble is to be aristocratic, that is to say a ruler. Thence it follows that aristocracy is multiple kingship, and to be an aristocrat is to partake both of the nature of philosopher and king. . . .

Yet it is manifest that the powerful people of this world are by no means necessarily noble, and that most modern kings, poor in quality, petty in spirit, conventional in outlook, controlled and limited, fall far short of kingship. Nevertheless, there *is* nobility, there *is* kingship, or this earth is a dustbin and mankind but a kind of skin-disease upon a planet. From that it is an easy step to this idea, the idea whose first expression had already so touched the imagination of Amanda, of a sort of diffused and voluntary kingship scattered throughout mankind. The aristocrats are not at the high table, the kings are not enthroned, those who are enthroned are but pretenders and *simulacra*, kings of the vulgar; the real king and ruler is every man who sets aside the naïve passions and self-interest of the common life for the rule and service of the world.

This is an idea that is now to be found in much contemporary writing. It is one of those ideas that seem to appear simultaneously at many points in the world, and it is impossible to say now how far Benham was an originator of this idea, and how far he simply resonated to its expression by others. It was far more likely that Prothero, getting it heaven knows where, had spluttered it out and forgotten it, leaving it to germinate in the mind of his friend. . . .

This lordly, this kingly dream became more and more essential to Benham as his life went on. When Benham walked the Bisse he was just a youngster resolved to be individually brave; when he prowled in the jungle by night he was there for all mankind. With every year he became more and more definitely to himself a consecrated man as kings are consecrated. Only that he was self-consecrated, and anointed only in his heart. At last he was, so to speak Haroun al Raschid again, going unsuspected about the world, because the palace of his security would not tell him the secrets of men's disorders. He was no longer a creature of circumstances; he was kingly, unknown, Alfred in the camp of the Danes. In the great later accumulations of his Research the personal matter, the introspection, the intimate discussion of motive, becomes less and less. He forgets himself in the exaltation of kingliness. He worries less and less over the particular rightness of his definite acts. In these later papers White found Benham abstracted, self-forgetful, trying to find out with an ever increased self-detachment, with an ever deepening regal solicitude, why there are massacres, wars, tyrannies and persecutions, why we let famine, disease and beasts assail us and want dwarf and cripple vast multitudes in the midst of possible plenty. And when he found out, and as far as he found out, he meant quite simply and earnestly to apply his knowledge. . . .

§ 3

The intellectualism of Benham intensified to the end. His definition of Prejudice impressed White as being the most bloodless and philosophical formula that ever dominated the mind of a man.

'Prejudice,' Benham had written, 'is that common incapacity of the human mind to understand that a difference in any respect is not a difference in all respects, reinforced and rendered malignant by an instinctive hostility to what is unlike ourselves. We exaggerate classification and then charge it with mischievous emotion by referring it to ourselves.' And under this comprehensive formula he proceeded to study and attack Family Prejudice, National Prejudice, Race Prejudice, War, Class Prejudice, Professional Prejudice, Sex Prejudice, in the most industrious and elaborate manner. Whether one regards oneself or others he held that these prejudices are evil things. 'From the point of view of human welfare they break men up into wars and conflicts, make them an easy prey to those who trade upon suspicion and hostility, prevent sane collective co-operations, cripple and embitter life. From the point of view of personal aristocracy they make men vulgar, violent, unjust and futile. All the conscious life of the aristocrat must be a constant struggle against false generalisations; it is as much his duty to free himself from that as from fear, indulgence, and jealousy; it is a larger and more elaborate task, but it is none the less cardinal and essential. Indeed it is more cardinal and essential. The true knight has to be not only no coward, no self-pamperer, no egotist. He has to be a philosopher. He has to be no hasty or foolish thinker. His judgment no more than his courage is to be taken by surprise.

'To subdue fear, desire and jealousy is the aristocrat's personal affair, it is his ritual and discipline, like a knight watching his arms; but the destruction of division and prejudice and all their forms and establishments is his real task, that is the common work of knighthood. It is a task to be done in a thousand ways; one man working by persuasion, another by example, this one overthrowing some crippling restraint upon the freedom of speech and the spread of knowledge, and that preparing himself for a war that will shatter a tyrannous presumption. Most imaginative literature, all scientific investigation, all sound criticism, all good building, all good manufacture, all sound politics, every honesty and every reasoned kindliness, contribute to this release of men from the heat and confusions of our present world. '

It was clear to White that as Benham progressed with this major part of his research, he was more and more possessed by the idea that he was not making his own personal research alone, but, side by side with a vast, masked, hidden and once unsuspected multitude of others; that this great idea of his was under kindred forms the great idea of thousands, that it was breaking as the dawn breaks, simultaneously to great numbers of people, and that the time was not far off when the new aristocracy, the disguised rulers of the world, would begin to realise their common bent and effort. Into these latter papers there creeps more and more frequently a new phraseology, such expressions as the 'Invisible King' and the 'Spirit of Kingship,' so that as Benham became personally more and more solitary, his thoughts became more and more public and social.

Benham was not content to define and denounce the prejudices of mankind. He set himself to study just exactly how these prejudices worked, to get at the nature and habits and strengths of each kind of prejudice, and to devise means for its treatment, destruction or neutralisation. He had no great faith in the power of pure reasonableness; his psychological ideas were modern, and he had grasped the fact that the power of most of the great prejudices that strain humanity lies deeper than the intellectual level. Consequently he sought to bring himself into the closest contact with prejudices in action and prejudices in conflict in order to discover their sub-rational springs.

A large proportion of that larger moiety of the material at Westhaven Street which White from his extensive experience of the public patience decided could not possibly 'make a book,' consisted of notes and discussions upon the first-hand observations Benham had made in this or that part of the world. He began in Russia during the revolutionary trouble of 1906, he went thence to Odessa, and from place to place in Bessarabia and Kieff, where during a pogrom he had his first really illuminating encounter with race and culture prejudice. His examination of the social and political condition of Russia seems to have left him much more hopeful then was the common feeling of liberal-minded people during the years of depression that followed the revolution of 1906, and it was upon the race question that his attention concentrated.

The Swadeshi outbreak drew him from Russia to India. Here in an entirely different environment was another discord of race and culture, and he found in his study of it much that illuminated and corrected his impressions of the Russian issue. A whole drawer was devoted to a comparatively finished and very thorough inquiry into human dissensions in lower Bengal. Here there were not only race but culture conflicts, and he could work particularly upon the differences between men of the same race who were Hindus, Christians, and Mahometans respectively. He could compare the Bengali Mahometan not only with the Bengali Brahminist, but also with the Mahometan from the north-west. 'If one could scrape off all the creed and training, would one find much the same thing at the bottom or something fundamentally so different that no close homogeneous social life and not even perhaps a life of just compromise is possible between the different races of mankind?'

His answer to that was a confident one. 'There are no such natural and unalterable differences in character and quality between any two sorts of men whatever, as would make their peaceful and kindly co-operation in the world impossible,' he wrote.

But he was not satisfied with his observations in India. He found the prevalence of caste ideas anti-pathetic and complicating. He went on after his last parting from Amanda into China, it was the first of several visits to China, and thence he crossed to America. White found a number of American press-cuttings of a vehemently anti-Japanese quality still awaiting digestion in a drawer, and it was clear to him that Benham had given a considerable amount of attention to the development of the 'white' and 'yellow' race hostility on the Pacific slope; but his chief interest at that time had been the negro. He went to Washington and thence south; he visited Tuskeegee and Atlanta, and then went off at a tangent to Hayti. He was drawn to Hayti by Hesketh Pritchard's vivid book, *Where Black Rules White,* and like Hesketh Pritchard he was able to visit that wonderful monument to kingship, the hidden fastness of La Ferrière, the citadel built a century ago by the 'Black Napoleon,' the Emperor Christophe. He went with a young American demonstrator from Harvard.

§ 4

It was a memorable excursion. They rode from Cap Haytien for a day's journey along dusty uneven tracks through a steaming plain of luxurious vegetation, that presented the strangest mixture of unbridled jungle with populous country. They passed countless villages of thatched huts alive with curiosity and swarming with naked black children, and yet all the time they seemed to be in a wilderness. They forded rivers, they had at times to force themselves through thickets, once or twice they lost their way, and always ahead of them, purple and sullen, the great mountain peak with La Ferrière upon its crest rose slowly out of the background until it dominated the landscape. Long after dark they blundered upon rather than came to the village at its foot where they were to pass the night. They were interrogated under a flaring torch by peering ragged black soldiers, and passed through a firelit crowd into the presence of the local commandant to dispute volubly about their right to go further. They might have been in some remote corner of Nigeria. Their papers, laboriously got in order, were vitiated by the fact which only became apparent by degrees, that the commandant could not read. They carried their point with difficulty.

But they carried their point, and, watched and guarded by a hungry half-naked negro in a kepi and the remains of a sky-blue pair of trousers, they explored one of the most exemplary memorials of imperialism that humanity has ever made. The roads and parks and prospects constructed by this vanished Emperor of Hayti had long since disappeared, and the three men clambered for hours up ravines and precipitous jungle tracks, occasionally crossing the winding traces of a choked and ruined road that had once been the lordly approach to his fastness. Below they passed an abandoned palace of vast extent, a palace with great terraces and the still traceable outline of gardens, though there were green things pushing between the terrace steps, and trees thrust out of the empty windows. Here from a belvedere of which the skull-like vestige still remained, the negro Emperor Christophe, after fourteen years of absolute rule, had watched for a time the smoke of the burning of his cane-fields in the plain below, and then, learning that his bodyguard had deserted him, had gone in and blown out his brains.

He had christened the place, after the best of examples, 'Sans Souci.'

But the citadel above, which was to have been his last defence, he never used. The defection of his guards made him abandon that. To build it, they say, cost Hayti thirty thousand lives. He had the true Imperial lavishness. So high it was, so lost in a wilderness of trees and bush, looking out over a land relapsed now altogether to a barbarism of patch and hovel, so solitary and chill under the tropical sky—for even the guards who still watched over its suspected treasures feared to live in its ghostly galleries and had made hovels outside its walls—and at the same time so huge and grandiose—there were walls thirty feet thick, galleries with scores of rust-eaten cannon, circular dining-halls, king's apartments and queen's apartments, towering battlements and great arched doorways—that it seemed to Benham to embody the power and passing of that miracle of human history, tyranny, the helpless bowing of multitudes before one man and the transitoriness of such glories, more completely than anything he had ever seen or imagined in the world before. Beneath the battlements—they were choked above with jungle grass and tamarinds and many flowery weeds—the precipice fell away a sheer two thousand feet, and below spread a vast rich green plain populous and diversified, bounded at last by the blue sea, like an amethystine wall. Over this precipice Christophe was wont to fling his victims, and below this terrace were bottle-shaped dungeons where men, broken and torn, thrust in at the neck-like hole above, starved and died; it was his headquarters here, here he had his torture chambers and the means for nameless cruelties. . . .

'Not a hundred years ago,' said Benham's companion, and told the story of the disgraced favourite, the youth who had offended.

'Leap,' said his master, and the poor hypnotised wretch after one questioning glance at the conceivable alternatives made his last gesture of servility, and then stood out against the sky, swayed, and with a convulsion of resolve, leapt and shot headlong down through the shimmering air.

Came presently the little faint sound of his fall.

The Emperor, satisfied, turned away, unmindful of the fact that this projectile he had launched had caught among the bushes below, and presently struggled and found itself still a living man. It could scramble down to the road and, what is more wonderful, hope for mercy. An hour and it stood before Christophe again, with an arm broken and bloody and a face torn, a battered thing now but with a faint flavour of pride in its bearing. 'Your bidding has been done, Sire,' it said.

'So,' said the Emperor unappeased. 'And you live? Well—— Leap again . . . .'

And then came other stories. The young man told them as he had heard them, stories of ferocious wholesale butcheries, of men standing along the walls of the banqueting chamber to be shot one by one as the feast went on, of exquisite and terrifying cruelties, and his one note of wonder, his refrain was, '*Here !* Not a hundred years ago. . . . . It makes one almost believe that somewhere things of this sort are being done now.'

They ate their lunch together amidst the weedy flowery ruins. The lizards which had fled their coming crept out again to bask in the sunshine. The soldier-guide and guard scrabbled about with his black fingers in the ruinous and rifled tomb of Christophe in a search for some saleable memento. . . .

Benham sat musing in silence. The thought of deliberate cruelty was always an actual physical distress to him. He sat bathed in the dreamy afternoon sunlight and struggled against the pictures that crowded into his mind, pictures of men aghast at death, and of fear-driven men toiling in agony, and of the shame of extorted obedience and of cringing and crawling black figures, and the defiance of righteous hate beaten down under blow and anguish. He saw eyes alight with terror and lips rolled back in agony, he saw weary hopeless flight before striding proud destruction, he saw the poor trampled mangled dead, and he shivered in his soul. . . .

He hated Christophe and all that made Christophe; he hated pride, and then the idea came to him that it is not pride that makes Christophes but humility.

There is in the medley of man's composition, deeper far than his superficial working delusion that he is a separated self-seeking individual, an instinct for co-operation and obedience. Every natural sane man wants, though he may want it unwittingly, kingly guidance, a definite direction for his own partial life. At the bottom of his heart he feels, even if he does not know it definitely, that his life is partial. He is driven to join himself on. He obeys decision and the appearance of strength as a horse obeys its rider's voice. One thinks of the pride, the un-controlled frantic will of this black ape of all Emperors, and one forgets the universal docility that made him possible. Usurpation is a crime to which men are tempted by human dirigibility. It is the orderly peoples who create tyrants, and it is not so much restraint above as stiff insubordination below that has to be taught to men. There are kings and tyrannies and imperialisms, simply because of the unkingliness of men.

And as he sat upon the battlements of La Ferrière, Benham cast off from his mind his last tolerance for earthly kings and existing States, and expounded to another human being for the first time this long-cherished doctrine of his of the Invisible King who is the lord of human destiny, the spirit of nobility, who will one day take the sceptre and rule the earth. . . . . To the young American's naïve American response to any simply felt emotion, he seemed with his white earnestness and his glowing eyes a veritable prophet. . . .

'This is the root idea of aristocracy,' said Benham.

'I have never heard the underlying spirit of democracy, the real true Thing in democracy, so thoroughly expressed,' said the young American.

§ 5

Benham's notes on race and racial cultures gave White tantalising glimpses of a number of picturesque experiences. The adventure in Kieff had first roused Benham to the reality of racial quality. He was caught in the wheels of a pogrom.

'Before that time I had been disposed to minimise and deny race. I still think it need not prevent men from the completest social co-operation, but I see now better than I did how difficult it is for any man to purge from his mind the idea that he is not primarily a Jew, a Teuton, or a Kelt, but a man. You can persuade any one in five minutes that he or she belongs to some special and blessed and privileged sort of human being; it takes a lifetime to destroy that persuasion. There are these confounded differences of colour, of eye and brow, of nose or hair, small differences in themselves except that they give a foothold and founda-tion for tremendous fortifications of prejudice and tradition, in which hostilities and hatreds may gather. When I think of a Jew's nose, a Chinaman's eyes, or a negro's colour I am reminded of that fatal little pit which nature has left in the vermiform appendix, a thing no use in itself and of no significance, but a gathering-place for mischief. The extremest case of race-feeling is the Jewish case; and even here, I am convinced, it is the Bible and the Talmud and the exertions of those inevitable professional champions who live upon racial feeling, far more than their common distinction of blood, which holds this people together banded against mankind.'

Between the lines of such general propositions as this White read little scraps of intimation that linked with the things Benham let fall in Johannesburg to reconstruct the Kieff adventure.

Benham had been visiting a friend in the country on the further side of the Dnieper. As they drove back along dusty stretches of road amidst fields of corn and sunflower and through bright little villages, they saw against the evening blue under the full moon a smoky red glare rising from amidst the white houses and dark trees of the town. 'The pogrom's begun,' said Benham's friend, and was surprised when Benham wanted to end a pleasant day by going to see what happens after the beginning of a pogrom.

He was to have several surprises before at last he left Benham in disgust and went home by himself.

For Benham, with that hastiness that so flouted his exalted theories, passed rapidly from an attitude of impartial inquiry to active intervention. The two men left their carriage and plunged into the network of unlovely dark streets in which the Jews and traders harboured. . . . Benham's first intervention was on behalf of a crouching and yelping bundle of humanity that was being dragged about and kicked at a street corner. The bundle resolved itself into a filthy little old man, and made off with extraordinary rapidity, while Benham remonstrated with the kickers. Benham's tallness, his very Gentile face, his good clothes, and an air of tense authority about him had its effect, and the kickers shuffled off with remarks that were partly apologies. But Benham's friend revolted. This was no business of theirs.

Benham went on unaccompanied towards the glare of the burning houses.

For a time he watched. Black figures moved between him and the glare, and he tried to find out the exact nature of the conflict by inquiries in clumsy Russian. He was told that the Jews had insulted a religious procession, that a Jew had spat at an ikon, that the shop of a cheating Jew trader had been set on fire, and that the blaze had spread to the adjacent group of houses. He gathered that the Jews were running out of the burning block on the other side 'like rats.' The crowd was mostly composed of town roughs with a sprinkling of peasants. They were mischievous but undecided. Among them were a number of soldiers, and he was surprised to see a policeman, brightly lit from head to foot, watching the looting of a shop that was still untouched by the flames.

He held back some men who had discovered a couple of women's figures slinking along in the shadow beneath a wall. Behind his remonstrances the Jewesses escaped. His anger against disorder was growing upon him. . . .

Late that night Benham found himself the leading figure amidst a party of Jews who had made a counter attack upon a gang of roughs in a court that had become the refuge of a crowd of fugitives. Some of the young Jewish men had already been making a fight, rather a poor and hopeless fight, from the windows of the house near the entrance of the court, but it is doubtful if they would have made an effective resistance if it had not been for this tall excited stranger who was suddenly shouting directions to them in sympathetically murdered Russian. It was not that he brought powerful blows or subtle strategy to their assistance, but that he put heart into them and perplexity into his adversaries because he was so manifestly non-partisan. Nobody could ever have mistaken Benham for a Jew. When at last towards dawn a not too zealous governor called out the troops and began to clear the streets of rioters, Benham and a band of Jews were still keeping the gateway of that court behind a hasty but adequate barricade of furniture and hand-barrows.

The ghetto could not understand him, nobody could understand him, but it was clear a rare and precious visitor had come to their rescue, and he was implored by a number of elderly, dirty, but very intelligent-looking old men to stay with them and preserve them until their safety was assured.

They could not understand him, but they did their utmost to entertain him and assure him of their gratitude. They seemed to consider him as a representative of the British Government, and foreign intervention on their behalf is one of those unfortunate fixed ideas that no persecuted Jews seem able to abandon.

Benham found himself, refreshed and tended, sitting beside a wood fire in an inner chamber richly flavoured by humanity and listening to a discourse in evil but understandable German. It was a discourse upon the wrongs and the greatness of the Jewish people—and it was delivered by a compact middle-aged man with a big black beard and long-lashed but animated eyes. Beside him a very old man dozed and nodded approval. A number of other men crowded the apartment, including several who had helped to hold off the rioters from the court. Some could follow the talk and ever and again endorsed the speaker in Yiddish or Russian; others listened with tantalised expressions, their brows knit, their lips moving.

It was a discourse Benham had provoked. For now he was at the very heart of the Jewish question, and he could get some light upon the mystery of this great hatred at first hand. He did not want to hear tales of outrages, of such things he knew, but he wanted to understand what was the irritation that caused these things.

So he listened. The Jew dilated at first on the harmlessness and usefulness of the Jews.

'But do you never take a certain advantage?' Benham threw out.

'The Jews are cleverer than the Russians. Must we suffer for that?'

The spokesman went on to the more positive virtues of his race. Benham suddenly had that uncomfortable feeling of the Gentile who finds a bill being made against him. Did the world owe Israel nothing for Philo, Aron ben Asher, Solomon Gabriol, Halévy, Mendelssohn, Heine, Meyerbeer, Rubinstein, Joachim, Zangwill? Does Britain owe nothing to Lord Beaconsfield, Montefiore, or the Rothschilds? Can France repudiate her debt to Fould, Gaudahaux, Oppert, or Germany to Fürst, Steinschneider, Herxheimer, Lasker, Auerbach, Traube and Lazarus and Benfey? . . .

Benham admitted under the pressure of urgent tones and gestures that these names did undoubtedly include the cream of humanity, but was it not true that the Jews did press a little financially upon the inferior peoples whose lands they honoured in their exile?

The man with the black beard took up the challenge bravely.

'They are merciful creditors,' he said. 'And it is their genius to possess and control. What better stewards could you find for the wealth of nations than the Jews. And for the honours? That always had been the rôle of the Jews—stewardship. Since the days of Joseph in Egypt . . .'

Then in a lower voice he went on to speak of the deficiencies of the Gentile population. He wished to be just and generous, but the truth was the truth. The Christian Russians loved drink and laziness; they had no sense of property; were it not for unjust laws even now the Jews would possess all the land of South Russia. . . .

Benham listened with a kind of fascination. 'But,' he said.

It was so. And with a confidence that aroused a protest or so from the onlookers, the Jewish apologist suddenly rose up, opened a safe close beside the fire and produced an armful of documents.

'Look!' he said, 'all over South Russia there are these!'

Benham was a little slow to understand, until half a dozen of these papers had been thrust into his hand. Eager fingers pointed, and several voices spoke. These things were illegalities that might some day be legal; there were the records of loans and hidden transactions that might at any time put all the surrounding soil into the hands of the Jew. All South Russia was mortgaged. . . .

'But is it so?' asked Benham, and for a time ceased to listen and stared into the fire.

Then he held up the papers in his hand to secure silence and, feeling his way in unaccustomed German, began to speak and continued to speak in spite of a constant insurgent undertone of interruption from the Jewish spokesman.

All men, Benham said, were brothers. Did they not remember Nathan the Wise?

'I did not claim him,' said the spokesman, misunderstanding. 'He is a character in fiction.'

But all men are brothers, Benham maintained. They had to be merciful to one another and give their gifts freely to one another. Also they had to consider each other's weaknesses. The Jews were probably justified in securing and administering the property of every community into which they came, they were no doubt right in claiming to be best fitted for that task; but also they had to consider, perhaps more than they did, the feelings and vanities of the host population into which they brought these beneficent activities. What was said of the ignorance, incapacity and vice of the Roumanians and Russians was very generally believed and accepted, but it did not alter the fact that the peasant, for all his incapacity, did like to imagine he owned his own patch and hovel and did have a curious irrational hatred of debt. . . .

The faces about Benham looked perplexed.

'*This*,' said Benham, tapping the papers in his hand. 'They will not understand the ultimate benefit of it. It will be a source of anger and fresh hostility. It does not follow because your race has supreme financial genius that you must always follow its dictates to the exclusion of other considerations. . . .'

The perplexity increased.

Benham felt he must be more general. He went on to emphasise the brotherhood of man, the right to equal opportunity, equal privilege, freedom to develop their idiosyncrasies as far as possible, unhindered by the idiosyncrasies of others. He could feel the sympathy and understanding of his hearers returning. 'You see,' said Benham, 'you must have generosity. You must forget ancient scores. Do you not see the world must make a fresh beginning?'

He was entirely convinced he had them with him. The heads nodded assent, the bright eyes and lips followed the slow disentanglement of his bad German.

'Free yourselves and the world,' he said.

Applause.

'And so,' he said, breaking unconsciously into English, 'let us begin by burning these *beastly* mortgages!'

And with a noble and dramatic gesture Benham cast his handful on the fire. The assenting faces became masks of horror. A score of hands clutched at those precious papers, and a yell of dismay and anger filled the room. Some one caught at his throat from behind. 'Don't kill him!' cried some one. 'He fought for us!' . . .

§ 6

An hour later Benham returned in an extraordinarily dishevelled and battered condition to his hotel. He found his friend in anxious consultation with the hotel proprietor.

'We were afraid that something had happened to you,' said his friend.

'I got a little involved,' said Benham.

'Hasn't some one clawed your cheek?'

'Very probably,' said Benham.

'And torn your coat? And hit you rather heavily upon the neck?'

'It was a complicated misunderstanding,' said Benham. 'Oh! pardon! I'm rather badly bruised upon that arm you're holding.'

§ 7

Benham told the story to White as a jest against himself.

'I see now of course that they could not possibly understand my point of view,' he said. . . .

'I'm not sure if they quite followed my German. . . .

'It's odd, too, that I remember saying, "Let's burn these mortgages," and at the time I'm almost sure I didn't know the German for mortgage. . . .'

It was not the only occasion on which other people had failed to grasp the full intention behind Benham's proceedings. His aristocratic impulses were apt to run away with his conceptions of brotherhood, and time after time it was only too manifest to White that Benham's pallid flash of anger had astonished the subjects of his disinterested observations extremely. His explorations in Hayti had been terminated abruptly by an affair with a native policeman that had necessitated the intervention of the British Consul. It was begun with that suddenness that was too often characteristic of Benham, by his hitting the policeman. It was in the main street of Cap Haytien, and the policeman had just clubbed an unfortunate youth over the head with the heavily loaded wooden club which is the normal instrument of Haytien discipline. His blow was a repartee, part of a triangular altercation in which a large, voluble, mahogany-coloured lady whose head was tied up in a blue handkerchief played a conspicuous part, but it seemed to Benham an entirely unjustifiable blow.

He allowed an indignation with negro policemen in general that had been gathering from the very moment of his arrival at Port-au-Prince to carry him away. He advanced with the kind of shout one would hurl at a dog, and smote the policeman to the earth with the stout stick that the peculiar social atmosphere of Hayti had disposed him to carry. By the local standard his blow was probably a trivial one, but the moral effect of his indignant pallor and a sort of rearing tallness about him on these occasions was always very considerable. Unhappily these characteristics could have no effect on a second negro policeman who was approaching the affray from behind, and he felled

Benham by a blow on the shoulder that was meant for the head, and with the assistance of his colleague overpowered him, while the youth and the woman vanished.

The two officials dragged Benham in a state of vehement protest to the lock-up, and only there, in the light of a superior officer's superior knowledge, did they begin to realise the grave fact of his British citizenship.

The memory of the destruction of the Haytien fleet by a German gunboat was still vivid in Port-au-Prince, and to that Benham owed it that in spite of his blank refusal to compensate the man he had knocked over, he was after two days of anger, two days of extreme insanitary experience, and much meditation upon his unphilosophical hastiness, released.

Quite a number of trivial incidents of a kindred sort diversified his inquiries into Indian conditions. They too turned for the most part on his facile exasperation at any defiance of his deep-felt desire for human brotherhood. At last indeed came an affair that refused ultimately to remain trivial, and tangled him up in a coil that invoked newspaper articles and heated controversies.

The effect of India upon Benham's mind was a peculiar mixture of attraction and irritation. He was attracted by the Hindu spirit of intellectualism and the Hindu repudiation of brutality, and he was infuriated by the spirit of caste that cuts the great world of India into a thousand futile little worlds, all aloof and hostile one to the other. 'I came to see India,' he wrote, 'and there is no India. There is a great number of Indias, and each goes about with its chin in the air, quietly scorning everybody else.'

His Indian adventures and his great public controversy on caste began with a tremendous row with an Indian civil servant who had turned an Indian gentleman out of his first-class compartment, and culminated in a disgraceful fracas with a squatting brown holiness at Benares, who had thrown aside his little brass bowlful of dinner because Benham's shadow had fallen upon it.

'You unendurable snob !' said Benham, and then lapsing into the forceful and inadvisable, 'By Heaven, you *shall* eat it ! . . .'

§ 8

Benham's detestation of human divisions and hostilities was so deep in his character as to seem almost instinctive.

But he had too a very clear reason for his hostility to all these amazing breaks in human continuity in his sense of the gathering dangers they now involve. They had always, he was convinced, meant conflict, hatred, misery, and the destruction of human dignity, but the new conditions of life that have been brought about by modern science were making them far more dangerous than they had ever been before. He believed that the evil and horror of war was becoming more and more tremendous with every decade, and that the free play of national prejudice and that stupid filching ambitiousness that seems to be inseparable from monarchy, were bound to precipitate catastrophe, unless a real international aristocracy could be brought into being to prevent it.

In the drawer full of papers labelled 'Politics,' White found a paper called 'The Metal Beast.' It showed that for a time Benham had been greatly obsessed by the thought of the armaments that were in those days piling up in every country in Europe. He had gone to Essen, and at Essen he had met a German who had boasted of Zeppelins and the great guns that were presently to smash the effete British fleet and open the Imperial way to London.

'I could not sleep,' he wrote, 'on account of this man and his talk and the streak of hatred in his talk. He distressed me not because he seemed exceptional, but because he seemed ordinary. I realised that he was more human than I was, and that only killing and killing could come out of such humanity. I thought of the great ugly guns I had seen, and of the still greater guns he had talked about, and how gloatingly he thought of the destruction they could do. I felt as I used to feel about that infernal stallion that had killed a man with its teeth and feet, a despairing fear, a sense of monstrosity in life. And this creature who had so disturbed me was only a beastly snuffy little man in an ill-fitting frock-coat, who laid his knife and fork by their tips on the edge of his plate, and picked his teeth with gusto and breathed into my face as he talked to me. The commonest of representative men. I went about that Westphalian country after that, with the conviction that headless, soulless, blood-drinking metal monsters were breeding all about me. I felt that science was producing a poisonous swarm, a nest of black dragons. They were crouching here and away there in France and England, they were crouching like beasts that bide their time, mewed up in forts, kennelled in arsenals, hooded in tarpaulins as hawks are hooded. . . . And I had never thought very much about them before, and there they were, waiting until some human fool like that frock-coated thing of spite, and fools like him multiplied by a million, saw fit to call them out to action. Just out of hatred and nationalism and faction. . . .'

Then came a queer fancy.

'Great guns, mines, battleships, all that cruelty-apparatus; I see it more and more as the gathering revenge of dead joyless matter for the happiness of life. It is a conspiracy of the lifeless, an enormous plot of the rebel metals against sensation. That is why in particular half-living people seem to love these things. La Ferrière was a fastness of the kind of tyranny that passes out of human experience, the tyranny of the strong man over men. Essen comes, the new thing, the tyranny of the strong machine. . . .

'Science is either slave or master. These people—I mean the German people and militarist people generally—have no real mastery over the scientific and economic forces on which they seem to ride. The monster of steel and iron carries Kaiser and Germany and all Europe captive. It has persuaded them to mount upon its back, and now they must follow the logic of its path. Whither? . . . Only kingship will ever master that beast of steel which has got loose into the world. Nothing but the sense of unconquerable kingship in us all will ever dare withstand it. . . . Men must be kingly aristocrats—it isn't *may* be now, it is *must* be—or these confederated metals, these things of chemistry and metallurgy, these explosives and mechanisms, will trample the blood and life out of our race into mere red-streaked froth and filth. . . .'

Then he turned to the question of this metallic beast's release. Would it ever be given blood?

'Men of my generation have been brought up in this threat of a great war that never comes; for forty years we have had it, so that it is with a note of incredulity that one tells oneself, 'After all this war may happen. But can it happen?'

He proceeded to speculate upon the probability whether a great war would ever devastate western Europe again, and it was very evident to White that he wanted very much to persuade himself against that idea. It was too disagreeable for him to think it probable. The paper was dated 1910. It was in October, 1914, that White, who was still working upon the laborious uncertain account of Benham's life and thought he has recently published, read what Benham had written. Benham concluded that the common sense of the world would hold up this danger until reason could get 'to the head of things.'

'There are already mighty forces in Germany,' Benham wrote, 'that will struggle very powerfully to avoid a war. And these forces increase. Behind the coarseness and the threatenings, the melodrama and the display of the vulgarer sort there arises a great and noble people. . . . I have talked with Germans of the better kind. . . . You cannot have a whole nation of Christophes. . . . There also the true knighthood discovers itself. . . . I do not believe this war will overtake us.'

'*Well!*' said White.

'I must go back to Germany and understand Germany better,' the notes went on.

But other things were to hold Benham back from that resolve. Other things were to hold many men back from similar resolves until it was too late for them. . . .

'It is preposterous that these monstrous dangers should lower over Europe, because a certain threatening vanity has crept into the blood of a people, because a few crude ideas go inadequately controlled. . . . Does no one see what that metallic beast will do if they once let it loose? It will trample cities; it will devour nations. . . .'

White read this on the 9th of October, 1914. One crumpled evening paper at his feet proclaimed in startled headlines : 'Rain of Incendiary Shells. Antwerp Ablaze.' Another declared untruthfully but impressively : 'Six Zeppelins drop Bombs over the Doomed City.' He had bought all the evening papers, and had read and re-read them and turned up maps and worried over strategic problems for which he had no data at all—as every one did at that time—before he was able to go on with Benham's manuscripts.

These pacific reassurances seemed to White's war-troubled mind like finding a flattened and faded flower, a girl's love-token, between the pages of some torn and scorched and blood-stained book picked out from a heap of loot after rapine and murder had had their fill. . . .

'How can we ever begin over again?' said White, and sat for a long time staring gloomily into the fire, forgetting forgetting, forgetting too that men who are tired and

weary die, and that new men are born to succeed
them. . . .

'We have to begin over again,' said White at last, and
took up Benham's papers where he had laid them down. . . .

§ 9

One considerable section of Benham's treatment of the
Fourth Limitation was devoted to what he called the
Prejudices of Social Position. This section alone was
manifestly expanding into a large treatise upon the psy-
chology of economic organisation. . . .

It was only very slowly that he had come to realise
the important part played by economic and class hostilities
in the disordering of human affairs. This was a very
natural result of his peculiar social circumstances. Most
people born to wealth and ease take the established industrial system as the natural method in human affairs; it is
only very reluctantly and by real feats of sympathy and
disinterestedness that they can be brought to realise that
it is natural only in the sense that it has grown up and come
about, and necessary only because nobody is strong and
clever enough to rearrange it. Their experience of it is a
satisfactory experience. On the other hand, the better
off one is, the wider is one's outlook and the more alert one
is to see the risks and dangers of international dissensions.
Travel and talk to foreigners open one's eyes to aggressive
possibilities; history and its warnings become conceivable.
It is in the nature of things that socialists and labour parties
should minimise international obligations and necessities,
and equally so that autocracies and aristocracies and pluto-
cracies should be negligent of and impatient about social
reform.

But Benham did come to realise this broader conflict
between worker and director, between poor man and
possessor, between resentful humanity and enterprise,
between unwilling toil and unearned opportunity. It is a
far profounder and subtler conflict than any other in
human affairs. 'I can foresee a time,' he wrote, 'when the
greater national and racial hatreds may all be so weakened
as to be no longer a considerable source of human limitation
and misery, when the suspicions of complexion and language
and social habit are allayed, and when the element of hatred
and aggression may be clean washed out of most religious
cults; but I do not begin to imagine a time, because I

cannot imagine a method, when there will not be great friction between those who employ, those who direct collective action, and those whose part it is to be the rank and file in industrialism. This, I know, is a limitation upon my confidence due very largely to the restricted nature of my knowledge of this sort of organisation. Very probably resentment and suspicion in the mass and self-seeking and dishonesty in the fortunate few are not so deeply seated, so necessary, as they seem to be, and if men can be cheerfully obedient and modestly directive in war time, there is no reason why ultimately they should not be so in the business of peace. But I do not understand the elements of the methods by which this state of affairs can be brought about.

'If I were to confess this much to an intelligent working man I know that at once he would answer "Socialism," but Socialism is no more a solution of this problem than eating is a solution when one is lost in the wilderness and hungry. Of course everybody with any intelligence wants Socialism; everybody, that is to say, wants to see all human efforts directed to the common good and a common end, but brought face to face with practical problems Socialism betrays a vast insufficiency of practical suggestions. I do not say that Socialism would not work, but I do say that so far Socialists have failed to convince me that they could work it. The substitution of a stupid official for a greedy proprietor may mean a vanished dividend, a limited output, and no other human advantage whatever. Socialism is in itself a mere eloquent gesture, inspiring, encouraging, perhaps, but beyond that not very helpful, towards the vast problem of moral and material adjustment before the race. That problem is incurably miscellaneous and intricate, and only by great multitudes of generous workers, one working at this point and one at that, secretly devoted knights of humanity, hidden and dispersed kings, unaware of one another, doubting each his right to count himself among those who do these kingly services, is this elaborate rightening of work and guidance to be done.'

So from these most fundamental social difficulties he came back to his panacea. All paths and all inquiries led him back to his conception of aristocracy, conscious, self-disciplined, devoted, self-examining yet secret, making no personal nor class pretences, as the supreme need not only of the individual but the world.

§ 10

It was the Labour trouble in the Transvaal which had brought the two schoolfellows together again. White had been on his way to Zimbabwe. An emotional disturbance of unusual intensity had driven him to seek consolations in strange scenery and mysterious desolations. It was as if Zimbabwe called to him. Benham had come to South Africa to see into the question of Indian immigration, and he was now on his way to meet Amanda in London. Neither man had given much heed to the gathering social conflict on the Rand until the storm burst upon them. There had been a few paragraphs in the papers about a dispute upon a point of labour etiquette, a question of the recognition of Trade Union officials, a thing that impressed them both as technical, and then suddenly a long incubated quarrel flared out in rioting and violence, the burning of houses and furniture, attacks on mines, attempts to dynamite trains. White stayed in Johannesburg because he did not want to be stranded up country by the railway strike that was among the possibilities of the situation. Benham stayed because he was going to London very reluctantly, and he was glad of this justification for a few days' delay. The two men found themselves occupying adjacent tables in the Sherborough Hotel, and White was the first to recognise the other. They came together with a warmth and readiness of intimacy that neither would have displayed in London.

White had not seen Benham since the social days of Amanda at Lancaster Gate, and he was astonished at the change a few years had made in him. The peculiar contrast of his pallor and his dark hair had become more marked, his skin was deader, his features seemed more prominent and his expression intenser. His eyes were very bright and more sunken under his brows. He had suffered from yellow fever in the West Indies, and these it seemed were the marks left by that illness. And he was much more detached from the people about him; less attentive to the small incidents of life, more occupied with inner things. He greeted White with a confidence that White was one day to remember as pathetic.

'It is good to meet an old friend,' Benham said. 'I have lost friends. And I do not make fresh ones. I go about too much by myself, and I do not follow the same tracks that other people are following.' . . .

What track was he following? It was now that White first heard of the Research Magnificent. He wanted to know what Benham was doing, and Benham after some partial and unsatisfactory explanation of his interest in insurgent Hindoos, embarked upon larger expositions. 'It is, of course, a part of something else,' he amplified. He was writing a book, 'an enormous sort of book.' He laughed with a touch of shyness. It was about 'everything,' about how to live and how not to live. And 'aristocracy, and all sorts of things.' White was always curious about other people's books. Benham became more earnest and more explicit under encouragement, and to talk about his book was soon to talk about himself. In various ways, intentionally and inadvertently, he told White much. These chance encounters, these intimacies of the train and hotel, will lead men at times to a stark frankness of statement they would never permit themselves with habitual friends.

About the Johannesburg labour trouble they talked very little, considering how insistent it was becoming. But the wide propositions of the Research Magnificent with its large indifference to immediate occurrences, its vast patience, its tremendous expectations, contrasted very sharply in White's memory with the bitterness, narrowness and resentment of the events about them. For him the thought of that first discussion of this vast inchoate book into which Benham's life was flowering, and which he was ultimately to summarise, trailed with it a fringe of vivid little pictures; pictures of crowds of men hurrying on bicycles and afoot under a lowering twilight sky towards murmuring centres of disorder, of startling flares seen suddenly afar off, of the muffled galloping of troops through the broad dusty street in the night, of groups of men standing and watching down straight broad roads, roads that ended in groups of chimneys and squat buildings of corrugated iron. And once there was a marching body of white men in the foreground and a complicated wire fence, and a clustering mass of Kaffirs watching them over this fence and talking eagerly amongst themselves.

'All this affair here is little more than a hitch in the machinery,' said Benham, and went back to his large preoccupation. . . .

But White, who had not seen so much human disorder as Benham, felt that it was more than that. Always he kept the tail of his eye upon that eventful background while Benham talked to him.

When the firearms went off he may for the moment
have even given the background the greater share of his
attention. . . .

§ 11

It was only as White burrowed through his legacy of
documents that the full values came to very many things
that Benham said during these last conversations. The
papers fitted in with his memories of their long talks like
text with commentary; so much of Benham's talk had
repeated the private writings in which he had first digested
his ideas that it was presently almost impossible to disentangle what had been said and understood at Johannesburg from the fuller statement of those patched and
corrected manuscripts. The two things merged in White's
mind as he read. The written text took upon itself a
resonance of Benham's voice; it eked out the hints and
broken sentences of his remembered conversation.

But some things that Benham did not talk about at all,
left by their mere marked absence an impression on White's
mind. And occasionally after Benham had been talking
for a long time there would be an occasional aphasia, such
as is often apparent in the speech of men who restrain
themselves from betraying a pre-occupation. He would
say nothing about Amanda or about women in general,
he was reluctant to speak of Prothero, and another
peculiarity was that he referred perhaps half a dozen times
or more to the idea that he was a 'prig.' He seemed to be
defending himself against some inner accusation, some
unconquerable doubt of the entire adventure of his life.
These half hints and hints by omission exercised the quick
intuitions of White's mind very keenly, and he drew far
closer to an understanding of Benham's reserves than
Benham ever suspected. . . .

At first after his parting from Amanda in London Benham
had felt completely justified in his treatment of her. She
had betrayed him and he had behaved, he felt, with dignity
and self-control. He had no doubt that he had punished
her very effectively, and it was only after he had been
travelling in China with Prothero for some time and in the
light of one or two chance phrases in her letters that he
began to have doubts whether he ought to have punished
her at all. And one night at Shanghai he had a dream in
which she stood before him, dishevelled and tearful, his
Amanda, very intensely his Amanda, and said that she

was dirty and shameful and spoilt for ever, because he had gone away from her. Afterwards the dream became absurd, she showed him the black leopard's fur as though it was a rug, and it was now moth-eaten and mangy, the leopard skin that had been so bright and wonderful such a little time ago, and he awoke before he could answer her, and for a long time he was full of unspoken answers explaining that in view of her deliberate unfaithfulness the position she took up was absurd. She had spoilt her own fur. But what was more penetrating and distressing in this dream was not so much the case Amanda stated as the atmosphere of unconquerable intimacy between them, as though they still belonged to each other, soul to soul, as though nothing that had happened afterwards could have destroyed their common responsibility and the common interest of their first unstinted union. She was hurt, and of course he was hurt. He began to see that his marriage to Amanda was still infinitely more than a technical bond.

And having perceived that much he presently began to doubt whether she realised anything of the sort. Her letters fluctuated very much in tone, but at times they were as detached and guarded as a schoolgirl writing to a cousin. Then it seemed to Benham an extraordinary fraud on her part that she should presume to come into his dream with an entirely deceptive closeness and confidence. She began to sound him in these latter letters upon the possibility of divorce. This, which he had been quite disposed to concede in London, now struck him as an outrageous suggestion. He wrote to ask her why, and she responded exasperatingly that she thought it was 'better.' But, again, why better? It is remarkable that although his mind had habituated itself to the idea that Easton was her lover in London, her thought of being divorced, no doubt to marry again, filled him with jealous rage. She asked him to take the blame in the divorce proceedings. There, again, he found himself ungenerous. He did not want to do that. Why should he do that? As a matter of fact he was by no means reconciled to the price he had paid for his Research Magnificent; he regretted his Amanda acutely. He was regretting her with a regret that grew when by all the rules of life it ought to be diminishing.

It was in consequence of that regret and his controversies with Prothero while they travelled together in China that his concern about what he called priggishness arose. It is a concern that one may suppose has a little afflicted every reasonably self-conscious man who has turned from the natural passionate personal life to religion or to public service or any abstract devotion. These things that are at least more extensive than the interests of flesh and blood have a trick of becoming unsubstantial, they shine gloriously and inspiringly upon the imagination, they capture one and isolate one and then they vanish out of sight. It is far easier to be entirely faithful to friend or lover than it is to be faithful to a cause or to one's country or to a religion. In the glow of one's first service that larger idea may be as closely spontaneous as a hand-clasp, but in the darkness that comes as the glow dies away there is a fearful sense of unreality. It was in such dark moments that Benham was most persecuted by his memories of Amanda and most distressed by this suspicion that the Research Magnificent was a priggishness, a pretentious logomachy. Prothero could indeed hint as much so skilfully that at times the dream of nobility seemed an insult to the sunshine, to the careless laughter of children, to the good light in wine, and all the warm happiness of existence. And then Amanda would peep out of the dusk and whisper, 'Of course if you could leave me——! Was I not *life*? Even now if you cared to come back to me——! For I loved you best and loved you still, old Cheetah, long after you had left me to follow your dreams. . . . Even now I am drifting further into lies and the last shreds of dignity drop from me; a dirty, lost, and shameful leopard I am now, who was once clean and bright. . . . You could come back, Cheetah, and you could save me yet. If you would love me. . . .'

In certain moods she could wring his heart by such imagined speeches, the very quality of her voice was in them, a softness that his ear had loved, and not only could she distress him, but when Benham was in this heartache mood, when once she had set him going, then his little mother also would rise against him, touchingly indignant, with her blue eyes bright with tears; and his frowsty father would back towards him and sit down complaining that he was neglected, and even little Mrs Skelmersdale would reappear, bravely tearful on her chair looking after him as he slunk away from her through Kensington Gardens; indeed every personal link he had ever had with life could in certain moods pull him back through the door of self-reproach Amanda opened, and set him aching and accusing himself of harshness and self-concentration. The very kittens of his childhood revived forgotten moments of

long-repented hardness.   For a year before Prothero was
killed there were these heartaches.   That tragedy gave
them their crowning justification.   All these people said
in this form or that, 'You owed a debt to us, you evaded it,
you betrayed us, you owed us life out of yourself, love and
services, and you have gone off from us all with this life
that was ours, to live by yourself in dreams about the rule
of the world, and with empty phantoms of power and
destiny.   All this was intellectualisation.   You sacrificed
us to the thin things of the mind.   There is no rule of the
world at all, or none that a man like you may lay hold
upon.   The rule of the world is a fortuitous result of in-
calculably multitudinous forces.   But all of us you could
have made happier.   You could have spared us distresses.
Prothero died because of you.   Presently it will be the
turn of your father, your mother—Amanda perhaps. . . .'

He made no written note of his heartaches, but he made
several memoranda about priggishness that White read
and came near to understanding.   In spite of the tugging
at his heart-strings, Benham was making up his mind to
be a prig.   He weighed the cold uningratiating virtues of
priggishness against his smouldering passion for Amanda,
and against his obstinate sympathy with Prothero's grossness and his mother's personal pride, and he made his
choice.   But it was a reluctant choice.

One fragment began in the air.   'Of course I had made
myself responsible for her life.   But it was, you see, such a
confoundedly energetic life, as vigorous and as slippery
as an eel. . .   Only by giving all my strength to her could
I have held Amanda. . . .   So what was the good of
trying to hold Amanda? . . .

'All one's people have this sort of claim upon one.   Claims
made by their pride and their self-respect, and their weaknesses and dependences.   You've no right to hurt them,
to kick about and demand freedom when it means snapping
and tearing the silly suffering tendrils they have wrapped
about you.   The true aristocrat, I think, will have enough
grasp, enough steadiness, to be kind and right to every
human being and still do the work that ought to be his
essential life.   I see that now.   It's one of the things this
last year or so of loneliness has made me realise; that in
so far as I have set out to live the aristocratic life I have
failed.   Instead I've discovered it—and found myself out.
I'm an over-strung man.   I go harshly and continuously
for one idea.   I live as I ride.   I blunder through my

fences, I take off too soon. I've no natural ease of mind or conduct or body. I am straining to keep hold of a thing too big for me and do a thing beyond my ability. Only after Prothero's death was it possible for me to realise the prig I have always been, first as regards him and then as regards Amanda and my mother and every one. A necessary unavoidable priggishness. . . .

'I do not see how certain things can be done without prigs—people, that is to say, so concentrated and specialised in interest as to be a trifle inhuman, so resolved as to be rather rhetorical and forced. . . . All things must begin with clumsiness, there is no assurance about pioneers. . . .

'Some one has to talk about aristocracy, some one has to explain aristocracy. . . . But the very essence of aristocracy as I conceive it, is that it does not explain nor talk about itself. . . .

'After all it doesn't matter what I am. . . . It's just a private vexation that I haven't got where I meant to get. That does not affect the truth I have to tell. . . .

'If one has to speak the truth with the voice of a prig, still one must speak the truth. I have worked out some very considerable things in my research, and the time has come when I must set them out clearly and plainly. That is my job anyhow. My journey to London to release Amanda will be just the end of my adolescence and the beginning of my real life. It will release me from my last entanglement with the fellow creatures I have always failed to make happy. . . . It's a detail in the work. . . . And I shall go on.

'But I shall feel very like a man who goes back for a surgical operation.

'It's very like that. A surgical operation, and when it is over perhaps I shall think no more about it.

'And beyond these things there are great masses of work to be done. So far I have but cleared up for myself a project and outline of living. I must begin upon these masses now, I must do what I can upon the details, and, presently, I shall see more clearly where other men are working to the same ends. . . .'

§ 12

Benham's expedition to China with Prothero was essentially a wrestle between his high resolve to work out his conception of the noble life to the utmost limit and his curiously invincible affection and sympathy for the earthliness of that inglorious little don. Although Benham insisted upon the dominance of life by noble imaginations and relentless reasonableness, he would never altogether abandon the materialism of life. Prothero had once said to him, 'You are the advocate of the brain and I of the belly. Only, only we respect each other.' And at another time, 'You fear emotions and distrust sensations. I invite them. You do not drink gin because you think it would make you weep. But if I could not weep in any other way I would drink gin.' And it was under the influence of Prothero that Benham turned from the haughty intellectualism, the systematised superiorities and refinements, the caste marks and defensive dignities of India to China, that great teeming stinking tank of humorous yellow humanity.

Benham had gone to Prothero again after a bout of elevated idealism. It was only very slowly that he reconciled his mind to the idea of an entirely solitary pursuit of his aristocratic dream. For some time as he went about the world he was trying to bring himself into relationship with the advanced thinkers, the liberal-minded people who seemed to promise at least a mental and moral co-operation. Yet it is difficult to see what co-operation was possible unless it was some sort of agreement that presently they should all shout together. And it was after a certain pursuit of Rabindranath Tagore, whom he met in Hampstead, that a horror of perfect manners and perfect finish came upon him, and he fled from that starry calm to the rich uncleanness of the most undignified fellow of Trinity. And as an advocate and exponent of the richness of the lower levels of life, as the declared antagonist of caste and of the uttermost refinements of pride, Prothero went with Benham by way of Siberia to the Chinese scene.

Their controversy was perceptible at every dinner-table in their choice of food and drink. Benham was always wary and Prothero always appreciative. It peeped out in the distribution of their time, in the direction of their glances. Whenever women walked about, Prothero gave way to a sort of ethnological excitement. 'That girl—a wonderful racial type.' But in Moscow he was sentimental. He insisted on going again to the Cosmopolis Bazaar, and when he had ascertained that Anna Alexievna had vanished and left no trace he prowled the streets until the small hours.

In the eastward train he talked intermittently of her.
'I should have defied Cambridge,' he said.

But at every stopping station he got out upon the platform ethnologically alert. . . .

Theoretically Benham was disgusted with Prothero.
Really he was not disgusted at all. There was something
about Prothero like a sparrow, like a starling, like a Scotch
terrier. . . . These, too, are morally objectionable creatures
that do not disgust. . . .

Prothero discoursed much upon the essential goodness
of Russians. He said they were a people of genius, that
they showed it in their faults and failures just as much as
in their virtues and achievements. He extolled the
'germinating disorder' of Moscow far above the 'implacable
discipline' of Berlin. Only a people of inferior imagination,
a base materialist people, could so maintain its attention
upon precision and cleanliness. Benham was roused to
defence against this paradox. 'But all exaltation neglects,'
said Prothero. 'No religion has ever boasted that its
saints were spick and span.' This controversy raged between
them in the streets of Irkutsk. It was still burning while
they picked their way through the indescribable filth of
Pekin.

'You say that all this is a fine disdain for material things,'
said Benham. 'But look out there !'

Apt to their argument a couple of sturdy young women
came shuffling along, cleaving the crowd in the narrow
street by virtue of a single word and two brace of pails
of human ordure.

'That is not a fine disdain for material things,' said
Benham. 'That is merely individualism and unsystematic
living.'

'A mere phase of frankness. Only frankness is left to
them now. The Manchus crippled them, spoilt their roads
and broke their waterways. European intervention
paralyses every attempt they make to establish order on
their own lines. In the Ming days China did not reek. . . .
And, anyhow, Benham, it's better than the silly waste of
London. . . .'

And in a little while Prothero discovered that China had
tried Benham and found him wanting, centuries and
dynasties ago.

What was this new-fangled aristocratic man, he asked,
but the ideal of Confucius, the superior person, 'the son
of the King?' There you had the very essence of Benham,

the idea of self-examination, self-preparation under a vague Theocracy. ('Vaguer,' said Benham, 'for the Confucian Heaven could punish and reward.') Even the elaborate sham modesty of the two dreams was the same. Benham interrupted and protested with heat. And this Confucian idea of the son of the King, Prothero insisted, had been the cause of China's paralysis. 'My idea of nobility is not traditional but expectant,' said Benham. 'After all, Confucianism has held together a great pacific state far longer than any other polity has ever lasted. I accept your Confucianism. I've not the slightest objection to finding China nearer salvation than any other land. Do but turn it round so that it looks to the future and not to the past, and it will be the best social and political culture in the world. That, indeed, is what is happening. Mix Chinese culture with American enterprise and you will have made a new lead for mankind.'

From that Benham drove on to discoveries. 'When a man thinks of the past he concentrates on self; when he thinks of the future he radiates from self. Call me a neo-Confucian; with the cone opening forward away from me, instead of focusing on me. . . .'

'You make me think of an extinguisher,' said Prothero.

'You know I am thinking of a focus,' said Benham. 'But all your thought now has become caricature. . . . You have stopped thinking. You are fighting after making up your mind. . . .'

Prothero was a little disconcerted by Benham's prompt endorsement of his Chinese identification. He had hoped it would be exasperating. He tried to barb his offence. He amplified the indictment. All cultures must be judged by their reaction and fatigue products, and Confucianism had produced formalism, priggishness, humbug. . . . No doubt its ideals had had their successes; they had unified China, stamped the idea of universal peace and good manners upon the greatest mass of population in the world, paved the way for much beautiful art and literature and living. 'But in the end, all your stern orderliness, Benham,' said Prothero, 'only leads to me. The human spirit rebels against this everlasting armour on the soul. After Han came T'ang. Have you never read Ling Po. There's scraps of him in English in that little book you have— what is it?—the *Lute of Jade*? He was the inevitable Epicurean; the Omar Khayyam after the Prophet. Life must relax at last. . . .'

'No!' cried Benham. 'If it is traditional, I admit, yes; but if it is creative, no. . . .'

Under the stimulation of their undying controversy Benham was driven to closer inquiries into Chinese thought. He tried particularly to get to mental grips with English speaking Chinese. 'We still know nothing of China,' said Prothero. 'Most of the stuff we have been told about this country is mere middle-class tourist's twaddle. We send merchants from Brixton and missionaries from Glasgow and what doesn't remind them of these delectable standards seems either funny to them or wicked. I admit the thing is slightly pot-bound, so to speak, in the ancient characters and the ancient traditions, but for all that, they *know*, they *have*, what all the rest of the world has still to find and get. When they begin to speak and write in a modern way and handle modern things and break into the soil they have scarcely touched, the rest of the world will find just how much it is behind. . . . Oh! not soldiering; the Chinese are not such fools as that, but *life*. . . .'

Benham was won to a half belief in these assertions.

He came to realise more and more clearly that while India dreams or wrestles weakly in its sleep, while Europe is still hopelessly and foolishly given over to militant monarchies, racial vanities, delirious religious feuds, and an altogether imbecile fumbling with loaded guns, China, even more than America, develops steadily into a massive possibility of ordered and aristocratic liberalism. . . .

The two men followed their associated and disconnected paths. Through Benham's chance speeches and notes, White caught glimpses, as one might catch glimpses through a moving trellis, of that bilateral adventure. He saw Benham in conversation with liberal-minded mandarins, grave-faced, bald-browed persons with disciplined movements, who sat with their hands thrust into their sleeves, talking excellent English; while Prothero pursued inquiries of an intenser, more recondite sort with gentlemen of a more confidential type. And, presently, Prothero began to discover and discuss the merits of opium.

For if one is to disavow all pride and priggishness, if one is to find the solution of life's problem in the rational enjoyment of one's sensations, why should one not use opium? It is art materialised. It gives tremendous experiences with a minimum of exertion, and if presently its gifts diminish one need but increase the quantity. Moreover, it quickens the garrulous mind, and steadies the happiness of love. Across the varied adventures of Benham's journey in China fell the shadow first of a suspicion and then of a certainty. . . .

The perfected and ancient vices of China wrapped about Prothero like some tainted but scented robe, and all too late Benham sought to drag him away. And then in a passion of disgust turned from him.

'To this,' cried Benham, 'one comes! Save for pride and fierceness!'

'Better this than cruelty,' said Prothero, talking quickly and clearly because of the evil thing in his veins. 'You think that you are the only explorer of life, Benham, but while you toil up the mountains I board the house-boat and float down the stream. For you the stars, for me the music and the lanterns. You are the son of a mountaineering don, and I am a Chinese philosopher of the riper school. You force yourself beyond fear of pain, and I force myself beyond fear of consequences. What are we either of us but children groping under the black cloak of our Maker?—who will not blind us with his light. Did he not give us also these lusts, the keen knife and the sweetness, these sensations that are like pineapple smeared with saltpetre, like salted olives from heaven, like being flayed with delight. . . . And did he not give us dreams fantastic beyond any lust whatever? What is the good of talking? Speak to your own kind. I have gone, Benham. I am lost already. There is no resisting any more, since I have drugged away resistance. Why then should I come back? I know now the symphonies of the exalted nerves; I can judge; and I say better lie and hear them to the end than come back again to my old life, to my little tin-whistle solo, my—effort! My *effort!* . . . I ruin my body. I know. But what of that? . . . I shall soon be thin and filthy. What of the grape-skin when one has had the pulp?'

'But,' said Benham, 'the cleanness of life!'

'While I perish,' said Prothero still more wickedly, 'I say good things. . . .'

§ 13

White had a vision of a great city with narrow crowded streets, hung with lank banners and gay with vertical vermilion labels, and of a pleasant large low house that stood in a garden on a hillside, a garden set with artificial stones and with beasts and men and lanterns of white porcelain, a garden which overlooked this city. Here it was that Benham stayed and talked with his host, a man robed in marvellous silks and subtle of speech even in the European languages he used; and meanwhile Prothero, it seemed, had gone down into the wickedness of the town below. It was a very great town indeed, spreading for miles along the banks of a huge river, a river that divided itself indolently into three shining branches so as to make islands of the central portion of the place. And on this river swarmed for ever a vast flotilla of ships and boats, boats in which people lived, boats in which they sought pleasure, moored places of assembly, high-pooped junks, steam-boats, passenger sampans, cargo craft, such a water town in streets and lanes, endless miles of it, as no other part of the world save China can display. In the daylight it was gay with countless sunlit colours embroidered upon a fabric of yellow and brown; at night it glittered with a hundred thousand lights that swayed and quivered and were reflected quiveringly upon the black flowing waters.

And while Benham sat and talked in the garden above came a messenger who was for some reason very vividly realised by White's imagination. He was a tall man with lack-lustre eyes and sunken cheeks that made his cheek bones very prominent, and gave his thin-lipped mouth something of the geniality of a skull, and the arm he thrust out of his yellow robe to hand Prothero's message to Benham was lean as a pole. So he stood out in White's imagination, against the warm afternoon sky and the brown roofs and blue haze of the great town below, and was with one exception the distinctest thing in the story. The message he bore was scribbled by Prothero himself in a nerveless scrawl; 'Send a hundred dollars by this man. I am in a frightful fix.'

Now Benham's host had been twitting him with the European patronage of opium, and something in this message stirred his facile indignation. Twice before he had had similar demands. And on the whole they had seemed to him to be unreasonable demands. He was astonished that while he was sitting and talking of the great world-republic of the future and the secret self-directed aristocracy that would make it possible, his own friend, his chosen companion should thus, by this inglorious request and this ungainly messenger, disavow him. He felt a wave of intense irritation.

'No,' he said, 'I will not.'

And he was too angry to express himself in any language understandable by his messenger.

His host intervened and explained after a few questions that the occasion was serious. Prothero, it seemed, had been gambling.

'No,' said Benham. 'He is shameless. Let him do what he can.'

The messenger was still reluctant to go.

And scarcely had he gone before misgivings seized Benham.

'Where *is* your friend?' asked the mandarin.

'I don't know,' said Benham.

'But they will keep him! They may do all sorts of things when they find he is lying to them.'

'Lying to them?'

'About your help.'

'Stop that man,' cried Benham, suddenly realising his mistake. But when the servants went to stop the messenger their intentions were misunderstood, and the man dashed through the open gate of the garden and made off down the winding road.

'Stop him!' cried Benham, and started in pursuit, suddenly afraid for Prothero.

The Chinese are a people of great curiosity, and a small pebble sometimes starts an avalanche. . . .

White pieced together his conception of the circles of disturbance that spread out from Benham's pursuit of Prothero's flying messenger.

For weeks and months the great town had been uneasy in all its ways because of the insurgent spirits from the south and the disorder from the north, because of endless rumours and incessant intrigue. The stupid manœuvres of one European 'power' against another, the tactlessness of missionaries, the growing Chinese disposition to meet violence and force with violence and force, had fermented and brewed the possibility of an outbreak. The sudden resolve of Benham to get at once to Prothero was like the firing of a mine. This tall, pale-faced, incomprehensible stranger charging through the narrow streets that led to the pleasure-boats in the south river seemed to many a blue-clad citizen like the White Peril embodied. Behind him came the attendants of the rich man up the hill; but they surely were traitors to help this stranger.

Before Benham could at all realise what was happening

he found his way to the river-boat on which he supposed Prothero to be detained, barred by a vigorous street fight. Explanations were impossible; he joined in the fight.

For three days that fight developed round the mystery of Prothero's disappearance.

It was a complicated struggle into which the local foreign traders on the river-front and a detachment of modern drilled troops from the up-river barracks were presently drawn. It was a struggle that was never clearly explained, and at the end of it they found Prothero's body flung out upon a waste place near a little temple on the river bank, stabbed while he was asleep. . . .

And from the broken fragments of description that Benham let fall, White had an impression of him hunting for all those three days through the strange places of a Chinese city, along narrow passages, over queer Venetian-like bridges, through the vast spaces of empty warehouses, in the incense-scented darkness of temple yards, along planks that passed to the dark hulls of secret barges, in quick-flying boats that slipped noiselessly among the larger craft; and sometimes he hunted alone, sometimes in company, sometimes black figures struggled in the darkness against dim-lit backgrounds and sometimes a swarm of shining yellow faces screamed and shouted through the torn paper windows. . . . And then at the end of this confused effect of struggle, this Chinese kinematograph film, one last picture jerked into place and stopped and stood still, a white wall in the sunshine come upon suddenly round a corner, a dirty flagged passage, and a stiff crumpled body that had for the first time an inexpressive face. . . .

§ 14

Benham sat at a table in the smoking-room of the Sherborough Hotel at Johannesburg and told of these things. White watched him from an arm-chair. And as he listened he noted again the intensification of Benham's face, the darkness under his brows, the pallor of his skin, the touch of red in his eyes. For there was still that red gleam in Benham's eyes; it shone when he looked out of a darkness into a light. And he sat forward with his arms folded under him, or moved his long lean hand about over the things on the table.

'You see,' he said, 'this is a sort of horror in my mind. Things like this stick in my mind. I am always seeing

Prothero now, and it will take years to get this scar off my memory again. Once before—about a horse, I had the same kind of distress. And it makes me tender, sore-minded about everything. It will go, of course, in the long run, and it's just like any other ache that lays hold of one. One can't cure it. One has to get along with it. . . .

'I know, White, I ought to have sent that money, but how was I to know then that it was so imperative to send that money? . . .

'At the time it seemed just pandering to his vices. . . .

'I was angry. I shall never subdue that kind of hastiness altogether. It takes me by surprise. Before the messenger was out of sight I had repented. . . .

'I failed him. I have gone about in the world dreaming of tremendous things and failing most people. My wife too. . . .'

He stopped talking for a little time and folded his arms tight and stared hard in front of himself, his lips compressed.

'You see, White,' he said, with a kind of setting of the teeth, 'this is the sort of thing one has to stand. Life is imperfect. Nothing can be done perfectly. And on the whole——' He spoke still more slowly, 'I would go through again with the very same things that have hurt my people. If I had to live over again. I would try to do the things without hurting the people, but I would do the things anyhow. Because I'm raw with remorse, it does not follow that on the whole I am not doing right. Right doing isn't balm. If I could have contrived not to hurt these people as I have done, it would have been better, just as it would be better to win a battle without any killed or wounded. I was clumsy with them and they suffered, I suffer for their suffering, but still I have to stick to the way I have taken. One's blunders are accidents. If one thing is clearer than another it is that the world isn't accident-proof. . . .

'But I wish I had sent those dollars to Prothero. . . . God! White, but I lie awake at night thinking of that messenger as he turned away. . . . Trying to stop him. . . .

'I didn't send those dollars. So fifty or sixty people were killed and many wounded. . . . There for all practical purposes the thing ends. Perhaps it will serve to give me a little charity for some other fool's haste and blundering. . . .

'I couldn't help it, White. I couldn't help it. . . .

'The main thing, the impersonal thing, goes on. One

thinks, one learns, one adds one's contribution of experience and understanding. The spirit of the race goes on to light and comprehension. In spite of accidents. In spite of individual blundering.

'It would be absurd anyhow to suppose that nobility is so easy as to come slick and true on every occasion. . . .

'If one gives oneself to any long aim one must reckon with minor disasters. This Research I undertook grows and grows. I believe in it more and more. The more it asks from me the more I give to it. When I was a youngster I thought the thing I wanted was just round the corner. I fancied I would find out the noble life in a year or two, just what it was, just where it took one, and for the rest of my life I would live it. Finely. But I am just one of a multitude of men, each one going a little wrong, each one achieving a little right. And the noble life is a long, long way ahead. . . . We are working out a new way of living for mankind, a new rule, a new conscience. It's no small job for all of us. There must be lifetimes of building up and lifetimes of pulling down and trying again. Hope and disappointments and much need for philosophy. . . . I see myself now for the little workman I am upon this tremendous undertaking. And all my life hereafter goes to serve it. . . .'

He turned his sombre eyes upon his friend. He spoke with a grim enthusiasm. 'I'm a prig. I'm a fanatic, White. But I have something clear, something better worth going on with than any adventure of personal relationship could possibly be. . . .'

And suddenly he began to tell White as plainly as he could of the faith that had grown up in his mind. He spoke with a touch of defiance, with the tense force of a man who shrinks but overcomes his shame. 'I will tell you what I believe.'

He told of his early dread of fear and baseness, and of the slow development, expansion and complication of his idea of self-respect until he saw that there is no honour nor pride for a man until he refers his life to ends and purposes beyond himself. An aristocrat must be loyal. So it has ever been, but a modern aristocrat must also be lucid; there it is that one has at once the demand for kingship and the repudiation of all existing states and kings. In this manner he had come to his idea of a great world republic that must replace the little warring kingdoms of the present, to the conception of an unseen kingship ruling the whole globe, to his King Invisible, who is the Lord of Truth and all sane loyalty. 'There,' he said, 'is the link of our order, the new knighthood, the new aristocracy, that must at last rule the earth. There is our Prince. He is in me, he is in you; he is latent in all mankind. I have worked this out and tried it and lived it and I know that outwardly and inwardly this is the way a man must live, or else be a poor thing and a base one. On great occasions and small occasions I have failed myself a thousand times, but no failure lasts if your faith lasts. What I have learnt, what I have thought out and made sure, I want now to tell the world. Somehow I will tell it, as a book I suppose, though I do not know if I shall ever be able to make a book. But I have away there in London or with me here all the masses of notes I have made in my search for the life that is worth while living. . . . We who are self-appointed aristocrats, who are not ashamed of kingship, must speak to one another. . . .

'We can have no organisation, because organisations corrupt. . . .

'No recognition. . . .

'But we can speak plainly. . . .'

(As he talked his voice was for a space drowned by the jingle and voices of mounted police riding past the hotel.)

'But on one side your aristocracy means revolution,' said White. 'It becomes a political conspiracy.'

'Manifestly. An open conspiracy. It denies the king upon the stamps and the flag upon the wall. It is the continual proclamation of the Republic of Mankind.'

§ 15

The earlier phases of violence in the Rand outbreak in 1913 were manifest rather in the outskirts of Johannesburg than at the centre. 'Pulling out' was going on first at this mine and then that, there were riots in Benoni, attacks on strike breakers, and the smashing up of a number of houses. It was not until July the 4th that, with the suppression of a public meeting in the market-place, Johannesburg itself became the storm centre.

Benham and White were present at this market-place affair, a confused crowded occasion, in which a little leaven of active men stirred through a large uncertain multitude of decently dressed onlookers. The whole big square was astir, a swaying crowd of men. A ramshackle platform improvised upon a trolley struggled through the swarming straw hats to a street corner, and there was some speaking. At first it seemed as though military men were using this platform, and then it was manifestly in possession of an excited knot of labour leaders with red rosettes. The military men had said their say and got down. They came close by Benham, pushing their way across the square. 'We've warned them,' said one. A red flag, like some misunderstood remark at a tea-party, was fitfully visible and incomprehensible behind the platform. Somebody was either pitched or fell off the platform. One could hear nothing from the speakers except a minute bleating. . . .

Then there were shouts that the police were charging. A number of mounted men trotted into the square. The crowd began a series of short rushes that opened lanes for the passage of the mounted police as they rode to and fro. These men trotted through the crowd, scattering knots of people. They carried pick-handles, but they did not seem to be hitting with them. It became clear that they aimed at the capture of the trolley. There was only a feeble struggle for the trolley; it was captured and hauled through the scattered spectators in the square to the protection of a small impassive body of regular cavalry at the opposite corner. Then quite a number of people seemed to be getting excited and fighting. They appeared to be vaguely fighting the foot-police, and the police seemed to be vaguely pushing through them and dispersing them. The roof of a little one-story shop became prominent as a centre of vigorous stone-throwing.

It was no sort of battle. Merely the normal inconsecutive-ness of human affairs had become exaggerated and pugnacious. A meeting was being prevented, and the police engaged in the operation were being pelted or obstructed. Mostly people were just looking on.

'It amounts to nothing,' said Benham. 'Even if they held a meeting, what could happen? Why does the Government try to stop it?'

The drifting and charging and a little booing went on for some time. Every now and then some one clambered to a point of vantage, began a speech and was pulled down by policemen. And at last across the confusion came an idea, like a wind across a pond.

The strikers were to go to the Power Station.

That had the effect of a distinct move in the game. The Power Station was the centre of Johannesburg's light and energy. There if anywhere it would be possible to express one's disapproval of the administration, one's desire to embarrass and confute it. One could stop all sorts of things from the Power Station. At any rate it was a repartee to the suppression of the meeting. Everybody seemed gladdened by a definite project.

Benham and White went with the crowd.

At the intersection of two streets they were held up for a time; the scattered drift of people became congested. Gliding slowly across the mass came an electric tram, an entirely unbattered tram with even its glass undamaged, and then another and another. Strikers, with the happy expression of men who have found something expressive to do, were escorting the trams off the street. They were being meticulously careful with them. Never was there less mob violence in a riot. They walked by the captured cars almost deferentially, like rough men honoured by a real lady's company. And when White and Benham reached the Power House the marvel grew. The rioters were already in possession and going freely over the whole place, and they had injured nothing. They had stopped the engines, but they had not even disabled them. Here too, manifestly, a majority of the people were, like White and Benham, merely lookers-on.

'But this is the most civilised rioting,' said Benham. 'It isn't rioting; it's drifting. Just as things drifted in Moscow. Because nobody has the rudder. . . .

'What maddens me,' he said, 'is the democracy of the whole thing. White! I *hate* this modern democracy. Democracy and inequality! Was there ever an absurder combination? What is the good of a social order in which the men at the top are commoner, meaner stuff than the men underneath, the same stuff, just spoilt, spoilt by prosperity and opportunity and the conceit that comes with advantage? This trouble wants so little, just a touch of aristocracy, just a little cultivated magnanimity, just an inkling of responsibility, and the place might rise instantly out of all this squalor and evil temper. . . . What does all this struggle here amount to? On one side unintelligent greed, unintelligent resentment on the other; suspicion everywhere. . . .

'And you know, White, at bottom *they all want to be decent!*

'If only they had light enough in their brains to show them how.

'It's such a plain job they have here, too—a new city, the simplest industries, freedom from war, everything to make a good life for men, prosperity, glorious sunshine, a kind of happiness in the air. And mismanagement, fear, indulgence, jealousy, prejudice, stupidity, poison it all. A squabble about working on a Saturday afternoon, a squabble embittered by this universal shadow of miner's phthisis that the masters were too incapable and too mean to prevent.

'Oh, God !' cried Benham, 'when will men be princes and take hold of life? When will the kingship in us wake up and come to its own? . . . Look at this place ! Look at this place ! . . . The easy, accessible happiness ! The manifest prosperity. The newness and the sunshine. And the silly bitterness, the rage, the mischief and miseries ! . . .

And then : 'It's not our quarrel. . . .'

'It's amazing how every human quarrel draws one in to take sides. Life is one long struggle against the incidental. I can feel my anger gathering against the Government here in spite of my reason. I want to go and expostulate. I have a ridiculous idea that I ought to go off to Lord Gladstone or Botha and expostulate. . . . What good would it do? They move in the magic circles of their own limitations, an official, a politician—how would they put it?—"with many things to consider. . . ."

'It's my weakness to be drawn into quarrels. It's a thing I have to guard against. . . .

'What does it all amount to? It is like a fight between navvies in a tunnel to settle the position of the Pole star. It doesn't concern us. . . . Oh ! it doesn't indeed concern us. It's a scuffle in the darkness, and our business, the business of all brains, the only permanent good work, is to light up the world. . . . There will be mischief and hatred here and suppression and then forgetfulness, and then things will go on again, a little better or a little worse. . . .'

'I'm tired of this place, White, and of all such places. I'm tired of the shouting and running, the beating and shooting. I'm sick of all the confusions of life's experience, which tells only of one need amidst an endless multitude of distresses. I've seen my fill of wars and disputes and struggles. I see now how a man may grow weary at last of life and its disorders, its unreal exacting disorders, its blunders and its remorse. No ! I want to begin upon the realities I have made for myself. For they are the realities. I want to go now to some quiet corner where I can polish what I have learnt, sort out my accumulations, be un-disturbed by these transitory symptomatic things. . . .

'What was that boy saying? They are burning the *Star* office. . . . Well, let them. . . .'

And as if to emphasise his detachment, his aversion, from the things that hurried through the night about them, from the red flare in the sky and the distant shouts and revolver shots and scuffling flights down side streets, he began to talk again of aristocracy and the making of greatness and a new great spirit in men. All the rest of his life, he said, must be given to that. He would say his thing plainly and honestly and afterwards other men would say it clearly and beautifully; here it would touch a man and there it would touch a man; the Invisible King in us all would find himself and know himself a little in this and a little in that, and at last a day would come when fair things and fine things would rule the world and such squalor as this about them would be as impossible any more for men as a Stone Age Corroboree. . . .

Late or soon?

Benham sought for some loose large measure of time.

'Before those constellations above us have changed their shapes. . . .

'Does it matter if we work at something that will take a hundred years or ten thousand years? It will never come in our lives, White. Not soon enough for that. But after that everything will be soon—when one comes to death then everything is at one's finger-tips—I can feel that greater world I shall never see as one feels the dawn coming through the last darkness. . . .'

§ 16

The attack on the Rand Club began while Benham and White were at lunch in the dining-room at the Sherborough on the day following the burning of the *Star* office. The Sherborough dining-room was on the first floor, and the Venetian window beside their table opened on to a veranda above a piazza. As they talked they became aware of an excitement in the street below, shouting and running and then a sound of wheels and the tramp of a body of soldiers marching quickly. White stood up and looked. 'They're seizing the stuff in the gunshops,' he said, sitting down again. 'It's amazing they haven't done it before.'

They went on eating and discussing the work of a medical mission at Mukden that had won Benham's admiration. . . .

A revolver cracked in the street and there was a sound of glass smashing. Then more revolver shots. 'That's at the big club at the corner, I think,' said Benham and went out upon the veranda.

Up and down the street mischief was afoot. Outside the Rand Club in the cross street a considerable mass of people had accumulated, and was being hustled by a handful of khaki-clad soldiers. Down the street people were looking in the direction of the market-place, and then suddenly a rush of figures flooded round the corner, first a froth of scattered individuals and then a mass, a column, marching with an appearance of order and waving a flag. It was a poorly disciplined body, it fringed out into a swarm of sympathisers and spectators upon the side walk, and at the head of it two men disputed. They seemed to be differing about the direction of the whole crowd. Suddenly one smote the other with his fist, a blow that hurled him sideways, and then turned with a triumphant gesture to the following ranks, waving his arms in the air. He was a tall lean man, hatless and collarless, gray-haired and wild-eyed. On he came, gesticulating gauntly, past the hotel.

And then up the street something happened. Benham's attention was turned round to it by a checking, by a kind of catch in the breath, on the part of the advancing procession under the veranda.

The roadway beyond the club had suddenly become clear. Across it a dozen soldiers had appeared and dismounted methodically and lined out, with their carbines in readiness. The mounted men at the club corner had vanished, and the people there had swayed about towards this new threat. Quite abruptly the miscellaneous noises of the crowd ceased. Understanding seized upon every one. These soldiers were going to fire. . . .

The brown uniformed figures moved like automata; the rifle shots rang out almost in one report. . . .

There was a rush in the crowd towards doorways and side streets, an inquiring pause, the darting back of a number of individuals into the roadway, and then a derisive shouting. Nobody had been hit. The soldiers had fired in the air.

'But this is a stupid game,' said Benham. 'Why did they fire at all?'

The tall man who had led the mob had run out into the

middle of the road. His commando was a little disposed to assume a marginal position, and it had to be reassured. He was near enough for Benham to see his face. For a time it looked anxious and thoughtful. Then he seemed to jump to his decision. He unbuttoned and opened his coat wide as if defying the soldiers. 'Shoot,' he bawled, 'Shoot, if you dare !'

A little uniform movement of the soldiers answered him. The small figure of the officer away there was inaudible. The coat of the man below flapped like the wings of a crowing cock before a breast of dirty shirt, the hoarse voice cracked with excitement, 'Shoot, if you dare. Shoot, if you dare ! See !'

Came the metallic bang of the carbines again, and in the instant the leader collapsed in the road, a sprawl of clothes, hit by half a dozen bullets. It was an extra-ordinary effect. As though the figure had been deflated. It was incredible that a moment before this thing had been a man, an individual, a hesitating complicated purpose.

'Good God !' cried Benham, 'but—this is horrible !'

The heap of garments lay still. The red hand that stretched out towards the soldiers never twitched.

The spectacular silence broke into a confusion of sounds, women shrieked, men cursed, some fled, some sought a corner from which they might still see, others pressed forward. 'Go for the swine !' bawled a voice, a third volley rattled over the heads of the people, and in the road below a man with a rifle halted, took aim, and answered the soldiers' fire. 'Look out !' cried White, who was watching the soldiers, and ducked. 'This isn't in the air !'

Came a straggling volley again, like a man running a metal hammer very rapidly along iron corrugations, and this time people were dropping all over the road. One white-faced man not a score of yards away fell with a curse and a sob, struggled up, staggered for some yards with blood running abundantly from his neck, and fell and never stirred again. Another went down upon his back clumsily in the roadway and lay wringing his hands faster and faster until suddenly with a movement like a sigh they dropped inert by his side. A straw-hatted youth in a flannel suit ran and stopped and ran again. He seemed to be holding something red and strange to his face with both hands; above them his eyes were round and anxious. Blood came out between his fingers. He went right past the hotel and stumbled and suddenly sprawled headlong at the opposite corner. The majority of the crowd had already vanished into doorways and side streets. But there was still shouting and there was still a remnant of amazed and angry men in the roadway—and one or two angry women. They were not fighting, Indeed they were unarmed, but if they had had weapons now they would certainly have used them.

'But this is preposterous!' cried Benham, 'Preposterous. Those soldiers are never going to shoot again! This must stop.'

He stood hesitating for a moment and then turned about and dashed for the staircase. 'Good Heaven!' cried White. 'What are you going to do?'

Benham was going to stop that conflict very much as a man might go to stop a clock that is striking unwarrantably and amazingly. He was going to stop it because it annoyed his sense of human dignity.

White hesitated for a moment and then followed, crying, 'Benham!'

But there was no arresting this last outbreak of Benham's all too impatient kingship. He pushed aside a ducking German waiter who was peeping through the glass doors, and rushed out of the hotel. With a gesture of authority he ran forward into the middle of the street, holding up his hand, in which he still held his dinner napkin clenched like a bomb. White believes firmly that Benham thought he would be able to dominate everything. He shouted out something about 'Foolery!'

Haroun al Raschid was flinging aside all his sublime indifference to current things. . . .

But the carbines spoke again.

Benham seemed to run unexpectedly against something invisible. He spun right round and fell down into a sitting position. He sat looking surprised.

After one moment of blank funk White drew out his pocket handkerchief, held it arm high by way of a white flag, and ran out from the piazza of the hotel.

§ 17

'Are you hit?' cried White dropping to his knees and making himself as compact as possible. 'Benham!'

Benham, after a moment of perplexed thought answered in a strange voice, a whisper into which a whistling note had been mixed.

'It was stupid of me to come out here. Not my quarrel. Faults on both sides. And now I can't get up. I will sit here a moment and pull myself together. Perhaps I'm— I must be shot. But it seemed to come—inside me. . . . If I should be hurt. Am I hurt? . . . Will you see to that book of mine, White? It's odd. A kind of faintness. . . . What?'

'I will see after your book,' said White and glanced at his hand because it felt wet, and was astonished to discover it bright red. He forgot about himself then, and the fresh flight of bullets down the street.

The immediate effect of this blood was that he said something more about the book, a promise, a definite promise. He could never recall his exact words, but their intention was binding. He conveyed his absolute acquiescence with Benham's wishes whatever they were. His life for that moment was unreservedly at his friend's disposal. . . . .

White never knew if his promise was heard. Benham had stopped speaking quite abruptly with that 'What?'

He stared in front of him with a doubtful expression, like a man who is going to be sick, and then, in an instant, every muscle seemed to give way, he shuddered, his head flopped, and White held a dead man in his arms.

LONDON AND GLASGOW: COLLINS' CLEAR-TYPE PRESS

H. G. WELLS

MESSRS. COLLINS have secured the cheap rights of almost all Mr. Wells's novels and short stories. Perhaps the most widely read author in the world, his work needs no introduction. The following books are in many cases already classics.

THE RESEARCH MAGNIFICENT	2/6 net
THE FIRST MEN IN THE MOON	2/6 net
TALES OF LIFE AND ADVENTURE	2/6 net
MARRIAGE	2/6 net
IN THE DAYS OF THE COMET	2/6 net
THE PASSIONATE FRIENDS	2/6 net
TALES OF THE UNEXPECTED	2/6 net

ALSO PUBLISHED

THE WIFE OF SIR ISAAC HARMAN	1/6 net
KIPPS	1/6 net
LOVE AND MR. LEWISHAM	1/6 net
THE WAR IN THE AIR	1/6 net
THE HISTORY OF MR. POLLY	1/6 net
WHEN THE SLEEPER WAKES	1/- net
THE INVISIBLE MAN	1/- net

J. D. BERESFORD

Has been described as " the best novelist in Europe."

THE PRISONERS OF HARTLING

Is a brilliantly told story of a tyrannical old man who bullied his family, using his will as the whip. There is a strong love interest.

OTHER FAMOUS BOOKS BY FAMOUS WRITERS

FOE-FARRELL   Sir A. QUILLER-COUCH

THE HALL AND THE GRANGE
         ARCHIBALD MARSHALL

THE ROMANTIC   MAY SINCLAIR

MAINWARING   MAURICE HEWLETT

THE CLUB OF QUEER TRADES
         G. K. CHESTERTON

MADE TO MEASURE
         Mrs. HENRY DUDENEY

THE DEATH OF SOCIETY
         ROMER WILSON
         (Winner Hawthornden Prize)

THE PROBLEM CLUB   BARRY PAIN

THE FOOLISH LOVERS   ST. JOHN ERVINE

THIS SIDE OF PARADISE
         F. SCOTT FITZGERALD

SALTY   CHARLES W. WESTRON

THE CARAVAN MAN   ERNEST GOODWIN

"WHERE'S JOSEPH?"   CHAS. W. HOPPER

MDLLE. DE MAUPIN
         THÉOPHILE GAUTIER

THE CHILDREN OF ALSACE
         RENÉ BAZIN